I'll Be
Your Sweetheart

I'll Be Your Sweetheart

JOAN JONKER

BCA

Hi to all my readers

I'm dedicating this book to you because I know you will enjoy it. Molly and Nellie are doing what they do best and that is lending a helping hand where needed, and bringing love and laughter wherever they go. In this book there is laughter on every page.

As Nellie would say, 'It costs nothing to laugh.' So make the bed, wash the dishes and then spend a few hours having fun with the loveable duo.

Take care now.

Lots of love to you and yours

Joan

Chapter One

The Bennett house was like bedlam on the Monday morning, for the alarm hadn't gone off and the family had overslept. While Molly busied herself making a pot of tea and toast, her husband, Jack, and youngest daughter Ruthie shared the kitchen sink for a cat's lick and a promise. And as they didn't have time for their usual leisurely breakfast, they each drank their tea standing up, and left for work with a piece of toast in their hand.

'They'll have indigestion all day, gobbling toast down like that,' Molly told the empty living room when she came back after seeing them off. 'I'll have to get another alarm clock; it's the second time that one's let us down in the last two weeks.' She began to clear the table. 'Mind you, we've had our money's worth out of it. I only paid a few bob for it when I bought it, and that was at the beginning of the war if my memory serves me right. So I shouldn't be moaning about it.'

However, when Molly walked through to the kitchen, and her eyes rested on the dolly tub, which was filled with clothes she'd left in steep over night, she decided a good moan was in order. 'Oh dear, oh dear, where shall I start? Would it be better to tidy and dust the living room, or get started on the washing?' She pondered for a while, her chin cradled in her hand as she leaned against the doorjamb. Then, with a sigh, she straightened up and told the kitchen of the decision she'd reached. 'I'll do the living room first, 'cos yer never know, I might just have a visitor. Not that it's very likely at this time of the morning. And if by some strange chance I did have one, they wouldn't get a very warm welcome. Still, as me ma always told me, yer should be prepared for any eventuality, so I'd better make the room respectable.'

When Molly stood back half an hour later, she felt very pleased with herself. The living room was as bright as a new pin. The hearth gleamed, the aspidistra looked satisfied that the table it stood on in front of the window was highly polished, and you could see yourself in the shine of the sideboard.

'Not bad going, even if I do say so meself.' Molly nodded to endorse the self-congratulation. 'I'll have a quick cup of tea with a round of toast, then get cracking on the ruddy washing. It's been in steep all night, in soapy water, so by rights it should be clean enough to rinse.' She hummed as she lit a match under the kettle. 'Then it'll go through the mangle and be ready to hang out. There's a decent breeze out, so it should be dry enough to iron tonight.'

All went according to plan, for Molly was very methodical in her work, and at ten o'clock she was opening the kitchen door with a sheet over her arm and four wooden pegs in her mouth. She was about to step down into the yard when she heard a familiar voice. It came from three yards up, and belonged to her best mate, Nellie McDonough. A smile came to Molly's face when she recognized the tune. It was a song Laurel and Hardy had sung in a picture the two mates had been to see a few weeks ago. They'd laughed till they cried in the picture house as they'd watched the antics of the two funny men, and they'd had many a laugh about it since.

Molly looked down at the sheet, was thoughtful for a second, then made a sudden decision. She did an about turn and made her way back to the kitchen where she spat the pegs into the sink before putting the sheet down on the draining board. Then, throwing off the washday blues, she hurried down the yard, closed the entry door behind her, and tiptoed over the cobbles to her mate's door. Nellie was still singing so loud she didn't hear her mate come up behind her, and she was startled when she felt a hand on her shoulder.

'Molly Bennett, yer stupid sod! Why did yer creep up on me like that? I nearly jumped out of me skin.'

'I didn't creep up on yer, sunshine, it was you what was singing so loud yer didn't hear me. Anyway, that was a nice welcome to give yer very best mate.'

Nellie's eyes narrowed. 'If yer were me very best mate, yer wouldn't have tried to give me a heart attack.'

'It would take more than me to give you a heart attack, Nellie McDonough, it would take a ghost . . . or the devil himself. Anyway, the reason I came up was for a bit of light entertainment. Anything is better than turning that ruddy handle on the mangle. And I could hear yer singing, so I thought I'd join yer. With the two of us, we could sing that song like Laurel and Hardy. You can be Stan, and I'll be Oliver.'

Nellie put the wet towel she was carrying over the clothes line. 'How can I be Stan, yer silly nit? He's as thin as a drink of water, while I've been blessed with this voluptuous body. So, I'll be Oliver, and you can be Stan.'

'Are we going to give it the full works, sunshine? The dance as well as the singing? It would cheer us up for the rest of the day.'

Nellie's eyes disappeared from view as her cheeks moved upwards in a smile. 'Just the job, girl, just the job. I hate bleeding washday.'

Nellie's next-door neighbour, Beryl Mowbray, had heard the exchange and knew whatever Molly and Nellie got up to would be a laugh. Just what she needed to take her mind off the mound of clothes waiting to go in the dolly tub. As she'd heard Molly say, a little light entertainment would brighten the day. So over the yard wall she called, 'Hang on a minute, ladies, while I fetch a chair out to stand on. I won't be two shakes of a lamb's tail.'

'Well, the bleeding cheek of her!' Nellie folded her arms and they immediately disappeared from view beneath her mountainous bosom. And when she heard the sound of a chair being scraped along the yard next door, and saw Beryl's head appearing over the wall, she snorted in disgust. 'Yer've got a ruddy cheek, Beryl Mowbray. I've a good mind to charge yer tuppence for a ticket.'

Molly jabbed her mate in the ribs. 'We haven't got no tickets, sunshine.'

'Well, if we did have, I'd charge the cheeky article at least threepence. Just look where she is, girl! She's up there in the best seat in the house, and will see more of us than we'll see of ourselves.'

Beryl leaned her elbows on the top of the wall. 'Yer're dead right there, Nellie. I'm definitely in the best speck. If yer like, I'll give Mrs Harris next door a knock. Then yer'll have a proper audience.'

'If there's any knocking to be done, it'll be me what's doing it.' Nellie rolled her sleeves up and made a fist to wave at Beryl. 'See this, missus? Well, if yer don't keep quiet and let me and me mate get on with a private performance, then this will knock yer off that ruddy wall. And it'll knock the bleeding smile off yer face, as well.'

'Nellie, will you and Beryl call a truce, please?' Molly asked. 'I came down for a little light-hearted amusement, to cheer meself up. But the mood is beginning to wear off.'

Nellie's face was transformed into a beaming smile. 'Yer've got a smashing way with words, girl. I wish I'd gone to the same school as you, 'cos then I'd be as clever as you, and understand what ye're talking about all the time.'

Her lips pursed and her head shaking slowly, Molly said, 'Nellie, sunshine, if I'd gone to the same school as you, and we were mates, I certainly wouldn't have the vocabulary that I have now. So as far as I'm concerned, it's thank God for small mercies.'

Nellie stared open-mouthed at her mate. Then, after she'd given the matter some thought, she asked, 'What was it yer said yer wouldn't have, girl? It sounded like "big belly" but I can't see yer saying that. Besides, it's me what's got the big belly, not you.'

Beryl was having the time of her life. At that moment she didn't care if the washing never got done. 'Molly said vocabulary, Nellie, but it's too big a word for you to understand, never mind get yer tongue round.'

Molly screwed up her eyes and through gritted teeth she groaned, 'Ooh, that was a bad move on your part, Beryl. Yer should have kept yer mouth shut. Nellie will have yer guts for garters now.'

The little woman was standing with her arms folded, looking up at Beryl. 'Okay, clever clogs, now spell it for me.'

'Spell what, Nellie?'

'Yer know what word I mean, Beryl Mowbray, the one yer said I wouldn't understand. Just spell it for me. If yer get it right I'll eat me hat. Get it wrong and I'll knock yer off that bleeding perch for poking yer nose in where it wasn't wanted.'

Beryl chuckled. 'Nellie, I couldn't spell the blinking word if yer paid me. It took me all me time to say it. Yer see, queen, the school I went to must have been like the one you went to.'

Nellie asked herself if that sounded like an apology. Then, after due consideration, she decided it was good enough to let Beryl off the hook. 'Okay, girl, I'll let yer off this time. But keep yer gob shut, eh?'

4

'Oh, sod this for a lark,' Molly said, making for the entry door. 'I could have had me clothes on the line by now. I've got more to do than waste me time listening to two grown-up women acting like a pair of spoilt kids.'

For an eighteen stone woman, Nellie was very light on her feet. With her lips set in a thin line of determination, she covered the few yards in seconds. Grabbing Molly's arm, she pulled her back. 'Where the hell are you off to, girl? If ye're desperate to go to the lavvy, yer don't need to go home, yer can use mine. I won't charge yer.'

This was the outcome Molly was reckoning on. There was no way she was going back home until she'd done her little turn with Nellie. She was going to cheer herself up even if she killed herself in the process. 'I'm going home, Nellie, to get the washing on the line before it goes dark.'

Her hand flat on the door keeping it closed so Molly couldn't escape, Nellie said, 'What are yer on about, girl? How can it go dark at bleeding ten o'clock in the morning?'

'It was ten o'clock when I left our house, sunshine. I was hoping to have a little singsong with yer, and a laugh, and be back putting me washing on the line by a quarter past ten. Thanks to you and Beryl playing silly beggars, I'm later than I expected to be, so I'm on me way to make up the time.'

'Over my dead body, girl, over my dead body.' Nellie did a perfect imitation of Oliver Hardy shaking his head and playing with his tie. 'Yer came here to visit me and have a laugh, Molly Bennett, and a laugh yer'll have. Even if I have to go upstairs and take that ostrich feather off me wedding hat to tickle yer with.'

Not to be outdone, Molly took on her Ethel Barrymore dramatic pose. With her body limp, and the back of a hand on her brow, she sobbed, 'Oh, not the ostrich feather, I beg of yer. Please have some pity on a poor widow who is about to be thrown out into the street because she won't let the landlord have his wicked way with her.'

'Don't be sad, girl, I won't let the landlord have his wicked way with yer.' This was right up Nellie's street and she was thoroughly enjoying herself now. 'I'll stand in front of yer, and I'll offer myself in your place. And when the landlord sets his eyes on my voluptuous body, he won't be able to resist my charm. So dry yer eyes, girl, for all is not lost. I am willing to sacrifice myself so you have a roof over yer head.' Nellie couldn't keep all the laughter back, and some escaped. 'While he's under my spell, I'll make a deal with him. He can have my body, in exchange for your roof.'

Beryl was quite taken with Nellie's performance, and she clapped with such gusto that the chair she was standing on toppled over, and she was left hanging on to the wall for dear life. But it didn't stop her from gasping, 'That was great, Nellie, yer surpassed yerself. Yer were so good, yer brought tears to me eyes.'

'Thanks, girl, it's nice of yer to say so.' Seeing the predicament her neighbour was in, Nellie offered some advice. 'That happened to me once, girl, and it's a bugger when ye're left swinging. But what I did, I let meself down slowly, and I found the drop not nearly as bad as I'd thought. I landed on me backside, like, but it didn't hurt.'

They could hear Beryl's shoes scraping down the wall, followed by a loud groan. 'It was all right for you, queen,' her voice sailed over the wall. 'With the size of your bottom, yer had plenty of flesh to cushion yer fall. I bet I'll be black and blue tonight.'

'Get your feller to rub some cream on it when yer go to bed,' Nellie suggested. 'It'll make you feel better, and your feller will think he's won the pools.'

'Sod off, Nellie! The day I let my feller rub cream on me backside is the day I'll have given up on life.' Beryl's left buttock had taken the brunt of the fall, and she rubbed it gently. 'Anyway, he might enjoy himself so much he'd want to make a habit of it. And I couldn't be doing with that.'

'Oh, stop yer moaning and get round here.' Nellie showed no sympathy. 'Ye're holding the performance up.'

'I thought I heard Molly say she was going home to put her washing out?'

'Molly Bennett is staying in this yard whether she likes it or not.' Nellie nodded, forgetting her neighbour couldn't see through a brick wall. 'Even if it means carrying her under me ruddy arm.'

'You carry me, sunshine?' Molly kept her face straight even though the faces Nellie was pulling were comical. 'That would be no mean feat.'

'I didn't say nothing about yer feet, girl. Where did yer get that from?'

'I didn't mean feet, as in the two things I've got at the bottom of

6

me legs. The feat I meant was when someone does an unusual act, sort of thing.'

Nellie threw her hands in the air. 'I give up. One of us is going daft, girl, and it ain't me. But before yer go completely gaga, can we bring Stan and Ollie on? They've been waiting in the wings and getting impatient.'

'Hang on a minute.' Beryl slipped through the yard door and closed it after herself. 'Wait until I've found meself a good speck, so I can see everything without getting in yer way.'

Nellie rubbed her hands together, a huge smile on her chubby face. 'Let's get the show on the road, girl.'

'Sure thing, sunshine.' Molly was always bucked up by one of her mate's smiles. 'Left foot forward and then step back, and sing in harmony.'

'In the blue ridge mountains of Virginia,
On the trail of the lonesome pine.
In the pale moonshine, our hearts entwine
As she carved her name, and I carved mine.'

Nellie moved like an eighteen stone ballerina, so light on her feet she seemed to float just above the ground as she and Molly gave a good imitation of the two much-loved comedians' well-known routine. And several back doors opened as neighbours left their washtubs to listen. The singing, plus their imagination, put a smile on their faces. It certainly chased away the washday blues.

Beryl watched with hands clasped and body swaying as she sang along with gusto. She would have loved to tag on next to Nellie, but knew she couldn't watch and take part as well. And watching really was a treat. For Molly and Nellie had the actions and the facial expressions of Laurel and Hardy off to perfection. And the pleasure written on their faces told of their fondness for each other. Theirs was a friendship that no one would ever come between.

When the performance came to an end, the two mates held hands as they bowed to the applause from Beryl and their neighbours, who called for an encore. 'Sorry, ladies,' Molly called. 'But if I don't get me washing on the line pronto, it'll put me behind all day. We'll do it again for yer some other time.'

7

Beryl followed Molly into the entry. She'd never known anyone like the two mates before. You never knew whether they were serious or acting the goat. But she wished she was one of them. And if Laurel and Hardy had had another partner, she could very well have been.

When Nellie called to Molly's later, for their usual cup of tea, she was in high spirits. 'Ay, girl, next time we entertain the neighbours, I think we should sell tickets. Then we could buy ourselves two second-hand men's suits from the market and dress up.' She'd had this brainwave while she was hanging a sheet on the clothes line, and really thought it was a brilliant idea. 'We wouldn't half look good if we could dress up like them. We'd bring the house down at the party.'

Molly's eyes widened. 'Which party is that, sunshine? Nobody has said anything about a party to me.'

Looking the picture of innocence, Nellie said, 'The party when our Paul gets married.'

'Your Paul!' Molly fell back on her chair. 'I didn't know he was getting married. Him and Phoebe have only just got engaged.'

'I know that, girl! He's too bleeding slow to catch a cold, that's his problem. But he's bound to be getting married some time, so we could start looking for second-hand suits so we'll be ready when the time comes. Ye're always telling me off for leaving things until the last minute.'

'Nellie, I've only ever said that to yer when ye're late calling for me to go to the shops. There's a lot of difference between buying a pound of sausage for the family's dinner, and two second-hand men's suits, which would only be worn once.'

Her face deadpan, Nellie answered, 'They wouldn't only be worn the once, girl, 'cos we could wear them for the christening party as well.'

'Which christening party is that, sunshine?'

'When our Paul and Phoebe get married, girl, that's when. I know I said our Paul was too slow to catch a cold, but I bet he's not slow when it comes to making a baby. Not if he takes after his dad, anyway.'

Molly shook her head as though dazed. 'I don't believe what I'm hearing. In five minutes flat, yer've married yer son off, and made

8

him a father into the bargain! That's going a bit too far, even by your standards, sunshine. For heaven's sake don't mention it in front of Phoebe, she'd die of embarrassment.' Molly drained her cup. 'Come on, drink up, Nellie, before yer come up with any more crackpot schemes.'

Nellie put the cup to her mouth, but she didn't drink from it. She was too busy muttering under her breath that her mate had no sense of humour, imagination or adventure.

When Molly and Nellie entered the butcher's shop, they were greeted by their neighbour, Ellen Corkhill, who worked behind the counter in the shop. 'Ye're late today, ladies. Was the wash load bigger than usual?'

Tony, the owner of the shop, came through from the stockroom. 'I bet they've been jangling over their morning cup of tea. It's nice for some people, who don't have to slave all day, like me.'

'Oh ay, Tony, I know someone who's worked a lot harder than you.' Molly put a hand on Nellie's shoulder. 'My mate, here, has not only married a son off, she's made him a father as well. I bet that makes you feel as though yer've been working in slow motion.'

'Is your Paul getting married then, Nellie?'

Nellie's eyes went to the ceiling as she tutted. 'Take no notice of this mate of mine, 'cos she's got a cob on. And all because I wanted to buy a man's suit each, so we could do our Laurel and Hardy act better.' She spread her chubby hands as though asking for understanding. 'Now that's nothing for her to get her knickers in a twist over, is it?'

Tony winked at his assistant. They were in for a laugh now. 'I don't think so, Nellie. It seems to me that Molly is being very unfair to yer. And I'd like to help yer out. I've got a suit in me wardrobe what I haven't worn for ages on account of me expanding waistline. It would fit Molly, so that would be her fixed up as Stan Laurel. And if she's getting it for nowt, I don't see how she can complain.'

Nellie glared at him. 'I'm Stan Laurel, soft lad.' She jerked her thumb at Molly. 'She's Oliver Hardy. So yer wouldn't be doing me no favours.'

Ellen leaned across the counter. 'While you two are fighting it out, I'd like a quiet word with Molly. I've heard something from a customer that I think she'd want to know about. So you two carry on, and we'll move down the counter.' She gave a slight jerk of her head. 'Come on, Molly, it won't take a few minutes, and I know yer'd go mad if I didn't tell yer.'

'It sounds serious, sunshine.'

'It is, Molly, and I'm blazing mad, as well as being worried to death.'

Nellie's ear was twitching. 'Tell yer what, Tony, why don't we talk about yer suit another time? For if there's something going on, like dirty work at the crossroads, then I've got to stay by me mate. Yer see, it might be a job for the McDonough and Bennett Private Detective Agency.' The little woman followed her mate's example and leaned her elbows on the counter. 'What's all the secrecy, Ellen?'

Ellen kept her voice low, and her eyes on the door for customers. Tony was a good boss and she would never take advantage of him. If a few customers came in, she wouldn't leave him on his own to serve them. He deserved as much for being so good to her over the years. 'Have yer heard what's happened to Mrs Parker? The old lady who lives at the back of us?'

Molly shook her head. 'Why, is she ill?'

Once again Ellen's eyes went towards the door before she answered. 'Mrs Clarkson was in before, and she told me Mrs Parker hadn't been feeling well for a few days, so this morning she decided to have a lie-in. She must have been in a deep sleep because she didn't wake up until eleven o'clock. And when she went downstairs, she found the living room had been ransacked and the front door was wide open.'

Molly's hand went to her mouth. 'Oh, the poor thing must have been petrified getting a shock like that. Especially at her age, and her not being well. Was anything stolen?'

'Whoever it was sneaked in, they must have got nerves of steel,' Ellen said. 'They stayed long enough to search every drawer and cupboard. Mrs Clarkson said things have been stolen, but Mrs Parker is too upset to look properly. She said she felt as though the house is dirty now some rotter has been through her things. One item she does know has gone, and she's breaking her heart over it, is her husband's fob watch. Yer know he was killed in the First World War, and that was the only thing she had left of his. And she's treasured it all these years.'

'What a lousy thing to do to anyone of that age.' Molly's anger was rising. 'The shock is enough to kill her.'

'I'll tell yer what, girl, I hope they find the bugger what done it.' Nellie's face was red with temper. 'I'll strangle him with me bare hands. Has anyone gone to the police to report it?'

'Mrs Clarkson's been to the police station,' Ellen told them. 'She was in a hurry to be served 'cos she wanted to be with the old lady when the police come. Not that Mrs Parker has been left on her own – all the neighbours are keeping an eye on her. There's been someone with her all the time, talking to her and making cups to tea.'

Molly stood upright. 'Serve us quick, will yer, Ellen, and me and Nellie will go there straight from here. We can get the rest of our shopping in this afternoon.'

'What did yer want, Molly?'

'I'll make do with three-quarters of stewing meat, sunshine, and I'll make a pan of scouse for quickness. Lots of veg and dumplings, it'll be easy to make and go down a treat.'

Ellen turned to Nellie. 'And what about you, love? What do you want?'

The little woman clicked her tongue and looked at Ellen as though she'd gone daft. 'What sort of question is that, soft girl? Yer know damn well I always buy the same as me mate.'

Ellen grinned. 'Only asking, Nellie! I mean, it's policy in any shop for the assistant behind the counter to ask a customer what they want to buy. Otherwise, we could spend the day just gazing into their eyes and trying to read their mind.'

Nellie's eyes narrowed and she touched Molly's arm. 'Would you say Ellen was being sarcastic, girl, or is it my bad mind?'

'I don't like taking sides, sunshine, but seeing as yer've asked for my opinion, then yer can hardly clock me one if I give it to yer. I would say that Ellen was well within her rights to ask yer what yer wanted to buy. After all, Tony pays her to stand behind the counter for that very reason.'

Nellie was all flustered. 'I've been getting the same as you every day for the last twenty years, girl, and she should know that by now.'

Tony leaned over the counter until his face was on a level with

Nellie's 'For your information, Mrs McDonough, Ellen has only worked here for five years, not twenty. In fact, I didn't own the shop twenty years ago.'

The heavy bosom was hitched up and the eyes became slits as Nellie pushed her face forward until her nose was almost touching Tony's. 'Listen to me, soft lad,' she hissed. 'You go and teach yer grandma how to milk ducks. I know yer haven't been here that long, 'cos me and me mate remember the man what had the shop before you. And a real gent he was too! Wasn't he, girl?' She glanced at Molly but didn't give her a chance to answer. 'Yeah,' Nellie repeated, 'he was a real gent. And he knew a real lady when he saw one, as well. Treated me and Molly like royalty, he did. And he always knocked a penny off anything we were buying. Whether it was a pound of stew or a leg of lamb, he never failed to knock a penny off.'

Molly, who was standing behind her mate, had eyes the size of saucers. 'In the name of God, Nellie, yer've either got a lousy memory, or ye're very good at making things up. I don't even remember the name of the man who owned the shop before Tony. But I do remember he was a miserable beggar. A smile would have cracked his face. And as for being a real gent, and very generous, well ye're miles out! I never looked forward to coming in this shop, 'cos there was never a smile or a greeting. And I don't know how yer can say he was generous with us, 'cos he was dead tight! He always sold us short, yer know that! At least yer should, for I still have a picture in me mind of you trying to climb over the counter threatening to strangle him. If yer legs hadn't been so short yer'd have made it, too, 'cos yer were blazing mad. Surely yer remember that, sunshine? Yer caused ructions in the shop.'

Nellie's smile was a sight to behold. 'Yeah, I remember that all right, girl. I really had me dander up that day. But it wasn't me short legs what stopped me getting over the counter, it was me knickers. I couldn't get me leg up high enough because the elastic had no ruddy give in it.'

Tony could picture the scene in his head. He knew Molly and Nellie very well; they were his favourite customers. He had also seen Nellie in action and was well aware of what she was capable of. 'Nellie, just so I don't make the same mistake as my predecessor, and in the knowledge that it is quite possible you are now wearing a

12

larger size in knickers, will yer tell me what the man did to bring about your probably justified anger?'

Nellie gaped. 'Bloody hell, girl, did yer hear that? He's either swallowed a dictionary or he made those words up as he went along. Would you mind translating them into plain English for me?'

'We haven't got all day, sunshine, 'cos I want to go and see Mrs Parker. So I'll make it short. Tony wants to know what made yer mad at the man who owned the shop before him. And make it snappy; we're in a hurry.'

'Right, snappy it shall be, girl.' Nellie stood to attention. 'Me and me mate were as poor as church mice in those days, lad, always counting the pennies. The day Molly's talking about, we'd asked for four sausage each, which is half a pound. And didn't the tight-fisted bugger cut half an inch off one of the sausages after he'd weighed them, 'cos he said they'd gone over on the scale.'

'And had they?' Tony asked.

'Had they hell! Me and Molly both had our eyes on the scale because we didn't trust him. And when I saw him cutting half an inch off one of my sausages, then off Molly's, well, I saw red. I would have throttled him if I could have got to him.'

'And that's it for now,' Molly said, pulling on her mate's arm. 'But so ye're not left wondering, Tony, I'll tell yer the end bit. The man really thought Nellie would do him an injury, so he put the two bits of sausage back in the wrapping paper. I imagine he thought it would be cheaper to do that than have Nellie wreck his shop, and him have a heart attack. And now yer know the outcome, we'll love yer and leave yer.' She propelled Nellie towards the door. 'Come on, sunshine, shake a leg.'

The two mates were walking through the door when Tony and Ellen roared with laughter as Nellie answered, 'I can't shake a leg, girl. Me knickers will fall down.'

Chapter Two

Nellie was puffing and blowing as her short chubby legs tried to keep up with Molly. 'In the name of God, girl, will yer slow down a bit? Anyone would think we were running in the Grand National.' She came to a halt and bent to put her two hands on her knees while she gasped for breath. Then she turned her head sideways and looked up at her mate. 'If yer want to get rid of me, there's easier ways to do it. A dose of arsenic would be quicker and much less bleeding painful.'

Trying hard not to smile, Molly said, 'Ye're out of condition, girl, that's your trouble. If yer kept off the custard creams and cream slices, it would help. And doing something a little bit more energetic every day.'

Had she thought before speaking, Molly would have chosen her words more carefully. But it was only when she saw the sly look in Nellie's eyes that she realized what she'd let herself in for. By then, of course, it was too late.

'You can be as energetic as yer like during the day, girl. Do bleeding handstands, or cartwheels for all I care. But yer'll have to excuse me if I don't follow suit, 'cos I preserve all me energy for bedtime. Not that I need energy to climb the stairs, 'cos I can be up them in ten seconds flat. The time I need the energy is when I'm in bed, between the sheets. And I'd have a bet with yer that I am more energetic in half an hour than you are in a whole day.' Nellie took a deep breath and straightened up. 'So put that in yer pipe and smoke it.'

'I'm not going to answer yer, or make any comment, sunshine. I'll leave that to your vivid imagination. But can I ask yer to empty yer head of everything except the task in hand? We are going to see an elderly lady who has been robbed. Naturally she will be very upset, so we need to be kind, caring and sympathetic. No jokes, just sympathy, and help if need be. Is that all right with you?'

'What d'yer take me for, girl? I'm not as thick as two short planks, yer know. Did yer think I'd go in there singing "Lullaby of Broadway", and doing the Charleston?'

Molly's shoulders shook with laughter as she imagined the scene in her mind. 'It would probably frighten the old lady to death, but it sure would cheer me up.'

Nellie's face was transformed by a radiant smile. There was nothing she liked better than to cheer her mate up. When Molly was happy, Nellie was happy. 'I'll behave meself, girl; I won't let yer down. We like Mrs Parker, she's a little love. And if the police find out who robbed her, then he'll have to answer to us, won't he?'

'He'll have to answer to the police, sunshine.' Molly linked her mate's arm and they carried on walking up the street. 'That's if they ever catch the blighter.'

'If they don't, girl, we could open up the McDonough and Bennett Private Detective Agency. I bet we could find him.'

When they reached Mrs Parker's house, it was to find the front door ajar. Molly drew her arm from Nellie's and pushed the door wider. Standing on the top step, she called, 'It's Molly and Nellie come to see yer, sunshine, and we're coming in.'

With Nellie close on her heels, Molly made her way into the living room to see the old lady seated in her rocking chair, sobbing as though her heart would break and wiping her red-rimmed eyes with a hankie sodden with tears. She looked so old and frail, Molly's heart went out to her. Two neighbours were sitting on the couch and Molly acknowledged them with a nod. 'Have the police been yet?'

Lily Swift shook her head. 'We've been expecting them for the last hour, Molly, but there's been no sign, has there, May?'

May Forest nodded. 'More like two hours. Yer'd think they'd have sent a bobby by now. They've been told what happened, and how old Flora is, so they should have made an effort.'

Molly undid the buttons on her coat and put her bag down at the side of the table. 'If you two want to catch the shops before they close for lunch, me and Nellie will stay with Mrs Parker until the bobby comes. We'll see she's all right.'

Nellie and her chins were in agreement. 'We'll see she's all right. We'll keep her company and make her cups of tea.'

Lily and May didn't show it, but they were very relieved. It wasn't that they didn't think the world of Flora, but the last two hours had been hard going. They'd done everything they could to try to stop her crying, but nothing had any effect. Flora Parker was inconsolable.

'If it wouldn't be too much trouble, Molly,' Lily said, 'it would give me and May a chance to run to the shops for something for our dinner. Once we've got that sorted, we could come back and see what messages Flora needs.'

'Don't worry about that,' Molly told them. 'We'll see to whatever shopping she needs. So yer needn't rush back. We'll be fine.'

Once the neighbours had left, Molly dropped to her knees at the side of Flora's chair. Stroking the fine, white hair, she spoke softly. 'There's some bad people in the world, sunshine, isn't there? They're not fit to be called human beings.'

The old lady sniffed and wiped at her tears. Her voice thick with emotion, she sobbed, 'The shock was bad enough, Molly. I got the fright of me life. But I'd have got over that eventually, and just been more careful in future about me door being safely locked. What I'll never get over is that they've stolen Wally's fob watch. It was the only thing I had left that belonged to him. I can still remember the day his father gave him that watch for his twenty-first birthday. He was so proud, 'cos there weren't many lads his age with a fob watch. His mother told me, on the quiet, that they'd scrimped and scraped to get the money together to buy it. They even had a small photograph of him put under the glass in the lid.'

The memories were too much for Flora to bear and her whole body shook with her sobs. Molly held her close, and spoke soothingly, as she would to a child. And at the same time she signalled to Nellie. 'Put the kettle on, sunshine. A cup of very weak tea, with plenty of sugar in, will do Flora a power of good. And we'll have one to keep her company.'

Nellie's facial contortions were laughable as she mouthed the words, 'We may as well, seeing as I'm boiling the kettle.'

'Don't fill the kettle, sunshine, just enough water for three cups.' Molly turned her attention back to Flora. She was quite concerned for the old lady, for a shock like this could bring on a stroke or a heart attack. It might be wise to send for a doctor, who could give her something to calm her nerves. But then again, sending for a doctor might just make matters worse. Best to wait until the police had been, and then mention it.

Molly took hold of the frail, wrinkled hand, and held it between hers. 'Don't give up hope, sunshine, 'cos the police might get the watch back for yer. They know all the tricks these robbers get up to, and yer never know, they might just get lucky, please God.'

'I wouldn't care, but it's the first time in years I've slept in until that time. I could kick meself for being so lazy.'

'You're not lazy, sunshine, far from it. This room is a damn sight cleaner and tidier than mine, and I'm not joking. Anyway, yer weren't feeling well, so there's nothing to be ashamed of for having a lie-in. Besides, things might have turned out far worse if yer had woken up and disturbed the robber. For all we know there might have been more than one.'

'Molly, I wouldn't have cared if they'd emptied me house, as long as they'd left Wally's watch. He really loved that watch, and was so proud of it. And I feel I've let him down. There's nothing in this house now that I can touch and bring back memories of a good husband, fine soldier, and a man I loved with all my heart. We didn't have long together, 'cos he was called up to serve in the army, but he was the only one for me. I never looked at another man after he was killed. I had a few chances, but not one of them came up to my Wally.'

'And yer'll never forget him as long as yer live, sunshine, for love like yours never dies. I hope with all my heart that they catch the blighter that did this to you, but even if they don't, yer'll always remember his face, his smile and his kisses. And that special look that told yer how much he loved yer. No robber can take those memories away from yer.'

· Nellie had been listening in the kitchen, and she could feel herself filling up at Molly's words. She had a way with words, did her mate, and always knew the right ones to use. The whistling of the kettle made her jump, and after telling herself she was a soft nit for letting herself be scared of a ruddy kettle, she soon set to and it wasn't long before she was carrying a cup of tea through to Flora. 'Get that down yer, girl. I've put plenty of sugar in and enough milk to cool the tea down for yer.'

She watched until the old lady had taken a few sips, then she hitched up her bosom and announced, 'If the police don't catch the bugger what did this to yer, then me and Molly will take the case on, and we'll soon be on his trail. We're very good at detecting.' She screwed up her face until there was little space between her lips and nose. 'That didn't sound right, girl, did it? Is there such a word as detecting?'

'I couldn't tell yer, sunshine. But because I've never heard of it doesn't mean that there isn't such a word. But just to be sure, why not put it another way, and tell Flora that you and me are good detectives?'

'That's it, girl. I knew I could count on you. So now yer know, Flora, that if the police fail, me and me mate will take the case over.'

While Nellie was talking, Molly heard a man's voice at the front door. She was trying to scramble to her feet at the same time as Nellie bent down, and the two women collided and ended up sprawled on the floor.

'Oh, ay, and what have we here?' the policeman's voice boomed, and Molly's face went the colour of beetroot as she pulled at her skirt, which was now riding so high she was showing plenty of leg. She could feel herself blushing, and was afraid to look up until a hand the size of a ham shank was put under her nose. 'Get hold, missus, and I'll pull you up.'

Nellie was on the floor, too, but she didn't care about the expanse of blue fleecy-lined knickers she was showing. If her mate was getting a hand up, then she wanted the same treatment. 'What about me, Mr Policeman?'

Chuckling loudly, the constable sized Nellie up before offering her his two hands. 'I won't ask why yer were both on the floor, but you can tell me if yer wish.'

Nellie brushed herself down. 'It was easy. I was going one way, and me mate was getting up. We couldn't miss each other, really.'

Molly glanced at Flora, and was relieved to see she was no longer crying. At least the collision hadn't upset her. 'Can me and me friend stay with Mrs Parker while you're here? She's had a big shock and is very upset. I think she'd feel better if we stayed.'

18

'Of course yer can. I understand.' He shook hands with the three women as he introduced himself as PC Peter Morgan. 'Perhaps we could all sit down while I ask Mrs Parker a few questions.'

He proved to be a very efficient officer, thorough, but gentle and understanding. And he was very sympathetic to Flora's plight. She couldn't give a list of things stolen, for she'd been too upset to search. But she explained about her late husband's fob watch and the sentiment attached to it. And she was able to describe it in minute detail, and the photograph inside. After the officer had written the details down, he asked if she knew of anything else that was missing. And Flora had to admit, tearfully, that her purse was gone. Unfortunately, it contained her rent money, which was due to be paid in two days' time when the collector called. Worse still, every penny she had in the world was in it also. Whoever the thief was, he'd left an old lady penniless.

'Would you mind if I take a look around, Mrs Parker?' When the constable stood up, he asked, 'You are sure you closed the front door before you went up to bed?'

Flora nodded. 'I'm positive I locked and bolted it before I went up to bed last night, as I always do. And I had no reason to open it this morning.'

'What about the back door, was that locked?'

'I can't remember, I'm sorry. Yer see, I locked it as usual last night, but unlocked it this morning because I needed to go down the yard. And me head is so much of a jumble now, I can't say whether I locked the door when I came in. I wasn't feeling too good, yer see; that's why I went back to bed.'

'Don't worry about it, Mrs Parker. I'll have a look at the back, see if I can tell how the intruder gained entry, and if he's left any clues.'

When the officer left the room, Molly was too angry to speak. Her whole inside was churned up at the injustice. Flora had never hurt a soul in her life. She'd suffered great sadness, and at her age she deserved to be treated better than this. The meagre pension she received wasn't enough to keep body and soul together, yet she didn't owe anyone a penny, and never complained.

After taking a few deep breaths to calm herself down, Molly said, 'Don't worry about money, sunshine. Me and Nellie will make sure yer have enough to pay yer rent and have some food to live on.'

Nellie was feeling angry too, and it showed in her flared nostrils and the way she was pinching at the fat on her arms. 'That's right, girl, don't worry. We won't see yer starve.'

'It's not food I'm worried about.' Flora's spirits were so low she was filled with despair. 'It's my rent money. I've never missed a week in all the years I've lived here. I don't know what to do, or where to turn.'

Molly had to force herself to speak lightly. 'Then yer've got a better record than me and Nellie, sunshine, for there's many a time we missed a week's rent when the kids were little and we were struggling. Yet never once did Mr Henry threaten to throw us out, for he knew he'd get his money eventually. He's a good landlord, and I'm damn sure he's not going to worry about a good tenant like yerself. I know it's easy for me to talk, but I promise yer, Flora, that things won't feel so bad in a few days' time. I can't promise yer'll get yer husband's watch back, although I wish I could, but yer don't have to worry about money. Me and Nellie know Mr Henry very well, and we'll sort yer rent out for yer. That's one worry less for yer.'

The bobby came back into the room then, and all eyes turned to him. 'The intruder climbed over the entry wall to gain entrance. There's marks on the wall made by his shoes as he's climbed up. Then he came in through the kitchen door, which you must have left unlocked, Mrs Parker. There's no sign of a forced entry. The yard door is still bolted, but I can't understand why he didn't go out that way instead of going out of the front door. Whoever he was, he doesn't appear to have been worried about being seen by the neighbours. He took a chance, for there was far more likelihood of him being spotted in the street than there'd have been if he'd used the back entry. Anyway, I've made a note of everything and will pass it on to the sergeant. I think yer'll be getting a visit from a detective, Mrs Parker, who will take the case on. He'll no doubt be questioning the neighbours to ask if anyone noticed anything suspicious, or any strangers hanging around.' When PC Morgan looked down at Flora, he was thinking of his own grandmother, who would be about the same age. And he felt emotional. This was one side of the job he didn't like. 'I'll call in some time when I'm in the area, just to see how you are. But I can see you have good friends who'll keep an eye on you.'

'You can rest assured that Flora will be well looked after, constable,' Molly said. 'There's a gang of us who'll be watching over her like a hawk, and waiting on her hand and foot.'

Not wanting to be left out, Nellie told him, 'Yeah, she'll be spoilt rotten. Treated like a queen, that's what she'll be.'

PC Morgan grinned. If the rest of the neighbours were like these two, Mrs Parker was in good hands. 'I'll keep yer to that. It may be a few days before I get a chance to call again, but when I do, I'll be expecting to see Mrs Parker wearing a diamond tiara. If she's not, then I'll want to know why.'

Molly saw him to the door. 'She will be well cared for, officer, yer can depend on that.'

'I'm concerned that she has no money to live on. How will she manage for food and any other necessities?'

'We'll make sure she doesn't go short, I can promise yer that. None of the families round here are well off, but they'll all muck in to help. She's well thought of in the neighbourhood, is Flora, and everyone will want her to know that.' She gave him a smile. 'It would be nice if yer called again to see her, she'd love that. But I'll say ta-ra for now, 'cos me and me mate have got work to do.'

Molly and Nelly sat with Flora until her two neighbours returned to take over. Lily Swift and May Forest had done their shopping, prepared the dinner for their families and were ready to sit with the old lady for a few hours. 'We're all right until about four o'clock, Molly,' Lily said as she and May draped their coats over the arm of the couch. 'So if the police come, we'll be here to see to them.'

'The police have been, sunshine,' Molly told her. 'A young constable came, and he's taken himself back to the police station. He said a detective will be calling, but couldn't say when. It could be today or tomorrow.' As she was putting her coat on, she looked knowingly at Flora. She'd had a good chat with the old lady, and told her not to mention to her neighbours that all her money had been stolen along with the fob watch. When Flora said they'd soon find out when she had to tell the rent collector she couldn't pay him, Molly had coaxed her into keeping quiet about it until later, when all would be revealed. They weren't asking her to tell lies, and there was nothing underhand about keeping silent. 'We'll be bringing a few groceries back for Flora. She's given us the money for them. Oh, and she fancies a meat pie from Hanley's, to eat with some bread and best butter.'

Lily pulled a face. 'Some hope you've got, queen, 'cos Hanley's will be well sold out by this time.'

'One can but try, sunshine, one can but try.'

Nellie's chins and mountainous bosom showed they were in agreement 'Yeah, God loves a trier, and as He's a mate, we're in with a chance.' She gave an exaggerated wink to Flora. 'See yer later, girl.'

Nellie didn't speak until they were halfway down the street. 'Why did yer tell Flora not to say anything about her money getting pinched? She'll need to borrow some money to live on. She can't live on fresh air, girl. And then there's the rent man. She'll have to tell him she can't pay, and then the whole street will know.'

'Nobody will find out if I've got anything to do with it. Seeing Flora in that state really got to me. I'm boiling inside with anger, that someone of her age has been made penniless by a low-down thug. Whoever he is, I'd like him to know I think he's the lowest of the low.' Molly bent her elbow. 'Stick yer leg in, sunshine, and I'll tell yer what I've got in mind. First, I'm going to get round Edna Hanley to give a meat pie and a loaf, without charging for them. She'll do that willingly, I know she will, 'cos she's like one of us. And that will be the start.'

'Good thinking, girl, good thinking. But that doesn't alter the fact that Flora's got no money. She's broke, skint, penniless.'

'I'm hoping she won't be any of those things by tonight, sunshine. If I pull it off, she'll have her rent money, and enough to live on.'

'How are yer going to manage that, girl? I think ye're letting yer heart rule yer head. I know yer feel sorry for Mrs Parker, I do meself. And if I could get me hands on the feller what robbed her, he'd wish he'd never been born. But to pay her rent, and money to live on, ye're talking about six or seven bob. And where are yer going to find that much money?'

Molly could imagine the look on her mate's face when she heard what the plan was, and was chuckling in advance when she said, 'I reckon it would take at least eight shillings to put Flora back on her feet. She could pay her rent, and the coalman, and have coppers for the gas meter, and enough for her food. And I know exactly how I can raise that much money without any trouble.'

Nellie's eyes slid sideways. 'Don't tell me ye're going to sell yer body! That would be taking things too far, even to help an old lady what's in distress.'

'You could probably raise eight shillings with your voluptuous body, but I wouldn't stand a chance. No, I've got a much easier plan than that. I'll do me rounds tonight, visiting me family. And I'll ask for a donation from Doreen and Phil, Jill and Steve, Tommy and Rosie, and your Lily and Archie. They'll all want to help when I tell them about Flora, and I'm hoping for two shillings from each house. That would make the eight shillings I think she needs to put her on an even keel. It won't help her get over the loss of her husband's watch, but it will take away the worry of not having a penny to her name.'

'I take me hat off to yer, girl, 'cos ye're very thoughtful and have got a heart of gold. There's not many people like you around.'

'Yes there is, sunshine, and you're one of them. The two shillings you're giving me, and my two shillings' contribution, will make it twelve shillings. That will take all the stress and strain away from the old lady. She'll feel secure having a few bob to fall back on.' Molly squeezed Nellie's arm. 'And you and me, sunshine, will feel much better for doing a good deed. Our conscience will be clear.'

Nellie pulled them to a halt. 'I haven't got a heart of gold, girl, and there's nowt wrong with my conscience. Me memory must be going, though, 'cos for the life of me I can't remember saying I'd give two shillings. And as for doing a good deed, well, I wouldn't know one if I fell over it.'

Molly had expected this response and was prepared. 'That's all right, sunshine, don't worry yer head about it. If yer don't want to help Flora, well, that's up to you. I'm not twisting yer arm. It's you that will have to live with yerself.' She began to walk on. 'Hurry up, I haven't got time to waste.'

'Hang on, girl, and give me a chance. I didn't say I wouldn't help Flora, now did I?'

'No, yer didn't, Nellie, that's quite true. But yer didn't say yer would help her, either. And like I said, I'm not going to twist yer arm and make yer do something yer don't really have the heart for. Yer have a mind of yer own, and yer must do as yer please.'

'I'll give yer the two shillings, girl, yer don't have to make a bleeding song and dance about it. I'll cough up, seeing as you are too!'

Molly shook her head. 'No, sunshine, if the money is begrudged, it won't do Flora any good. She'd have nothing but bad luck.'

Nellie snorted. 'She hasn't had much bleeding good luck without it, has she? Anyway, girl, what are yer being so snooty about? Isn't my money good enough for yer?' Once again she snorted, before muttering under her breath, 'What a bloody palaver this is! Much more of it and I'll ask for me money back.'

Molly chuckled. This was a scene she could have written the plot of, for she knew her mate inside out. 'How can I give yer back what I haven't yet been given?'

'I'll give it to yer tonight when I'm doing the rounds with yer. I'll make sure I've got a two bob piece in me pocket.'

'Who said yer could come with me on me rounds? It's manners to wait until ye're asked, sunshine.'

'If you're going round collecting money, then I'm going to make sure yer don't short change them what have the same blood running through their veins as I have.' Nellie gave a sharp nod to confirm. 'So there, clever clogs.'

'Doreen and Phil don't have the same blood as you, sunshine, they're not related to yer. And neither are Tommy and Rosie.'

'That's what you say, girl, but I think different and I'm not taking your word for it. I saw a picture once, I can't remember now what it was called but I can remember the hero saying that families had blood ties what bind them together. And I'd rather believe Randolph Scott than you.'

Molly's jaw dropped. That was a long speech for Nellie, and she hadn't used one swear word. She'd made the story up as she went along, like, but Molly gave her full marks for initiative. Nevertheless, she wasn't going to let it stop her pulling her mate's leg. 'Oh, I remember that picture, sunshine. It was a real weepy. And I clearly remember Randolph Scott saying what you just said.'

Nellie's eyes darted from side to side. She'd never seen Randolph Scott in her life. He was always in Western films and she hated cowboys and Indians. 'I'd like to stand talking, girl, but if we don't make a move my feet will be stuck to the pavement, Hanley's will have sold out of meat pies, and Flora will have died of starvation.'

'Yeah, we better put a move on, 'cos I'd like to be with Flora when the detective comes. Lily and May are smashing neighbours, but they're a bit on the shy side. They wouldn't speak out or ask questions.'

After linking her mate's arm, Nellie said, 'Ye're not the only one with ideas, girl. My brain might not be as big as yours, but now and again it surprises me and comes up with some useful information. And while we were sitting with Flora, right out of the blue, it came up with a brilliant idea. If the police don't find the thief, then we should open up our detective agency and take on the job ourselves.'

'That's exactly what I was thinking, sunshine, so it just goes to show that great minds do think alike.'

That was praise indeed. And to show her appreciation, Nellie's back straightened, her head was held high, and her bosom stood to attention. 'What time are yer doing the rounds tonight, girl? Just so I can be ready when yer call for me. And I'll have me money ready. I'll be the first one to make a contribution. The first name on yer list. That's good, isn't it, girl?'

'Marvellous, sunshine, absolutely marvellous. And I'll make sure you get yer full title. Helen Theresa McDonough.'

Chapter Three

Jack Bennett pushed his dinner plate away. 'I'm sorry, love, I couldn't eat any more. There's nothing wrong with the dinner, it's me, me tummy's upset. Listening to yer telling us about Mrs Parker has taken me appetite away.'

'I know how yer feel, sunshine, 'cos my tummy's been upset since I walked in her house and saw the state she was in. She looked so lost and alone, as though she had nothing left to live for. Even Nellie was affected, but yer know what she's like, she never lets anyone see the soft side of her.'

Ruthie, their fifteen-year-old daughter, had been really moved by what her mother had told them, and there was a catch in her voice when she asked, 'Won't she ever get her husband's watch back, Mam? She might, yer know, 'cos the police might find out who stole it.'

'I don't think there's much chance of that, sunshine. I doubt she'll ever see it again.' Molly let out a heartfelt sigh. 'The detective that came didn't hold out much hope, though he didn't say that to Flora. I have to say the young bobby and the detective were very good with her. They really treated her with respect. They were patient and kind, treated her like a real lady, as though she was someone special. They asked the neighbours if they'd noticed anyone strange hanging around the entry, or coming out of Flora's front door, but no one had seen anything out of the ordinary.'

'Whoever it was must be young, because I certainly couldn't scale a yard wall. I might have done twenty years ago, but not now.' Jack reached for his packet of Woodbines, which was unusual because other nights he didn't light up until dinner was over, the table cleared, and he was in his fireside chair with the evening paper. 'The rotter is probably patting himself on the back right now for picking a house where there was no resistance and he was able to walk off with cash and a gold fob watch which must be worth a few pound.'

'It was worth more than all the money in the world to Flora.' Molly was angry and sad at the same time. 'Nellie said she'd wring the neck of the robber if he ever gets caught, and the way I feel now, I'd hold him while she did it.'

'That's the sad part about it,' Jack said. 'He's probably in some pub right now, trying to flog it for a few bob. He won't keep hold of it, in case he gets caught with it on him. So he'll sell it for the price of a few pints. He won't give a thought to the heartbreak he's caused, just for the sake of a few beers. And he wouldn't even feel guilty if he was told the man who had owned the watch was killed in the First World War, fighting for his country.' He shook his head in disgust. 'Fighting to protect people like him.'

Ruthie shivered as though someone had walked over her grave. 'Mam, it's a good job Mrs Parker was fast asleep in bed, or he might have hurt her if she'd tried to stop him from stealing from her.'

'I did tell her that, sunshine, but it was no consolation. I can't find the words to explain how she looked, for she was in a world of her own. Her head must have been in turmoil, what with the loss of the watch, and being left without a penny to her name. It's enough to send a young person out of their mind, never mind someone of her age.'

'If ye're going round the family asking them to chip in and help, then I'm more than willing to put me hand in me pocket,' Jack said. 'I can't give much, yer know that, but Mrs Parker is welcome to what I've got.'

Ruthie leaned forward, her blue eyes wide. 'I could give yer sixpence as well, Mam. Every little helps.'

Molly left her chair and rounded the table to hug her daughter. 'That's good of yer, sunshine, but I'll manage without taking money off you or yer dad. Me and Nellie are giving two bob each, and I'm going round the family tonight with a hat. They'll all chuck a few bob in, I know, and I'll be able to sleep easy in me bed. It should be enough for Flora to pay her rent and the coalman, plus coppers for the gas meter, and her food. The family are all generous, and when they know why I'm calling with a begging bowl, they'll be only too pleased to help.'

'It's a good idea to have Nellie with yer,' Jack said. 'She can keep them laughing while they're parting with their money.'

'Oh, she insisted on coming with me, to make sure I didn't fiddle any of her family what are blood relatives.' Molly smiled as she patted the back of his hand. 'There's a story attached to that, love, a very funny story. But if I start telling yer now, I won't leave meself enough time to do the rounds. I can't call in each house, grab their money off them and then run like hell. I'll have to explain why I'm asking them for money, and that will take time. Then there'll be the problem of Nellie wanting a cup of tea and a custard cream in every house. And she won't leave until she gets it. My mate is definitely not backward in coming forward. By no stretch of the imagination could yer call her shy, or bashful.'

'You get yerself ready, now, love, and me and Ruthie will wash the dishes and tidy up.'

Molly cupped his face in her two hands, and gave him a noisy kiss. 'It was my lucky day when I met you, Jack Bennett. The best husband in the world, bar none. And I love every hair on yer head, and the bones of yer.'

Ruthie was swinging her legs under the chair and giggling. 'Mam, what about his eyes, ears, nose and teeth? What have yer got against them that they don't measure up to his hair and his bones? If they were listening to what yer said, they may get a cob on and decide to fall out. Then where would me dad be?'

'I'd better make amends, then, love, just in case.' Molly was asking herself who was the daftest, her or her daughter. But her four children all had a wacky sense of humour, which they'd inherited from her. And she wouldn't have them any different, for their home had always been a warm and happy one. 'So I'll start all over again, and give yer dad another kiss while I tell him there isn't a part of him that I don't love to bits.'

'Don't overdo it, love,' Jack laughed, 'or yer'll make me bigheaded. I can feel me cheeks blushing already.'

'They'll soon stop blushing when yer start clearing away and washing the dishes. Nothing like a bit of work to bring yer down to earth.' Molly stood up and pushed her chair under the table. 'I'd better make tracks if I want to catch everyone in. I'll try not to stay too long in each house, 'cos we're calling to Flora's when we're finished to give her whatever money we collect. She knows to expect us, because after the fright she's had, I didn't want to knock on her door and give her another. She'll be afraid of every sound now, God love her. Anyway, if we give her enough money to pay her rent and other things, that might make her feel a bit better. And Nellie said she's got an old purse Flora can use until she's able to buy a new one.'

Molly was slipping her coat on when Jack said, 'Yer never know, love, the police might catch the thief before he's had time to spend the money or flog the watch. We never hear about them catching criminals, but they do a good job on the quiet. And they have the advantage of knowing who the local thieves are.'

'It would be wonderful if they did catch him. But I won't say that to Flora 'cos I wouldn't want to raise her hopes, and then have them dashed.' Taking the front door key out of the glass dish on the sideboard, Molly dropped it into her pocket. 'I'll see yer later, sunshine. I'll try not to be out too late.' She raised a brow to her daughter. 'And as for you, young lady, no later than ten o'clock. Tara for now.'

Molly's hand had barely touched the knocker when the door was opened and Nellie greeted her mate with a smile. 'I'm all ready for yer, girl, 'cos I knew yer didn't want to hang around.' She pushed Molly aside and banged the door after herself. There was nothing Nellie liked more than a little excitement in her life. 'It's all go, isn't it?'

'It certainly is, sunshine, especially when it's to help someone. And it'll give us a chance of seeing all our families in one night.' Molly took her mate's arm and they turned to cross the cobbles to a house opposite, where her daughter Doreen lived with her husband Phil, their baby son Bobby, and Victoria Clegg. The name on the rent book was Victoria's, as she had lived in the house for over fifty years. A spinster, she'd lived a lonely life until she'd offered to share the house with Doreen and Phil when the only thing stopping them getting married was the lack of a place to live. She counted her blessings that at her age she now had a family. And when the baby came along nine months ago, her cup of happiness overflowed. She had a family she loved, and who adored her in return.

Doreen opened the door, and with a stern look on her pretty face she wagged a stiffened finger at her mother. 'Where have you two been all day? We've had the kettle on the boil, expecting yer any minute.'

'Me and Nellie have had a busy day, sunshine, and if yer'll stand aside and let us in, we'll tell yer all about it.'

Doreen held the door wide. 'Keep yer voices down, please, 'cos I've not long put Bobby in his cot. If he hears yer voices he'll scream the place down. He missed yer today,'

When she walked into the living room, the first thing Molly did was cross the floor to Victoria, who was sitting in her rocking chair with a smile of welcome on her face for the two friends who had been so good to her over the years. She was very frail, with thin white hair, faded blue eyes, and skin as sheer as gossamer. But while age had slowed her down physically, she was very alert mentally. And she was what Molly called a real old-fashioned lady. No bad language and a house like a little palace.

'Hello, sunshine.' Molly's hug was gentle, her kiss loving. 'I'm sorry me and Nellie missed our usual visit, but when yer hear the reason, yer'll understand.'

Her son-in-law, Phil, was leaning against the kitchen door. 'What have you and Auntie Nellie been up to, Mrs B?'

'It hasn't been the best of days,' Molly told him as she straightened up. 'If yer sit down, we'll put yer in the picture.'

Doreen and Phil sat on the couch, holding hands, while Molly pulled two chairs from the table for herself and Nellie. 'Do you want to start, sunshine, or shall I?'

Nellie didn't even consider the question. 'Oh, you tell them, girl, ye're much better at it than me. Besides, I'll probably hear things what I missed meself. Yer see, I can't take as much in as you can. My George is right when he says I've got a big mouth and a small brain.'

Rubbing an ear lobe, Molly said, 'Your George doesn't say that to yer, sunshine, does he? If he does, it's only in fun. He doesn't mean it.'

Nellie's chins were so busy listening, they missed seeing her head shake, and went off in all directions. 'No, my feller doesn't say that to me face, girl, he wouldn't have the nerve. But I can tell it's what he thinks. Not that it worries me, 'cos he's not exactly a brainbox himself. He thinks he knows it all, but there's some things I know what he doesn't, so that makes us quits.'

'What are yer talking about, Nellie McDonough? Yer've used a lot of words there, and managed to say nothing! Not everyone can do that, so I suppose that lurking in that head somewhere there must be some form of life. But before yer baffle us all with science, can I ask yer to let me get on with telling them what we came for?'

Folding her arms, Nellie hitched up her bosom. 'The floor is yours, girl, don't let me stop yer. Go right ahead.'

When Molly saw her mate's chubby face take on that look of innocence, she felt like giving her a kiss. But she had to put the impulse aside and deal with the matter in hand, otherwise they wouldn't be home before midnight. 'The day started off well, with me and Nellie having a bit of fun with Beryl Mowbray and Laurel and Hardy. But I'll tell yer about that tomorrow, when we've got more time.' She ran her eyes over those waiting to hear what she had to say. 'It was when we were in the butcher's that the day took a bad turn. For Ellen was waiting for us with some bad news. You all know old Mrs Parker from the next street? Well, she's been broken into and robbed. Ellen was worried about her, but of course she couldn't leave the shop. So me and Nellie hot-footed it round to Flora's to see if she needed any help.' A glance at the clock told Molly she didn't have much time to spare. 'I'll have to be as quick as I can, and I'll tell yer why when I've finished.'

For the next fifteen minutes, the only sound in the room was Molly's voice. Even Nellie was silent, though she kept nodding her head and hitching her bosom to show she agreed that her mate was telling the truth.

After she'd given a short version of the day's events, Molly sighed. 'I could go on all night about how sad Mrs Parker looks, and how upset she is. And how good the neighbours are, 'cos they've all rallied round. I could also tell yer what I think of the scum who robbed her, but I'll leave that until I'm a bit more calm.'

When Victoria spoke, they all turned to her. 'Flora Parker is the same age as myself. We used to be very friendly, when we were younger. Neither of us had any family, and we used to go to the

31

shops together. But as we grew older we saw less of each other. I'd go to her now, if I was able, for that is a dreadful thing to happen to her. She must be out of her mind.'

'She is, sunshine, but I can assure yer she's being well looked after. I'll tell you how she is, and how she's managing, when me and Nellie call tomorrow. Right now, though, we've got a big favour to ask the family. I want to know if each house can spare any money to put in a kitty for Flora. I wouldn't ask, but she hasn't got a penny to her name, and I couldn't see her like that without trying to help. Going round with a begging bowl isn't my idea of a good night out, but I'm not too proud to ask for help for a woman of Flora's age.'

Phil leaned forward, his elbows resting on his knees. He had a good job as a floorwalker, and earned a good wage. Having gone through a rough childhood himself, he was sympathetic to someone in need. And he never forgot that when he was in need, it was Doreen's family and friends who took him in. 'Yer don't have to beg, Mrs B. We all admire you and Mrs Mac for the good works yer do. And I know yer well enough by now to know yer will have a sum in mind that you would like to be able to give Mrs Parker to set her straight. Would it help if I offered to pay her rent money?'

Molly's eyebrows shot up. 'No, sunshine, I couldn't let yer do that! That's far too much. I wouldn't dream of taking that off yer.'

Nellie's eyes rolled to the ceiling. She couldn't make her mate out sometimes. 'Tell him, girl, and get it over with.' She leaned forward to stare at Phil. 'She's hoping to get two bob in each house, lad, but we'll be sitting here all bleeding night before she'll ask for it.'

He chuckled. 'Is two bob enough, Mrs Mac?'

'Don't ask me, lad, I'm leaving the money side of this to me mate. But there's one thing I can tell yer, which might help. She's not getting a penny more than two bob off me.'

'I'd like to give something as well,' Victoria said. 'Is that all right with you, Molly?'

Molly's head nearly came off her shoulders when she shook it. 'Certainly not, Victoria! I'll give Flora yer best wishes and that's all. And I hope I don't have the same trouble in the other houses we're going to, or it'll be time for bed, and I'll be sorry I started. I'm getting a flipping headache now.'

'Where else are yer going, Mam?' Doreen asked. 'Or is that a secret?'

'Yer don't think I can have secrets with Nellie around, do yer?' Molly winked at her daughter. 'I'm terrified to keep a secret in case she finds out.'

The little woman sat back in her chair, hitched her bosom, and closed her eyes while she mulled over what her mate had said. Then one eye opened. 'I don't get that, girl. You are terrified to keep a secret in case I find out? Doesn't make sense, that. And there's another thing I don't get, either.'

'What's that, sunshine?'

'Why we've been sitting here for so long, and the kettle hasn't even been put on. That's bad manners, that is. Fancy having visitors and not giving them a drink. Some people don't know what heticat is.'

'Yer mean etiquette, don't yer, sunshine?'

The chins went one way, the bosom went the other. 'No, girl, that might be what you mean, but me, I mean I'm so thirsty I'm spitting bleeding feathers.'

While the others were laughing at Nellie speaking her mind, Molly jumped up. 'On yer feet, sunshine, before I die of embarrassment. And please carry on spitting feathers until yer've got enough to fill a pillow. Then I'll buy them off yer.'

Nellie hunched her shoulders. 'Ooh, me mate's getting a cob on with me. She takes things to heart too much, and I keep telling her she won't live to a ripe old age unless she learns how to stay calm. Me, I don't get ruffled like her. I mean, if I don't get a cup of tea and a custard cream, I'm not going to bawl me eyes out and throw me dummy out of the pram.'

Molly bit on her bottom lip to keep a smile away. 'Can I have yer two bob, Phil, and we'll be on our way.'

Phil stood up and put a hand in his trouser pocket. He picked a two-shilling piece from the coins in his hand, and was about to pass it over when he saw what Nellie was doing behind his mother-in-law's back. She had a thumb in each ear and was wiggling her fingers, while her tongue was sticking out and her eyes were crossed. She looked so comical, he really found it hard to keep the laughter back. 'Here's the money, Mrs B, and I hope all goes well with yer good work.'

Molly kissed his cheek. 'Thank you, sunshine, I'm sure all will go well. And now would yer tell that clown behind me that I'm on me way now, but if she wants to stay for tea and a biscuit she can do. I can manage on me own. In fact, I can get round a damn sight quicker without her.'

Nellie's change of expression was quick. Out came the thumbs, in went the tongue, and the eyes returned to normal. 'Oh, no, yer don't, Molly Bennett! I said I'd keep an eye on yer, and I intend to do just that. Two eyes, in fact. The next stop is our Lily's and I'm going to make sure my family don't get diddled. Everything has got to be seen to be above board. Two bob here, two bob there.'

'That's right, sunshine, you keep tabs on me. And to let Phil see that yer intentions are good, why don't yer give me your two bob in front of him?'

'I'll do that, girl, just to make you look daft.' Nellie leaned sideways to put a hand down her deep pocket. Unfortunately, Molly failed to notice the sly look on her mate's face. Nellie had the ability to put on an expression that suited any particular purpose, and when she withdrew her hand from the pocket, her face the picture of innocence, she said, 'I've got a hole in the lining of me pocket, and the bleeding two bob piece must have fallen out.'

And Molly fell for it, hook, line and sinker. 'Ah, yer poor thing! But we've only come across the street, sunshine, so it must be on the cobbles somewhere. Come on, we'll go back over again and I'll help yer look for it. And don't worry if it doesn't turn up, it's just one of those things and can't be helped.' She pulled on her mate's arm. 'Come on.'

'No, girl, I can't get on me knees on the cobbles, I'd never get up again. Besides, it could take all night, and you're in a hurry.'

'I'm not in so much of a hurry I won't help yer look for yer money. And you needn't get on yer knees, I can do that for yer. After all, two bob is two bob. So, come on, before it's time to go to bed.'

'No, girl, I'm not going to let me best mate get down on her hands and knees for me, it wouldn't be right. Particularly when I've just remembered I didn't put the two bob in the pocket with the hole in, I put it in the other pocket.'

Phil's loud guffaw filled the room, while Doreen giggled and Victoria tittered behind the hand she held to her mouth. And what did Molly do? She put her arms round Nellie and the two mates shook with laughter. 'What would I do without you, sunshine? I'm going to feel really mean taking the two bob off yer now. But I'll force meself. So put yer hand in the pocket without the hole, and pass the money over. Then we can thank these kind people, give them a kiss, and tell them we'll see them tomorrow. And once we're outside, we'll have to go like the clappers to make up for lost time.' As she was walking towards the door, Molly said over her shoulder, 'Oh, and don't pull the hole in the pocket stunt again, Nellie, please. I'd like to be in and out of the other houses in record time.'

Nellie was lowering herself down to the pavement when she muttered, 'Sod off, Molly Bennett. The next stop is our Lily's house, and I'll be giving the orders. So there, clever clogs.'

Lily Higgins, nee McDonough, opened the door and waved the couple in. As her mother squeezed past, she gave her a kiss. 'We weren't expecting visitors. This is a nice surprise.'

'I wouldn't speak too soon, girl, if I were you.' Nellie screwed up her eyes and her head swayed from side to side. 'No, let me put that another way.'

Lily's husband, Archie, came through from the kitchen, a smile on his face at the sound of his mother-in-law's voice. Over six foot tall, with jet black hair, a winning smile and strong white teeth, he thought the world of Nellie. He often joked he'd married Lily because of her mother. He thought she was the funniest thing on two legs and they got along like a house on fire. 'Go on, Mrs Mac, what did yer want to say?'

Nellie craned her neck and grinned up at him. 'Well, it's like this, lad. When I said to our Lily that I wouldn't speak too soon, I should have said it's never too soon.'

Molly had taken a seat on the couch. Wriggling her bottom until she was comfortable, she asked, 'Never too soon for what, sunshine?'

'To make a bleeding cup of tea, that's what.'

'Give us a chance, Mam,' Lily said. 'Yer've only just walked through the door.' She was a pretty girl, with a nice trim figure and possessing her mother's gift of seeing the funny side of life. 'I'll put the kettle on, but what's the big hurry?'

'I'm dying of thirst, that's what the big hurry is. My mate has got me running around like one of those flies what have a blue bottom. Her and her good deeds will be the death of me.' She spread out her hands and appealed to Archie, knowing he would be sympathetic. 'I mean, lad, it should be a pleasure to go visiting. A nice cup of tea, a few custard creams and light conversation. All sociable, like.'

'I'll stick the kettle on, Mam, 'cos I've got a feeling we're in for one of yer tales.' Lily winked at Molly. 'I hope it's not a woeful one, 'cos all me hankies are in the wash.'

'It's not my tale we've come with, and don't yer be so sarky, Lily McDonough. Yer won't be laughing when yer've heard what we've come for. Me mate will tell yer, 'cos all this is her doing.'

Archie smiled at Molly. 'What is it, Mrs B? Not bad news, I hope?'

When Molly began to tell the tale of why they were there, Lily came in from the kitchen to listen. 'That's terrible!' she said when Molly had finished. 'I've known Mrs Parker since I was a baby. I can remember she always gave me a biscuit if she saw me playing in the entry. She's a nice quiet woman who wouldn't hurt a fly.'

Archie, who had been mentioned in dispatches for his bravery during the war, looked grim.

'The lout who did that is a coward. If I knew who he was, he'd be sorry he'd been born. A couple of years in the army would sort him out, make a man of him. I'll be happy to help the old lady out, Mrs B. How much d'yer want?'

'I'm hoping for two bob from each house, Archie. That will be plenty to keep the wolf from Mrs Parker's door.'

'Me and Archie will give yer two bob each,' Lily said, reaching for her bag. 'We can afford it; we're both working.'

But Molly was adamant. 'No, we all pay the same. Phil wanted to give more, but I think it only fair if we stick to the two bob. The old lady doesn't know I'm doing this, and I'd rather she didn't find out I've been going round with the hat. I'll have to be very careful how 1 explain where we got the money from. But if I have to lie to save her pride, then I'll do that. She hasn't got much left in material possessions, so I'd hate to take her pride and dignity from her as well.'

'That's right, Mrs B,' Lily said. 'And she won't find anything out from us. But yer know we're always here if yer want us, and in a case like this we'd want to help.'

'I knew I could count on our gang.' Molly shuffled to the edge of the couch. 'We've got another two calls to make, and I want to be at Mrs Parker's before it gets too late. So although it looks awful to take yer money and run, I know yer'll understand.'

Nellie's face was a picture, and her voice a squeak. 'What d'yer think ye're playing at, girl? We haven't had a cup of tea yet!'

'Listen, sunshine, will yer think of something else beside yer ruddy tummy? Yer don't want to be knocking on Mrs Parker's door too late, yer'd give her a fright.'

'Five minutes won't make any difference.' Nellie turned to Archie for support. 'Aren't I right, son?'

'I'm going to have to let yer down for once, Mrs Mac, 'cos I think Mrs B is right in not wanting to be out late. Any other time, I'm on your side, yer know that.'

Through narrowed eyes, Nellie glared at him. 'Turncoat, that's what yer are,' she said, following Molly out into the tiny hall. 'I had yer down in me will, but I'm going to see me solicitor and have yer crossed off.'

'Oh, don't tell me I've missed a fortune, Mrs Mac? Me and my big mouth. Were yer going to leave me one of the family heirlooms?'

'That's for me to know and you to find out, smart arse.' Nellie linked Molly's arm. 'Yer'd kick yerself if yer knew what ye're missing.'

Molly grinned up at the young couple standing on the step. They hadn't been married very long, and their joy in each other was there for all to see. 'I wouldn't lose any sleep over it, Archie, because I already know what's in me mate's will. And none of us are mentioned in it. All her money is going to a home for stray cats.'

'No, it's not, girl, I was only pulling yer leg.' Nellie chuckled. 'It's going to a home for loose women.'

Chapter Four

When the door closed on Lily and Archie, the two mates headed for their next port of call, which was a house opposite. It was a house in which the two women had an equal footing, for it was the home of Molly's eldest daughter, Jill, and Nellie's son Steve. They had been married on the same day as Doreen and Phil, in a double wedding which was still talked about in the streets. It had been a big affair, the like of which had never been seen before in the neighbourhood. With the two sisters being so well known, and very popular, the neighbours had lined the streets and filled the church to give them a good send-off. And what a pretty pair they were, with their long blonde hair and vivid blue eyes, and looking radiant in their long flowing dresses. The handsome grooms with their smart clothes, buttonholes and smiling faces completed the perfect picture. Even the weather had been kind, the sun shining in a bright blue cloudless sky.

As the two friends reached the far pavement, Nellie put her hand on Molly's arm. With her feet firmly planted on the ground, and a determined expression on her face, she said, 'Yer can't give yer orders to me in this house, girl, so bear that in mind.'

Molly gasped. 'When have I ever ordered you around, sunshine? Yer wouldn't let me, even if I wanted to, which I don't.'

'Well, I can only say, girl, that yer've got a very short memory. Twice tonight yer've given me orders which stopped me from having a cup of tea. Me mouth is as dry as that sandpaper what's used for rubbing paint down, and I can hardly speak.'

'Ye gods and little fishes, sunshine, for someone hardly able to speak, ye're not doing so bad. And if ye're so thirsty, have a cup of water. That will quench yer thirst.'

'I don't want a bleeding cup of water, I want a nice cup of tea and a custard cream biscuit. And as this is my son's house, I'm going to do as I like. So there!'

'There's a small detail yer've overlooked, sunshine.' In the glow of the street lamp, Molly could see the determination on her mate's face. Lips were clamped together and eyes narrowed to slits. 'Two little details, in fact. My daughter also lives here, and has as much right to her opinion as Steve has. But leaving them aside, it seems to have slipped your memory that neither of them have the right to say what goes on. Lizzie Corkhill is the tenant, and it's her name on the rent book. It was through the goodness of her heart she offered to share the house with Jill and Steve when they got married. And I have to say I will be eternally grateful to Lizzie for her kindness.'

Nellie's eyes widened as her expression changed. 'I know that, soft girl, I haven't forgot. She's one in a million is Lizzie, and the last person in the world to begrudge anyone a cup of tea.' She held out her chubby hands. 'Now yer can't say yer don't agree with that!'

The two women were so intent on staring each other out, they failed to notice the door opening and a figure appearing on the top step. 'I thought it was your dulcet tones I could hear, Mam.' Steve was smiling, happy as ever to see the mother he loved and the mother-in-law who had always been like a second mother to him. She'd been part of his life from the time he was born, and the one he ran to for comfort when he was little and fell over and hurt himself. It was she who wiped his tears away. And he loved her more than ever now, since he'd married her beautiful daughter and became one of the family. 'What's me mam been up to, Mrs B? It must have been serious by the looks on yer faces.'

Nellie put a hand somewhere in the region of her heart. 'Yer daft nit, yer nearly gave me a heart attack! Why didn't yer cough, or something, to let us know yer were there?'

Steve was blessed with the same sense of fun as his mother, and with a straight face he said, 'I did knock on the door, Mam, but yer were too busy gassing to hear me.'

That gave Nellie food for thought, and she closed her eyes for a few seconds to sort it out in her head. 'What was the good of you knocking on the door, soft lad, when me and Molly are in the street talking? How did yer expect us to hear yer?'

'Jill heard me.' Steve's dimples were deep. 'She's been to the door three times to see if yer'd come to blows yet.'

Nellie was quick to take advantage. 'Well, next time she comes out, tell her to put the bleeding kettle on, 'cos I'm dying of thirst.'

'Oh, I'm sorry to disappoint yer, Mam, but we don't possess a bleeding kettle. We wouldn't want to, either, because me and Jill go weak in the knees at the sight of blood. But we've got a very nice whistling kettle, if that'll do.'

Molly was thinking of the time ticking away, and what they still had to do before nine o'clock. 'Shall we all go inside and discuss the advantages of an ordinary kettle which serves the purpose?' She pushed Nellie towards the door. 'And we can also discuss why a cup of tap water does yer more good than ten cups of tea.'

'You can discuss what yer like, girl, and for as long as yer like.' Nellie pushed her son aside. 'Me, now, I'm going straight to the kitchen to make meself a cup of tea. And while I'm waiting for the water to boil, I'm going to rummage in the biscuit tin.'

Lizzie Corkhill was sitting in her rocking chair with a smile on her face and anticipation in her eyes. The arrival of the two mates meant there'd soon be laughter in the room. 'Visitors to this house are not allowed to make their own tea, it's in the rules. It's manners to wait on visitors, my old ma used to say.'

Jill came to stand beside her husband and she linked arms with him. 'Forget about cups of tea and manners, doesn't anyone get a kiss? Considering we haven't set eyes on yer all day, I think kisses are called for.'

Steve leaned towards his wife and puckered his lips. 'I'm ready, willing and able, sweetheart.'

Jill pushed him playfully. 'You've had enough kisses to last yer until yer bedtime kiss.'

Molly forgot about the time; her family always came first. 'I'm sorry, sunshine, but me and Nellie have had a very hectic day.' She hugged and kissed her firstborn, who was the most gentle of all her children, and loved by everyone. 'With a bit of luck we'll be back to normal tomorrow.'

While Molly hugged and kissed Steve and Lizzie, Nellie made her way to the kitchen, saying, 'I'm dying of thirst and hunger, and haven't even got the strength to pucker me lips.'

Jill slid her arm from Steve's and was about to follow her mother-in-law when Molly stopped her. 'She's in one of her moods, sunshine, so leave her to it. She knows where yer keep things, she'll manage. Leave her to it and sit down.'

They heard the tap being turned on, the striking of a match, then the plop of gas being ignited. A second later, Nellie's head appeared round the door. 'I'm not in one of me moods, Molly Bennett, ye're only saying that to ease yer guilty conscience. If yer hear a noise, it'll be me pegging out through thirst and hunger.'

Steve chuckled. 'Don't pass out, Mam, 'cos we wouldn't be able to pick yer up. If yer feel yerself going dizzy, hang on to the sink for support.'

'Come and sit down, Nellie,' Lizzie said. 'Jill will make the tea and bring the biscuit tin in.'

Nellie shook her head. 'I'll do it, Lizzie. Don't worry, I'm not in a bad mood. It was only me and me mate having a slight difference of opinion, like what we often have. I've been with her all day, and believe me, she's having one of her good deed days, trying to help someone in need. That's why we couldn't come earlier. We've been to Doreen's, and we've been to our Lily's, so I know all about the tale she's going to tell yer; I've heard it twice in the last hour. That's why I'm making meself a cup of tea. And I warn yer, it's a sad tale, so have yer hankies ready.' She nodded to Molly. 'Go on, girl, the floor is yours. But don't forget we've got to go to yer ma's house yet, so get on with it before it's time to go to bed.'

Her eyes on Nellie's retreating back, Molly said, 'I don't know what she's got against water. It's cold, quenches the thirst, and is free. Three good reasons for having a cup of clear, fresh water.'

A voice from the kitchen quickly responded. 'I can give yer three good reasons for not drinking tap water, girl.' Nellie poked her head round the door. 'It's cold, got no taste, and yer can't dunk a biscuit in it. So there!'

Molly chuckled. 'I can't win, can I? She's got an answer for everything. Still, if she doesn't want to hear me asking how our granddaughter is, that's her lookout.'

Now being a grandmother was an honour in Nellie's eyes, and she delighted in it. So she wasn't going to miss out on any conversation about the six-month-old baby girl who had been christened Molly

Helen McDonough, after her and Molly. 'The kettle's not boiled yet, so I may as well rest me legs for a minute.'

Molly smiled inwardly, but wasn't going to spoil her mate's pleasure by being petty. 'How is the baby, sunshine? Me and Nellie didn't half miss seeing her and Bobby.'

'She's fine, Mam. Hardly ever cries, except when it's getting near feeding time. And she's getting big for six months.'

Lizzie, who been granted the honour of being an adopted granny, leaned forward in the chair. 'She's the most contented baby I've ever known in me life. Jill lets her lie on the floor now, and she loves it. With legs and arms thrashing about, she's in her element. And if we go near her, she shrieks with laughter, as though to say she's having a whale of a time.'

Steve couldn't be any more proud. He thought himself the luckiest man alive, with a beautiful wife and an adorable baby. 'She's starting to look like me, isn't she, Jill? Yer can see the resemblance, and I'll swear she's going to have dimples.'

'Me and Molly will be here to see that for ourselves, lad,' Nellie said. 'But please God she doesn't take after yer, 'cos I'd hate to see me granddaughter with big muscles and a hairy chin.'

The second the kettle began to whistle, Nellie was off her chair like a shot from a gun. 'You get on with it, girl, and I'll be ready for the off when you are.'

Molly apologized for having to be so brief with the details, but what she did tell them shocked them to the core. They'd known Mrs Parker all their lives and were horrified by what had happened to her. Particularly Lizzie, who knew Flora well. Although ten years younger, Lizzie hoped she never experienced the same treatment at the hands of a thug. And Jill, tender-hearted Jill, who cared for everyone, was near to tears as she clung to Steve's arm. In fact Molly wondered if it would have been better not to tell them, with Jill and Lizzie getting so upset, but she realized they would have found out anyway. In such a tight-knit community, where most people cared for each other, nothing could be kept secret.

After letting out a sigh, Molly pushed herself off the chair. 'Come in now, sunshine. We'd better be making tracks.'

'Are yer sure two shillings is enough, Mrs B?' Steve asked. 'We're not exactly rolling in money, but we could give a few bob more without starving ourselves.'

'There's no need to, lad,' Nellie said. She'd had her drink of tea and washed the cup and saucer. And three custard creams were now missing from the biscuit tin. But she wasn't going to tell them; they'd find out for themselves if they kept count. 'We've all given two bob, and when we've collected Tommy's money we'll have a grand total of twelve shillings. That'll take care of all Flora's money worries.' She could feel Molly's eyes on her and pulled a face. 'I'm not taking over from yer, girl, I just thought yer voice was getting a bit hoarse, and I'd help yer out.'

'There's something important yer've left out, sunshine. I don't mind yer taking over, but yer must do a proper job of it.'

In trying to remember what had been left out, Nellie's face contorted into every humanly possible shape. Then, almost as though someone was standing over her with a magic wand, her face returned to normal, then broke into a beaming smile. 'Oh, yeah, girl, I've got it.' She waved a hand around the room. 'You lot haven't got to mention the money to anyone, because it might get back to Flora, and she'd be very embarrassed. So lips tightly sealed, and mum's the word.'

'Where will yer tell Flora yer got the money from, Molly?' Lizzie asked. 'She's a very proud, independent woman.'

Molly nodded. 'I'll think of something, Lizzie, before we give it to her. I won't upset her, yer can rely on that. She's had enough upset without me adding to it.' Molly gave each of them a kiss, then put Steve's money in her purse. 'We'll have to move, Nellie, it's half past eight now.'

'Ready when you are, girl. And I'm refreshed after me drink, so I'll be able to keep up with yer.'

After hasty farewells, the two mates left, and once outside they walked at a brisk rate. Nellie didn't link arms, as she could walk faster with her arms free to swing. 'What are yer going to tell Flora, girl?'

'I've got an idea, sunshine, that might work. I'll tell yer after we leave me ma's.'

'What kind of idea, girl?'

'It's only a glimmer of an idea, sunshine. I'll have to give it a lot

43

of thought before I could even give yer a hint. But needs must when the devil drives, so I'll come up with something.'

Tommy's face showed surprise when he answered the knock on the door and found his mother and Auntie Nellie there. 'What are you two doing out at this time of night? There's nothing wrong, is there, Mam?'

Molly quickly mounted the step. 'No, son, there's nothing wrong. Not with our family, anyway. But this isn't a social call, and me and Nellie can only stay for about ten minutes for we've another last call to make.'

Tommy stood aside and let them pass. 'Sounds very mysterious, Mam. And seeing as yer haven't got yer usual happy, glad to see yer smiles on yer faces, it must be serious.'

Molly entered the living room to find her ma and da sitting at the table with Rosie, and they were each holding a hand of cards. 'Sorry to interrupt, Ma, but don't put yer cards down 'cos me and Nellie aren't staying.'

Bridie Jackson laid her cards face down anyway. She sounded anxious when she said, 'There's something wrong with one of the babies, isn't there, me darling?'

Molly was quick to reassure her. 'No, Ma, the babies are fine.' She kissed Bridie, then her da, Bob. 'The family are all well, so don't look so worried.'

Tommy's beautiful wife Rosie laid her cards down and rounded the table to crush her mother-in-law in a bearlike hug. 'Sure, it's a scare yer've given us, Mrs B.' Her Irish accent was like music. 'It's very late for yer to be calling, so it is.'

This was all too much for Nellie, who was feeling left out. 'Excuse me, like, but don't I get a look in? No welcome, no smile, no kiss? Or are yer trying to give me one of those things what me mate can say, but I can't get me tongue round?'

'D'yer mean inferiority complex, sunshine?'

Nellie's head nodded so fast, her chins couldn't keep up with her and went their own way. 'That's what I meant, girl. Funny how I can never remember those two words! I've got a big voculbry, but somehow those words escape me.'

The apprehension on faces turned to smiles. 'Why don't yer write it down, Auntie Nellie, and keep the piece of paper in yer pocket? Then yer'll have the words to hand if yer need them.'

Nellie gave him a narrow-eyed glare. 'Because, smart Alec, I can't spell it, can't say it, and don't know what it means. So a fat lot of good it would do me to have it written down on a piece of paper in me pocket. Yer mam would soon get fed up with me finding it in me pocket and asking her if it was me shopping list.'

Bob Jackson was holding his wife's hand when he said, 'I'd forget about it, Nellie, for an inferiority complex is something you'll never have, thank God. Don't you agree, Bridie?'

'Sure, a truer word yer've never spoken, me darlin'. Nellie has a gift more precious than any words. She has the ability to make people smile and be happy, and not many folk have that gift. And that's the truth of it.'

Nellie's face was a sight to behold. 'Oh, what joy to receive such a compliment, Bridie,' she said. 'How come yer didn't pass yer brains and common sense on to yer daughter? Yer see, my mate Molly doesn't appreciate my gift like what you do. So the way I see it, it's Molly what should have that piece of paper in her pocket. And for two pins I'd write it out for her. The only thing is, I can't spell it.'

Rosie's laughter filled the room. 'It's a case yer are, Auntie Nellie, and don't we all love yer for it? We'd be very sad if yer ever changed.'

Molly was moving from one foot to the other. 'I'm sorry to have to break this up, for I can see me mate is lapping up all this praise. Much more and she'll forget what we came for.'

'No, I haven't forgotten, girl, 'cos I've got Flora and our mission at the back of me mind. I'm just waiting for you.'

The smile faded from Bridie's face. 'Is that Flora Parker from down the street? We heard the poor soul had had her house broken into. What a dreadful thing to happen at her age. Sure, I hope the dear lady hasn't been too affected by the ordeal?'

'She has, Ma, she's in a terrible state.' Molly decided to get it over quickly. 'Flora is the reason we're here, and why we're in a hurry.' Molly kept it brief, but couldn't keep the emotion from seeping into her voice when she looked at her mother. For Bridie and Bob had so much to enrich their lives, with grandchildren and now two new great-grandchildren. They had Tommy and Rosie living with them, and were very much loved by all the family and their friends. And Molly was happy, for this was how life should be for the older generation, who had worked hard and scrimped and scraped when times were hard. But Flora Parker had no one to turn to for solace. No shoulder to lay her head on, no arms to hold her tight. It didn't seem right that someone who had had her fair share of trouble and heartache should be alone in the winter of her life.

'Ma, you and Lizzie Corkhill have both known Flora for donkey's years, so wouldn't it be nice if yer paid her a visit? I'm sure she'd be delighted to see old friends, and talk to people of her own age. I don't mean yer should be in and out of each other's houses, but it would do her good to have a visitor now and again. She has no relations of her own.'

'Sure, wouldn't I be happy to do that, sweetheart, it would be my pleasure. Me and yer da are very lucky, and we know that. One way of repaying the good Lord for His bounty would be to help someone less fortunate. If yer can find out when it would be convenient, me and Lizzie will pay her a visit.'

While this conversation was going on, Nellie hadn't been idle. Not one to beat about the bush, she had told Tommy and Rosie of Molly's determination to help Flora, and soon the little woman was clutching a two shilling piece in her hand, given to her by Tommy, who said, 'My mam's a smasher. I don't half love her.'

'So do I, lad, so do I.' Nellie grinned up at him. 'Yer don't think I'd pick a rotter for a mate, do yer? I might look daft, but I know a good thing when I see it.'

Chapter Five

'We're nearly there, girl,' Nellie said, puffing as she tried to keep up with Molly. 'Have yer decided what ye're going to tell Flora about how yer came by the money? If yer haven't it's too late, 'cos we're only two doors away now.'

'I've got one idea, sunshine, but how it'll sound I haven't a clue. I'm going to play it by ear, and make it up as I go along. And I hope yer'll go along with whatever I say, Nellie, even though I'll be lying through me teeth. We'll both have to say a prayer when we go to bed, and ask God to forgive us. After all, we're only doing it to help someone, so I think He will understand.'

They were outside Flora's front door when Nellie said, 'Oh, He will forgive us, girl, 'cos He's a friend of mine.'

Molly lifted the knocker and tapped softly. 'I hope we get away with it, and Flora believes what I tell her. If she does I'll sleep with an easy mind.'

A voice came from behind the door. 'Is that you, Molly?'

'It is, Flora. Me and Nellie.'

They heard the bolt being drawn, then as the door was opening a frail voice said, 'When it got so late, I thought yer weren't coming and I bolted up for the night.'

'We got held up, sunshine.' Molly pushed Nellie ahead of her. 'I'm sorry we're late, but with promising to come, I wasn't going to let yer down. We won't stay long, though, 'cos yer must be worn out after the day yer've had.'

The living room looked cold and unwelcoming. The gas light was turned down low, and the few dying embers in the grate were giving out no heat. But the mates made no comment, as they were well aware the old lady had no money for the gas meter or the coalman.

'I'm sorry I can't make yer a cup of tea,' Flora told them as she sank into her chair with a weary sigh. 'But yer can sit down; at least that doesn't cost any money. And I am glad of a bit of company.'

Molly was nervous, worrying she might use the wrong words and make Flora think they were there because they felt sorry for her. And pity was the last thing she needed, 'It's money we've come to talk about, sunshine, and I don't want yer to get the wrong idea and fly off the handle. Listen to what me and Nellie have got to say.'

Nellie's eyes widened with surprise. Why did her mate have to bring her name into it, when she was in the dark about what was in Molly's mind? In fact she knew no more than Flora did! 'I'll leave the talking to you, girl. It's no use two of us talking at the same time.'

Molly sat forward on the wooden chair and took hold of one of Flora's hands. 'We've thought of a way to get round yer money worries, Flora, but it's up to you whether yer agree or not. We don't want to talk yer into something yer don't agree with; yer must do what is best for you.'

'I don't know how anyone can help me, queen, for I've nothing of any value to sell, and if I borrowed I couldn't pay them back. Everything in the house, like the furniture, was bought when I got married. I've looked after it well, but if I sold or pawned it I wouldn't get enough to pay me way for this week. And I'd be in the same boat next week. In fact I'd be worse off 'cos I'd have an empty house. Besides, I couldn't sell it. It's all I've got left to remind me of me parents and husband.'

'Just listen to what I've got to say, sunshine, and yer may find there is a way out. Far better than selling yer home up. The only one to gain from that would be the pawnbroker.' Molly shook her head. 'No, what me and Nellie have in mind would make it much easier for yer, and no one would be any the wiser. So just listen until I've finished, and then yer can say yes or no. Will yer do that?'

Flora nodded. 'Go on, Molly. I know yer mean well, and Nellie. But I doubt anyone can help. Still, I will listen to yer.'

'Well, it's like this, sunshine. Me and Nellie always put a bit of money away each week to help towards clothes, and birthday presents, or for Christmas.' Molly shot a warning glance at Nellie, who had sat forward in her chair with her mouth open. This was all news to her, and the warning was to remind her not to interrupt or show surprise. 'Now we've got twelve shillings in the kitty, six shillings each, and right now we have no need of it. So me and Nellie have had a good talk, and as the money is just lying in a box, not doing anything, we thought it would help you over this difficult time. It would be better to put the money to good use, rather than have it sitting there doing nothing.'

Flora had a hand to her throat, and was shaking her head. 'It's thoughtful of yer, Molly, and you, Nellie, but I couldn't even consider what yer've said. I could never pay twelve shillings back, for where would I get that much money from? I can barely live on the pension I get. By the time I've paid me way there's very little left.'

'We have thought of all that, sunshine. We know a widow's pension doesn't go far. Whoever is in charge of pensions wants shooting. I'd like to see them living on it. There'd soon be some changes if those in the government had to try and manage on a paltry few bob a week.' Molly moved to kneel next to Flora's chair. 'We can manage without the money we've got saved; there's nothing we're desperate for. We would really like yer to take it, so yer could pay yer dues, as usual, and buy yer food. We haven't told a soul, so it would be our secret. And if ye're too proud to take it from us as a gift, then yer could pay us back. Me and Nellie thought threepence a week would be about right, and you wouldn't feel beholden to us. We understand that yer have yer pride, Flora, and this way would mean yer could keep yer pride, and live without worrying about yer rent and coal money.'

Flora was shaking her head long before Molly finished. 'As I said Molly, it's very kind of you and Nellie, but at threepence a week it would be years before yer got yer money back. I could be dead and buried by then.'

It wasn't a time for humour, but Nellie couldn't resist. 'Oh, yer won't be dead, girl, I'll see to that. I'll be round here every day to make sure ye're looking after yerself. Keeping warm and eating well.'

Molly chuckled. 'Take no notice of her, sunshine, she's not as tight as she sounds. Or as hard-hearted. In fact she was over the moon at the idea of us being able to help yer. And it wouldn't take for ever to pay the money back, for threepence a week comes to a shilling every month. And yer'll have paid us back before yer know it.'

Flora was giving the offer much thought. She was being offered a life-line, but old habits die hard, and she'd never borrowed or owed anyone a penny in her life. 'Would the neighbours know I'd borrowed off yer?'

It was Nellie who was quick to say, 'Only me and Molly would know, girl, and we won't snitch. Take the money and don't be so ruddy stubborn. Ye're as bad as me mate. She's stubborn when she likes. Digs her heels in and won't budge.'

There was silence as the old lady gave the matter more thought. She'd been worrying all day about having to tell the rent collector she couldn't pay. Or the coalman that she didn't want her usual sack of nutty slack. And if she was very careful, she could repay the loan at sixpence a week, then it wouldn't take so long. And if the neighbours didn't know, she wouldn't have to lower her head in shame. 'I wouldn't want twelve shillings, Molly, that's far too much. Eight shillings would be plenty to see me through. And I don't know how to thank you and Nellie. You're very kind.'

Molly opened her handbag. 'We've brought the twelve shillings, Flora, so yer may as well have it. And don't worry that we'll be leaving ourselves skint, 'cos we won't. You take it and do what yer like with it.'

Nellie watched her mate put the six two-shilling pieces on the table. And feeling like Lady Bountiful, she said, 'Take it, girl, and after yer've put enough aside to pay yer way, go out tomorrow and treat yerself to something. It bucks yer up when yer've got a couple of coppers spare to treat yerself.' When she finished speaking, Nellie reflected on her words. And she gave herself a fright. If she didn't watch out, she'd end up as good-hearted as her mate, and that was taking things too far.

Flora was staring at the stack of silver coins. 'Molly, if ye're quite sure, then I'm beholden to yer. But I'll pay yer back at sixpence a week. I could manage that.'

'I've never been so sure of anything in me life, sunshine. Do as Nellie says and treat yerself.' Molly stood up and ran a hand down the front of her coat to smooth the creases. 'Oh, by the way, most of the people in the neighbourhood know yer've been broken into. But no one knows me and Nellie are here tonight.' And to give the old lady a thought to buck her up, Molly added, 'Ye're very well thought of, Flora. Yer should be proud. So don't be surprised if yer keep getting stopped in the street. People are not being nosy, they're concerned for yer.'

It was when Flora followed them to the door, so she could bolt up again, that Molly pretended she'd just thought of something. 'Oh, I nearly forgot, sunshine. Me ma said she'd like to come and see yer, and so did Lizzie Corkhill. I said I'd let them know when yer were up to having visitors. And yer can tell me to mind me own business if yer like, Flora, but if I was in your shoes I'd welcome visits from old friends. A good natter would be something for yer to look forward to. If yer don't feel up to having visitors, I could take you to see them.' Molly kissed her cheek. 'We'll call tomorrow, so yer can let me know then. Goodnight, sunshine, and God bless.'

Nellie wasn't one for kissing, so when she found herself kissing Flora's cheek a voice in her head said if she carried on the way she was, she'd become another do-gooder like her mate. And seeing as she couldn't remember having one good belly laugh that day, she muttered under her breath as she stepped down on to the pavement, 'Sod that for a lark. Being bountiful might be good for yer soul, but it doesn't do nothing for yer social life.' If you didn't have time for a laugh and a bit of fun, what was the point of living? No, she'd leave Molly to do the good deeds, and she'd provide the laughs and entertainment. As her old ma used to say, 'A good laugh does yer more good than a pan of scouse any day. And it's cheaper.'

The mates were deep in conversation as they turned the corner into their street. Molly was delighted at the way things had worked out; it was a load off her mind. And Nellie seemed happy with herself as she did a hop, skip and jump to keep up. 'Ay, girl, that sixpence a week will come in handy, won't it?'

Molly stopped in her tracks. 'What sixpence?'

'The sixpence off Flora, of course, what else?'

'Nellie McDonough, have yer lost the run of yer senses? Yer don't think for one minute that I'd take money off her, do yer? After what she's gone through, and at her age, I wouldn't dream of it. And I think yer should be ashamed of yerself.'

'Ay, keep yer hair on, girl, I've got nothing to be ashamed of. It's you what said Flora could pay the money back at sixpence a week, so why take off on me for mentioning it? If she's giving the tanner, I want to know where it's going.'

'I know where it would go if you got yer hands on it, sunshine, and that's Hanley's cake shop. An extra cream slice, is that what ye're after, greedy guts?'

'For your information, girl, I could get three cream slices for sixpence. And why ye're getting yerself all wound up over it, I don't know.'

Molly looked up at the star-filled sky. 'God, give me patience. I don't want to fall out with me best mate, 'cos she doesn't know any better. But it's hard sometimes.' Then she looked down at Nellie. 'Let's make this short and sweet, sunshine, 'cos I don't want to be standing here all night. I have no intention of taking any money off Flora. Now, is that understood, or do I have to spell it out to yer?'

'It wouldn't be no good yer spelling it out, girl, 'cos yer know very well I can't spell. But will yer tell me, without getting yer knickers in a twist, why and how ye're not taking the money off Flora? Yer said yerself that she's very proud, so what are yer going to do when she holds out a hand with a tanner in it?'

There came a deep sigh from Molly. 'I don't know, sunshine. I haven't had time to sort it out in me head. In fact, I've done that much talking tonight in five houses, me head's in a whirl. The only thing I'm certain of now is that our families have been eager to help the old lady, and there's no way I'm taking it back off her. They gave it in the goodness of their hearts, and that's how it will stay. I'll think of a way when me head is clear.'

Nellie's conscience was pricking her. Perhaps she could be half a do-gooder; that wouldn't be so bad. 'I'm sure yer'll come up with a good reason or excuse, whatever yer call it, 'cos yer always do, girl. I've never known yer fail to do something when yer've set yer mind to it. Yer have a way of knowing what words to use, and yer'll come up trumps this time, I bet. I wouldn't bet on meself 'cos I'm bleeding hopeless, but I'd put me money on you any time.'

A bell rang in Molly's head, and she could feel herself getting excited. 'That's it, Nellie! Oh, let me give yer a hug, yer clever thing.'

'What's got into yer, girl?' Nellie took a step back so she could look into her mate's face. 'Have I suddenly got a halo over me head, or has the day been too much for yer and yer've become hysterical?'

Molly cupped her chubby cheeks. 'Nellie, you little love, you! Ooh, I could kiss yer to death.' Kisses rained down on Nellie's face. 'Ye're a little beauty. I'll love yer for ever more.'

'Listen, girl, ye're beginning to frighten me now. Have yer seen a sign over me head, and an angel telling yer me halo's ready and there's a chair on the front row waiting for me?'

'Nothing like that, sunshine. And haven't we always said that as we go everywhere together, we may as well go to heaven together?'

'Yes, we have, girl, and I'm all for it. But not just yet, eh? In another forty years I'll go quietly, 'cos I'll have had a good innings, but not right this minute. Yer see, girl, I can't go right now 'cos I haven't got a clean pair of knickers on.'

A huge figure came up behind them, and a deep male voice said, 'Nellie McDonough, I'm ashamed of yer. Didn't yer mother ever tell yer never to go out without changing yer knickers?'

Nellie jumped. 'In the name of God, Corker, I've had enough frights off me mate without you having a go at me as well. The size of yer would put fear into anyone.'

Jimmy Corkhill was indeed capable of putting fear into the strongest of men. Molly's next door neighbour, he was six foot five inches tall and built like a battleship. But Lizzie Corkhill's son was a gentle giant. He was known as Corker to everyone for miles around, and was very popular. To the kids in the area he was known affectionately as Sinbad, because of his bushy head of hair, beard and moustache. To Molly, he was her best friend and often her confidant. Always ready to help, generous and caring. He was all those things rolled into one, and Molly thought the world of him. He had married Ellen when her husband died, and become father to her four children, who idolized him.

'Have yer been for a pint, Corker?' Molly asked. 'It's just about throwing out time, isn't it?'

'No, I've been waiting for you, me darlin'. Ellen told me about old Mrs Parker, and as soon as I'd finished me dinner I called on you to get the full story. Jack told me you and Nellie were out and wouldn't be in until after nine, so I stayed talking to him for a while, then went up to me ma's.'

'So yer know the whole story, then, Corker?'

'I do that, me darlin', and I wish yer'd called to our house for a contribution. I would gladly have given enough for the poor dear to pay her rent. It's not often I feel as angry as I do now, but right this minute I just wish I had the robber in front of me. I can promise yer that by the time I'd finished with him, he'd never rob another old lady who couldn't defend herself. What a coward he must be.'

'Corker, don't mention me and Nellie collecting money, for heaven's sake. I've made up a tale for Flora, 'cos she didn't want to take the money off us. I spun her a tale, and that's the only way I got round her. But if she finds out the truth, she'd be so humiliated she'd fling the money back in me face and never speak to me again. So don't let me down, Corker, please. And tell Ellen to keep it to herself, as well.'

'I'll do as yer ask, me darlin', and I'll tell Ellen not to repeat it. But I do want to help, Molly, for there's six working in our house, so we're not short of money. The kids don't earn much, I admit, but we are still well off compared to Mrs Parker. And knowing the old lady for so long, and what sadness she's had in her life, I'll feel guilty if I can't help in some way.'

'You can help, Corker, definitely! In fact ye're the answer to a prayer. Nellie can take the credit for my thinking up this idea of how best to help Flora, but you're the one who can make it sound possible and plausible. So can yer come back to our house so I can put yer in the picture?'

Nellie piped up. 'And me, girl, yer can put me in the picture.'

'Won't George be expecting yer home, sunshine? I think yer've left him on his own long enough tonight.'

Nellie squared her shoulders, which caused her bosom to stand to attention. 'What I say, Molly Bennett, is sod you and sod George. I've stuck with yer all day, thirsty, hungry and tired, so I'm buggered if I'm going to miss the end of the story. So, march on, McDuff, and me and Corker will follow. And the first thing yer do when yer get through the door, is to tell your feller to put the kettle on. And tell him to fill the ruddy thing, so I can make up for all the cups I've been robbed of.' Over Corker's loud guffaw, she shouted, 'And show him where the biscuit tin is, while ye're at it.'

Jack had the door open ready. 'Nellie,' he said, 'I wish yer wouldn't shout so loud. Yer'll have the whole street lined up for tea and biscuits.'

Nellie marched past him into the living room. She went straight to the carver chair standing at the side of the sideboard and carried it to the table. To make room for it, she pushed one of the dining chairs out of the way with her foot. Then, once seated in the chair she always claimed as her own, she pointed a stiffened finger at Jack. 'If yer had any nous about yer, Jack Bennett, yer'd welcome a queue outside yer door wanting tea and biscuits. Charge them tuppence for a cup of tea and a ginger nut and yer'd be laughing sacks. And if they preferred custard creams, yer could up the price to threepence.' She rolled her eyes. 'If yer put a smile on yer face, yer'd do a roaring trade.'

Molly hung her coat up before saying, 'Don't you be ordering my husband about, Nellie McDonough. And when he puts a cup of tea and a biscuit in front of yer, pay him the threepence before yer partake of them.'

Nellie screwed up her face. 'Before I what?'

'Before yer scoff them, soft girl.'

With a loud click of her tongue, Nellie shook her head. 'I'm sure my mate makes words up just to confuse me, Corker. Half the time I'm nodding or shaking me head, when I don't understand what she's said. The best I can do is try and look intelligent.'

'I don't believe that, Nellie, me darlin'. I bet yer've got more brains in that head of yours than half the people in this room.'

With Jack in the kitchen making a pot of tea, there was only Molly and Corker in the room with Nellie. And after giving the matter careful thought, she said, 'There's three of us here. How can yer have half of three people, unless one is a cannibal?' There was a smirk on her face as she laughed inwardly at her own joke. 'A hungry cannibal!'

Corker slapped his leg as he roared with laughter. 'There yer go, Nellie, yer've just proved how clever yer are. Who but yerself would have thought the best way to even things up would be to introduce a hungry cannibal?'

When Nellie laughed and threw her head back, the chair almost toppled backwards, and it was only her quick reaction that prevented it. 'I'm sorry about that, girl, but I got carried away. It was the mention of cannibals, yer see, and you and Corker sitting there looking all smug. And I got to thinking yer wouldn't be sitting there if yer knew how hungry I was, yer'd be pushing each other aside to be first out of the door.'

When Jack came through from the kitchen, his tongue was sticking out of the side of his mouth as he tried to keep the tray he was carrying straight. He set it down carefully on the table before speaking. 'It grieves me, Nellie, that I can only offer yer a couple of custard creams. It's a bit late to go out looking for a human sacrifice for yer to boil in the dolly tub.'

With her eyes on the plate of biscuits, Nellie thought she could afford to be generous. 'Ye're a smasher, Jack Bennett, and no mistake. If it was left to yer wife, I'd starve to death and she wouldn't bat an eyelid! She'll be sorry, though, 'cos I'm going to cut her out of me will and put you in. You'll be the one I leave this chair to. This prize possession of mine, what I love dearly.'

'Except it's not yours to give away, sunshine,' Molly said. 'It's yours when ye're in this house, yer make sure of that. But I'm the one that bought it.'

Nellie's expression was one of disgust. 'Oh, well, if there's going to be any squabbling over the chair between you and Jack, then the best thing I can do is take it to heaven with me when I die. I'll give Saint Peter prior notice, so he can have a space made for it next to my chair and me harp.'

'I know it's a good chair, sunshine, but I doubt it'll still be here in forty years' time. And yer did say, sometime today, that yer wanted to live for another forty years, didn't yer?'

The little woman didn't want to talk, not when there were a few biscuits on the plate and nobody else seemed interested in them. 'Enough messing around now, girl. Why don't we get down to business?'

'Yes, that's a good idea,' Molly agreed, and faced Corker. 'Do yer still have a bet on the gee-gees, Corker?'

The big man looked surprised at the question. But knowing Molly, he knew there would be a good reason for it. 'I do, me darlin'. I like a flutter if there's a horse running that I fancy. Why?'

'Are yer lucky? I mean do yer ever win?'

Jack looked astonished. 'Molly, that's Corker's business. Yer have no right to ask something so personal.'

'I'm not being nosy, sunshine, as yer'll know when I tell yer why I'm asking. So bear with me while I explain.'

Corker leaned forward and clasped his hands between his knees. He had liked Molly from the time he first set eyes on her, and over the twenty-odd years they'd lived in the same street, his admiration had grown. When he was going to sea, it was always Molly he looked forward to seeing when he came home. And she'd been the one to bring him and Ellen together. He would trust her with his life. 'I'm all ears, me darlin', so fire away.'

While Jack and Corker focused on her mate, Nellie focused her attention on the plate of custard creams. She told herself she could eat and listen at the same time, there was no harm in that. Molly curled her hand and held it to her mouth as she gave a nervous cough. 'I don't quite know where to start, but here goes. It's like this, Corker: I'm in a bit of a quandary. Yer see, I had to concoct a story that Flora would believe, or she never would have taken the money from us, 'cos yer know how proud she is.' After taking a deep breath, Molly went on. 'Anyway, me and Nellie told her that we always put a few coppers away every week in case of an emergency, and as we'd had no reason to delve into the pot, it had mounted up. I said we now had the grand sum of twelve shillings, and as we had no need of it, she could have it to pay her rent and that, and buy her food. Of course she wouldn't hear of it at first, until we told her she could pay it back at sixpence a week. Even then it took some doing to talk her into accepting, but we managed it, so she'll be able to pay her dues and have money over to live on.' Molly looked across the table to see if her mate would like to add to what had been said, but Nellie's eyes were on the last biscuit on the plate, which was testing her will power.

'Now comes the problem, Corker, for there is no way I can take sixpence a week off Flora. The money wasn't mine anyway, for six families had contributed towards it. And I've been racking me brains to find a solution to the problem. As me and Nellie were walking home, however, me mate passed a remark that lit a spark. She said something like, "I bet yer come up trumps, yer always do."'

The plate now empty, Nellie was dusting the crumbs off the front of her coat. 'Well, yer do, don't yer, girl? I've never known yer be stumped for a way out.'

'Listen, sunshine, I may have me moments, but I'm not a ruddy genius. It's just that this situation is one I want to get right, for it's a long time since I felt as emotional or as strongly as I do over Flora Parker. She's too old to fend for herself, and hasn't got a soul to turn to. So I'm hoping and praying that this idea of mine, brought on by you, Nellie, bears fruit. Otherwise I don't know what I'll do.'

'Molly, me darlin', if yer tell me what yer have in mind, I'll help. I'm on your side, remember that,' Corker told her. 'We've helped each other many a time over the years, and long may we carry on doing so.'

'It may not be possible, Corker,' Molly said, looking doubtful and feeling rather stupid, 'but I wondered if we could tell Flora that we'd put a bet on a horse, in her name, and the horse had won the race? Would we get away with it, or is it beyond the realms of possibility?'

Corker looked thoughtful as he stroked his beard. 'Have you ever put a bet on, Molly?'

'Only on the Grand National once, when me and Nellie put threepence each on a horse that is still running.'

Corker, who had given the matter some thought, reached a decision. 'It's a miracle if yer can pick the horse which is going to win before the race starts. If it was so easy, Molly, I'd be a very rich man. But I've hit on an idea that would solve the problem to suit everyone. Yer see, I'm quite friendly with the bookie, so I may be able to cadge a blank betting slip off him. If I explain the reason, and let him know there'd be no cheating so he wouldn't get into trouble with the law, or lose money, then I'm almost sure he'll go along with it. He should do, he's made enough off me over the years.'

'How would a betting slip help?' Molly asked. 'Yer've lost me, Corker.'

'Let me explain, then. I'll make it as simple as possible. If I can get a blank betting slip, I can fill it in after the race, when we know the name of the winning horse. I can put it down at whatever odds yer need to make up the amount of money yer gave Flora. Not the exact amount or she'll think it's too good to be true, and she won't believe yer. And although what I'm suggesting isn't illegal, and no one is being robbed, I would rather yer didn't mention it to anyone. Yer don't need to worry, we're doing it for the very best of reasons.'

'No one will breathe a word, Corker, I promise yer. Me and Jack won't, and when I've told Nellie about the terrible food the prisoners in Walton Jail get, she'll keep quiet. The thought of no cream slice after her dinner will be enough to strike her dumb.'

Corker stood up and stretched his huge frame. 'I'd better make tracks or Ellen will be wondering where I've got to.' He looked at the three serious faces, and throwing back his head he roared with laughter. 'If yer could just see yerselves! My partners in crime, and looking as though we've been plotting to rob a bank. Yer really don't have to worry, I know what I'm doing.'

'I'm glad you do, Corker,' Nellie said, 'cos I'm blowed if I do. Me head won't take it all in, so I couldn't tell anyone when I don't know meself. But I'll ask a favour of yer, if yer don't mind, lad?'

'Fire away, Nellie me darlin', your wish is my command.'

'Ooh, ye're a good lad, Corker. I knew I could rely on yer. What I'd like yer to do, and there's a pint in it for yer, is that when yer know the name of the winning horse, will yer put a tanner on it for me?'

There was complete silence for a few seconds as three pairs of eyes focused on Nellie's face, waiting for her to show a sign that she was joking. But her face was as innocent as a newborn baby's. Then Molly said, 'She's not with us, Corker, and perhaps it's just as well. Where Nellie is concerned, ignorance is most definitely bliss.'

Chapter Six

At two o'clock on the Saturday afternoon, Nellie stood on Molly's top step and lifted her hand to the knocker. But before she brought it down, she narrowed her eyes and moved her head several times from left to right, making sure there were no people about. She was taking Corker's words very seriously, and wasn't going to let the cat out of the bag. When she was satisfied the coast was clear, she brought the knocker down with full force.

Molly opened the door, and her eyes widened in surprise. 'What have yer got against this door, Nellie, that yer punish it every time yer come? I'm sure it would appreciate a nice gentle tap instead.'

Nellie's eyes looked up to the sky. 'Gentle tap be buggered, girl, it's a ruddy wooden door.'

'Okay, it's a wooden door. Silly me thinking it was the stop for the tram into Lime Street.'

'Don't be so bleeding sarky, girl, it doesn't suit yer.'

'Right! I won't be sarky any more, sunshine. I'll ask nicely and gently, why are yer standing on my step at this time on a Saturday afternoon? Or, if yer want me to butter yer up, I could ask why I am having the pleasure of seeing you.'

Before answering, Nellie made a great show of being sure there was no one within earshot. 'There's a lot of questions there, girl, but I'll answer the first one. I'm standing on yer step because I can't get in yer house when ye're blocking me way.'

'I don't want yer in me house, Nellie, 'cos I'm in the middle of a stack of ironing, and I don't want to stop until I've finished. So tell me what yer want and then I can get back before the iron gets too hot. Anyway, whatever it is can't be important, or yer'd have mentioned it when we went to the shops this morning.'

'I can't tell yer standing in the bleeding street, girl, 'cos yer never know who might be listening.'

Molly sighed. 'Just for five minutes, Nellie, then I'm going to chase yer. So make it snappy.'

'Well, seeing as I can't walk through yer, girl, wouldn't it be a good idea for yer to stand aside and let me in?'

Molly wasn't feeling very happy as she closed the door. She had her whole afternoon planned in her head, with a visit to her two daughters, Jill and Doreen, and then to her ma's. But she could say goodbye to her timetable now, for five minutes to Nellie could be anything up to an hour or more.

As she followed her mate into the living room, Molly gave herself a lecture. She'd have to be firm, hard even, and put her foot down. Yes, that's what she'd do. But her heart sank when Nellie made straight for the carver chair, picked it up and carried it to the table. Without a by-your-leave, she used her foot to push one of the dining chairs aside to make room for the carver.

'Nellie, I told yer I could only spare five minutes, so what are yer making yerself comfortable for?' Molly put her hands on the back of a chair, and even though she knew she was wasting her time, she tried again. 'Nellie, will yer tell me what yer want me for, and make it quick 'cos I've got an iron on a gas ring.'

Cool as a cucumber, Nellie said, 'Well, turn it off, girl, for it's costing yer money. And yer know darn well I can't talk quick, 'cos I've got to think in case I come out with something I shouldn't.'

'If yer don't stop messing around, sunshine, I'll be doing something I shouldn't, never mind saying it. So just tell me, in plain English, and not a lot of words, what are yer here for?'

Nellie took her elbows off the arms of the chair, and folded her arms under her bosom. And the set expression on her face said she had no intention of moving until she was ready. 'I'm waiting for Corker to come, to tell us the name of the horse what is going to win the race.'

Molly was flabbergasted. 'You what! There's nothing wrong with yer hearing, Nellie, and yer were here when Corker said it would be about six o'clock before the races were over. And if yer think I'm going to let yer plonk yer backside down on that chair, and stay there until six o'clock, then yer better think again, sunshine, 'cos

I can't spare the time to entertain a visitor. I've got too much work to do.'

'It'll be nice for yer to have company, girl. While yer do the ironing, I can talk to yer and keep yer amused. And that's a ruddy good offer; yer'll not get a better one. Yer'll be so busy listening to me, yer'll have yer work done before yer know it.'

Molly opened her mouth, but the retort died on her lips as she remembered the iron was still on the gas ring. 'Oh, my God.' She fled to the kitchen, switched off the gas, and reached for a towel to move the red-hot flat iron. 'Nellie McDonough, I could wring your ruddy neck. Yer've upset me whole routine. I should never have opened the door to yer. And I want me bumps feeling for letting yer in.'

Nellie wasn't a bit put out. 'I would have gone round to the back door, girl, 'cos I know that's always on the latch, and just walked in.'

'D'yer know the thought that has just entered my head?' Molly was trying her level best to stay calm, but it was hard going. 'When anyone asks me how many children I've got, I always say four, 'cos I forget about you. So for twenty-odd years I've been telling fibs. With that record, there's not much chance of me getting into heaven.'

In her devious mind, Nellie was telling herself that Molly was coming round. It wouldn't be long before there was a pot of tea on the table, and a plate of custard creams. 'Of course yer'll get into heaven, girl, yer'll walk it! As soon as Saint Peter knows ye're my mother, he'll welcome yer with open arms.'

Molly knew she was mad and wanted her head testing, but she couldn't stop the giggle that escaped through her lips. And this paved the way for a gale of laughter. Holding her tummy, she bent over the table. 'Nellie McDonough. Ye're priceless, that's what yer are. A bloody nuisance as well, like, but priceless none the less.' She nearly choked on a bout of laughter. 'Me, your mother, indeed!' Wiping a tear of laughter away, Molly pointed a finger. 'I think I can safely say, sunshine, that if I was your mother, God forbid, then yer'd have far more on top than yer've got. And yer'd be better mannered, saying please and thank you occasionally. Also, yer conversations wouldn't be peppered with swear words.'

A frown creased Nellie's forehead as her mind ticked over. Why didn't her mate use little words, like what everyone did? In the end, after much deliberation, she said, 'Yer've lost me altogether now, girl. Where does pepper come into it? I don't like the ruddy stuff, it's too hot for me, makes me sneeze and sweat like nobody's business.'

'I didn't mean pepper what yer sprinkle on yer food, soft girl, I meant peppered as in— Oh, forget it, sunshine, it would take too long to explain.' Molly threw her hands in the air. She gave in, surrendered, capitulated, lost the will to argue any more. It was her own fault, anyway, for opening the front door in the first place. Served her right for being so nosy. 'I know when I'm beat, Nellie, but as I'm not completely knocked out, I'll only meet yer halfway. So I'll put the kettle on and make a pot of tea. We'll have a cup each, with a biscuit, and then I'm sending you on yer way. Yer can go peacefully, or I can chuck you out. The choice is yours.'

When her mate walked through to the kitchen, Nellie's face lit up and her short, chubby legs swung happily under the chair. She didn't know why Molly had got herself all het up when the outcome had been plain from the second she'd knocked on the door. 'Don't forget, girl,' she called, 'I like two sugars in me tea, and two biscuits in the saucer.'

A voice came back. 'Sod off, sunshine. Yer'll have what I give yer and like it.'

'Oh, I'll like it, girl, as long as the tea's sweet and the biscuits are custard creams.'

Corker was a happy man when he walked into Molly's house at six o'clock. He'd managed to get a blank betting slip off the bookie, which he'd write out in front of his neighbours so they'd know what he was doing. He was pleased he'd be able to help Molly out, but his huge smile owed more to his win on the gee-gees.

Jack looked up from his fireside chair at the giant of a man who seemed to fill the small living room. 'Yer have the look of a man who has something to be cheerful about, Corker. Did yer back a winner?'

'Three of them, Jack.' Corker rubbed his hands together. Hands that could lift a ton weight, yet were gentle when holding a baby. 'It's been a good day for me, all right, and I'm dead chuffed. The bookie had a bad day, though; he must have paid some money out. Still, it's not often any bookmaker is out of pocket. I had a six to one winner, a three to one and a two to one. Not bad in one day, eh?'

'You lucky beggar! Still, they say much gets more,' Molly said, affection in her eyes for the man who had always been a good friend. 'I couldn't even win a blinking coconut at the fairground.'

Her husband chuckled. 'To win, love, yer have to have a bet. And I can't see you putting money on a horse.'

'Not likely,' Molly said with conviction. 'I've got better things to do with me money.'

They all turned their heads when Nellie came barging in. 'Have I missed anything?'

Mollie's eyes were wide. 'How the heck did you get in?'

'Through the bleeding door, soft girl. How else could I have got in?'

Corker looked sheepish as he raised a hand. 'I'll take the blame for that, Molly me darlin'! I was so pleased with meself, I couldn't wait to brag about me good fortune, and I must have forgotten to close the door behind me.'

'I'll let yer off,' Molly told him, 'but only because ye're bigger than me. If I wanted to clock yer one, I'd have to stand on a chair and I haven't got the energy.'

Nellie tutted. 'Why don't yer tell the truth, girl, and shame the devil? Yer won't stand on a chair because ye're afraid of showing yer bloomers.'

Molly's voice was shrill. 'Bloomers! Nellie, bloomers went out with the ark. No one wears them these days, and I hope yer haven't come just to embarrass me.'

'No, I haven't come for that, girl, I wouldn't want to embarrass me best mate.' Nellie allowed her bosom to blossom when she squared her shoulders. 'I came because I saw Corker coming, and I knew yer wouldn't knock for me, like yer promised to.'

Corker looked forward to these exchanges between the friends. He thought they were hilarious. They'd been like this since he'd known them, yet never once had they fallen out. 'Nellie, I didn't pass your house, so how did yer see me?'

'I was looking for yer, soft lad, that's how. If I'd waited until me mate knocked, like what she said she would, then I'd still be waiting when it was time for bed.' Then her eyes lit up with devilment 'Not that I mind going to bed, Corker, don't get me wrong, Bed is me favourite place, where I get all the excitement and pleasure I need to round off a good day. And my George, well he has the best times of his life in bed.'

Molly knew this was intended to wind her up, and she didn't know whether to laugh or cry. So she settled for a happy medium. 'Nellie McDonough, it's a good job for you that our Ruthie is over in her mate's. I'll not have her listening to talk like that at her age. Honest, the things yer come out with would make the devil himself blush. I don't know where to put meself sometimes.'

'I know where yer can put yerself, girl, and that's on the couch. I'll get me chair and put it by the table, and we'll all make ourselves comfortable while Corker tells us whether our horse won, or fell at the first hurdle.' She turned her head slightly, so she could give Corker a sly wink before going on. 'Oh, don't bother putting the kettle on yet, girl. We'll wait until Corker's finished.'

Molly put her hands on her hips and asked, 'Who was yer servant before I came along, sunshine? Sitting on that throne of a chair giving yer orders out. Talk about Lady Muck isn't in it.'

Her mate didn't turn a hair. Putting on her innocent expression, she said, 'I didn't have no servant before you came along, girl. Didn't even have any friends. So yer can imagine how happy I was when I met you. I went from having nothing to having a friend, a servant, and a throne, all in one go. Then I knew my ship had come in.'

Molly looked at Corker and shrugged her shoulders. 'I don't know why I bother, 'cos it's just a waste of breath. Unlike your horses, I can't win.'

Nellie's mouth formed several contortions before she could get her words out. 'Ooh, did our horse win, Corker?'

'It wasn't our horse, Nellie,' Molly said. 'I've told yer a dozen times but it doesn't seem to sink in. If Corker has managed to find a solution regarding Flora, there'll be no money involved, and every-thing will be hunky dory. You and me will be off the hook, and Flora will have no money worries.' She looked at Corker. 'Put us out of our misery, sunshine, but keep yer own business to yerself, or it'll be round the street in no time.'

'I'm so chuffed with meself, Molly, I'll probably be blowing me trumpet in the pub tonight. So the whole neighbourhood will know without Nellie telling them. There'll be a few pints for Jack and George, and a couple of bottles of milk stout for you good ladies.'

Nellie was all ears. 'Have yer had a win, then, Corker?'

'I've won a few bob, Nellie, yes, but I'm not telling yer how much. If Ellen and the kids get to know, it'll be gone before I know it.'

'Don't let them cadge it off yer before me and Molly get our milk stouts, Corker.' Nellie had it in her mind to say if he'd give her the money she'd run up and get them, because the pub would be open now. But common sense prevailed when she considered what her mate would have to say.

'Trust you to think about yerself, sunshine,' Molly said, her head shaking slowly. 'To hell with everyone else as long as you're happy.'

'It was meant as a joke, girl. Have yer got no bleeding sense of humour? Yer've got a gob on yer that would stop a ruddy clock.'

Molly took it in good part. 'Ooh, what clock is that, Nellie? There's some beautiful-looking clocks. Like that one in Cookson's window. I passed the shop the other day and thought how lovely it was, and how I'd buy it if I had the money.'

Nellie's tummy was shaking with silent laughter. 'Okay, girl, I think we're about even now, so shall we be quiet and listen to what Corker has to say?'

It didn't take the big man very long to show how he had filled in the blank betting slip. 'I've made a bet in Mrs Parker's name, see, for two shillings. The horse I've put down is the one that came in at six to one, and she'd placed her bet on it to win. So, in theory, she won twelve shillings.'

'Oh, that's marvellous, Corker, ye're very kind. That lets me and Nellie off. I know I've got to tell a lie to Flora when I show her the betting slip, but it's a damn sight better than trying to find excuses every week for nearly a year. That betting slip is a godsend, and I owe you one big favour.'

'You owe me nothing, Molly me darlin'. I was thinking of giving you some of me winnings for the old lady, but although I'd be only too pleased to help, I know it would be too awkward for you to explain.'

Nellie piped up. 'She wouldn't take any money off yer, lad. She's too proud.'

Molly was looking down at the betting slip she was holding. 'The money has made her independent, Corker, and allowed her to pay her way. At least we know she'll have gas, coal and food. But if starving herself would get her husband's watch back, then she'd starve to death with it in her hand.'

'I've been giving that some thought,' Corker said. 'I'll go out a bit earlier tonight, and visit a few of the local pubs. I'll ask the landlords to spread the word, and yer never know, something might turn up. Whoever the rotter was who stole it, he must be fairly local. He must have known the old lady lived on her own. He'd probably been keeping tabs on her house for a few days to see who comes and goes. That's why he picked on Flora. And the only places he's going to be able to sell the watch is in the pubs. It's worth a try, anyway. As yer know, yer have to be tough to be a pub landlord, and some of them would turn a blind eye to crooked dealing in their pubs. But not when the stolen goods have been taken from the house of a woman in her eighties. They certainly wouldn't defend or protect such a rotter. Anyway, as I said, it's worth a try.'

'The police said something along the same lines, Corker,' Molly told him, 'And they mentioned pawnshops.'

Corker pushed himself off the couch. 'Most pawnbrokers are straight. They wouldn't entertain stolen goods in case the police raided their shops. But I know two who buy anything that's going. They sell from under the counter, and in my eyes they are lower than the robbers.' He ran two fingers down the crease in his trouser legs, then stretched to his full height. 'Anyway, I'll love yer and leave yer, or Ellen will have strong words with me if the dinner gets cold. Don't forget to give me that slip back after yer've shown it to Flora.'

'We'll go round and see her now, shall we, girl?' Nellie was all for a little diversion in her life. 'She'd be made up to see us.'

Molly had other ideas, though. 'Not tonight, sunshine, I think we've seen enough of each other for one day. Don't forget this is your third time here. No, we'll go tomorrow. Sunday is a nice peaceful day, just the day for bearing good news to a lovely old lady.'

'Come on, Nellie, I'll see yer home,' Corker said, taking her arm. Her head back as far as it would go, Nellie looked up at him.

'But yer only live next door.'

'I know that, Nellie me darlin', but I'll see yer to yer door to make sure yer come to no harm.'

'I don't want yer to save me from harm, yer big daft ha'p'orth.' Nellie's eyes rolled. 'If some handsome man comes along, and fancies my voluptuous body, I don't want yer frightening him off.'

Molly chuckled. 'Nellie, the chances of a handsome man coming along between here and your house, which is about ten yards away, are more remote than the chances would be of a horse we put money on winning a blinking race.'

Corker put his arm across the little woman's shoulder. 'Come on, me darlin'. And I promise I'll make meself scarce if I see a man of any shape or size on the horizon.' As he led Nellie towards the door, Corker called over his shoulder, 'I'll see yer about eight o'clock, Jack. Then we'll pick up George.'

Walking behind them to see them out, Molly heard her mate say, 'If yer don't get an answer, lad, yer'll know me and George are in bed. I don't see why yer should have all the fun. I'll tell him to follow yer on, though, but don't be surprised if he hasn't got the energy to lift his pint up.'

Chapter Seven

Jack let out a sigh of satisfaction as he pushed his empty dinner plate out of the way so he could rest his elbows on the table. 'That dinner was really tasty, love. It's not often we have a whole chicken for our dinner.'

His daughter nodded in agreement. 'It was last Christmas we had a chicken.' Ruthie rubbed her tummy. 'I liked the stuffing best, though. It wasn't half tasty, Mam. I don't suppose there's any left?'

'Yer suppose right, sunshine, the bowl is empty. Besides, yer eyes must be bigger than yer belly, 'cos after the dinner yer've just had, I'll bet yer couldn't eat another bite.'

Ruthie grinned. 'I could try, Mam.'

'Seeing as there's none left, yer'd have a job. And the reason we don't have chicken often is because I can't afford it. And for your information, the only reason we had one today is because Tony had ordered too many.'

Jack raised his brows. 'How on earth did he come to do that? He's had that shop for so many years yer'd think he'd know exactly what to order.' He began to chuckle. 'Mind you, I'm not sorry he slipped up. If we can benefit from it, he should slip up more often.'

'I felt sorry for him, 'cos he's a good scout is Tony,' Molly said. 'He's been good to me and Nellie over the years, and that means he's been good to our families. When he does us a favour, he's doing you one as well. So I did feel sorry for him yesterday when he was telling me and Nellie what a lousy day he was having. His customers were spending coppers on stew and cheap mutton chops, instead of joints of meat, or chickens.'

'He won't lose out, love,' Jack told her. 'I bet he had a rush of customers after you left.

'I don't think so, sunshine, because there were no other customers in the shop, and there weren't many people about in the streets. It wasn't only Tony's shop that was quiet; all the other shops were slack.'

'He won't lose out, love, don't you worry. What he didn't sell yesterday can be sold next week. He's got a good-sized storeroom, and the meat will come to no harm.'

There was a smile hovering around Molly's lips when she answered. 'Yeah, he's got a big storeroom. Me and Nellie have been in it a few times when Ellen's made a pot of tea and the shop's been quiet. Tony's good like that, he doesn't mind Ellen giving us a cuppa.'

Jack was nodding knowingly. 'Yer see, I told yer the meat will come to no harm. If it's put in the storeroom it'll be fine, and Tony can flog it tomorrow.'

Molly was trying to keep the laughter back, and her face straight, when she informed her husband, 'Oh, it wasn't the meat Tony was worrying about, it was the number of chickens. There weren't enough hooks in the storeroom for him to hang them all in there.'

'Good heavens, love, what's wrong with the man?' Jack raised his eyes to the ceiling. 'I always thought Tony ran that shop like clockwork, but he can't be very organized if he buys more than he can sell, or store.'

Ruthie had been sitting as quiet as a mouse. She really wasn't interested in what was being said, and couldn't understand why her mam and dad were wasting so much time talking about the butcher. What difference did it make to them whether he sold his meat or not? Then the girl caught a glint in her mother's eye, and she sat up straight. There was something in the wind, and she bet that whatever it was involved her mam, Auntie Nellie, and Tony. Which meant there was bound to be laughter on the way.

'Oh, Tony's not behind the door for brains, Jack. He knows the butcher's business inside out. He knows his customers by name, what meat they buy, and what he should have in stock. Anyway, with the help of my mate Nellie, everything was sorted out to suit all concerned.'

Jack rested his chin on a clenched fist. 'I do believe you've been having me on, Mrs Woman, haven't yer?'

'Ye're very easy to fool, sunshine, 'cos ye're too trusting, that's your trouble. But just wait until I tell Tony that yer think he's incompetent, disorganized and doesn't know how to run a shop properly. It's a dead cert there'll not be another chicken on this table for the foreseeable future. Yer've blotted yer copybook good and proper.'

Jack's deep brown eyes stared into eyes as blue as the sky on a summer's day. 'Am I to understand that my own wife is going to snitch on me?'

'The thought was crossing my mind, sunshine, until I remembered that I'd be cutting me nose off to spite me face. You don't get any chicken, then me and Ruthie would have to go without as well. So we'll leave well alone and give praise and thanks to Nellie for the very nice meal we've just enjoyed.'

'I'm afraid yer've lost me again, love,' Jack said, looking slightly bewildered. 'Where does Nellie fit into all this? Unless she bought the chicken for us, but I can't believe yer'd let her do that.' After a moment's thought, he chuckled. 'Come to think of it, I can't believe Nellie would do that anyway.'

'Listen, Jack, if Nellie ever bought us a chicken, she'd expect to be invited to dinner. And the amount she can eat, we wouldn't stand a dog's chance. She'd scoff the lot before we had time to pick up a knife and fork.' Molly rubbed the side of her nose. 'I've been talking a load of rubbish for the last twenty minutes, and seeing as Nellie will be calling for me soon to go to Flora's, I'd better leave the true story until I come back.' She caught and held her daughter's eye. 'Unless Ruthie will be an angel and clear the table for me and wash up?'

The girl looked horrified. 'Ah, ay, Mam! I want to know what happened as well as me dad. I know you and Auntie Nellie have been up to something, I can tell, and I can't hear yer if I'm in the kitchen with the tap running. So I'll do a deal with yer. You let me hear what yer've got to say, then I'll help yer with the dishes and tidy up. That's fair, isn't it?'

Molly knew her daughter to be a good little worker, and between them they'd have the jobs done in no time. What they didn't do, Jack would finish off. 'It's a deal, sunshine, so here goes.' She took a deep breath before beginning to relate what happened in the butcher's shop the day before. 'Tony did have a lot of chickens hanging up, that part was true. And he did say he couldn't understand why they

71

weren't selling as well as they usually did on a Saturday. He wasn't moaning, like, 'cos he's not like that. He was just telling us in the course of conversation. But yer know what Nellie's like, she doesn't miss a trick and is not backward in coming forward.'

Pushing her chair back, Molly got to her feet. 'I may as well do the job properly, so imagine I'm Nellie, and this is how it went.' Although Molly wasn't endowed with a bosom of the same magnitude as her mate's, she had her facial expression and her stance off to perfection. 'Here goes. "Ah, I am sorry for yer, lad, and I hope trade picks up for yer, 'cos chickens are funny buggers. They're not like meat, what will keep for a few days. No, chickens go a funny colour and start to smell in no time. And they don't half pong. Yer have to open all the doors to let the smell out and the fresh air in." ' Molly hitched up an imaginary bosom and her face took on an expression of sweet innocence. ' "I don't like to see yer stuck, lad, so me and Molly will help yer out by taking two of the chickens off yer hands. That's if we can have them cheap, of course, 'cos we'd be doing yer a favour. Otherwise, when yer open up on Monday, the place will stink to high heaven and yer customers will run like hell to the butcher's in Stanley Road." ' Molly's head gave a sharp nod which was a habit of Nellie's when she was in full flow. ' "And they wouldn't come back to yer, 'cos the butcher in Stanley Road is the spitting image of Clark Gable." ' Molly dropped her pose, moved to one side and became Tony the butcher.

' "Nellie, the butcher in Stanley Road looks more like Charles Laughton than Clark Gable. But as yer seem to be losing yer eyesight, I'll take pity on yer. I'm a sucker for sad cases, so I'll knock sixpence off a chicken for you and Molly." '

Jack's guffaw was loud. 'He didn't, did he?'

'Oh, that's not all,' Molly told him. 'Nellie wasn't satisfied and leaned over the counter. "I've always said yer were a smasher, Tony, I'm forever singing yer praises. Me and Molly are going to get our spuds and things from the greengrocer's now, so while we're away, will yer cut the heads off the chickens for us?" Tony was looking at her as though she'd gone mad. I think he was about to tell her to take a running jump when she added, "Oh, before I forget, lad, would yer stick yer hand up their backsides and take out the giblets? I hate that job." And before the poor man had time to answer back, she pulled me out of the shop and I was dragged to the greengrocer's. I don't think me feet even touched the ground. And when Nellie saw me open me mouth to tell her what I thought of her, she beat me to it. "I thought it best to make a hasty retreat, girl, before he had time to change his mind.'"

Ruthie was holding her tummy while she shook with laughter. 'Ooh, I wish I'd been there. Me Auntie Nellie's not half funny.'

'I can laugh at it meself, now,' Molly admitted, 'but I was embarrassed at the time. I wouldn't have dared to ask Tony to sell us the chickens with sixpence knocked off the price. Not after him being so good to us over the years. I look on him as a friend. And if there'd been other customers in the shop there would have been a stampede, with them all demanding a cheap chicken.'

Jack was afraid Nellie might knock and he wouldn't get to hear the ending until much later. So he decided to hurry things along. 'And what happened when yer got back to Tony's? Did he have the birds cleaned and ready for yer?'

Molly began to laugh so hard she couldn't speak for a while. Then, after she'd composed herself enough to get some words out without spluttering, she said, 'That was the funniest stunt Tony has ever pulled on us, and yer should have seen Nellie's face! Talk about a picture no artist could paint, well, me mate's face went through every emotion humanly possible. For when we got to the counter, and I asked him if we could have the chickens now, he bent down and brought out two chickens with their heads and feathers intact, and their feet tied together with string. I looked from Tony's face to Nellie's, and I felt sure she was going to burst a blood vessel. The veins in her neck and her temples were blue.

' "What the bleeding hell do yer think ye're playing at, yer stupid bugger? If yer think I'm paying good money for them, well, yer've got another think coming. Just look at them! The poor buggers should have been left on the farm to live out their lives in peace. It wouldn't have been long, for the poor sods look as though they were dead before they got killed. And now I come to look at them, at their faces, like, and their skinny legs, they remind me of someone. Are you related to them by any chance, lad?'"

Jack and Ruthie were doubled over, their eyes running with tears of laughter. 'Oh dear, oh dear, oh dear.' Jack gulped. 'So Nellie had to put her hand inside the chicken's backside after all? Or did you do them both?'

'Did I heckers like.' Molly wrinkled her nose. 'Couldn't cut the head off a chicken if yer paid me. Or pluck it and take out the giblets. Me tummy is turning over now, just at the thought of it.'

'Well, come on, out with it, what happened?' Jack asked. 'Nellie will be here before yer know it.'

'All ended well, sunshine, 'cos while Tony removed the chickens from the counter, Ellen came through from the storeroom, and she was carrying a chicken in each hand, which she'd prepared while me and Nellie were doing the rest of our shopping. She'd chopped their heads off, plucked them and cleaned them. They were all ready to put in the roasting tin. And she'd slipped a piece of dripping inside each one. Whether Tony knew about that I don't know. I didn't mention it in case we got Ellen into trouble. But me and me mate were more than satisfied with the way things worked out. As Nellie said when we were walking home, "Not bad at all, eh, girl? A chicken all cleaned ready for the oven, plus the dripping to roast it in, and all for a shilling each. That's what I call a good day's work. But yer know why Tony's so generous with us, don't yer? Yeah, yer must do 'cos it's sticking out a mile every time he looks at me. It's me voluptuous body what does it." '

Nellie stood on the Bennetts' top step and brought the knocker down hard. It was the second time she'd knocked without getting any response. 'Are they all bleeding deaf?' she muttered. 'I know they're in 'cos I can hear them.' She waited a few seconds, then stepped down on to the pavement. 'Bugger this for a joke.' She walked to the window, balled her fist and banged on one of the panes of glass. 'They'll hear that all right, unless they've all pegged out during the night.'

'What the hell are yer playing at, Nellie?' Molly looked down at her mate. 'Yer nearly put the window in! I'm fed up telling yer to use the knocker on the door. That's what it was put there for.'

'Well, all I can say, girl, is that whoever the silly bugger was what put the knocker on the door, he must have thought we were all giants. I have to stand on the top step and stretch me arm out of its socket to reach up to it.'

74

Molly bit on the inside of her mouth to keep herself from laughing at Nellie's face. 'Well, sunshine, if I have a choice between one of my windows being smashed, or your arm being stretched out of its socket, I'll settle for the latter. That way it won't cost me anything.'

'How many times do I have to tell yer that being sarky doesn't suit yer? It doesn't go with yer face. Anyway, girl, aren't yer going to ask me in?'

Molly shook her head as she reached for her coat from a hook on the wall. 'No, I'm all ready, sunshine, so we can be on our merry way.'

The little woman stepped back a pace. 'Yer mean ye're not inviting me in? Have yer forgotten it's Sunday?'

Molly stepped on to the pavement and pulled the door shut behind her. 'Even if me and Ruthie hadn't gone to church this morning, I'd know it's Sunday. But seeing as your curtains were still drawn when me and Ruthie passed on our way to ten o'clock mass, I'm surprised yer haven't still got sleep in yer eyes.' Molly smiled and linked her arm through Nellie's to show she was only kidding. 'The reason I didn't invite yer in, sunshine, is because Jack is clearing the dinner table and Ruthie is washing the dishes. The place is a mess and I'd have been ashamed if yer'd have seen it.'

Nellie's face cleared and she squeezed Molly's arm as they began to walk up the street. 'Girl, if yer think your place is bad, yer should see mine. It's like a muck midden. We all slept in this morning 'cos it was after twelve when we got to bed. Once our Paul starts gabbing there's no shutting him up. Him and his flaming dancing, it's all he thinks about.'

'And Phoebe, sunshine; he thinks the world of her. She's been a good influence on him. He's slowed down a lot since they started courting. Is there any mention of marriage yet?'

'They are supposed to be saving up, girl, but our Paul likes gadding about, so whether he's saving up I wouldn't like to say. Phoebe is, I know that. She goes to the post office every week and puts money away. But our Paul, well, I don't think I'll be needing a wedding hat in the near future.'

Molly chuckled. 'Yer've still got the two wedding hats from when the girls got married, and your Lily. Yer don't need to buy another.'

Nellie brought her to a halt. 'Listen, girl, when our Paul gets married I'll definitely be pushing the boat out. Nothing but the best for the last one of me children to leave home.'

'And what makes yer think he'll be leaving home when he gets married?' Molly asked. 'Where would he and Phoebe live? They couldn't move into Corker's, 'cos there's no room. There's six living there now; they'd have to knock a wall down if they took anyone else in. Besides, a newly married couple need some privacy. And they'd get that in your house. Plus they wouldn't need to buy any furniture because Paul's room is already furnished. All they need to do is get married and walk into yours.'

'Bloody hell, girl, yer've got all that figured out, haven't yer? All I'm thinking about is getting a new hat, while you've got them married off and living with me.'

'It was just a thought, sunshine, for Paul and Phoebe have been courting over a year now. And it's not as though they're not serious about each other because never a night passes that they aren't off out together. They walk down the street arm in arm and gazing into each other's eyes. If they aren't crazy about each other, then all I can say is they are ruddy good actors.'

Nellie was giving serious thought to Molly's words, her lips in a straight line and her eyes narrowed. 'I have known for a long time that they would eventually get married, girl, but never gave a thought about them coming to live with me and George. It wouldn't half put a halt to my gallop.'

Molly tutted. 'Yer've got time to think of a new hat for yer son's wedding, but no time to consider, or wonder, where he and his new bride will live. And it wouldn't be a case of them putting you to any trouble if they did move in with you, 'cos Paul lives with yer already. The only difference is that a double bed would be required to replace the single already in the room.' Molly was getting into her stride now. 'Phoebe Corkhill is a smashing girl, everyone in the street likes her. Paul couldn't find himself a better wife. She's pretty, well mannered, a good worker and very quiet. What more do yer want?'

'That's the only thing I'm afraid of, girl, she's too quiet.'

Molly gasped. 'Too quiet! How can anyone complain because a girl is too quiet? I've heard of some objections from mothers whose son or daughter wants to get married, but that one takes the cake,

Nellie, it really does. Yer don't half come up with some cockeyed ideas.'

'I've got nothing against Phoebe, girl, I think she's lovely and will make Paul a good wife. But yer know what I'm like. I don't like quietness.'

'She's not a mouse, sunshine, Phoebe does talk and laugh like the rest of us.'

'Even when she's in bed, girl? That's where I do most of my laughing. Me and George have high jinks nearly every night. If there was someone lying in the next room, it wouldn't half put me off me stroke.'

'Paul sleeps in the next room to yer now, always has done, and Steve did too before he married Jill. So what difference would Phoebe make?'

'The snoring, girl, that's the difference. Yer see, all the men in me family snore so loud it's like an orchestra playing. We didn't half notice the difference when Steve went to live at Lizzie's. George and Paul still made a racket, but the orchestra didn't sound as loud without the trumpet.'

It only took Molly one second to realize she'd been taken for a ride. But seeing the devilment in her mate's eyes, she couldn't help but roar with laughter. 'Nellie McDonough, what am I going to do with yer? Yer really had me going there. I fell for it like a ton of bricks. Just wait until I get home and tell Jack.'

Nellie hadn't finished with her yet, though. 'We could tell Flora. She could do with a good laugh.'

Molly's mouth opened in horror. 'Don't yer dare, Nellie McDonough, or I'll never speak to yer again. Flora Parker is an old-fashioned lady, and she'd be shocked if yer repeated talk like that in front of her. So when we get there . . . if we ever do . . . keep your mouth firmly closed, d'yer hear me?'

'I heard yer, girl, I'm not deaf.' Nellie walked with her head down, muttering under her breath, 'No sense of humour, that's her trouble. It's a good job we don't live next door to each other, or she'd be complaining about lack of sleep because of the noise. Me and George would probably end up on the living-room floor.'

Molly cocked an ear, and pretended she hadn't heard every word. 'What did yer say about the floor, sunshine?'

'Not the floor, yer daft nit. Yer need yer ears cleaning out. What I said was that I hoped I'd remembered to close the front door.'

Molly chuckled inwardly, thinking her mate was as crafty as a boxload of monkeys. 'I'm sure yer did, sunshine, I'm sure yer did.'

Chapter Eight

Flora Parker felt a stab of fear when she heard the knock on the door. It was Sunday afternoon, she wasn't expecting visitors, and the street would be deserted, as parents didn't allow their children to play out on the Sabbath. What if it was the burglar? He knew she was old and lived alone, and if she opened the door he could push her inside and close the door without being seen by any of the neighbours. She gripped the arms of her rocking chair and told herself to stay where she was. Whoever it was would go away when their knock wasn't answered.

Outside, Molly and Nellie looked enquiringly at each other. 'She might be lying down, girl,' Nellie said. 'A lot of people do on a Sunday after a big dinner.'

'Yer could be right, sunshine, but on the other hand, it could be she's nervous about opening the door. After the fright she's had, it'll be a long time before she trusts anyone.' Molly glanced at the window. 'I don't like peeping in, but I'll give a light tap on the glass.'

'Why don't yer shout through the letter box, girl, to let her know it's only us?'

'I'll do both, sunshine.' Molly stretched her arm and tapped on one of the panes of glass. Then she bent down and lifted the letter box. 'It's Molly and Nellie, sunshine. But if yer don't feel up to visitors, we'll leave yer in peace and call back tomorrow.'

They heard the shuffle of feet, then the bolt being drawn. 'I'm sorry I kept yer waiting,' Flora apologized as she held the door wide. 'It's a terrible way to live, but the fact is, I don't trust anyone now.'

Molly gave her a hug. 'Me and Nellie understand, sunshine, yer don't need to apologize to us. We did think yer might not want to be disturbed on a Sunday, but as we have good news for yer we decided it would cheer yer up.'

Flora waved a hand towards the couch. 'Sit down and make yerselves comfortable. I'm glad to see you, 'cos it gets very lonely when ye're on yer own, with no one to talk to. The neighbours have been marvellous, but yer can't expect them to be here all the time. After all, Sunday is a day of rest, with no work for the husbands and no school for the children.'

'We haven't passed one soul on our way round here,' Molly said. 'Have we, Nellie? The place is like a graveyard.'

Nellie decided a wooden dining chair would be easier to get off than the low couch. And as she pulled a chair out from under the table, she said, 'If yer'd given me a chance to answer yer, girl, I'd have said we hadn't seen a body, never mind a soul.'

'I have had one visitor today,' Flora told them. 'It was this morning, before I'd had time to make meself presentable. Yer know Annie Cosgrove, Molly, who lives at the very top of the street?'

Molly nodded. 'Yes, I know her. A little woman who scurries along as though she hasn't a minute to spare. I've never seen her walking yet; she always seems to be in a hurry.'

The chair Nellie was sitting on began to creak in protest when her body shook with laughter. 'She's got a gang of children, that's why she never stands still for long.'

'I know she's got five or six children, sunshine, but what's that got to do with her always being in a hurry?'

The chair was really suffering now with eighteen stone of shaking fat on top of it. 'I know why she's always on the run, girl, it's 'cos she's frightened to stop. She thinks if she stands still for a minute, her feller will creep up on her and make her pregnant again.'

Molly wanted to laugh but didn't think she should. Flora, however, had no such inhibitions and she laughed until the tears ran down her cheeks. 'Oh, Nellie McDonough, yer never change, do yer? Always quick with an answer for anything that comes your way.' The old lady ran the back of a hand across her eyes. 'I know yer've got three children, so does that mean your husband caught you standing still three times?'

Afraid that if encouraged, her mate might come out with something really shocking, Molly said, 'Careful, Flora, don't lead her on or yer might regret it.'

Nellie was in her element. There was nothing she liked better than to make people laugh. The groans from the chair told her that it wasn't laughing, but she ignored it by silently saying it wasn't much of a chair if it couldn't carry an eighteen-stone woman what had a voluptuous body. 'Just the opposite, Flora; it was my feller who was frightened to stand still. If I'd left it to him, we wouldn't have had no children. It's me what's filled with passion, girl; my George is all for a quiet life. Not that he gets it, like, but he's man enough to keep me happy.'

Time to interrupt before she brings Paul and Phoebe into the conversation, Molly told herself. It was good to see Flora laughing, and she'd had a good chuckle too, but now a change of subject was called for. 'Yer said yer had a visitor early this morning, sunshine, so d'yer want to tell us what Mrs Cosgrove called for before we give yer our news?'

Flora was eager to pass on the information. 'Annie said she didn't know anything about me being robbed until this morning. She doesn't bother with the neighbours much; having a husband and five children to care for keeps her busy. But she walked home from church with Lily this morning, and that's when she found out. And guess what? She actually saw the robber coming out of my front door. Only she didn't know he was a robber, she just thought he'd been visiting me.'

'Go 'way.' There was surprise in Molly's voice. 'Is she sure about this? I mean, did she have the time right, and that it was your door he came out of?'

'She's positive. There was no one else in the street; that's how she came to notice him. She even walked past him. He banged my door shut and began to walk up to the main road, while she was going down to the corner shop.'

'Well, I'll be blowed.' Molly pulled on the lobe of her ear. 'Did she say what he looked like?'

Flora nodded. 'She said he had a cloth cap on, pulled down low on his forehead so she didn't get a good look at his face. Young, though, she said, about twenty. Yer can't blame her for not taking much notice of his appearance, 'cos it wouldn't occur to her, or anyone else for that matter, that he was a burglar.'

'She would have known if he lived round here, though, wouldn't she? Even if she didn't know him to speak to, she'd have known him by sight.'

'I asked her that, Molly, but as far as she can remember she'd never set eyes on him before. She was really upset about it, said she'd have kicked up a right stink if she'd known, and he would have been caught.'

'She'll have to go and tell the police,' Nellie said. 'They ask the proper questions, and they'd get more out of her than she thought she saw. A lot could come back to her, yer know, when she has a good think.'

'I can't see her walking into the police station, queen, she's not the type.' Flora jerked her head in disgust. 'Come to think of it, we're all the same. We live a respectable life, do the best we can with what we've got, and never think about burglars or police. It's the way we've been brought up.'

'I'd go to the police station with her if she didn't want to go on her own. There's nothing to be afraid of. The police are here to help us, and we should tell them all we know,' Molly said. 'If she doesn't fancy going to the station, we could always ask that nice young bobby to call to her house.'

Flora became very flustered at the idea, and her hands waved her objection. 'Oh, don't do that, Molly, for heaven's sake. The poor woman would die of fright if she opened her front door and found a policeman standing there.'

'We all would, sunshine, because a copper usually brings bad news with him. But I still think the police should be told about the bloke because what Annie saw might just help them. Otherwise we'd all be guilty of withholding information.'

'Leave it as it is for now, Molly, and I'll have a word with her when I can.' Flora didn't like the idea of involving someone against their will. 'She passes here every morning on her way to the shops, so I'll keep an eye out for her.'

'Her back yard door must be facing Lizzie Corkhill's if I'm not mistaken,' Molly said, seeing the top entry in her mind's eye. 'Yeah, it is. I can remember bumping into Elsie Flanaghan one day when I was going on a message for Lizzie, and Elsie lives next to Annie.'

Nellie bristled at the very mention of her sworn enemy's name

'God help her if she lives next to that Flanaghan woman. She's a cow, that one.'

'Nellie, sunshine, I'm sure Flora has got more on her mind than listening to you telling of the tussles yer've had with Elsie.'

That remark cut Nellie to the quick. 'Tussles, did yer say? It's not tussles with me and Elsie Flanaghan, it's all-out war.'

'Have it your way, Nellie, but let the matter drop. We still haven't told Flora why we came, and I'm sure she's wondering but too shy to ask.'

'I'm sure yer'll tell me in your own good time, Molly. And I'm in no hurry, for I've nowhere to go. But I could make yer a nice cup of tea.' The old lady saw Molly's mouth open to protest, and she got her words out first. 'I'm longing for a cup of tea meself, so yer wouldn't be putting me to any trouble.'

Ignoring Nellie's nodding head and happy face, Molly put a hand on Flora's chair. 'Let me tell yer our news first, Flora, because I've been holding it in since we knocked on the door. And I can't wait any longer to see your face when we tell yer what we've done. So sit back an' listen. I'll let Nellie tell yer if she wants to.'

But Nellie didn't want to, for she couldn't understand how Corker had worked the trick. She'd tried to make sense of it, but couldn't. 'No, girl, I'll let you tell her. It was your idea, after all. Besides, I know yer won't forget to say it was me what gave yer the insperoton.'

Molly caught Flora's eye and winked. 'It was Nellie we can thank, sunshine, for it was her who had the *inspiration*! That's what yer meant, wasn't it, sunshine?'

'That's it, girl, yer know me inside out. I bet when I'm in me own house yer know when I go to the lavvy.'

'I'm not that clever, sunshine. I may hear the chain being pulled occasionally, but I can honestly say I've never heard yer spending a penny.'

'I don't go very often, girl, 'cos it's too much bother. The seat is too high. I can't sit in comfort with me knickers round me ankles.' Nellie squinted through narrowed lids. 'I don't think it's worth a penny. I wouldn't go if I didn't have to.'

'None of us would if we didn't have to, Nellie, but when nature calls one has to obey. And now we've agreed on that, can I go ahead and tell Flora about our good fortune?'

Nellie waggled her bottom on the poor suffering chair. 'I'm all ears, girl. I don't half like tales about good fortune.'

Molly had prepared a tale which she thought sounded believable. 'D'yer know when me and Nellie told yer about how we put money away every pay day, in case of a rainy day? Well, after we'd lent you some money for yer rent and other things, we had four shillings left in the tin box. And yesterday dinnertime, we were standing talking outside our house, waiting for the family to come home, when Corker came up the street. We usually have a good laugh and a natter with Corker, but he didn't have much time to chat because he'd gone to work without his wallet, and he had no money to go to the bookies. He likes his bet, does Corker. Anyway, he wasn't going to stop and talk because there was a horse running in one of the races which he said was a cert. He'd been keeping his eye on this horse for weeks and said it was in good form.'

Flora shook her head. 'I'm surprised at Corker. I thought he had more sense. Gambling is a mug's game.'

'I've always thought the same, sunshine, and Jack doesn't gamble at all. But I'm very glad we threw caution to the wind yesterday. While Corker went home to get his money, me and Nellie decided that because he was so sure of this horse winning, we'd kick ourselves if we didn't back it and it won. So I nipped in the house, took two shillings out of the tin, and gave it to Corker to put on the horse for us. A shilling each from Nellie and me, and we put it to win. I didn't tell Jack, 'cos he'd have called me all the silly things going for throwing money away. Yer can imagine me and me mate were on pins all afternoon. We had to wait until Corker came back from the bookies at half five, to find out if we'd won.'

Flora was a bag of nerves by now. 'Well, hurry up, Molly, and put me out of me misery. Did the horse fall, or come in last?'

Molly and Nellie burst out laughing. But Nellie couldn't resist a bit of fun. 'The bleeding horse is tied up outside yer house, girl. Yer know how the cowboys tie up their horses outside a saloon? Well, as we haven't got no saloons or cowboys round here, we've left Silver tied up to a lamp post and being watched over by half the kids in the neighbourhood. All we need is John Wayne and a feeding bag, and it would be like the Wild West.'

The old lady's head was moving from one to the other. The couple were noted for bringing laughter with them wherever they went, but surely losing money on a horse was nothing to laugh about. She'd always been of the opinion that gamblers had more money than sense. 'When you two can calm yerselves down, would yer mind telling me what is so funny about throwing hard-earned money away?'

Molly wiped her eyes. 'There's nothing funny about losing money on a horse, sunshine, I agree. But there's every reason to laugh and be happy when the horse romps home the winner at six to one!'

Flora's mouth opened and closed several times, and she wet her lips before croaking, 'Ye're pulling me leg.'

Nellie was in her applecart. Sunday afternoons were usually dull, with Paul out with Phoebe, and George sat with his head in the *News of the World*, giving an occasional grunt when she spoke to him. But today was more to her taste and she was enjoying it. 'We're not pulling yer leg, girl, it's true. And the only one more surprised than me and Molly was the horse! Corker didn't half gloat, partly because he was right, and more so because he'd had a good win. He wouldn't tell us how much he had on, like, but as he had a smile a mile wide, I'd say he'd had a good day.'

'Oh, I am pleased for both of yer,' Flora said. 'Yer deserve it 'cos yer've both been very good. I know I'd have been in Queer Street without yer. There was no one I could turn to, so you saved me life.'

'I wouldn't go as far as to say that, sunshine, for the neighbours would have rallied round. They wouldn't have let yer starve, or go without coal.'

'I know they've got hearts of gold, Molly, and I appreciate the way they've looked after me. But most of them are living hand to mouth, robbing Peter to pay Paul every week. I'd starve rather than take off them, knowing they were going without to give to me.'

'Yer don't have that worry now, do yer, sunshine?' The laughter gone from Molly's face, she reminded herself that it would be a long time before Flora got over the shock she'd had. That a stranger had been in her home, rummaging through her personal belongings, was bad enough, but the one thing she would never get over was the loss of her dead husband's fob watch. And no amount of kindness could put that right.

Molly stood up to put a hand in her pocket. 'I've got something to show yer, sunshine.' She opened the betting slip and passed it over. 'Have yer got a pair of glasses, or can yer see without?'

Flora took the piece of paper, saying, 'I've got a pair of glasses, I think they're in the drawer. I don't need them now, but I do if I'm reading for long. Then me eyes get tired.' She looked down at the piece of paper, stared for a while, then lifted it to her eyes. 'This has got my name on it. Why is that?'

Nellie saw Molly fidget with the button on her coat, and knew her mate was worried about how the old lady would react to what she had to say. Nellie knew she herself couldn't help, for she didn't have the right words, or the gentle voice, and she'd put her foot in it. But her best mate was good at saying the right thing at the right time. 'Go on, girl, tell Flora. She can't eat yer.'

Molly sat back in the couch. 'Relax, Flora, 'cos I can tell by the way ye're sitting on the edge of yer seat that yer nerves are all strung up. I don't know why, 'cos there's only me and Nellie here. And as we've lived near yer for around twenty years, yer should know us well enough by now. We act daft a lot, but we do have our serious side.'

'I know that, queen, and so does everyone around here. I've never heard anyone say a wrong word about yer.'

Nellie couldn't keep back the thought that had crossed her mind. 'Not even Elsie Flanaghan?'

Much to the surprise of both friends, a hearty chuckle came from Flora. 'I'm not going to make any comment on Elsie Flanaghan. My mother had a saying, "Least said, soonest mended", and I'm sticking to that.'

This seemed a good opening, and Molly took advantage. 'Nellie's mam was very young when she died, and we often talk about her and wish she was here. We were only talking about it yesterday morning, as we walked to the shops. Nellie was saying she'd spoil her, and look after her like I try and look after my mam and dad. So, me and me mate decided that if yer would let her, Nellie will adopt yer.' When Flora sat forward, words ready on her lips, Molly held up a hand. 'Let me finish, sunshine, then yer can have your say.'

Nellie was amazed at what her mate was saying, for it was the first time she'd heard it. So, like Flora, she sat back to listen.

'That piece of paper in yer hand has your name on it because Nellie wanted to do something for yer . . . like I would do if what happened to you happened to my mam. If the horse was an old nag and came in last, well, that couldn't be helped and yer would never be told. However, thanks to our good friend Corker, the horse did as he said it would, and it romped in ahead of the field.' Molly chuckled to lighten the tension. 'My Jack went mad when he heard, said he would have put a tanner on himself if he'd known the horse was so good.'

'But surely yer'll share yer winnings with him, Molly?'

Now for it, thought Molly, and rushed in before she could change her mind and chicken out. 'But it's not our winnings, sunshine. Me and Nellie put the bet on for you. And before yer tell us yer don't want our charity, let me finish the whole story.'

Flora wasn't the only one to sit back and listen, because Nellie felt as though she was sitting in the stalls at the Carlton picture house, watching Bette Davis. In fact her best mate beat Bette Davis hands down.

Molly cleared her throat before speaking. 'The twelve shillings the horse won for yer, that will clear the money we lent to yer. So yer don't have to worry about giving us money every week. And we're doing this with a good heart, sunshine, we really want to help. Yer wouldn't be mean enough to throw it back in our faces, would yer?'

Flora was torn. She'd always prided herself on paying her way in life, and been beholden to no one. But it had been a lonely life, with no family or close friends. And there'd been times when she wasn't feeling well, but was too proud to ask anyone to run to the shops for her. Pride was one thing, pig-headedness was another. 'I don't know what to say to yer, Molly, or you, Nellie. I've never known such kindness in me life. I've been too proud, too stubborn and too bloody-minded since my Wally died, and been lonely because of it. But I'm not stupid enough to throw your kindness back in yer faces. I thank yer from the bottom of my heart for the money you gave me. Without it I wouldn't have known where to turn.' She cast her eyes down for a few seconds, then said shyly, 'I think I'd love being your adopted mother, Nellie. Thank you for the privilege.'

Nellie thought her heart would burst. She'd gone along with her mate's do-gooding, and had enjoyed the praise showered on them. She wasn't blind to the fact she wasn't as good-hearted as Molly, never had been and never would be. But she had learned to be more tolerant of people's faults, and to care for people like Flora. She didn't show it, but inside she knew she wasn't as rough or tough as she used to be. 'It's not all milk and honey, yer know, Flora. Being an adopted mother has ties attached to it.' Having used all the big words she could think of, she wanted to pass the rest over to Molly. 'You tell her what she's letting herself in for, girl, then she can't blame us afterwards.'

'If Flora is agreeable, sunshine, yer could make a pot of tea while I finish off.'

Flora nodded. 'Yer'll find the tea and sugar easy, queen, 'cos yer've been in the kitchen before. The milk is in a jug in the larder.'

Nellie's head popped back into the room. 'Are the biscuits in the larder, too, girl?'

Molly gasped. 'You cheeky article, Nellie McDonough. Don't be so forward.'

The grin on Nellie's face stretched from ear to ear and her cheeks nearly covered her eyes. 'Well, I did warn her that being an adopted mother had ties attached. Start as yer mean to go on, that's what I say.'

'The biscuits are in a tin, Nellie, so help yerself. And I'll try to remember to have a few in all the time, in case yer call.'

'Don't be spoiling her, Flora, 'cos she's a real guzzle guts. She'd eat yer out of house and home. But she got one thing right about being an adopted mother. It does come with ties. Taking Nellie on board means taking on both of our families, because we are one big happy family. And that is a lot of people, believe me. Not that yer'll see so much of them that they'll make yer life a misery. Me and Nellie will bring our grandchildren to see yer, and yer'll be sick of hearing us brag about them. Then there's the old friends who would be delighted if yer would visit them, or they came to you, I can promise yer that. Yer know Victoria Clegg of old, and Lizzie Corkhill. And of course yer know my mam, Bridie.'

Nellie came in then with a tray set with cups, saucers and a plate of biscuits. 'That's all the biscuits yer've got, Flora, and it only runs to three each.'

'There's many poor people who would think it was their birthday if they had half a biscuit, Nellie,' Flora said, winking at Molly. 'So count yerself lucky.'

Nellie put her hands on her wide hips and planted her feet a foot apart. 'Blimey, she's giving orders and she's only been me mother for ten minutes!'

Chapter Nine

'I warned yer years ago about your Ruthie having a liking for the boys, didn't I, girl?' Nellie's swaying hips pushed Molly nearer to the edge of the pavement. 'Fifteen years of age and she's a real flirt. If she carries on the way she is, she'll get a name like a bad penny. Always hanging round with lads.'

Molly pulled them to a halt. 'You be careful with that tongue of yours, Nellie McDonough, or yer'll find yerself at the end of mine, and yer'll be sorry yer signed. I know it's only a joke with yer, but if anyone happened to overhear, it would be round the neighbourhood in no time and set tongues wagging.'

The mates were on their way home from Flora's and had just turned into their street. 'Our Ruthie will be sixteen in a couple of weeks, and she's no different to what I was like at that age. And heaven only knows what you were like. I bet yer were more of a flirt than me and Ruthie put together.'

Nellie was having a good laugh to herself. It was so easy to wind her mate up. 'Yeah, I was, girl. I had me first boyfriend the day I started school; we were both five. But I chucked him the next day, 'cos the boy next to me in class gave me a jelly baby. I gave him a kiss for it, and after that I never went short of boyfriends or sweets.'

'And yer have the nerve to make jokes about Ruthie, saying she hangs around the street with boys?'

'Yer don't need to take my word for it, girl, yer can see it for yerself.' Nellie pointed a chubby finger. 'There she is, outside the Watsons' house, and she's making eyes at Gordon and Peter Corkhill, and that Johnny Stewart from the next street. They're all over her, like bees round a honey pot.'

Molly pulled her arm from Nellie's, and stood on tiptoe to crane her neck. After a few seconds she turned on Nellie with sparks coming from her eyes.

'You only see what yer want to see, Nellie McDonough. It didn't serve yer purpose to see Bella was there as well. Or that the Watsons' door was wide open and Mary was standing on the top step, arms folded and talking and laughing with the youngsters. Too tame for yer, a scene as innocent as that, isn't it?'

Nellie and her chins agreed. 'Yeah, I hate to say it, but that little scene is too tame for me. I'd rather have this little scene, it's more to my liking. Your face is the funniest sight I've seen since Laurel and Hardy joined the Foreign Legion.'

Molly saw the glint in her mate's eyes and a little voice in her head told her that the little woman might be her best mate, but right now she was having the time of her life. At my expense, too, Molly answered that little voice, adding that two could play at that game. So as they were nearing her house, which was almost facing the Watsons', Molly called over, 'Yer should hear what my mate's saying about yer, Mary. She said yer should be ashamed of yerself, running after young lads at your age.'

The young boys and Ruthie and Bella looked across to where the friends were standing, smiles on their faces. But it was Molly and Nellie who got their eye wiped, and the surprise of their life. For the usually quiet and strait-laced Mary shouted back, 'Nellie's only jealous. She's too late though, tell her, 'cos we've all paired off now. Gordon and Peter are going to court Ruthie and Bella, and I'm paired off with Johnny. Sorry, Nellie, but better luck next time.'

The little woman was flummoxed. 'Well, I never! She's coming out of her shell, isn't she? She'll be swearing next, and walking down the street with a ciggy dangling out of the side of her mouth.'

'Well, how does it feel to get a dose of yer own medicine, sunshine? Yer expected Mary to go all red-faced and embarrassed, but she turned the tables on yer, and it's not before time.'

Nellie wasn't given time to think up a smart retort, as all the youngsters said goodnight to Mary before crossing the cobbled street. 'Mam, can we ask a favour of yer?' Ruthie put her arm round her mother and her voice was coaxing, 'Wait until yer hear it all before yer give us yer answer.'

The boys were standing behind Ruthie and Bella, and Molly could see they were eager to hear what she had to say. 'I'm outnumbered five to one, so the odds are weighted against me.'

Nellie moved nearer and put her arm through her mate's. 'No ye're not, girl, 'cos I'm here and that makes it two and a half to one. I'll stick by yer through thick and thin.'

Ruthie, the spitting image of her mother, chuckled. 'We're not going to war, Auntie Nellie, only to a church dance. And that's not even certain yet. It all depends upon me mam. I just hope she takes into account that I'll be sixteen years old very soon.'

Bella, very shy compared to her friend, plucked up the courage to say, 'And me, Auntie Molly. I'll be sixteen as well.'

'I was going to say that perhaps yer mother should be here in case I say something she wouldn't agree with. But as she's gone in and closed the door, perhaps it would be best if we all went inside so yer dad can hear what this vital favour is.' She looked down at her mate. 'Yer may as well go home, Nellie, and see to George. He'll be wondering where yer've got to.'

That was the last thing on Nellie's mind. If there was any news to hear, then she wanted to hear it first hand. Not a watered down version that Molly would give her. 'No, George will be all right, girl, he won't have even missed me yet. I bet any money he's only up to page twelve of the *News of the World*. I'll come in yours with yer, it'll pass half an hour away.'

Jack was listening to the wireless when he heard the key in the door, and switched the set off before turning to the hall with a smile on his face. The house never seemed the same when Molly wasn't in it, not as homely or comfortable, as though the main ingredient was missing. But she was here now, and his heart felt lighter. 'I expected yer home earlier, love.' His mouth closed and his eyes widened when his wife was followed into the living room by Nellie, then Ruthie, Bella, and the three lads. 'I see yer've brought company with yer.'

Molly bent down to kiss him before slipping off her coat. 'I didn't have much choice. Nellie refused point-blank to go home, and Ruthie and Bella want to ask a favour, so the lads came with them for moral support.'

Nellie made a beeline for her carver chair. From the sound of things there were issues to discuss, and she may as well listen in comfort. And comfort to Nellie included tea and biscuits. 'Put the kettle on before business gets under way, girl, save breaking off halfway through the proceedings.'

'If you think this is going to be a party, sunshine, then yer've got another think coming.'

'I'm only asking for a cup of tea, so don't be so miserable.'

'No, sunshine, ye're asking for eight cups of tea, 'cos yer don't think I'd make you a cup and not everyone else. And the plain fact is, I don't possess eight cups and saucers.'

The youngsters' eyes were moving from Molly to Nellie as though hypnotized. Then Ruthie broke the spell. 'Mam, we only want to ask yer something. At least I want to ask you, 'cos Bella has already asked her mam. So if you and Auntie Nellie could call a truce for a few minutes, we could get it over with and leave yer in peace.' The girl's eyes were bright and her laughter filled the room. 'If yer go back to war, I bet Auntie Nellie will win, she always does.'

This pleased the little woman no end. 'I won't be fighting tonight, girl, 'cos I've left me pistol at home. But thanks for having faith in me.'

Molly looked at Jack's face and knew right away he wasn't in the mood for so many visitors. 'Can we get down to the favour yer want to ask, Ruthie, or the alarm clock will be going off to tell us it's time to get up before we go to bed.'

There was much chuckling from the youngsters, who thought Molly and Nellie were funnier than anyone in the pictures.

'Well, it's like this, Mam. Yer know me and Bella's birthdays are very close together, and we'd like to have a joint party. Will yer let us?'

'In this house, yer mean, sunshine, for you and yer mates?' Molly's hand swept round the circle of friends. 'It's fine by me, and I can't see your dad objecting.'

Ruthie pulled a face. 'I can't have a birthday party and not invite my sisters and brother. They would think I was mean and didn't love them. And I do love them, Mam, I really do.'

'Of course yer do, sunshine, but yer can't ask Jill without Steve, Doreen without Phil, or Tommy without Rosie. And what about your grandma and granda? That comes to eight and I haven't even started. There's me and your dad, plus Bella's mam and dad, as well. Twelve people so far.'

'More than that, girl,' Nellie said, sitting with her hands on the arms of the chair and her face serious. She reminded Molly of a judge presiding over a courtroom trial. 'What about me and George and Corker and Ellen? We'd all be very hurt if we were left out.'

The look of anticipation on five young faces had now turned to one of disappointment as they did some silent mental arithmetic. 'That comes to sixteen, I think.' Gordon Corkhill had been ticking off on his fingers. 'You'd never get sixteen to fit in this room, and that's not counting us.'

'Don't you be putting a damper on things, lad,' Nellie said. 'We've had twenty-odd in this room many times. And we've had a ruddy good time. If you had a party without me, yer'd have no entertainer and would be sat looking at each other all night, as miserable as sin.'

Five young faces lit up as one when Molly said, 'I've got the very solution to the problem. Nellie's house is exactly the same size as this. So as she's volunteered to do the entertaining, we may as well have the party in her house.'

Blessed with her mother's sense of humour, Ruthie didn't take long to get in on the act. 'That's a marvellous idea, Mam. Why didn't we think of that before? Me, Bella and the boys will see to the pop, you and Auntie Mary can buy the food as a birthday present, and Auntie Nellie can entertain and keep the party going.'

Nellie's eyes were almost popping out of her head as she sought an answer to get her out of the hole she'd dug herself into. Then she had guidance from above. 'Sorry, girl, but that is out of the question. Yer see, when your mam has a party here, the men carry this table to my house. And as yer can tell by just looking round, there's bags of room then.'

'That was a nice try, sunshine, but you really didn't think things through properly. Yer see, what's good for the goose is good for the gander. I'll get Corker to give Jack a hand carrying your table down here! There's an answer to everything if yer use your brains.' Molly moved her head slightly so she could wink at the youngsters, who were taking in every word and wondering what the outcome would be. Would there be a party or not? The only one without a care was Ruthie. She never had any doubt her birthday party would be in her own home. But she enjoyed these exchanges between her mam and

Auntie Nellie, and felt her life would have been poorer without them.

'It's not only the space, girl, there's other reasons why I can't have the party in my house. One is that I haven't got enough cups to go round, haven't got enough plates with no cracks, haven't got enough glasses, with or without chips. And I haven't got nowhere near twenty spoons.'

'And what, pray, would yer need twenty spoons for, sunshine?'

'For the trifles yer'd have to make, girl, that's what.'

Molly leaned her clenched fists on the table. 'While you've been telling us all the things yer haven't got, so you can't have the party in your house, I too have been giving thought to the matter. And I have reached a decision which all the talking in the world won't persuade me to alter.' She stood up straight and eyed each one in the room before saying, 'Ruthie and Bella can have their party in this house, but only for the seven friends. Parents, sisters, brother, and all other relatives and friends can call with cards and presents, and give their best wishes to the birthday girls. But they cannot stay for a party. There's too many, and I just couldn't cope. Besides which, I think the youngsters would enjoy themselves without going overboard. I don't want the neighbours complaining.'

Molly had hardly finished speaking before she was being hugged by her youngest daughter. 'Oooh, thank you, Mam, that's a lovely idea. It means I get to see everyone I love on me birthday, but me and Bella can have our own party for our mates.' Ruthie giggled. 'I can be hostess, and Bella can be assistant hostess, just like you and Auntie Nellie.'

The little woman wasn't too happy with the compromise, 'Yer said for Ruthie's six friends, but I can only see five. So were yer including me, girl?'

'No, I wasn't! If me and Jack are not coming to our daughter's birthday party, I'm damn sure you're not. The boys who will make up the seven are Ken and Jeff. I know Ruthie wouldn't leave them out.'

'I hadn't forgotten them, Mam, I just took it for granted they'd be invited, seeing as they're part of the gang.'

Molly gazed down at Jack. 'Is that all right with you, sunshine, or do yer have other ideas?'

'Suits me fine, love. Like yer said, the youngsters are better on their own. If yer invite all and sundry, it wouldn't be their party. But we grown-ups could make a night of it and go out somewhere for a change. Pictures, or the pub on the corner, anywhere the ladies fancy.'

This was more like it, and Nellie sat forward. 'I'm all for that, lad, it sounds good to me. What had yer in mind?'

But Molly put her foot down before Jack could answer, 'That's enough for tonight, Nellie, it's getting late. We've plenty of time to decide where we'd like to go. As long as the kids know their party is definitely in here, then they're fixed up. So I suggest all those who don't live here should go home now, and let those who do live here have half an hour's peace and quiet before going to bed.'

The three boys and Bella were smiling and all talking at once as they made their way into the street. Gordon Corkhill, at seventeen, was the oldest, and he tried to look nonchalant, as though a party for two sixteen-year-old girls was kids' stuff. But inside, he was looking forward to it. He'd make sure he sat next to Ruthie at the table, even if he had to push the other lads away. And seeing as it was his dad's gramophone and records that were going to provide the music, then it was only fair that he got to dance with her. If they thought he was going to spend the night putting records on and turning them over just for them to dance to, then they had another think coming. The subject of going dancing hadn't been discussed tonight because everyone's mind was full of the party. But he was pretty certain that since Mrs Watson had given Bella permission to go to the local church dance with them, then Auntie Molly was bound to allow Ruthie to join them. And like the other lads, he thought that was great. However, he hadn't told his mates he had a secret agenda that didn't include them. He'd waited a long time for the day Ruthie was sixteen, and unless his courage deserted him, he intended to ask Auntie Molly if she would let him take her daughter to the pictures one night. Without the rest of the gang, of course. And if she gave her consent, then he'd ask Ruthie.

While he was climbing the stairs to bed that night, he argued with himself that it should be the other way round. He should ask Ruthie first, then ask her mam. He still couldn't make up his mind as he lay in bed next to his brother, Peter. Then, when he could no longer keep his eyes open, he muttered softly that he'd ask his dad what he should do, and drifted into a slumber that brought a smile to his face. He dreamt that he was sitting in the back row of the stalls at the Broadway, and he was holding Ruthie's hand.

Unfortunately, his brother was still awake, and listened as Gordon, blissfully unaware he was talking in his sleep, told of his hopes and plans.

Peter grinned and spoke his thoughts aloud. 'I don't think much of yer chances, mate, not with Ken and Jeff in the running with the same idea. Me now, I've got me eye on Bella, and there's no one else in the picture.'

A knock came on the partition which divided the back bedroom into two. On the other side of the partition was the bed shared by his sisters Phoebe and Dorothy. It was Phoebe's voice coming through the thin wall. 'Will you two stop gabbing so I can get some sleep? It'll be time to go to work before I've closed me eyes.'

'It's not me, our kid.' There was a grin on Peter's face. 'It's our Gordon talking in his sleep. Don't be moaning at me, he's keeping me awake as well.'

'Give him a kick, that will shut him up. Or turn him on to his side.'

'Ah, ay, sis, he's a lot bigger than me, and I'm not taking me life in me hands. If I kick him, he'll kick me back so hard I'll go through the wall and end up between me mam and dad. And me dad would be so mad, he'd kick me back to me own bed. And I don't fancy playing football at this time of night. Especially if I'm the ball.'

Gordon stirred, turned on his side, and, his voice drowsy, said, 'Will yer shut up and let me get some sleep? Yer can't half talk, Peter, ye're worse than a blinking woman.'

In the next room, Corker chuckled softly before putting his arm round Ellen's waist and making himself comfortable for a good night's sleep. Life was wonderful when you had a wife and children you adored.

Chapter Ten

'I enjoyed that cup of tea, girl,' Nellie said as she put her cup back on the saucer. 'It's funny how your tea always tastes better than mine. D'yer think it's the way yer hold yer mouth?'

Molly gazed into her mate's eyes for a few seconds before answering. 'No, sunshine, it's got nothing to do with the way I hold me mouth. If yer asked me to make a suggestion, I'd say an extra spoonful of tea would help. It would give the water a bit of colour, like, instead of looking and tasting insipid. Another thing that would greatly improve your idea of a good cuppa would be to give the kettle a chance to boil, instead of whipping it off the stove before it can let yer know it's ready for the pot. Ye're too impatient, sunshine, that's your trouble.'

Nellie's chins were quick to agree. They knew only too well how impatient she was, for when she swilled her face every morning, she forgot they were there. Many's the time they went a full week before seeing a bar of soap. 'Yeah, ye're right, girl, I am inpetous. Always have been. I just can't help meself.'

'You're impetuous, sunshine.'

'I just told yer I was.'

'No, Nellie, yer told me yer were inpetous. I don't know what that means, but if you say so, I'll go along with yer to save any argument.'

Nellie's eyes became slits. She didn't know if her mate was being funny or sarky, but she wasn't going to ask because she had other things on her mind. 'Life is too short to be arguing all the time, girl, it's not worth the effort. But talking of tea, and how to make it, is there another cup left in the pot? Me mouth's gone all dry just thinking about it.'

Molly tutted. 'Tea tank, that's what yer are. If there is any tea left in the pot, it'll be stiff by now.'

'I don't mind cold tea, girl, not to drink, anyway. If I had biscuits to dunk I wouldn't like it, though.'

'I'm going to tell yer to help yerself, sunshine, while I put me ironing away. But that only applies to the tea, it does not mean I've given yer the go-ahead to the biscuit tin as well.'

The little woman was wearing a smile as she reached for the teapot. A custard cream would be nice, but at least she got half of what she was after. And when Molly had her back to her as she placed her ironing in neat piles on the shelves of the cupboard set into the wall at the side of the fireplace, Nellie put an extra spoonful of sugar in the cup of tepid tea. 'Have yer thought what ye're having for dinner tonight, girl?'

'Not yet, Nellie,' Molly called over her shoulder. 'I get a bit fed up trying to find something different for a change.'

'Yeah, me too! George likes tripe, but me and Paul hate it. Another thing he likes that we don't is pig's belly. Ask Paul if he'd like that for a change, and he'd be straight out to the grid in the yard to be sick.'

Molly closed the cupboard door, happy in the knowledge that the week's laundry had been washed, ironed and put away. 'I think I'll settle for sausage, liver and onions. It's easy and quick to cook, and the three of us like it. I might do a bit of mashed potato to go with it.'

Right on cue, Nellie said, 'Well, fancy that, now! I was thinking of getting the same meself. Yer must be a mind reader, Molly Bennett.'

'I'm not a mind reader, sunshine, but I always know what you're going to say next. I can't do it with anyone else, only you. Funny that, isn't it?'

'Ye're pulling me leg, girl. Yer must think I'm doolally to fall for that. There's no way yer can tell what I'm going to say next, when I don't even know meself.'

'I've spoilt things now, by telling yer.' Molly walked to the sideboard and pulled open a drawer. 'I'll tell yer what I'll do to prove I'm telling the truth.' She took a small notebook and pencil from the drawer, then closed it with her hip. 'You stay where yer are, sunshine, and I'll sit the opposite end of the table. That way we both know there's no cheating. Is that all right with you?'

'Of course it's all right with me, girl. I don't know what the hell

99

ye're talking about, but you go ahead and tell me what ye're on about.'

'Well, it's like this,' Molly told her. 'I'm going to write something down on this piece of paper, and I'm going to make sure you don't see what I'm writing. Then I'm going to put the paper, folded over, mind, into me coat pocket. And I bet that before we leave this house, you will have spoken the very words that I've written down. Then perhaps yer'll believe that I always know what ye're going to say before yer say it.'

'That is one load of double Dutch to me, girl. Are yer trying to tell me that ye're going to write some words on that paper that I'll say before we go out?' Nellie watched as her mate made a circle of her arm around the paper, and began to write. 'Either I'm going crazy, girl, or you are.' She watched the pencil moving, and muttered, 'I hope we both end up in the same asylum for the insane.'

Molly put the pencil down and lifted the paper for Nellie to see. 'Watch, girl, while I fold it once, then twice. Keep yer eyes on me while I walk to the hall and place the paper in the pocket of my coat.' The paper in the pocket, Molly returned to stand behind her chair. 'It's nearly time for us to go to the shops, sunshine, so I won't make meself comfortable. Pass me yer cup and saucer so I can rinse them before we go. I hate going out and leaving dirty dishes.'

'Ye're too fussy, you are, girl,' Nellie said, passing her cup over. 'I don't care what me house looks like during the day, no one sees it. As long as it's tidy for George and Paul coming home from work, that's the main thing.'

Molly came back from the kitchen after rinsing the dishes, and she made straight for the hall to take her coat down from a hook. She looked calm enough, but her inside was doing somersaults. Had she slipped up by making that forecast about knowing what Nellie was going to say before they went out? She'd look a fool if she was wrong, but it would serve her right for being so big-headed. 'Come on, sunshine, I want to call to Doreen's and Jill's, to see if they need anything from the shops, save them going out.'

Nellie lumbered to her feet. 'They probably won't, 'cos they take the babies out every day for some fresh air. Still, we like to see our grandchildren every day, don't we, girl?'

As Molly put the front door key in her pocket, her hand touched the piece of paper. Oh dear, she thought, my mate will have a field day. Everyone we meet, even strangers, will be told how I'm not as clever as I make out to be.

Nellie was behind Molly when the front door was opened, and as Molly was about to lower herself on to the top step, she heard a voice asking, 'If we're having liver and onions, girl, how many sausages will we get to go with it?'

Molly stepped back so quickly she trod on Nellie's toes, and the little woman cried out, 'Bloody hell, girl, yer've broken half me toes! And woke me corn up as well.'

'I'm sorry, sunshine.' Molly cupped the chubby face and planted a kiss on each cheek. 'Come back into the living room and I'll rub yer toes better.'

'Sod off, yer've caused enough trouble as it is.' Nellie would have been delighted to have her toes rubbed. It would have been a real luxury, if it wasn't for her big toe sticking out of the ruddy big hole in her stocking. 'What were yer messing at, stepping back like that? Yer knew I was right behind yer.'

'I stepped back because I'm thoughtless, big-headed, and full of me own importance, that's why,' Molly said. 'And I wouldn't blame yer if yer stamped on my foot, for spite.'

'I wouldn't do that, girl, even though a couple of me toes are still throbbing. What would I want to spite yer for? Yer didn't do it on purpose.'

'I feel ashamed to tell yer, Nellie, but if I told yer a lie it would haunt me all day. So why don't we go and sit down for a few minutes so I can show yer something and your toes can have a rest.'

'Me toes would feel better if I could have a cup of tea while I was resting them.' Nellie kept her eyes averted so her mate couldn't see the laughter there. She may as well milk the situation for all it was worth. 'We can make up the time by doing our shopping without dawdling in each shop.'

Molly closed the door and followed Nellie back into the living room. She knew her mate was making the most of the situation, as she walked with a limp. 'You sit down, sunshine, and I'll put the kettle on.' She took the piece of paper from her pocket, waited until Nellie was seated, then handed it to her. 'While I'm making the tea, you can be reading this.'

'I didn't know the postman called this morning, girl. Yer didn't say.' Nellie screwed her eyes up and read aloud. ' "If we're having liver and onions, girl, how many sausages will we get to go with it?" '

Molly came to stand by the kitchen door waiting for the water to boil. 'That's right, sunshine, those are the exact words yer used.'

Her brow furrowed, Nellie said, 'I know that, girl, I'm not daft, but I can't remember what yer said about the sausages. Did yer say three? Or didn't yer answer me at all?'

Molly put a hand to her forehead and closed her eyes. And leaning against the doorjamb, she asked herself why she had bothered. Had it been worth it? As far as Nellie was concerned it hadn't been worth it, for the little woman hadn't twigged what the words on the paper meant. She was sitting on her favourite chair, with her legs swinging back and forth as though she didn't have a care in the world. Then she turned her head towards where Molly was standing, and asked, 'Shall we get four sausages each? One and a half for the men, and one for us women. You'd have a spare one that yer could cut up and share out. That's us sorted out, then, girl.'

By this time Molly had lost the will to live. With a heartfelt sigh, she said, 'If yer say so, sunshine. The kettle's boiling so yer'll have yer cuppa in a minute.'

What Molly didn't see was the crafty look in her mate's eyes. And it wasn't until they were facing each other across the table, a cup of steaming tea in front of them, that Nellie, her face as innocent as a baby's, said, 'It's a good trick, that, girl, 'cos it'll save the wear and tear of me tongue.'

'What's that, sunshine?'

'Ah, don't be acting the goat, yer know very well what I'm talking about. At least yer should do if yer can really read me mind. Or was this,' Nellie lifted the piece of paper up and waved it over her head, 'just a fluke, and yer were winding me up?'

Molly wondered whether to let things stay as they were and leave her mate to think what she wanted to. Then a stubborn part of her mind told her to salvage something from the long drawn out situation. She might even get a laugh out of it. 'If it was a fluke, sunshine, then tell me how I know exactly what's in your mind and what yer next words will be?'

Nellie wasn't falling for that! Oh, no, she wasn't that daft. If she told Molly what she was about to say, her mate would say she knew that already. So the chubby face creased, eyes narrowed and lips clamped. And there was complete silence in the room except when Molly yawned. It lasted five minutes, the longest time in living memory that Nellie had gone without saying one word. But the strain was telling, and her bottom couldn't keep still on the chair. In the end she could stand it no longer and banged a clenched fist on the table. Then, staring at her mate, she opened her mouth.

Molly anticipated what was coming, and spoke before the first word left Nellie's lips. 'Is there any bleeding tea left in the pot?'

Nellie's facial contortions had to be seen to be believed. Her lips were touching her nose, and her eyebrows nearing her hairline. There were plenty of words she wanted to say, like calling her mate a clever bugger, and other swear words. But her mate wouldn't like the air turning blue. 'Well, is there?'

'Is there what, sunshine?'

'Any bleeding tea in the pot?'

'No there isn't. And even if there was I wouldn't let yer have it 'cos we've wasted so much time acting like a couple of kids, we'll be lucky to catch the shops before they close for dinner, so get yer bottom off that chair, and we'll be on our way. At long last. I was beginning to think we wouldn't be home before the sun goes down.'

'What sun, girl? There's no sun in the sky, only big black clouds.'

'All the more reason to run like hell then, sunshine. So get yer skates on.' Molly was quick to add, 'Before yer say it, I know yer haven't got no skates.'

Nearly tripping over herself to get down the steps quickly, Nellie muttered under her breath. 'This bleeding mind reading is beginning to get on me nerves. If it carries on like this I won't need to open me ruddy mouth.'

When Doreen opened the front door, Molly was wearing a smile as she put a foot on the bottom step. 'We're late this morning, sunshine, and yer can blame yer Auntie Nellie for holding us back.'

Doreen pulled the front door to and put a hand out to stop her mother from entering the house. 'Don't come in, Mam, 'cos Bobby isn't very well.'

It was then Molly noticed her daughter's red-rimmed eyes. 'What's wrong, sunshine? If the baby isn't well, I'd like to see him. Yer might be getting yerself all upset for nothing. I know I used to when you and the others were babies. Move back, sunshine, and let me have a look at him.'

'I was the same with mine, girl,' Nellie told her. 'I used to knock for yer mam when one of the kids was sick, and she always knew what to do if they were feverish or sickly.'

'I can't let yer in, Mam 'cos Bobby has got the measles or chickenpox. He's come out in a rash all over. He was restless through the night, and me and Phil didn't get a wink of sleep. We thought he must be teething, but this morning we found him covered in this rash.'

'Poor little love, he must be feeling rotten. But there's no reason to keep me and Nellie out, sunshine, because we both had the measles and chickenpox when we were babies, so we're not likely to catch it off him.'

'It's not you I'm worried about, Mam, 'cos I know you won't catch it. But yer could pick the germ up on yer clothes and pass it on to little Molly. That's what I'm afraid of. Mind you, she might have caught it already, 'cos they were playing on the floor together yesterday.'

'Yer were right not to let us in, love, 'cos it is very contagious and I'd hate little Molly to get it if it can be helped. We'll go up there now and see how things are. But if yer need any shopping, will yer make a list and we'll pick it up on the way down?'

'Can I ask yer a favour, Mam? I'd have done it meself, but with Bobby being so restless I didn't want to leave him with Aunt Vicky, it wouldn't be fair. Would yer ask Maisie if yer could use her phone to ring the doctor for us? I'd feel better if the doctor saw him, just to know what it is he's got, and what he needs to make him better.'

'I'll go to Jill's first, before ringing the doctor. Could be he'll need to make a call there while he's in the street.' Molly put her hand on Nellie's shoulder and turned her to face the top of the street before telling her daughter, 'When ye're making yer list out, sunshine, put camomile lotion on it. It's the best thing to cool a rash and it eases the pain.'

Doreen nodded, concern for her baby written on her pretty face.

'Okay, Mam, but don't forget to ring the doctor for us. I'll be on pins until I know Bobby's going to get better, that it isn't anything really serious. And I'm not the only one. Aunt Vicky is worried to death.'

Molly was already walking away. 'There's no need to worry or panic, sunshine. It's very upsetting for you and the baby, but it's not life-threatening. All babies, including yerself when you were one, catch it. And in a week or so it'll be gone and forgotten.' Over her shoulder she called, 'Go in, close the door, tell Victoria there's nothing to worry about, and give Bobby a kiss from his grandma and adopted grandma. Tell him we love the bones of him.'

Nellie pulled them to a halt so she could have her say. 'And we love every spot he's got, as well as his bones. You tell him that from me.'

Jill's face lit up when she saw who her visitors were. 'I was going to call in and see you, Mam, on me way to the shops. But it's nice yer've come, 'cos Auntie Lizzie likes to have a joke and a natter. Come on in, both of yer.'

Molly got a kiss and a hug, then Nellie demanded the same. 'How come your mam gets special treatment? She gets a longer kiss and a tighter hug than I do. And don't forget, girl, when yer married my son yer became a member of the McDonough family. That means I'm yer mam as well.'

Molly, in the living room by now, called, 'Let her have her way, Jill, agree with everything she says. There's been enough upset for one day, without starting World War Three.'

Lizzie looked from Molly to Nellie. 'Don't tell me you two have fallen out? That's unheard of, that is, and I'm really surprised.'

'We haven't fallen out, Lizzie,' Molly said. 'We have our differences, like anyone else, but never fall out. No, I wasn't referring to me and me mate when I said there'd been enough upset. It's baby Bobby. He's not very well, and seeing Doreen upset, well, me and Nellie got upset as well.'

'What's wrong with Bobby?' Jill picked little Molly up from the couch and held her tight. 'He's not ill, is he?'

'I can't say for certain because Doreen wouldn't let us in. She thinks he's got measles or chickenpox, 'cos he's got all the symptoms. High temperature and rash. The reason Doreen wouldn't let us in was because she was afraid we might pass it on to Molly. The baby doesn't have any signs, does she?'

Little Molly was like a porcelain doll, she was so beautiful. And it was easy to see she was going to inherit her mother's looks and colouring. She was laughing and gurgling now as she tried to catch hold of Jill's nose. 'There doesn't seem to be anything wrong with her, Mam, thank goodness, she's as bright as a button. Slept right through the night without a murmur.'

'Doreen was concerned because the two babies were playing together yesterday. But it doesn't necessarily mean that Molly will also get it, so don't sit watching and waiting for her to break out in spots.' Molly glanced at the clock. 'We're going to have to love yer and leave yer, I'm afraid. I've promised Doreen I'll ring for the doctor from the corner shop. And I've told her to have a list of shopping ready, so we can make the shops before they close for dinner. Is there anything we can get for you?'

Jill shook her head, sending her long blonde hair swinging across her face. 'No, thanks, Mam, I'll go to the shops meself. I like to take the baby out in the pram every day so she gets some fresh air. And I'll call to Doreen's later, to see what the doctor had to say.'

Lizzie Corkhill shot forward in her rocking chair. 'Oh, I don't think that would be wise, sweetheart. If Bobby has got the measles, it's very catching, and I don't think yer should risk Molly catching it. I know she'll get it some time, all babies do, but she's such a little tot, and if it can be avoided until she's a bit older and stronger, then I'd advise yer to steer clear.'

Nellie's chins, bosom and tummy were in agreement. 'Lizzie is right, girl, so heed her advice.'

Molly also agreed. 'I know you and Doreen are very close and yer want to help her. But just think how bad she'd feel if the baby did catch whatever Bobby's got. She'd blame herself and be very upset. So leave it until we hear what the doctor has to say. And how d'yer think I feel? Doreen is me daughter, Bobby me grandson, and because I can't do anything to help I feel useless. If I could take away Bobby's pain and Doreen's worry, and go through it for them, I would do so willingly. But as it isn't possible, I'll have to sit back and watch while saying a prayer for it to be over soon.'

Nellie, not usually emotional, was trying to swallow the lump in her throat. 'I'll be sitting with yer, girl, yer won't be on yer own.'

'I won't call to Doreen's, I'll do as yer say, Mam,' Jill said. 'I can see it would be unwise. But yer will tell her how sorry I am, won't yer? And I hope I'll see them very soon.'

'I'll do that, sunshine, even though there's no need. Doreen knows we all love her and Bobby without being told. Whether we're Bennett, McDonough or Corkhill, we all know we're loved without a word being spoken. And that makes us very lucky people. Very special people.' Molly fastened the buttons on her coat, then her eyes slid sideways to Nellie. 'I can't blame you for holding us back now, can I? Since I crossed the threshold I've never stopped talking. But I'll have to put a stopper on it now, if I want to catch the doctor before his surgery closes, and the shops pull their shutters down. I'll be back later, though, Jill, to let you and Lizzie know what's going on. I promise to keep yer informed.'

Jill passed the baby over to Lizzie. 'Mind her for us, please, while I see me mam and Auntie Nellie out. Then I'll get her ready to go out. We both need some fresh air.'

'I'll come with yer today, if yer don't mind.' Lizzie looked on Jill, Steve and little Molly as the family she never had. Oh, she had Corker, and she adored him, but he had always been away at sea and Lizzie had known what it was to be lonely. She was never lonely now, though, with a young family bringing her home to life. 'I could do with some air to blow the cobwebs away.'

Chapter Eleven

Jack was washing his hands in the kitchen sink and had his back to Molly, who was struggling to lift the large cast iron frying pan from the stove. 'This ruddy thing weighs a ton. It's enough to break me back.'

Ruthie was standing by the door, quiet for once. 'Mam, leave it on the stove and I'll hold the plates for yer to put the dinner on. That would be much easier.'

'Why didn't I think of that?' Molly sighed with relief when the frying pan was back on the stove. 'Pass me one plate at a time, sunshine, there's a good girl.'

Turning the tap off, Jack shook the water from his hands before reaching for a towel. 'It's only natural for yer to be at sixes and sevens after the day yer've had. It's not only the running around, but the worry on top of it.'

'Take those two plates in, sunshine,' Molly told her daughter. 'That one's yer dad's, the other is yours. I'll bring me own in.' She walked into her husband's open arms and laid her head on his chest. 'It's been a day and a half, love, or at least it felt like it. I've heard the expression "running around like a headless chicken", well, I know now what it means.' She lifted her face for a kiss, then drew away. 'Come on, don't let the dinner go cold.'

As Jack followed his wife into the living room, he asked, 'It's definitely the measles, is it?'

Molly put her plate down, then dropped on to her chair. 'Yes. The doctor said it's in the early stages yet, and it will get worse over the next three days. All Doreen can do is try to ease the pain by dabbing camomile lotion all over the rash. Doreen said he was very good with Bobby and thought he was big and bonny for his age.'

'The poor little blighter, he must be wondering why his mammy isn't making the pain go away.' Jack clamped his lips as he shook his head. 'It couldn't have come at a worse time, either, with him teething.'

Ruthie was playing with the food on her plate, for she had lost her appetite. 'Can't I go and see Bobby, Mam? He'll think I've forgotten him if I don't go.' Then, before her mother had time to respond, she voiced the fear in her heart. 'He's not going to die, is he, Mam?'

'Of course he's not, sunshine. In a week or two he'll be as right as rain. You had it when yer were a baby, and you're alive and kicking. And yer sisters and Tommy had it. In fact, ninety-nine children out of a hundred get measles or chickenpox. Many of them get both.'

Jack stood his knife and fork like sentinels at the side of his plate. 'I can remember, as though it was only yesterday, the day I came home from work to find Jill had chickenpox.' His eyes were tender as he gazed at Molly. 'You were out of yer mind, love, because yer didn't know what to do for the baby, to stop the pain. And I thanked God for yer ma that day, because she gave yer a good talking to, explaining like, and put our minds at rest. She said the worst would be over in a week, and by golly she was right.'

'I don't remember getting it, Mam,' Ruthie said, feeling slightly better. 'And I should do, shouldn't I?'

'Not really, sunshine, yer were too young to remember. The girls and Tommy will remember when you had it, 'cos they didn't get much sleep with you crying all through the night. They'd forgotten Tommy had been as bad when he had it. I can laugh at it now, but I didn't think it funny at the time, the way Jill and Doreen gave yer a wide berth in case they caught it off yer. I told them they wouldn't, but looking at you covered in spots and a rash, they weren't taking any chances.'

Ruthie's legs began to swing back and forth. 'That was mean of them. I couldn't help having spots. Just wait until I see them, I'll tell them off.'

Jack chortled. 'I think ye're fourteen years too late to tell them off, sweetheart. Don't forget there's seven years between you and Tommy, then a year extra between him and Doreen. And as yer well know, Jill is a year older than Doreen. They'll have long forgotten your spots. Besides, yer mam exaggerated a bit. They all felt sorry for yer. That's 'cos they knew what yer were going through.' He reached for Molly's hand. 'And for every pain you had, yer mam suffered with you. She nursed every one of you; wouldn't even let me take over so she could get some sleep.'

'Yer didn't have to sit all night with me, did yer, Mam?'

Molly nodded and squeezed her husband's hand. 'I sat up with each of my children. Nursing isn't a man's job, that's what mothers are for.'

'Will Doreen have to stay up all night, Mam?' Ruthie's mind was ticking over. 'I'll sit with her tonight, and I could look after Bobby while she has a sleep. Would she let me do that, 'cos I want to help.'

'Ah, that's a lovely thought, sunshine, and I'm really proud of yer. I'll be giving Doreen a knock later, and I'll tell her about yer kind offer.' When Molly looked into the face of one of her daughters, it was like looking into a mirror. Through them, she could see herself at different stages, from Ruthie at nearly sixteen to her eldest, Jill, who was now twenty-three. And looking at her wonderful son, Tommy, she could see her husband, for they were very alike, both in looks and nature. 'I know Doreen will be grateful to yer, sunshine, for being so thoughtful, but my girls all take after me. And when one of yer were sick or in pain, I would never have let anyone but me nurse my babies better. When you are older, and married to the man of your dreams, the day will come when you'll understand what I'm telling you now.'

Jack leaned across the table and ruffled Ruthie's hair. 'Yer've got a long way to go before then, love, and I hope yer get a lot of pleasure out of life while you're young. Plenty of time before yer worry about meeting the man of your dreams.'

Ruthie giggled. 'I hope I've learned to do the waltz before then, Dad. And the quickstep.' Her eyes brimming with mischief, she asked, 'How d'yer know I haven't met the man of my dreams already?'

'Ay, young lady, we'll have less of that.' Molly tried to put on a stern face, but her effort was in vain. 'Me and yer dad have to vet any boy you go out with. And if he wants to steal yer away from us, he'll have to pass a very hard test.'

'Even if he comes down our street riding a white horse, and he wants me to hop on behind him?'

Jack chortled. 'Hop on behind him? Ay, sweetheart, a knight of old wouldn't be talking to yer like that. He'd jump from his horse, sweep yer up in his arms and place yer tenderly on the saddle. Then he'd jump on himself, take off the hat with an ostrich feather on, and wave a farewell to me and yer mam.'

'Oh, it would be more exciting than that, love,' Molly said. 'I mean, it would be a rare sight to see, a man wearing a big hat with an ostrich feather on, riding a white horse down this street. The word would spread like wildfire and everyone in the street would be out. In fact I'd go as far as to say the whole neighbourhood would hear, and the people would be coming from all directions. They'd have to send for the police to form a cordon, so no one would be trampled under the horse's hooves. The poor thing would be frightened by all the people shouting. Especially if yer Auntie Nellie tried to stop the knight from capturing you. If she stretched up to pull yer off the horse, and he caught sight of her knickers, well, it would scare the life out of him and he'd bolt.'

'It's good to hear yer laughing, love,' Jack said. 'When I came in yer looked worried to death.'

'I was, love. Have been since I knocked on Doreen's front door this morning. My heart went out to her 'cos she was out of her mind. She's only young, it's her first baby, and she didn't know what to do. And of course, seeing her in such a state, well, I lost all sense of proportion. But sitting here now, going back to when our kids were Bobby's age, it's put me back on an even keel. Doreen will fret with her baby, but it will teach her how to cope in future. Every mother goes through it, and she is no exception.'

'I doubt if Doreen will see it like that, love. She'll be too worried to think rationally.'

'Don't I know it! I've been through it four times, don't forget. In fact, six times because two of them got chickenpox as well.'

This gave Ruthie food for thought. 'It's not easy being a mother, is it, Mam?'

'It's all worth it in the end, sunshine. It would be a lonely life without a family. I wouldn't change my life for anything in the world. My ma couldn't have any more children after me, but just think of the huge family we've got now, thanks to her.'

'Ooh, I didn't know that, Mam. Grandma's never mentioned it.'

'There was never any reason to. Anyway, me ma wouldn't discuss such a delicate matter in front of a youngster.'

'I'll soon be sixteen, Mam, and then I won't be a youngster any more. I'll be a young lady, like you were when yer courted me dad. Sweet sixteen yer were when he fell for yer at a dance.'

Molly tutted. 'I should never have told yer about that, 'cos yer'll keep harping on it.' She could almost see her daughter's mind ticking over. 'And before yer ask, the answer is the same as the last time yer asked. Me and yer dad have given in to yer having the birthday party here, but don't ask any more favours or yer'll be pushing yer luck.' She smiled to soften her words. 'Quit while ye're ahead, sunshine, and take my word for it, that is good advice.'

'Always take yer mam's advice, pet,' Jack told her, 'and yer won't go far wrong. And shall we offer to clear up for her, 'cos I'm sure she'll be going over to Doreen's.'

Molly pushed her chair back. 'No, I'll wash up tonight. I can't expect you and Ruthie to do it all the time, not after yer've both been working all day. It won't take me long once I get stuck in. I will be calling to Doreen's to see how things are, and make sure she's got everything in that she needs, then I'm going to me ma's, to put the family there in the picture. They'd have me guts for garters if I didn't tell them. Yer know what me ma and da are like, their lives revolve around the family. She'll give me the third degree tonight, right down to the last detail.'

'I think I'll come with yer, love,' Jack said. 'I know it's not far, but the walk and fresh air will do me good. I know I see our Tommy every day, but I don't get to see yer ma and da, or Rosie, that often. We could have a game of cards.'

'Hey, hold yer horses, love, what about our daughter? We can't both go out and leave her. If we start playing cards at me ma's, it could be well after ten before we get back, and I'm not leaving Ruthie to come into a dark house from Bella's.'

'Mam, if it makes yer feel better, I could bring Bella over here to sit with me until yer come in.' Ruthie thought that a good idea because it meant she and Bella could talk freely without grown-ups listening. 'Me dad could walk her home and her mam wouldn't worry if she knew that.'

'Okay, sunshine, as long as none of the lads are coming in, 'cos Mary wouldn't be happy about it.'

'They won't be, Mam, I promise. Me and Bella are going to do each other's hair, see what we look like with a different style.'

'Go and ask her now, sunshine, while me and yer dad clear away. We'll be ready for the off in ten minutes, so don't stand gabbing.'

Ruthie was off like a shot, leaving Molly and Jack grinning at each other. 'They'll be made up having the house to themselves,' Molly said. 'I bet their tongues will be going fifteen to the dozen with no old fogies listening in. Hair, make-up, shoes and clothes, in that order. They can't wait to be old enough to buy and wear what they want. I was the same at their age, and I didn't listen when me ma told me I was wishing me life away.'

'Whatever yer did, or we did,' Jack said, tenderness and love in his eyes, 'it was the right thing. We've had a good life, yer must admit. The kids have all grown up well mannered and respectful, and not one of them has caused us any worry or brought trouble to our door.' He put his arms round her waist and held her tight. 'And I love yer now as much as the day I married you. More, if it's possible.'

Molly rubbed noses with him. 'Ye're a soppy beggar, Jack Bennett, but I wouldn't have yer any different. I love the bones of yer and every one of our family. Which of course includes Nellie's tribe and the Corkhills.' She gave him a peck on the cheek before pulling away. 'I'd say we are well blessed, and pray it stays that way.'

Girlish laughter had the couple turning towards the tiny hall, where Ruthie and Bella had their hands across their mouths to deaden the sound of their laughter.

'How long have you two been there?' Molly asked, her face flushed with embarrassment. 'It's bad manners to listen in to other people's conversation.'

'Not when it's you and me dad, Mam,' Ruthie said. 'We're only laughing because when we were coming out of Bella's house, her mam and dad were kissing and cuddling. We said it must be catching.'

'Ay, well, young ladies,' Jack told them, 'let's hope that when you've been married as long as we have, you still love your husbands enough to want to kiss and cuddle.'

'I'll make sure of that, Dad,' Ruthie said, pulling a chair out for Bella to sit on. 'I've been watching you and me mam since I was a baby, and I'm a quick learner. And it hasn't slipped my notice that Jill and Steve, Doreen and Phil, and our Tommy and Rosie have all learned from you.'

Molly slipped her coat on and dropped the door key into her pocket. 'I hope yer have learned something, sunshine. We've tried to set yer a good example.'

'Oh, yer have, Mam. That's why I'm not going to marry any boy until yer've given him the once over, and tell me he's good enough for me.'

Jack butted in. 'If we don't get a move on the night will be over. We'll be getting to yer ma's just as they're going to bed.'

'Okay, keep yer hair on, sunshine, we're on our way.' Molly turned at the living-room door to tell her daughter, 'We'll discuss your future husband another time. But you and Bella make yerselves a drink and we'll see you around ten to half past.'

When Phil opened the door to his mother and father-in-law, they could hear the baby's screams of pain and distress. 'The poor love,' Molly said. 'I'd have the pain for him if it was possible.'

Phil pulled the door to behind him, and stepped down on to the pavement. 'He really is in a sad state. And Doreen is really upset because nothing she does makes it any better. She said the baby is looking at her as though he's asking what she's doing to him.'

'I know it's not much consolation, son, but it will start to ease off after three days. Not that he'll be over it, but he'll be through the worst.'

'I won't ask yer in, Mrs B, 'cos Doreen has got her hands full. We're trying to keep Bobby away from Aunt Vicky, as well, which doesn't help. The doctor told Doreen not to let her near the baby, because of her age. Not that she's likely to catch the measles, but, as he said, better to be safe than sorry.'

The screaming continued and Molly linked her arm through Jack's. 'We'll let yer get back in, son, but if yer need us during the night, don't hesitate to knock. And tell Doreen I'll be over first thing in the morning.'

'Once Aunt Vicky goes to bed, I'll make Doreen go and lie down for a couple of hours while I nurse Bobby. She needs to get some sleep or she'll be ill herself.'

'Just keep telling each other it's only for a few days,' Jack said, putting a hand on his son-in-law's shoulder. 'In a week or so the worst will be over.'

Phil stepped into the hallway. 'I hope so, 'cos it's hard to see someone so young in pain and not be able to help. I'll give Doreen yer message, Mrs B., and she'll see yer tomorrow.'

'All right, sunshine, but don't forget yer only have to cross the street if yer need us. We'll always be there for yer.' Molly pulled on Jack's arm as she added, 'Goodnight and God bless, son.'

'Yer feel helpless, don't yer, love?' Jack said, as they walked up the street. 'And yer wonder how Bobby caught the measles when he can't walk yet, and only ever goes out in the pram.'

'I'm not clever enough to answer that, sunshine. All I know is it's a germ which can be passed on just by standing by someone. And once caught, there's no getting rid of it until it's run its course. I'm just hoping baby Molly doesn't get it, 'cos she's a lot more delicate than Bobby. I couldn't bear to see both me grandchildren in pain.'

'Are we calling to Jill's?'

Molly nodded. 'I promised to let her know. Yer know how close all our children are. When one hurts, the others feel the pain. We won't stay long, though, 'cos I want to call and see how me ma and da are.'

The first words out of Steve McDonough's mouth when he saw his in-laws on the step were: 'How is young Bobby, Mrs B.?'

Molly squeezed past him. 'I haven't seen him, sunshine, but there's no change since this morning. He's very much out of sorts, poor little beggar.'

Steve gave his father-in-law a pat on the back before closing the door. 'Keeping yer wife company tonight, Mr B.?'

'I like to keep in touch with all the family, son.' And, to Jack, Steve was just like a son. He'd been part of their family since the day he was born, and they couldn't have wished for a better husband for Jill. He was honest, straight as a die, a good worker, and could be trusted to take care of their daughter. 'If I don't keep coming now and again I'll forget what you all look like. And when one of yer opens the door yer'll think I'm a stranger and ask me what I want.'

Jill was delighted to see her beloved parents, and hurried towards them. It was well over a year now since she'd left home, but she still missed them. And she missed her sisters and brother, for their lives had been filled with love, warmth and laughter. Mealtimes had been the best, when they all sat round the table vocally recalling the events of the day, and exaggerating at times to make their tale funnier than it really had been. No matter how funny they all were, though, none could beat their mother, who kept them in stitches as she impersonated Auntie Nellie in words and actions. Those scenes would never be forgotten. They were etched on her memory for ever, together with the warmth and love of her parents.

'How is Bobby, Mam?' Jill held her mother close as she kissed her. 'I was going to walk down to see her, 'cos I feel mean for not showing my face when she's in trouble. But Auntie Lizzie said Doreen probably wouldn't thank me for calling when she's got so much on her plate.'

'I haven't seen the baby, sunshine, never mind you. Me and yer dad called before we came here, but we only saw Phil. We could hear Bobby crying, and I just wanted to push Phil out of the way so I could hold the baby and give him a kiss. But I know I'm daft for a woman of my age, who has had four children who went through what Bobby's going through now. I'll have to learn to be patient, and tell meself that in a few days the worst will be over.' Molly smiled over Jill's shoulder. 'How are yer, Lizzie?'

'I'm fine, Molly, thank God.' Lizzie Corkhill planted her feet firmly on the floor to stop the rocking of the chair. 'It's a shame for Doreen's baby, though, him being so young. Corker was about four when he caught it. At that age he could tell us where he hurt, and how to make him comfortable. Not that he didn't cry so loud the whole street could hear him.' She smiled as she conjured up an image of her son as he was at that age, then as he was now. 'He was big for his age then, but I never dreamt he'd grow into the giant he is today.'

Jack was leaning against the sideboard, having refused his daughter's offer of a chair. He knew Molly didn't want to stay long, and if they sat down and made themselves comfortable they'd be late getting to her ma's. 'Was yer husband a big man, Lizzie?'

She shook her head. 'Not as big as Corker is. He wasn't small, mind, about the same height as you I'd say at a guess.'

116

Steve came and stood shoulder to shoulder with Jack. 'I'm the same height as you, Mr B., there's only an inch in it either way. If I had a penny for every time I wished I'd grow to be as tall as you, I'd be a rich man.'

Jill slipped her arm through her husband's, her blue eyes showing her love for him. 'Yer've never mentioned it before, love. Why were yer wishing that?'

'I'll only tell yer if yer promise not to laugh. I don't mind making a fool of meself as long as nobody tells me I am a fool.' Steve's dimples were deep in his handsome face. 'And I need a promise that what I say won't be repeated.'

Four heads nodded, and Molly acted as spokeswoman. 'Yer've got our word on it, sunshine, so let's into the big secret.'

'Well, it's no secret I fell in love with Jill when I was two and she was a baby in her pram. I didn't know what love was then, of course, I only remember thinking I wished I could make her smile at me like she smiled when she saw this tall man walking up the street every night on his way home from work. She used to get really excited, clapping her hands and holding her arms out for him to lift her out of the pram. I wanted to be that man, so she would smile at me and be as happy to see me as she was to see him. I waited twenty years for my wishes to come true, and here I am standing next to that man, with my arm round that little girl in the pram.'

Jill, always the most tender and emotional of the Bennett children, had tears in her eyes. 'Oh, that was a lovely thing to say, love, really romantic. I don't know what my thoughts were when I was that baby in the pram, but I do know that I can't remember a time when I didn't love you. And I always knew I would marry yer. There was never anyone else for me.'

Molly jerked her head at Jack. 'I bet you can't come up with anything as romantic as that.'

Jack chortled. 'I can't go back to the days when yer were in yer pram, love. Steve has the advantage over me there. But I can go back to when yer started work at fourteen, and were the prettiest girl I'd ever seen. I noticed you right away, but you were very shy and never looked my way. I wasn't going to be put off, though. I made up my mind I was going to chase you until I caught you. The going wasn't as easy for me as it was for Steve. I lived a few tram stops away from your street, and I had to run the gauntlet with yer ma and da, I was a stranger to them, and they weren't going to let their daughter go out with anyone unless they knew everything about me. Steve had an easy time winning his fair lady, I had to work hard on it. But it was worth it, and I'd do it all over again if needed.'

'Well, look what yer got for yer trouble, sunshine. A wonderful family, and a mother and father-in-law in a million.' Molly winked at Lizzie. 'We're all soppy, Lizzie, it runs in the family. But that's the way we like it.' She turned to her firstborn. 'The baby goes to bed early, doesn't she? I thought we might have caught her before yer took her up.'

There was pride on Jill's pretty face. 'Half past six every night now, Mam. Once she's been washed and fed, she's tired out and goes to bed without a murmur. And most nights she sleeps through until six.'

'They don't know they're born with little Molly,' Lizzie said. She was an adopted granny for the baby and took her role seriously. 'She's a credit to them.'

'As all my children are a credit to me, Lizzie.' Molly made a move towards the door. 'We're going round to me ma's now, to keep them up to date with events. But I'll be up again tomorrow, after I've spoken to Doreen.'

'I'll see you out, Mrs B.' Steve followed her and Jack to the door. 'Don't forget to tell Doreen and Phil that we're here if they need us.'

'We won't, son. I'll definitely pass the message on.' With her arm through Jack's, Molly turned in the direction of her parents' home, which was also the home of her beloved son and his wife. 'I'd say you are two of the luckiest people alive, sunshine. We've got a family in a million.'

Jack squeezed her arm. 'I'll second that, love.'

Chapter Twelve

Jack threw his hand of cards into the middle of the table, his tut-tut a sign of pretend disgust. 'Talk about the luck of the Irish! We've had five hands of rummy, Bridie won two, and Rosie O'Grady won three. Now if that isn't a fiddle I'll eat me hat.'

Rosie's blue Irish eyes were shining as she gathered the cards in and patted them into a neat pile. 'It's wrong on two counts yer are, Mr B. Sure, haven't I been the same name as yerself since I married yer son, who is the finest figure of a man yer'll see if yer walked the length and breadth of Ireland and England? And isn't it proud I am to have been given the honour of being his ever-loving wife?'

Tommy tapped his beautiful wife on the shoulder. 'What about you being called a fiddler, pet, are yer going to answer that?'

'If yer'll give me a chance, Tommy Bennett, then I'll be after telling me father-in-law that it wasn't meself that was sliding a card along the table when no one was looking. It was my dearly beloved husband, who happens to be his son.'

Tommy feigned shock. In a whisper loud enough for all to hear, he said, 'It's a sneak yer are, Rosie Bennett, and I'm blushing with shame for yer.'

Molly caught Jack's eye and jerked her head to where her ma and da were sitting on the opposite side of the table. Both in their late seventies, Bob and Bridie Jackson were smiling as they listened to the banter from the young couple who had enriched their lives since the day they got married and moved into the back bedroom of the small house. It was history repeating itself. Fifty years ago, Bridie had left her home in Ireland to seek work in England. She met Bob, they fell in love and were married. Half a century later, a shy fifteen-year-old girl came to England seeking work. She fell in love with Tommy at first sight, but the boy needed coaxing for he thought girls were cissies. Rosie had her work cut out to make him change his mind. But she refused to be put off, and eventually she stole his heart. And no one was more pleased than Tommy, who now adored his beautiful Irish colleen.

'I bet watching them takes yer back a bit, Ma?' Molly smiled at the mother whom she loved so much, she could always feel a lump in her throat when she looked at her and her da. 'It's like you and me da all over again.'

'It is that, me darlin'.' Bridie reached for her husband's hand, 'Me and Bob often say we're living our youth again through them.'

Jack chortled. 'Ay, Bridie, I wouldn't let the neighbours see yer with a skipping rope, or playing hopscotch. They'll ask yer what pills ye're on.'

Bob took the pack of cards from the table and began to deal. 'We'll have time for another hand before it's time to call it a day. And if yer watch me hands carefully, yer'll know there's been no sleight of hand.'

'Da, I'd trust yer with me life,' Molly said, winking at the man who was, in her eyes, the perfect husband, father and gentleman. Then she remembered something she'd promised herself she'd do. 'Oh, before I forget, Ma, would you and me da walk down to Flora's one day? I'm sure she'd be delighted to see yer. With her having no family to look out for her, me and Nellie are going to keep an eye on her. In fact, we've told her we've adopted her. But with you being nearer to her age, I'm sure yer'd have lots to talk about. And having company would do her the world of good.'

'Of course we will, me darlin'. Sure, we were only saying last night we should pay her a visit. Me and yer da appreciate how lucky we are, and it's beholden upon us to share what we have. So if yer see the dear lady, would yer be after telling her we'll call tomorrow afternoon, say two o'clock?' She turned her gaze on to her husband. 'Is that all right with you, sweetheart?'

'Anything you say is all right with me, love, yer know that. And wouldn't it be nice if yer baked some of your delicious fairy cakes, and we took them with us?'

'What a lovely idea, Da.' Molly was pleased. 'I'll let Flora know you're coming, but I'll not tell her about the cakes. I'll let that be a surprise.'

It was Tommy who asked, 'Have the police not found the rotter who stole from her?'

'No, son, not to my knowledge. And with me and Nellie calling in every day, Flora would have told us if she'd had any news.'

'Well, whoever it was,' said Bridie, 'I hope God pays him back. I don't know how he can sleep at night, and that's the truth of it.'

Rosie, who had a heart as beautiful as her face, said, 'Me and Tommy will call and visit her, so we will. Just to let the poor soul know that not all people have hearts as black as the divil himself.'

Molly smiled. 'That would be wonderful, sunshine. She'd enjoy the company of young people. But let her know when yer'll be calling, 'cos otherwise she won't open the door.'

'We'll give a knock at Doreen's as well,' Tommy said. 'I know we won't be able to go in the house, but we can talk to Doreen on the step. I want her to know we're thinking about Bobby, and hoping he's soon better.'

'It'll be at least a week before the poor mite shows any sign of being himself again, so it will.' Bridie nodded. 'And it's meself that'll be happy, for won't we miss seeing the little love with his bonny smile, and arms outstretched to be lifted up for a cuddle.'

Bob had been waiting patiently to start the game. Now he asked, 'Are we having a last game of cards or not? It'll soon be time for bed.'

Cards were lifted, fanned out and sorted into the right order. 'I think it's my turn to go first,' Molly said. 'And I hope I have better luck than I had earlier.' She was smiling inwardly, for she had a good hand. Two pairs she had, and a joker, so surely she was in with a chance. In her mind she had her fingers crossed as she reached to pick the top card off the pack in the centre of the table. And when she picked up the two of spades she couldn't believe her luck. She was dealt the two of diamonds and hearts, so she could lay three of her cards down now. Her face alight with pleasure, and with a grand flourish, she laid the cards down. 'How about that, then, folk? Looks like my luck has changed, and I'm due for a winning streak.'

'Don't brag too soon, love, 'cos it's bad luck.' Jack jerked his head back as his eyes scanned the cards in his hand. He had no pairs or runs; it was a lousy hand. So with a sigh of disgust he threw down the king of hearts. 'I couldn't win an argument.'

The only thing Jack got right in that last game was his warning to Molly. She did brag too soon, for the good start she had didn't last long, and the game ended with Bob being the winner. 'I don't feel bad about yer winning Da,' Molly said, 'but I would have cried like a baby if me ma or Rosie had won again. I'd have demanded a check to make sure none of their cards were fake.'

Tommy's shoulders began to shake. 'None of the cards are fake, Mam, I can say that with me hand on me heart. But I can't say the same for the little marks on the cards what no one would notice, only me and Rosie. We have a secret code, and know exactly, by the tiny code marks, what cards yer've all got in yer hands.' His shoulders shook even more when he saw the look on his mother's face as she scanned one card after another. 'Yer can't see them, Mam, that's why only me and Rosie know. There's no point in cheating if the other players know our secret.'

'Well, yer've done a good job of it, 'cos I'm blowed if I can see a mark on any of the cards.' She looked up to catch Tommy winking at his wife, then lowered her eyes so they wouldn't know they'd been rumbled. 'Well, actually, that's not true. I can't tell a lie, sunshine, so I've got to tell yer that yer didn't fool me for one second. In the other hands yer did, but not in this last one. I was suspicious, thinking no one could be lucky all the time, like Rosie, and I gave me cards a good going over. At first I couldn't see anything wrong, then suddenly I noticed a little mark on the eight of hearts in me hand. That had me checking each card, and there was a mark on every card in me hand. If I didn't have good eyesight I'd have missed it.' Molly knew she was talking a load of rubbish, but if someone was pulling her leg then it was payback time. She threw her cards into the centre of the table and sat back in her chair. 'I'm glad about that. At least I now know I lost every hand because someone was cheating, not because I'm unlucky.'

'How can yer be unlucky when yer've got me for a husband?' Jack asked. 'The day yer met me was the luckiest day of yer life. Out of the dozens of pretty girls I had to choose from, I picked you.'

Molly slapped an open palm on her forehead. 'At last the mystery has been solved. How can I have gone through the last twenty-odd years thinking I must have done something really bad to be so unlucky, when all the time a curse had been put on me by those dozens of girls yer turned down. I should have remembered the old saying, "Hell hath no fury like a woman scorned."' Sighing heavily, and making it look like an effort to push herself to her feet, she gazed at her husband. 'You've let me walk round all these years carrying this heavy burden, and not said a dickie bird. One curse would have been bad enough, but dozens is far more than one person can endure. In fact I feel bereft of all my senses, weary and tired out. So tired, I'm afraid yer'll have to carry me home. And for your sins, I'll remind you that not only are you carrying me, but also a dozen curses. A heavy weight to bear, Jack Bennett.'

There was a burst of applause from those sitting round the table, and Bridie said, 'Very good, me darlin'. Ethel Barrymore at her best.'

'Oh, no, Grandma,' Tommy said. 'Definitely Bette Davis. What do you think, Granda?'

Bob smiled at his beloved daughter, who had always been there for him and Bridie. 'I think your mam knocks them all into a cocked hat. She can be anyone she chooses, and be as good as them. Her and Nellie have a rare gift. That's why their friendship has lasted so long and is as steady as a rock.'

The mention of her mate brought a grin to Molly's face. 'If I start talking about Nellie, we'll be here all night. But I'd like to say, quickly, that there are some things in which she leaves me standing miles behind her. This is just one of them. We've been going into the butcher's shop nearly every day for over twenty years. And every day Nellie has a tale for him. It's all made up, mind, but she's never told the same tale twice. When she walks in the shop she doesn't know what she's going to say, and I certainly don't. She just opens her mouth and spins a tale which has Tony and Ellen almost believing her. She's so good that even I find meself believing her for a while. She might not be able to spell a word with more than six letters in, but by golly she is one good storyteller, with a fantastic imagination.'

With her lips pursed, Bridie nodded her head slowly. 'Sure, in His wisdom, didn't the good Lord dispense His gifts far and wide. To each creature He gave a talent, and it's up to us what we do with that talent, so it is.'

'Ye're right there, Ma,' Molly said, pushing her chair back under the table. 'It's up to each and every one to make the best of what we've been given. I think I can safely say that every member of our clan does that.' She looked across at Jack. 'Come on, sunshine, or Bella's mam will be having a fit. Yer know what Mary's like. I bet she's standing at her front door waiting for you to take her daughter home.'

Tommy scratched his head. 'But she only lives opposite. Fifteen steps at the most. Surely Bella couldn't come to any harm crossing the street on her own?'

'Mary Watson can't help the way she is, sunshine. And although she's always molly-coddled Bella, it's better that way than letting a child run wild.'

Jack slipped on his coat. 'You said ten to half past, love and we've got ten minutes to the deadline. We can make it with a few minutes to spare.'

After hugs and kisses were exchanged, and Molly had promised to let them know every day how Bobby was, Molly and Jack were on their way home.

'Yer ma and da look good for their age, love,' Jack said, crooking his arm for Molly to link. 'I hope we look like them when we're nearly eighty, please God.'

'It's Tommy and Rosie who keep them young. They adore them, wait on them hand and foot, and make sure they eat a proper meal and keep warm. They get on like a house on fire and it takes a lot of worry off me, knowing Ma and Da are in good hands.'

They were turning into their street when they heard the sound of men's voices and laughter. 'The pub must have had a stay-back for a few of their regulars,' Jack said. 'It happens once a week, but only for about six of the best customers.'

'Corker's with them.' Molly chuckled. 'If I didn't recognize his laugh, I couldn't miss him 'cos he's head and shoulders above all the other men.' She raised her voice and shouted over to the group. 'Haven't you got homes to go to, yer dirty stop-outs?'

'Molly, me darlin'.' Corker excused himself and left the group to cross the street to his neighbours. 'I did knock for yer, Jack, but Ruthie said you and Molly were out visiting.'

'We're just keeping the family informed of the situation with young Bobby,' Molly told him. 'Doreen doesn't want any visitors while the poor baby is so fretful, so I'm doing the rounds each day with the news.' She suddenly remembered she still had the betting slip in her pocket. 'Oh, before I forget, here's the slip you asked me to give you back once Flora had seen it. I should have let yer have it sooner, but things have been a bit hectic the last few days.'

'That should have been the least of yer worries.' Corker tore the slip and put the pieces in his pocket. 'Did it go well with Mrs Parker? She believed what yer told her?'

Molly nodded. 'It took some talking, and quite a few lies, but she accepted it eventually. And I've arranged for some members of the family to visit her, so she isn't left on her own too much. Me ma and da are going, your mother is going another day, and Tommy and Rosie one night. Plus me and Nellie will be calling most days, so she'll have plenty of company. And when Bobby is better, I'll be bringing her out to visit some of her old friends.'

'Has she heard any more from the police about the robbery?' Corker asked 'They haven't caught the culprit?'

'Let's walk down while we're talking, Corker, 'cos we've left Bella in with Ruthie and Mary Watson will be on pins. We didn't expect to be out so late, but we had a few games of rummy at me ma's and it's amazing how quickly time can pass.'

'I'll run on, love, and take Bella home.' Jack began to walk ahead. 'You fill Corker in with the news.'

'There's not much to tell yer, Corker, 'cos the police haven't been back to see Flora. But there was something unusual happened that I don't think anyone has told the police yet. D'yer know Annie Cosgrove, who lives at the top of the street?'

'The lady with the large family, who always seems to run instead of walk? Yes, I know Annie. Why?'

'Well, she didn't know about the break-in until Sunday, and when she heard, she told Lily that she'd seen a man coming out of Flora's front door on the Monday morning. She didn't think anything of it at the time, she just thought he'd been visiting the old lady. And yer can't blame her; how was she to know any different?'

'Mmm, that's interesting. Whoever the burglar was, he had a nerve showing his face in the street.' Corker stroked his beard while he digested the latest development. 'I'm surprised no one informed the police and gave a description.'

'Ah, well, there wasn't a description as such. Yer just said yerself that Annie is always on the run, and she didn't give the bloke more than a glance. She was mad with herself when she knew, said she'd have screamed the place down and the bloke would have been caught. Flora's next door neighbours either side, Lily and May, they quizzed her on what he looked like and what he was wearing, but all Annie could remember was that he looked young and was wearing a cap pulled low over his eyes. After all, it was over a week ago now.'

'The police should have been told this information, Molly. They have ways of jogging people's memory. They know how to ask the right questions.'

'To tell yer the truth, Corker, me and Nellie did have a go at Annie, and we got a bit more out of her. Not much, like, but enough to help the police identify the bloke. He was young, according to Annie, probably eighteen to twenty. He had a sallow complexion, thin build, and was wearing a dirty-looking knee-length coat and an old cap which Annie now remembers thinking should have been thrown in the midden long ago. And before yer say any more about the police not being informed, well, me and Nellie are definitely going to the police station in the morning. We'll get through our housework on the double, knock to see how things are in Doreen's, then if all is well we'll go to the police station before we do our shopping.'

Jack came to join them, saying, 'Bella is home safe and sound with a new hairstyle which had Mary's eyes popping out of her head.'

Molly tutted. 'Don't tell me our Ruthie has cut Bella's hair short, or bleached it blonde? I wouldn't put it past her.'

Jack chuckled. 'As a matter of fact, love, our daughter had done an excellent job, and Mary was as pleased as Punch. And yer won't know yer daughter; she's got her hair in pigtails. It suits her, too.'

'God knows what they'll be up to next,' Molly said, rooting in her pocket for the front door key in case Ruthie had gone to bed. 'It's this double birthday party, they can't sit still for excitement. They talk of nothing else but what dress they'll wear, or what hairstyle suits them best. They're only having the party in our house, but listening to them talk, yer'd think it was going to be a big posh do in the Adelphi.'

'I bet you were just the same at their age, Molly me darlin',' Corker said. 'It's a big step in their lives, being sixteen. And they'll have as much fun at a party in your house as they would in the Adelphi. More, in fact, because they would be so awestruck at the chandeliers in the grand hotel, they'd be afraid to open their mouths.'

Molly handed the key to Jack. 'Put the kettle on, love, I'm gasping for a cuppa. And I'll say goodnight to yer, Corker. I'll let yer know how me and Nellie get on at the police station.'

'Goodnight and God bless, Molly.' Corker walked two steps to his own front door. He wasn't going to tell his neighbour that the information she'd given him about the rotter who had robbed Flora Parker would be used by himself. Tomorrow night he'd visit all the local pubs he'd called at when he first heard of Flora's plight. This fuller description of the thief may ring a bell with one of the managers. It was certainly worth a try.

Molly shivered as they stood outside the police station. 'It's queer, sunshine, but I always have a funny feeling when I see a bobby, even though I've done nothing wrong. And I feel like shaking in me shoes now I've got to walk into the station. If they don't attend to us right away, I'll pass out.'

Nellie hitched her bosom and shook her head to give her chins a breath of fresh air. 'I know a good way of making sure they attend to us on the double, girl. Don't you worry, I'll see to it that we're in and out in no time.'

There was suspicion on Molly's face. 'For heaven's sake, sunshine, don't make a show of me, not in a police station. There's a time and place for everything, and this is neither the time or place.'

'Oh, stop being so fussy, girl, and let's get on with it. If we stand here much longer they'll arrest us for loitering.'

Molly gave herself a mental shake, took a deep breath, and mounted the steps into the police station. The sooner the ordeal was over the better, and she could relax. But if Molly had known what her mate was planning, she'd have turned on her heel and run for all she was worth.

The policeman sitting at the desk behind the window stopped writing when the two women walked in. 'Good morning, ladies. Can I help you?'

127

Nellie pushed herself in front of Molly and leaned an elbow on the window shelf. 'Well, it's like this, lad. I don't want no help, but me friend might. And her husband definitely doesn't want no help 'cos he's past it. Yer see, she's just murdered him.'

Molly gasped as she watched the policeman's jaw drop so fast his top set of false teeth fell out and on to the desk. He recovered his teeth before his composure, and he couldn't get his words out without stuttering. 'Wait there until I fetch the sergeant. Don't go away.'

Molly didn't know whether to faint or run like hell. She thought of another option she had, and that was strangling her mate. But strangling someone in a police station wasn't a very good idea. 'What the hell did yer tell him that for? This is a joke too far sunshine, and that bobby's boss might not have a sense of humour.'

'I told yer I would get them to attend to us right away, and I did. So what are yer moaning for? Left to you, we'd have been here all day.'

Molly didn't know where to start. 'Nellie, the chances are that I might be here for a very long time, behind bars. Yer've pulled some stunts in yer life, but yer've gone too far this time and landed us both in trouble.'

But Nellie wasn't the least perturbed. 'Don't be piling the agony on, girl, there's nothing to worry about. When the bobby comes back I'll tell him I was only pulling his leg, and I bet yer any money he'll see the funny side.'

However, he wasn't on his own when he came back. He was accompanied by a very serious-looking plain-clothes detective, who happened to be the one who had visited Flora. He nodded briefly to acknowledge he remembered them, then said, 'If what the constable has told me is true, it's a very serious accusation. I'd like yer to come through to the interview room and explain to me in detail what happened.'

'We won't come through if yer don't mind, lad,' Nellie said, rising to her full four foot ten inches. 'We're on our way to the butcher's, yer see. We only called in to give yer some information we've been given about the bloke what robbed Mrs Flora Parker.'

The detective frowned. 'I am more interested in what you told the constable, which was a very serious accusation. So please come through and make a statement.'

By this time Molly was in a state of panic. Her mate had surpassed erself this time, and landed them both in hot water. She'd have to ut a stop to it before it went too far. 'I'm sorry, inspector,' she said, fter taking a deep breath. 'I really have to apologize for my friend, vhose sense of humour has for once gone too far. I had no idea she vas going to tell the constable what she did, and I can understand if ou are angry at us for wasting your time. The real reason we are ere is, as Mrs McDonough said, to pass on information we've been ,iven about Mrs Parker's burglary.'

The detective, Steve Willard, was, against his better judgement, eginning to see the funny side. It certainly made a change from lealing with women moaning about nosy neighbours, kids breaking vindows, drunks, vagabonds and thieves. 'So, you haven't murdered our husband? What your friend told the constable wasn't true?'

Molly's eyes sent an apology to Nellie before she said, 'No, it's ot true. But Mrs McDonough didn't mean any harm. It was only a oke.'

Nellie was silent while all this was going on. She thought the vhole episode was hilarious and she deserved a pat on the back for hinking up something so funny. And she couldn't understand why ier mate was giving her daggers. After all, she'd done what she said he would, hadn't she? They'd been attended to right away.

The detective had a problem keeping his face straight, but he was letermined to play a joke himself, something to tell the missus when ie got home.

'Making such a serious accusation knowing it to be untrue, and vasting police time, are actions the police don't take lightly. I'm fraid I'm going to have to charge Mrs McDonough with both offences. And when the constable has written out her statement, illing in her full name, address, next of kin and so on, I'm afraid she vill have to be taken to a cell. She'll be released when my superior ias weighed up the situation and is convinced she is not a threat to he general public. And before she is released she will be cautioned.' Ie turned to the constable, who had never known anything like this n the twelve years he'd been in the police force. 'Take the statement, hen put Mrs McDonough in a cell. She'll only be released on the uper's say-so.'

If Molly hadn't noticed the laughter lurking in the detective's eyes, she would have moved quickly to stand four square next to her mate. But she was beginning to liken the episode to a Laurel and Hardy film. And as it appeared nothing drastic was going to happen to Nellie, perhaps the fright would teach her a lesson.

The detective touched Molly's elbow. 'Come this way, Mr Bennett.'

They had only taken two steps when they heard Nellie's voice, and they both turned to see a sight that had them chuckling. The constable was six foot two inches in height, and Nellie four foot ten inches. They made an unlikely pair. Nellie was craning her neck to look up at the bobby, and at the same time she was half running to keep up with his long stride. 'Ay, lad, will yer put me in a cell what has a nice soft seat? I'm used to a very posh chair, yer see. And when yer've locked me in, so I can't escape, like, be a good lad and fetch us a cuppa. I like two sugars and plenty of milk. Oh, and d'yer think there's any chance of a couple of biscuits? Custard creams are me favourites.'

As the detective told his wife as they were having their evening meal that night, he had never known a day like it in all the years he'd been with the force.

The constable didn't tell his wife, because he knew she wouldn't believe him. She never did see the funny side of life.

Chapter Thirteen

'Oh, come on, love, yer don't really expect me to fall for that, surely?' Jack speared a carrot and popped it into his mouth. 'Even by Nellie's standards, that is beyond belief.'

Ruthie agreed with her father in her head, but didn't voice it. For her mother was so good at telling stories, the girl could see her Auntie Nellie in her mind's eye, and she was hoping everything her mother had said was the truth. 'Go on, Mam, cross yer heart and hope to die, if this day you tell a lie.'

'I will not, indeed! If you and yer dad think I'm a liar, then that's all there is to it. It's no skin off my nose, and I've no intention of making excuses for a piece of information which was word for word the truth.'

'Don't be like that, love,' Jack said, his tone soothing. 'You must admit it's hard to believe that Nellie went in the police station and told the bobby you'd murdered me. And then she gets put in one of the cells. Even by her standards it sounds too far-fetched to be true.'

'If yer think what I've told yer is far-fetched, I'd love yer to be next door, listening to Nellie's version of events. I bet her story's a belter.'

'Why don't yer take her off for us, Mam, like yer usually do when she does something funny?' Ruthie was certain now that what her mother had told them was the truth. Otherwise she would have owned up before now. 'Go on, give us a laugh.'

'I'll tell yer what, sunshine, I thought I'd never laugh again when I heard Nellie telling the bobby I'd murdered me husband. I couldn't breathe, I felt as though all the breath had left me body. And while I'm dithering in me shoes, me mate is having a ball! Even when the constable went to get a senior officer she didn't bat an eyelid.' Molly closed her eyes and relived the scene in her mind. 'I'll never forget it as long as I live. And when the detective – his name was Steve Willard, I found out later – said he would have to charge her for making a false accusation and wasting police time, I thought I was going to faint.'

His wife looked too serious to be making it all up, and Jack was now convinced that, although the story sounded beyond the realm of possibility, Molly was definitely telling the truth. 'She was lucky to get away with it, love. Police don't have time to spare to be messed around.' He suddenly had a thought and burst out laughing. 'Nellie certainly got away with murder.'

Molly screwed her face up. 'I keep telling meself not to laugh, because it's not a laughing matter. But I keep getting this picture in me mind of Nellie walking next to the very tall constable, looking up at him and asking if she could have a cell with a nice soft seat, 'cos she was used to a very posh chair. "And when yer've locked me in, so I can't escape, like, be a good lad and fetch us a cuppa. I like two sugars and plenty of milk. Oh, and d'yer think there's any chance of a couple of biscuits? Custard creams are me favourites." She's being taken to a cell where they put drunks and thieves who are probably filthy dirty, and she doesn't give a toss. And the fact that she could really have been in trouble never entered her head.'

'They say where there's no sense there's no feeling,' Jack said. 'Does Nellie come into that category?'

'Definitely not! My mate has got more on top than any of us. She's crafty, and knows exactly what she can get away with.'

'With all that going on, did yer manage to do what yer set out to do?' Jack asked. 'Did yer tell the detective about the bloke that was seen coming out of Flora's house?'

Molly nodded. 'Yeah. He wrote the description down and said he'd pass it on to all the police stations in the area. He thinks there's a fair chance it might ring a bell with a local constable. Although he did say there wasn't much hope of Flora getting her money back. He reckoned that would have been well spent by now.'

'And the watch? Does he hold out any hope of that ever turning up?'

'He was very honest because he didn't want to build Flora's hopes up. Burglars don't hang on to the stuff they pinch, apparently. They get rid of it in case anyone saw them. If the police find it on them, they can charge them and they could end up in prison. But without proof, there's little the police can do.'

Ruthie had been listening with interest, and now she frowned. 'That's not fair, is it, Mam? They must be wicked to take something that doesn't belong to them. Especially from someone as old and frail as Mrs Parker. They're cowards, and deserve to go to prison.'

'There are some bad people in the world, sunshine, and ye're right, they should be punished. But thank goodness they're in the minority. There's far more good people than bad.'

A knock came on the door and Molly gave a start. 'Oh, my God, who can this be? Look at the state of the place! You open the door, Jack, and me and Ruthie will clear the table. Keep them at the door as long as yer can.'

Jack was shaking his head as he opened the door. He could never understand why women worried if the house wasn't spick and span. 'Hello, Corker, come on in.' Jack let the big man pass, then closed the door, saying, 'Molly will have me life. I was told to keep whoever it was at the door, to give her time to tidy up.'

Corker's hearty laugh ricocheted off the walls. 'That's typical of a woman, Jack, they don't like to be caught on the hop. Ellen's the same. When there's a knock on the door she moves like a whirlwind. And most of the time it's either someone selling the *Watchtower*, or a neighbour wanting change for the gas meter.'

Molly came through from the kitchen rubbing her hands down her apron before patting her hair into place. 'I heard that, Corker, and yer'd soon have something to say if yer came home from work and found the table littered with dirty dishes, and Ellen brushing the dirt under the carpet.'

'Oh, is that what she does?' Corker boomed. 'Here's me thinking I'm getting taller, when all the time it's the dirt lifting the carpet up.'

'Sit down, yer make the place look untidy.' Molly waved her arm towards the couch. 'You've got yer dinner over early.'

'I'm surprised any of the dinner got eaten, we were all laughing so much. Ellen was telling us about the encounter you and Nellie had with the law. And I had to come and ask if it was true, or one of Nellie's pranks.'

'Oh, it was true all right, Corker. In fact it was twice as bad as anything Ellen told yer.' Molly quickly reeled off a couple of the most embarrassing moments. 'The only one who thought it was funny at the time was Nellie, the troublemaker herself.'

'Was she actually put in a cell?' Corker couldn't stop his huge frame shaking with laughter, causing the couch to groan and the floorboards to shiver.

'Oh, yeah, she was put in a cell, and then served tea with two sugars and plenty of milk.' Molly dropped her head into her hands. 'I was sick with worry because I really thought we were in deep trouble. Me head was buzzing, me tummy was churning over and my legs felt like jelly. But when I'd been interviewed by the detective over Flora, he took me along to the cell Nellie was in, and we both peeped through that lid thing they have in the door for the police to keep an eye on any prisoner. And I'll never forget, until the day that I die, the sight of my mate sitting on a bench kind of seat, swinging her little chubby legs and singing "Show Me The Way To Go Home". Honestly, there are times I feel like strangling her, then she looks at me with that innocent expression on her chubby face, and I want to hug her. She's full of bravado, but she'd never knowingly hurt anyone just for the sake of it. All she wants is to put a smile on the face of someone she likes, then she's happy.'

'You certainly hit the nail on the head, Molly, for that is exactly what Nellie is about. She's entertained us for years, and can you imagine one of our parties without her?'

Ruthie had finished washing the dishes and they were stacked neatly on the shelf. She glanced around to make sure there was nothing she'd overlooked, then, after satisfying herself, she made her way into the living room. 'Hello, Uncle Corker.' She gave him a kiss and wrinkled her nose when his moustache tickled her cheeks. 'I love my Auntie Nellie, she is the funniest person I know, and she always makes me laugh. But she wouldn't be as funny without me mam. Where me mam is the straight one, Auntie Nellie is the comic, and they both need each other.'

'I couldn't have put it better meself, darlin'. Yer have a very astute mind for your age.'

'Oh, I listen carefully, Uncle Corker, and I tell Bella everything. Yer see, me and her are going to be like me mam and Auntie Nellie when we're older. We often practise in Bella's bedroom and I think we're very good.'

Molly and Jack looked at each other in astonishment. 'That's the first I've heard of this. I can't imagine Bella doing a turn, she's far too shy.'

'That's what you think, Mam, but she's not a bit shy when there's just the two of us. And she can do a good impersonation of you, considering she doesn't see as much of you and Auntie Nellie as I do. With more practice, we'll give yer a run for yer money, Mam.'

'You cheeky little monkey! Me and Nellie have got a long way to go yet before we retire, so don't get any big ideas of knocking us off the top spot at parties. Auntie Nellie would have yer guts for garters if yer tried to steal her thunder.'

'Yer won't be the only one seeking to take over from Nellie, me darlin',' Corker told Ruthie. 'Her daughter Lily is coming up on the rails fast. And another contender is yer own sister, Doreen. She does a very good impression of both Nellie and yer mam. So we've got years of wonderful, lively parties to look forward to. And at the very next one, I'll bring you on to show how good you are. It will be yer very first time on stage in front of an audience.'

Ruthie shook her head and bottom at the same time. 'Sorry, Uncle Corker, but you won't be having the pleasure at the very next party. There's no adults coming to that 'cos there isn't enough room for everyone. It's a double birthday celebration for me and Bella, and we'll be sixteen. But your Gordon and Peter will be here, and they can report back to you on our performance.'

Molly pulled a face. 'I think I'll live to regret telling you all the tricks me and Nellie get up to. And don't you dare try using today's events in the police station as one of your acts. I'd be ashamed to show me face in the street if the whole neighbourhood learned what we'd been up to. Yer'd only need to tell one person and it would spread like wildfire. I know it was very funny, and nothing came of it because we were lucky enough to have a detective with a sense of humour. None the less, I don't want it broadcast.'

'We won't be doing that, Mam, 'cos it only happened today and we haven't rehearsed it. We've chosen, or should I say I chose, one where Auntie Nellie plays a trick on Tony, in the butcher's. You remember, Mam, the one with the chickens.'

Molly chuckled. 'For the life of me, sunshine, and with the best will in the world, I can't see Bella standing in the butcher's with her hands on her hips, squinting out of half-closed eyes, and turning the air blue with her language.'

Corker was grinning from ear to ear as he winked at Jack. He loved every member of the Bennett family. He'd known Molly and Jack since they moved into the street as newly-weds. They were soon friends. And the big man had seen the children grow from babies to adults. He'd lived at the top end of the street then, with his widowed mother Lizzie, although most of the time he was away at sea. When he docked in Seaforth Docks after a short or long trip, his first call was to his mother's, then the Bennetts'. To him they weren't just a friend or neighbour, they were more like family.

'It looks as though your youngest is going to be a chip off the old block, Jack. In fact all your children are. The girls are just like their mam, in looks and nature. And Tommy is the spit of you. They are a credit to you and Molly, you've done a good job and are loved for it.'

'Ay, what about yerself, Corker?' Molly said. 'You've got four smashing children who love the bones of yer. I know ye're not their real father, but you've given them something they never had before, and that's love and respect.'

Ruthie had been following the conversation with interest, and she now joined in. 'The children do love yer, Uncle Corker, and they're not half proud of yer. Gordon says he wants to be like you when he's older, but he'll never be as big as you.' She began to giggle. 'I told him he better hadn't grow a moustache and beard, or I'll not be going dancing with him.'

Molly leaned forward. 'Ay, young lady, it's manners to wait until ye're asked. I bet there's a line of girls at the church hall waiting and hoping Gordon or Peter ask them up for a dance. They're both presentable young men.'

'Oh, I think Gordon already has a girl in mind,' Corker said in an off-hand manner. 'He spends so much time on his appearance, I'd say there was something in the wind. Hair slicked down with Brylcreem, clothes brushed religiously, white hankie in his pocket and shoes so highly polished yer can see yer face in them. He wouldn't spend so much time on his appearance if there wasn't a girl involved.'

Ruthie pursed her lips. Gordon couldn't have a girlfriend, could he? She could feel her heart sinking, for if he did it would mean the end of their gang. And it would change everything. 'I don't think Gordon has a girlfriend, Uncle Corker, or he would have told us. When I said me and Bella were having a party here for our birthdays, he said right away that he'd love to come. Peter is coming as well, and Jeff and Ken. Besides all that, in our gang we tell each other everything, so if Gordon has got a girlfriend and not told us, then I think it's mean of him.'

Corker was sorry he'd spoken now, for the only girl Gordon had his eye on was Ruthie herself. He was even talking in his sleep about her, so he must be dead serious. However, it wasn't up to his father to discuss his affairs of the heart. A young lad wanted to do his own wooing.

'I think you are right, me darlin', for he's never mentioned any names. And if he did have a girl, Peter would know and spill the beans. He'd pull his brother's leg soft.'

'This time next year everyone in the gang will be courting,' Molly said. 'The lads will be turned eighteen and most lads that age are courting.'

Corker nodded his agreement. 'Ye're right, Molly. I just hope none of mine stray far from home. Like yours, I hope they stay local so me and Ellen see them often.'

Ruthie decided not to say any more. After all, actions speak louder then words. And just wait until the night of the party. She would make sure Gordon noticed her in earnest, for she intended to dress herself up to the nines. The same with Bella, who had eyes for no one but Peter. Her situation was easier than Ruthie's, though, because for ages Peter had been telling everyone that Bella was his girlfriend. Suddenly a thought came into her head and she lowered her eyes so the laughter shining in them couldn't be seen. A picture had flashed into her mind of Auntie Nellie standing in front of Gordon with her hands on her hips, telling him, 'Ye're too bloody slow to catch a cold, you are, lad. Yer need a kick up the backside.' Corker getting to his feet brought Ruthie back to reality. 'Are yer going, Uncle Corker?'

'I've got a couple of calls to make, me darlin', and if I don't put a move on I'll miss them. I only intended to stay ten minutes, but I always make meself so comfortable here, I never want to move.' When he stretched his arms over his head, his fingers touched the ceiling. 'I'll be on me way now, and leave yer in peace. I'll see meself out, Molly, you've had a busy day and must be tired. I'll close the door, and likely as not I'll see yer tomorrow.'

Ruthie jumped to her feet. 'What! No kiss, Uncle Corker?'

He slapped his forehead with an open palm. 'It's forgetful I'm getting in me old age. Fancy me saying goodbye to two of the prettiest girls in the street, and not taking advantage of the situation. So if Jack has no objection, I'll kiss you both and then take my leave.'

Corker covered the ground to the main road quickly. He hadn't intended staying so long in the Bennetts', but it was one house he could never run in and out of. He'd have to make up for lost time now, for he'd promised Ellen he wouldn't be late home. She liked to go to bed at a reasonable time after being on her feet in the shop all day, and then coming home to make a dinner for six people. That was hard going, and Corker was always telling her to pack in the job at the butcher's. He had a good job, and the four children were working, so they could manage without her wages. But no amount of coaxing could change Ellen's mind. Money didn't come into the equation, it was the job she enjoyed.

There was a pub at the end of nearly every one of the narrow streets, and it was into the second pub that Corker turned. The saloon was noisy and smoke-filled, crowded with men who would stand talking to their mates and making the pint of beer in their hands last them until closing time, for it was all they could afford. Corker was welcomed by the landlord, who pulled a pint of bitter and carried it to the end of the bar where the big man was standing. 'Wasn't expecting you tonight, Corker, but it's always a pleasure to see yer.'

'I wanted a word with yer, Bill.' Corker raised the glass to his lips, and with two gulps emptied half of it. He ran the back of his hand across his moustache to wipe away the froth. Then he gave the landlord a sign to move closer, so their conversation couldn't be overheard. 'It's about the robbery I told yer about last week, when an old lady was broken into. You said yer'd keep yer ears open for any leads on the robber.'

'Not a peep, Corker. I did mention it to a couple of me regulars, but they didn't know anything. And I've kept me eyes open, but no one has tried to flog a watch in here.'

'I've got a description of the bloke now,' Corker told him. 'One of the old lady's neighbours saw a man coming out of her house, but she didn't twig anything was wrong, she just thought he was a visitor. And it wasn't until Sunday she heard about the robbery. I've written the description down, 'cos I think it's likely someone will know who he is.' He took a slip of paper from his pocket. 'A bloke about twenty, tall, slim, sallow complexion, dirty cap pulled down to cover his eyes, and a knee-length scruffy coat.'

The landlord reached out and took the slip of paper from between Corker's fingers. His eyes scanned the few lines of writing, then he looked up. 'I know who this is, Corker. I barred him from this pub about two months ago for flogging stolen goods. He's a rotter through and through. Twenty-one years of age, and he's never worked since the day he left school. He's crafty, and earns his money by stealing. He's pig ignorant, can't read or spell properly, but he's never without money. Other people's money. And he's a loner, works on his own. If yer'd given me this description when yer were in last, I could have told yer right away who he is. He'll pinch anything that's not screwed down, and flogs it in pubs. I know he still goes in the pub on the next block, Les Simpson's place, but it's no good me telling yer to go and see Les, for I'd be sending yer on a wild goose chase, 'cos he's as bent as the thieves. He lets stolen goods be sold in his pub, and he pockets a percentage of the money the lad gets.'

'What's the lad's name, Bill? And does he live local?'

The landlord nodded. 'He's the son of Ted and Flo Blakesley, and his name's Sid. They live four streets away across the main road, and the whole family are rotten. They'd steal the eyes out of yer head if they thought they'd get a few coppers for them. They're a bad lot. Wouldn't trust them as far as I could throw them.'

Corker frowned. 'Ted Blakesley. Did he work on the docks a few years back?'

There was sarcasm in the landlord's voice. 'I wouldn't say he worked there, Corker. He got taken on there, but he only lasted a couple of weeks. They sacked him for stealing and taking too much time off. He's a lazy sod, won't do a hand's turn. There's hundreds of men round here who would have given anything for that job, men who would have worked their fingers to the bone for a job that put a wage packet in their hands every week. But not Ted Blakesley. He prefers to sit on his backside all day, then get his beer money from selling stolen stuff. And his wife is the same, a real fishwife, with a filthy mouth, and so fat she waddles from side to side. They never clean the windows or the step, so yer can imagine their house must be like a pigsty. The neighbours haven't got a good word for them, 'cos the state of their house spoils the others.'

The barman had been left to serve, and was run off his feet. Now he called for help. 'Can yer give us a hand, Bill? I can't serve and wash glasses as well.'

'Be with yer in two seconds, Dan.' Bill shrugged his shoulders at Corker. 'I can't leave him any longer, it's bad for business. Men don't like to be kept waiting. But let's know if yer find out anything, Corker.'

'I'll do that, Bill, and yer've been a great help.' He tapped his forehead. 'Me mind has been ticking over as I've listened to what yer were saying. I've got half an idea in me head, which is a good start.' Corker began to edge his way through the group of men standing near. His progress was slow, for everyone knew him and he was highly respected. Comments and greetings were exchanged with humour, and their laughter was still in his ears as he reached the door. He turned to wave a hand to Bill, who was pulling pints for the men leaning on the bar counter, and trying to make up for lost time.

Once out in the fresh air, Corker stood for a while deciding what his next move should be. He didn't have any reason for visiting the other pubs on his list, for Bill had supplied him with enough information to begin the task he'd set himself. And that was to find the rotter who had broken into Flora Parker's house. He knew there was no possibility of getting her money back; that would have been spent over the counter in a pub the night it was stolen. It was the fob watch she treasured that was in his mind. It may be an impossible task to get that back now, after the lapse of time, but it was a task he was determined to take on.

Corker's eyes looked across the main road to the streets opposite. Bill had said the Blakesleys lived four streets away, but hadn't given the name of the street. Besides, this wasn't the time of night to seek out a family who could be sitting boozing in any of the dozens of pubs in the area. And approaching them in a crowded pub wasn't the way to go about it. He needed a bit more information on the family first.

A smile crossed Corker's face, and he turned his steps in the direction of home. Ellen wasn't expecting him back so soon, so he would have time to visit the two people who were the most likely to be able to help him out. This was right up their street; they liked nothing better than putting their detecting skills to the test. He'd give Molly a knock, and she could bring Nellie down. He'd tell them what he'd found out, and ask for their help. Not anything that would get them into trouble, just the exact address and sort of people the family were. The two friends excelled at that, and they'd be only too glad to do what they could seeing as it was for Flora. They might even know people who lived in the Blakesleys' street, and that would be a help.

Corker was aware that he really should report his findings to the police, but he was of the opinion that he would move quicker than the police could, and time was important in the case of the watch. If it had been sold to someone in a pub, or to an unscrupulous pawnbroker, there was a chance the thief could be frightened into giving the name of the buyer. And Molly and Nellie were his best bet when it came to getting information for him. A man asking questions would draw attention, but not two local women. Especially two women who were good at detective work. Turning the corner into his street, Corker chuckled softly. He could see Nellie's face in his mind's eye, saying to Molly, 'This is a case for the McDonough and Bennett Private Detective Agency, girl.' And Molly answering, 'How many times do I have to tell yer, sunshine, it's Bennett and McDonough. I'm the senior partner.'

Chapter Fourteen

Doreen saw her mother and Auntie Nellie come out of the house opposite, and she hurried to open the front door before they had time to knock. 'I've just put Bobby down on the couch, Mam, and I was afraid you'd waken him up.'

'How is he, sunshine?'

'He slept a few hours through the night, which was a godsend, 'cos Phil got a good night's sleep. And after I fed and bathed him this morning, he dropped off again. He's still irritable and cries a lot, but his temperature doesn't seem as high. I won't ask yer in, if yer don't mind, 'cos he'd only wake up, and I'm hoping he sleeps long enough for me to get some washing done.'

Molly tutted. 'I don't know why yer won't let me do some washing for yer. It would give yer less to worry about, and I could have it washed and out on the line in no time.'

'I can manage, Mam. I've got to get used to being a mother and coping with all the baby ailments Bobby's bound to get. I won't say no to yer doing me shopping, though, 'cos I wouldn't leave the baby with Aunt Vicky, it wouldn't be fair to her. So I've made a list out, and I've put enough down to last me two days. Hang on till I get the list for yer.' Doreen was gone for a matter of seconds, and when she came back she passed a piece of paper over to her mother, and a ten shilling note. 'Aunt Vicky said to give yer her love. We both miss yer, 'cos we haven't had a good laugh for days.'

Molly chuckled. 'Me and Nellie are making a list of all the things ye're missing, so don't worry, sunshine. And some of the incidents are so unbelievable yer'll think we've made them up.'

Nellie decided she'd been left out long enough. 'You'll never guess where I ended up yesterday, girl, not in a million years.'

'Doreen hasn't got a million years right now, sunshine,' Molly said. 'But she will have in a week's time. Right now we'll let her get back to her work, she's got enough on her plate.' She reached up and stroked her daughter's face. 'Ye're doing a good job, love, and I'm proud of yer.'

'If I take after you, Mam, I'll be going through this another three times, so I may as well get used to it.'

'If yer Mam hadn't been so daft, then yer'd only have to go through it twice, girl,' Nellie piped up. 'She should have been satisfied with three children like me, and kept her legs crossed.'

Doreen hadn't had a good laugh for the last few days, but the look on her mam's face brought forth a giggle. She looked so embarrassed, if looks could kill, Auntie Nellie would have been as dead as a dodo. And her mam couldn't get away quick enough so she could tell her mate off.

'We'll be on our way, sunshine, 'cos we've got a few messages to go on.' Molly gripped Nellie's arm tight and began to frogmarch her down the street, while calling over her shoulder, 'Ta-ra for now.'

Nellie did a little skip to get into step. 'What's the big rush, girl? And let go of me arm before yer cut off me circulation.'

'I'll cut off more than yer circulation if you ever again embarrass me in front of one of me children,' Molly told her. 'Me and Jack never talk like that in front of the children. Never have and never will.'

Nellie feigned innocence. 'Talk like what, girl? I never said nothing to embarrass yer. I only told the truth. Yer can't deny that what I said was true. If yer'd kept yer legs crossed yer wouldn't have had your Ruthie.'

Molly pulled her to a halt. 'What you think is funny doesn't always amuse other people, Nellie, so while ye're talking to any one of my children, watch yer words.'

The pair carried on walking in silence. It didn't last long, however, for Nellie liked to hear herself talk. 'Have yer fallen out with me, girl?'

'Of course I haven't fallen out with yer, soft girl, I wouldn't be so childish. I was telling yer what I think, and now it's over and done with.'

'I'm glad about that, girl, 'cos I don't like it when ye're not speaking to me.' Nellie tripped along by Molly's side, happy now.

'Are we going to do some detective work for Corker first, or get our shopping in?'

'What I was thinking of doing, sunshine, was asking in Irwin's if they knew of a family named Blakesley. My first idea was to ask Tony in the butcher's, 'cos he knows nearly everyone around here. But I scotched that idea, 'cos Ellen would be bound to hear, and Corker might not want her to know what he's up to. There's no way we could get Tony on his own, so we'd better not mention we even saw Corker the other night. If he wants Ellen to know, he can tell her himself. Our best bet is Irwin's.'

Nellie nodded, adopting her private detective stance. 'I agree with yer, girl. That is definitely our best bet. But if we aren't in luck there, we could always try our corner shop routine.'

Molly looked surprised. 'There is no corner shop that I know of. Not on the main road, anyway. If it is the fourth street along, as Corker said, there's a pub on each corner. And nothing yer say, Nellie, would coax me to go in a pub to ask questions.'

Nellie tutted. 'I know ye're clever, girl, but now and again yer can be as thick as two short planks. Have we got a corner shop at the end of our street?'

'No, sunshine, we haven't. We do have one on a corner, but it's on the street which runs through the middle of our street.'

'And that's how it is in every street in the neighbourhood. Honest, girl, haven't yer lived round here long enough to know the layout? I bet if we walk down the fourth street, we'll find a corner shop halfway down. And I think we'd be better off trying that before Irwin's. There's always customers in there, and the manager doesn't like the girls behind the counter to spend too much time talking to customers. He's a miserable bugger at the best of times. Let's try walking down the fourth street, which is Spencer Street, by the way. I'm surprised yer didn't know that. You and Corker must walk around with yer eyes closed.'

'All right, Nellie, I don't take as much notice as you do, mainly because I'm not interested in the layout of the neighbourhood. As long as I can find me way to my own house, and to my family and friends, then I'm happy. I don't ask much out of life, sunshine, only that me and mine are warm, have enough to eat, and love each other.'

The expression on Nellie's face was comical. 'Yer don't half go on when yer start, girl. Ye're worse than Miss Harrison.'

'And who is Miss Harrison, for heaven's sake? I've never even heard of the woman.'

'She was my teacher in school, that's who. She used to drone on something woeful. Half the class would go to sleep during her lesson, and she never even noticed. The trouble with her was, she liked the sound of her own voice.'

Molly pulled on her ear lobe as she stared into her mate's face. 'It's thirty years since yer left school, Nellie, and I didn't know yer then. So can I ask why yer felt the need to bring Miss Harrison into the conversation? I expect she's forgotten you ever existed. In fact I'm sure she made a deliberate effort to put you out of her mind.'

'I've told yer many times that being sarcastic doesn't suit yer, girl. It's the way you hold yer mouth. If yer want to be good at being sarky, yer have to curl yer top lip, and ye're hopeless at that.'

'I never knew a curl of the top lip meant yer were being sarcastic, Nellie, 'cos to me it looks like a snarl.'

'Look, yer'll be telling me off in a minute for talking too much,' Nellie said, 'when it's you what's wasting time. Let's get walking, and we can make our plan when we see the corner shop. Ten minutes' walk, and we'll be there.'

Molly tucked her arm in. 'Okay, sunshine, let's put the open for business sign out, and Bennett and McDonough are ready for work.'

Oh, how Nellie loved the sound of that. 'Ready, willing, and able, girl, that's us. Best foot forward and we'll tackle any case, no matter how hard. And we'll win. We've never failed yet'

The pair were in confident mood as they walked down Spencer Street. It was a replica of their own street, and hundreds of others in Liverpool. The only difference to the mates was they knew every one of their neighbours, while here they didn't know a soul.

Nellie pulled on Molly's arm to slow her down. Nodding her head, she said, 'There's the corner shop, girl, on the other side. I told yer there'd be one, didn't I?'

'Yes, yer did, sunshine, and I should have had more faith in yer. But finding the shop was the easy part. Now we have to decide what our plans are, and how best to carry them out.'

Nellie looked up into her mate's face. 'Ay, girl, ye're beginning to talk like a real detective. If yer talk like that to the woman behind the counter, she'll twig there's something fishy going on. Our best chance of finding out what we want is if yer let me do the talking.'

'I'll let yer do the talking, sunshine, with pleasure. As long as we both agree how to go about it. For instance, I don't think we should just barge in and ask if they know a family called Blakesley, and where do they live. We need to be a bit more subtle, like, and talk about something else for a minute or two. Or use a name near enough to Blakesley, so we don't land ourselves in trouble. We could perhaps shorten the name to Blake. What do you think, Nellie?'

'I think that if yer don't fancy doing the talking yerself, and yer want me to do it, then yer should shut up and let me do it in me own way. Find out the lay of the land, like. I'll buy something first, just to get talking.'

Molly nodded and looked through the shop window. 'There's two customers in now, and just a woman behind the counter. We'll go in, eh? I'll buy a packet of tea, as well.'

When Nellie pushed the shop door open, the bell inside tinkled just like the one in Maisie's shop. They stood to one side to let the two customers who had been served get past, then they walked to the counter. The first thing to catch Nellie's eye was the tray of cakes, and this paved the way to start up a conversation. 'Ay, these cakes look nice, girl. Shall we buy two to have with our cup of tea when we get home?'

The shopkeeper walked down to where the mates stood. 'They're all fresh today. We get a tray delivered every morning with our bread.'

Nellie was licking her lips. 'I'll have that cream slice. What about you, Molly?'

Molly wasn't as crazy about cakes as her mate was, but she had to agree it was a good way of making conversation easier. 'I'll have the Eccles cake, it looks very tasty. I like them with sugar on top.'

The woman pulled a white paper bag from the nail at the side of the counter, and was putting the cakes in when she asked, 'Not from around here, are yer?'

Molly left the talking to Nellie, who didn't find it a problem. 'Not far away, girl, just ten or fifteen minutes' walk.' Then, with her

146

mouth watering, she said, 'Ay, girl, will yer put that cream bun in as well? My feller is very partial to cream buns.'

For a split second, Molly forgot she was supposed to be the silent partner. 'You big fibber, Nellie, that cake's for you. George won't even get to see it.'

'What he doesn't see he'll never miss, girl. Unless you snitch on me, that is. But as me so-called best mate, I don't think yer'd be lousy enough to tell tales.'

While the two mates were facing up to each other, the shopkeeper was looking on with more than a little interest. There was something familiar about the scene, but she couldn't for the life of her think what it was. 'Was there anything else you ladies wanted?'

Nellie grinned at her. 'There's loads of bleeding things I want, girl, like a very rich man in his eighties. I'd love him to death and then have a bloody good time on the money he left.'

Molly tutted. 'That's a terrible thing to say, and it's to be hoped Saint Peter wasn't listening, Nellie Mack, or he'll have moved yer chair to the back row and given yer harp and halo to someone more deserving.'

They both turned when the woman behind the counter said, 'Well, I'll be blowed! I knew there was something familiar about yer, but the last time I saw yer, yer were half the size. It is Nellie, isn't it? Used to live in Cedar Street until yer got married?'

Nellie pulled a face. 'That's me, girl, but how do yer know me? Did I go to the same school as yer?'

The woman shook her head. 'No, but I used to play skipping with yer. I lived at the top of the street. Me name was Ena Martin.'

There was a loud gasp from Nellie. 'Bloody hell, Ena Martin! Yeah, I remember yer now. Ye're a few years younger than me, aren't yer?'

'Only two years. I went to see yer getting married in St Anthony's.' Ena chuckled. 'That must be twenty-five years ago, if not more. Yer were nice and slim in those days.'

It was Nellie's turn to chuckle. 'Yeah, I didn't have this voluptuous body in those days. And it was nearly twenty-five years ago, it's our silver wedding anniversary this year. Time flies over, doesn't it, girl? But it's nice to see yer again, and the more I look at yer, I can see yer in me mind as yer were then.'

'What a coincidence, you walking in here. Me and Ralph, he's me husband, we bought this shop about fifteen years ago. We manage it between us, and we don't make a bad living out of it. But tell me, what are yer doing down this neck of the woods?'

Nellie sought Molly's advice. 'What d'yer think, girl?'

'The truth, sunshine, seeing as she's an old friend. It's nice that yer've met up again after so many years.'

Her head nodding, Nellie pushed the cake bag out of the way, then leaned her elbows on the counter. 'Ena, do yer know of a family round here by the name of Blakesley?'

'Are yer having me on, Nellie? It must be a joke, for I don't think there's anyone in the district who hasn't heard of the Blakesley family. They live in this street, but they're known by everyone in the surrounding area for the tricks they get up to. What business do you have with them?'

'I don't have no business with them, girl, I wouldn't know them if I fell over them. It's a very good friend of ours who asked if we could get some information on them. But it's all hush-hush, girl; we don't want them to know we're looking out for them.' Nellie stood up and rubbed her elbows, which were getting sore with leaning on the counter. 'Can yer tell us about them, so we can pass it on to our friend? You know, are they goodies or baddies, nice to know or horrible?'

'They are the family from hell, Nellie. There's only the three of them, father, mother and son. The father is a layabout, sits on his backside all day and never does a hand's turn. Only to go to the pub every night with his good-for-nothing son, who I'll come to later. And the mother is a big fat slob, with a mouth on her that turns the air blue right down from here to the docks. The house is filthy; yer can smell the dirt when yer pass it. The windows never get cleaned, and the curtains are falling to pieces. The house is a dump and spoils the other houses which are all neat and tidy.

Molly had been listening with every intention of leaving the talking and questioning to her mate. But she couldn't hold back any longer. 'It's a wonder the neighbours aren't up in arms. I would be if the house next door was so dirty it smelled.'

'Oh, the neighbours have had murder with them, and with the landlord. But as long as they're paying their rent they won't put them out. The police are often there, 'cos things are stolen from back yards nearly every day, but the police have no evidence that it's the Blakesleys' lad who steals them. They're a crafty bunch, all right. Liars, cheats and thieves. The lad is out robbing every day, and sells the stolen goods to anyone who'll buy them. Then the three of them are out boozing every night.' Ena sighed. 'The people who buy things off them, knowing they've been stolen from people who are living hand to mouth, are worse than the robber in my eyes.'

'It's the son our friend is interested in,' Nellie said. 'He thinks the lad robbed an old lady. She's in her eighties, alone in the world, and was left penniless and terrified.'

The tinkle of the bell when the door was pushed open put a stop to the conversation. 'Hang on until I serve these two customers, Nellie. I won't be long.' Ena walked down the counter with a smile on her face. 'What can I do for yer, ladies?'

Molly whispered, 'I think we should go now, sunshine. We've heard enough to pass on to Corker.'

Nellie shook her head. 'He couldn't do much on what we've been told. The address for one thing. And the lad's movements, times and suchlike. We may as well stay another five minutes, girl, it won't hurt us. In that five minutes we could find out enough for Corker to catch him. We do the footwork, Corker can do the rest.'

Molly could see the reasoning behind her mate's words, and nodded. 'Ye're right, sunshine. It's just that I feel conspicuous standing here. But wasn't it a stroke of luck finding the shopkeeper was a friend of yours? And that she knows what goes on in the street?'

Nellie was feeling very important that she was the one who was able to make their search easier. Corker really would be proud of her. She smiled at Molly now. 'I bet Saint Peter had a hand in this. I must thank him when I say me prayers tonight.'

The two customers had been served and Ena came back to the end of the counter. 'I'll have to be quick now, Nellie, because I start to get busy around this time. So tell me about the old lady that was robbed. It sounds like something Sid Blakesley's known for. He picks on old people who he knows live on their own. And anyone who leaves their back yard door open round here is bound to come home to find the place ransacked. But how did yer friend come by Sid Blakesley's name?'

'A neighbour saw him leaving the old lady's house. She described him as being about twenty, cap pulled down over his eyes, scruffy coat down to his knees.'

Ena banged a clenched fist on the counter. 'That's him! That's all he ever wears. Yer can tell yer friend he need look no further.'

'A few details would help, sunshine,' Molly told her. 'His address, which pub the family drink in, is the lad, Sid, out all day? Does he have a set routine?'

Ten minutes later, the shop was getting busy, and Nellie and Molly walked through the door with the answers to all their questions written down.

Chapter Fifteen

Molly closed the shop door behind her and mouthed the words, 'Let's walk up the street a bit, sunshine.'

Nellie nodded knowingly. She was taking her detecting work seriously, and looked left and right to make sure there was no one in earshot. 'Should we cross over, girl, 'cos the odd numbers are on that side?'

Molly linked arms. 'We don't want to cross over, sunshine, we'll be better off on this side.' She lowered her voice to a whisper. 'We'll see more from this side 'cos we'll have a better view. If we stopped outside their house to have a good look, one of them would be bound to see us, and they'd come out and start asking awkward questions.'

'Good thinking, girl, good thinking. From what we've heard, the whole family are ruffians.' Nellie squared her shoulders, like a boxer. 'Not that they'd frighten me, I'd take the three of them on and think nothing of it. But I know you don't like to see anyone fighting, so for your sake I'll go careful and not let them see us.'

'That's very thoughtful of yer, sunshine, but I won't say any more right now, 'cos we're almost facing number twenty-seven. So let's slow down, then we can have a good look.'

'Oh, my God, will yer look at the state of the house! Even a pig would turn its nose up at that,' Nellie hissed. 'The dirty buggers.'

Molly pulled on her mate's arm. 'Let's move on, sunshine, before they spot us. You can tell by just looking at the state of the house that they're the lowest of the low. Fancy living next door to that. They should be ashamed of themselves. Three grown-ups, and living in filth.'

The pair quickened their steps and didn't speak until they were on the main road. 'Well,' said Molly, 'we've got a few scruffy houses in our street, but they are palaces compared to what we've just seen. I feel sick in me tummy now.'

'Let's go to the butcher's first, girl, and tell Tony and Ellen about it. Not that they'll believe what we tell them about the state of the house, 'cos I wouldn't believe it if I hadn't seen it with me own eyes.'

'Nellie, we're doing this to help Corker, and most of all to help Flora. If Corker can prove it was the Blakesley boy, then Flora will feel better. But we must not breathe a word to anyone, not even Ellen or Tony. We'll just pass the information on to Corker and let him carry on from there.'

'Yeah, I know ye're right, girl, but I got a bit carried away there. Too enthusiastic, that's my trouble. I was so chuffed at seeing Ena again, and getting all we wanted to know from her without spending days walking round asking questions, well, as I say, I got carried away.'

'And yer had every right to be, sunshine, 'cos yer did a fantastic job.' Credit where it was due, Molly thought. Her mate had made their success possible, while she herself had done nothing but stand and listen. 'I didn't need to lift a finger to help, you did it all by yerself, and I'll tell Corker so.'

Nellie's face was pure bliss. That was praise indeed from her best mate. But because Molly was her best mate, she wasn't going to leave her out. 'There's no need to do that, girl, we share and share alike. Sometimes you're the best detective, sometimes it's me. But it doesn't matter really, does it? As long as the baddie is caught, that's the main thing.'

'That's a long speech for you, sunshine, and without one swear word, or any of the words that nobody but you has ever heard before. However, in this case I don't believe yer should try to hide yer light under a bushel. Praise where praise is due. Yer did an excellent job today, and I'm really proud of yer. If we were a bona fide detective agency making money, then I'd definitely vote yer a good pay rise.'

'Ay, girl, all this praise is turning me head.' Nellie transferred her shopping basket to her other arm. 'Yer'll be turning me into a snob and I'll be looking down me nose at people, thinking I'm better than they are.'

'I can't see yer turning into a snob, sunshine, 'cos yer'd have to give up too many of the things yer like.'

Nellie's eyes squinted up at Molly. 'I wouldn't have to give anything up, girl, why should I? And as I don't get many things now, what could I give up?'

Molly was enjoying the changing expressions on Nellie's chubby face. 'I can think of only a few off-hand, but I'm sure I can come up with more while we're doing our shopping. The first to come to mind is swearing, yer'd have to give that up. Next comes fighting. No more boxing matches with Elsie Flanaghan. Then there's the ladders in yer stockings, they're a definite no-no.'

'All right, girl, yer've made yer point. Me head will stay the same size as it's always been and I won't brag or show off. Life wouldn't be worth living if I couldn't swear now and again, or give Elsie Flanaghan a belt once in a while.' Nellie was fed up keeping a straight face, and she told herself that if God hadn't intended people to laugh and have fun, then He wouldn't have invented jokes, would He?

'What are yer smiling at, sunshine?' Molly asked. 'Let me in on the secret, 'cos I could do with a good laugh.'

'Well, yer see, girl, I was smiling because in me head I've sorted out a lot of things. I was brought into this world with eyes to see with, ears to hear with, a heart to keep me alive, and arms and legs to get me around. A face and head to go on top of my voluptuous body, a nose to smell with, and a mouth and tongue. And there were no strings attached to any of these gifts, was there, girl?'

To say Molly was flabbergasted would be an understatement. 'Of course there were no strings attached, sunshine, but what on earth brought all this on? Are yer feeling all right, or would you like to go home and have a little rest before we start our shopping?'

'No, I'm fine, girl, now yer've confirmed that I can do what I like with any part of me. Like swearing if I feel like it, or telling a joke to make people laugh. Even making up a story to make someone happy. And I'm free to give Elsie Flanaghan a belt if she deserves it.'

'Okay, okay, sunshine, yer've made yer point. There's no need to make a meal of it. Give yer head a good shake to clear it, then we'll set about buying food to feed the families.'

Nellie was laughing inside. She was surprised her friend hadn't shut her up before now. 'Ready when you are, girl. Like the corporal said to the major, "All shipshape and ready to sail, sir."'

If Molly didn't know her mate seldom drank a milk stout unless someone bought it for her, and that was only now and again, she would have thought Nellie was under the influence of drink. 'Nellie, a major and corporal would be in the army, nothing to do with ships and sails.'

'Oh, silly me! I meant to say the captain said to the first officer, "Squad ready for inspection, sir."'

Molly flung out a hand in disbelief, and, unfortunately for her, a woman who was about to pass them was hit in the eye. It was not a hard slap, but the woman was not well pleased. Nor was she a woman who at the best of times had a sunny nature. 'You stupid woman, you did that deliberately.' The woman was holding a hand to her eye when the two mates turned. 'I've a good mind to report you to the police.'

Molly was full of apologies. 'I'm sorry, but I had my back to you. I didn't see yer coming. Let me have a look at your eye, see if I've bruised it.'

The woman pushed her away. 'Don't you dare touch me with your dirty hands. Haven't you done enough damage?'

Nellie didn't like anyone talking to her mate like that, and she wasn't going to stand by and not do something. 'Don't you talk to my friend like that. She hasn't got eyes in the back of her head, and she didn't hit you on purpose. She couldn't have hurt yer that much, not with the back of her hand. If she'd punched yer in the face, then yer'd have something to moan about.'

'All right, Nellie, let me sort this out,' Molly said, before appealing to the woman. 'Let me see your face, please.'

'I will not remove my hand.' The stranger backed away. 'I would like your name and address, and if you have caused any damage, I will report you to the police.'

Nellie was sharp-witted. 'Oh, there's no need for you to bother, missus, I'll go and fetch a policeman for yer. There's the station over there.' She gave Molly's arm a squeeze. 'Shall I ask for the inspector, girl? The man in charge? Wasn't his name Steve? Yeah, I remember, Detective Inspector Steve Willard.'

Nellie had only taken two steps when the woman called her back.

'There's no need to bring a policeman, I'm sure my eye will get better after a while. Besides, the police have more to do with their time. Just give me your address in case I need to be financially compensated.'

But Nellie had smelled a rat from the very start, and she wasn't going to let the woman wriggle out of it. 'You just keep yer hand over yer eye, missus, until the inspector gets here, and he'll put it back in its socket. He's really good at that, and yer won't feel a thing.'

Nellie was stepping off the pavement when Molly caught hold of her arm, and said softly, 'Ye're not really going to the police station, Nellie, are yer? I'd die of shame if the same bobby comes over. He'd think I'm a real troublemaker.'

'No need to worry yer head, girl,' Nellie said, stepping back on to the pavement. 'The bird has flown.'

Molly turned quickly, and sure enough there was no sign of the woman. 'Where's she disappeared to? Talk about the Vanishing Lady, she's certainly one.'

'She's vanished right enough, girl, but she's certainly no lady. I knew from the beginning she was out to take yer for a ride. She was after a few bob, and thought if she kept it up long enough, yer'd be daft enough to give it to her.'

'Well, I'll be blowed.' Molly said. 'We've only been out of the house about three-quarters of an hour, and there's been more shocks and surprises than we normally get in a whole week. That flaming woman gave me a fright. I really thought I must have hurt her, the way she carried on.'

'I twigged what she was up to right away, girl, the way she wouldn't take her hand away from her face. Anyway, it was a bit of excitement, and she's gone now and taken her eye with her.' Nellie linked her mate's arm. 'It's a funny old world, isn't it, girl? Yer never know what's round the next corner.'

'Today has been an up and down day, sunshine. I was feeling good when yer old friend in the shop was so forthcoming with information on the Blakesleys. Then I was mad and disgusted when I saw the state of their house, knowing they didn't do a hand's turn to earn money, yet they're living the life of Riley on what they steal from honest, hardworking folk.' Molly let out a deep sigh. 'Then to top it off, that mad woman frightened the life out of me. Me tummy is really upset, and it's not like me to get meself all worked up.'

'Calm yerself down, girl, and then perhaps yer'll see the funny side.'

Molly huffed. 'The funny side! What funny side?'

'Oh, yer will see things in a different light when yer tummy settles down and yer can think clearly.' Nellie tapped the side of her temple. 'There's a word I want to use, but I can't think what it is. I'm not as clever with words as you are, but I know this one would help me explain what's in me mind. D'yer know when a person believes everything she's told, even though it's not true? Well, that's the word I'm looking for. To describe someone a bit simple.'

Molly's brow furrowed as her brain worked. 'Is the word ye're looking for naive, by any chance?'

Nellie stopped in her tracks. 'That's the one, girl, and it's not a long word, so wouldn't yer think I'd be able to remember it? Still, we can't all be clever, can we?'

'No, we can't, sunshine, that's true. And now we've agreed on that, will yer tell me why the word naive will be of help to yer? It certainly doesn't apply to you.'

'Oh, I know that, girl, I'm not daft enough to fall for everything someone tells me. But you are, Molly Bennett, yer'd fall for the bleeding cat, you would.'

They were nearing the greengrocer's by this time, and Nellie would have walked into the shop if Molly hadn't pulled her to a halt. 'Let me get this straight, sunshine. Am I right in thinking you had me puzzling me brains out to try and remember a word to describe someone soft enough to believe everything she was told? Someone a bit simple? Only to be told that it's meself yer were referring to?'

Nellie moved a step back. 'I'll get out of yer way before I answer that. After seeing the way yer belted that woman, I'm keeping out of harm's way. I didn't think yer had it in yer. But now I'm out of reach, I'll admit that I do think ye're—' Nellie slapped a chubby palm on her forehead. 'Bloody hell, I've forgotten the word again. But you know what it was, you're the brainbox. And I mean what I said, 'cos you really believed yer'd done that woman an injury. It never crossed yer mind that she was a con merchant, out to frighten yer into giving her money to shut her up.'

'I'm not as bad-minded as you, Nellie, I don't look for wickedness in people. Most people are good, there's not many bad apples in a barrel, as the saying goes. Besides, I'd hate to go through life distrusting everyone I meet. That would be a miserable existence.'

Nellie moved closer and looked up into Molly's eyes. 'Don't be downhearted, girl, we've got each other. And while we might pull each other's leg in fun, we'd never do anything to hurt each other. Only just remember, next time yer belt someone, make them show yer their injuries before yer start panicking.'

The greengrocer, Billy, came out of his shop and began to carry a box of cabbages inside. Over his shoulder he called, 'If ye're coming in, Molly and Nellie, yer better be quick 'cos I'm closing for me dinner hour in ten minutes.'

The information came as a shock. 'Oh, my God, I had no idea it was that time, sunshine,' Molly said. 'Will you get the potatoes and cabbage, while I run to the butcher's? I'm getting a sheet of bacon ribs. What do you want?'

'Same as you, girl, same as you. We'll have to come out again later, for our bread.'

Molly was already heading to the butcher's shop on the next block. 'You wait there for me, Nellie. I'll be as quick as I can.'

The two mates faced each other across the table. They each had a cup of tea in front of them, and a plate with a cheese butty on. Molly sighed. 'That was one mad dash. The morning gone, and we'd not done a blinking thing except natter.'

'Oh, come off it, girl!' Nellie took a bite out of her sandwich and chewed on it for a few seconds before continuing. 'We've got all that information for Corker. I bet a real detective agency would charge a few pound for that. They probably charge by the hour.'

Molly looked amused when she asked, 'Oh, are yer thinking of charging Corker, then?'

'Of course not. I was just saying. I mean, if we'd been charging for the detecting jobs we've done over the years, we'd be quids in. New clothes instead of Paddy's market, and getting our hair set every week.'

'Ay, I'm glad yer mentioned Paddy's market, sunshine, 'cos we haven't been for ages. And I'm sure Sadie was due to get married round about this time. I hope we haven't missed the wedding. We always said we'd be at the church the day she got married.'

'Ooh, ay, I'd forgotten about that. There's been so much going on.' Nellie pushed the plate out of the way so she could rest her bosom on the table. 'I'd like to see her getting married, girl, she'd make a beautiful bride. Shall we take the tram down to the market tomorrow and get her news? And see Mary Ann, we always have a laugh with her.'

Molly nodded. 'Yeah, I'd like that, it would cheer me up. Once we've finished the housework, seen how Bobby is and got Doreen's list of shopping, we can get our shopping at the same time and be ready to go to the market by twelve o'clock. How does that sound sunshine?'

'Sounds great, girl, sounds great. And we could take a few bob in case Sadie has some bargains for us.'

'That's a good idea. I could look for something for Ruthie's birthday present while I'm at it. I couldn't get anything from the second-hand stall for her, 'cos she'll be a young lady and wanting to show off. Me and Mary have agreed to buy them both the same so there's no jealousy. New dresses and silver dancing shoes, and they won't call the Queen their aunt.'

'What shall I get them, girl? I can't let their birthdays pass without giving them a present, but I haven't got a ruddy clue.'

'Get them a necklace each from Woolies. That would certainly be appreciated, it would be the icing on the cake.'

'Ay, d'yer know what, girl, I used to have a necklace when I first went dancing. I thought I was the whole cheese when I had that round me neck. But the clasp must have broken one night while was dancing, 'cos when I got home I didn't have it. I went back to the dance hall the next day in me dinner break, but there were only two cleaners there, and they said nothing had been handed in. Cried meself to sleep for a week, I did. And called those two cleaners all the bad names I could think of.'

'That wasn't fair, sunshine. Yer had no proof they weren't telling the truth. The poor women could have been as honest as the day is long for all you knew.'

The last of the cheese butty disappeared into Nellie's mouth and she sat swinging her legs, hoping a couple of custard creams would soon be on the way to her plate. She gave Molly a few minutes, and when there was no movement she asked, 'Aren't we having any afters, girl? I'm surprised ye're not offering me a biscuit to finish the meal off. Where's your heticat, Molly Bennett? Ye're not half letting the side down. In all the best houses they have afters.'

Molly pretended she'd been deep in thought and hadn't heard all her mate had said. 'I'm sorry, sunshine, I had something on me mind, and I was miles away.'

Now that was a dilemma for the little woman. What was her best bet? Two custard creams, or knowing what her mate had on her mind that took her miles away? Oh, why was life so complicated? Why couldn't Molly just have said, 'I'm sorry, I was miles away, sunshine, I'll get the biscuits for yer now. How many would you like?'

'What did you say, sunshine? I'm sorry, but I wasn't paying attention.'

'So yer said, girl. And I'd like to know what yer were thinking about when yer mind was miles away. It must have been bleeding interesting if yer ears were shut to what I was saying. Me, yer best mate, and I'm left sitting talking to meself.'

'Actually, Nellie, it was you I was thinking of. This picture flashed in me mind, of you dancing with a handsome man, and a shining blue necklace on your slim, lily white neck. Ooh, yer didn't half look pretty, sunshine, and a little voice in me head asked why yer didn't buy yerself a necklace from Woolies while ye're buying two for our Ruthie and Bella? They're only sixpence, and that wouldn't skint yer.'

Nellie's eyes lit up. 'Ay, that's a good idea, girl. Why didn't I think of that meself? I could ask George to pay for it. He won't mind, he can afford a shilling.'

'They don't cost a shilling, Nellie, they're only sixpence.'

'George won't know that, girl, and what he doesn't know won't hurt him.' Nellie legs were swinging fifteen to the dozen. 'I'll get one blue one, and a pink. Then I can swap them every day. D'yer know, Molly, this is turning out to be a good day. When our Paul and Phoebe get married I'll not only have a big hat on, I'll have a necklace to show off as well. People will think me and George have come into money.'

'If George ever came into money, he'd never even have time to count it before you had it off him. It would be cream slices every day after breakfast, dinner and tea. And morning coffee would be served with a selection of biscuits with cream in.'

'Mmm,' Nellie cupped her chin. 'I could even have a maid to do all me cleaning and cooking.' Her chins anticipated her nod and they started a slow foxtrot. 'After giving it some thought, girl, I think I'd offer you the position of maid. After all, you know all me likes and dislikes, so I wouldn't have to train yer. Don't yer think that's a belting idea, girl? I mean, I wouldn't be mean with the money, I'd pay yer a decent wage.'

'I don't know how to answer that, sunshine, but I do know I want yer to toddle off home now, while I prepare the dinner. If the ribs are left to simmer for a few hours they'll be so tender they'll melt in the mouth.'

'Yeah, I better make a move.' Nellie lumbered to her feet. 'I'll come about seven o'clock. Corker should be here by then. Ye've got everything written down, haven't yer, girl?'

Molly smiled. 'Every single thing, sunshine. I haven't left anything out. I've even put the colour of the filthy curtains down, and the crack in the bedroom window pane.'

Nellie looked pleased. 'That's real detective work for yer, girl: never miss the little details.'

'I won't forget to tell Corker that you played the biggest part in this operation, sunshine. He'll be really delighted with yer.'

Pushing her chair under the table, Nellie's chest swelled with pride. But she wasn't going to exclude her friend from the success they'd had. 'It was team work, girl. We make a good team.'

Chapter Sixteen

Nellie was sitting by the table in her carver chair when Corker called. And he didn't come alone, which was a surprise, for Ellen was with him. 'I've come to keep an eye on my feller, to make sure there's no dirty work at the crossroads.' Ellen slipped her coat off and draped it over the arm of the couch. 'Yer don't mind, do yer, Molly, having an extra one for a cup of tea?'

Nellie got in before Molly had time to answer. 'This is a private meeting, Mrs Corkhill, and what we'll be discussing is not for the ears of outsiders.'

Molly winked at her next door neighbour. 'I'll get some cotton wool so yer can plug yer ears, sunshine, then there'll be no complaints from the chairman of the committee. She's afraid that if any information we've got falls into the wrong hands, it could start World War Three.'

'Then my wife should use the cotton wool so she can't hear what's being said.' Corker lowered his huge frame on to the couch. 'How about blindfolding her, Nellie? D'yer think we should, just to be on the safe side?'

Nellie pretended to give this some thought. Then she said, 'I think my partner and I should confer on this. It has to be a joint decision.'

Molly gawped. 'In the name of God, sunshine, have yer swallowed a dictionary? Or have yer been practising with George?'

Ellen pursed her lips. 'No, I blame that chair. I've always thought she looked like a court judge sitting in it. All she needs is a red robe, white curly wig, and one of those wooden gavels they have. They bang them down when they want silence.'

Nellie brought a curled fist down on the table. 'The prisoner has been warned. One more outburst, while the court is in session, and I'll have her removed.'

161

'Tell the truth and shame the devil, sunshine,' Molly said. 'Yer've been practising those big words, haven't yer?'

The legs of the table left the floor when Nellie's tummy began to shake with laughter. 'Yer should see the faces on yer. Oh, dear, oh dear! It was worth getting George and our Paul to fight with each other over who could come out with the most words used by a judge in court. They didn't realize I was egging them on, and although it started off as a joke, the two of them got serious. Neither of them wanted to be the loser, so they went through all the police and detective films they'd seen.'

'You mean they didn't twig yer were having them on?' Molly tutted and raised her eyes to the ceiling. 'I'm surprised at George. He should be used to your tricks by now.'

'Plug me ears with cotton wool and blindfold me,' Ellen said. 'But do it right away, and get this committee meeting over with as soon as possible, 'cos Corker has promised to take me to the second house at the Atlas. June Allyson is on, and she's one of me favourite film stars. She's not as glamorous as some of them, more the girl next door type.'

'Oh yeah, I like her as well,' Molly said, keeping her eyes away from Nellie. She knew the chubby legs were swinging faster and faster, and could guess her mate was losing patience. 'Let's know if it's any good, and I'll try and coax Jack into taking me tomorrow night.'

That was the last straw for Nellie. 'Bloody hell! Have you two got nothing better to do than natter about a ruddy film star? I've got vital information on this piece of paper in front of me, and while I was under cover, getting this information, me life was in danger. I could have been bumped off any time, but it didn't stop me carrying out the orders I'd been given.' Her beady eyes covered the room. 'No detective worth their salt would leave his mission to go to the ruddy pictures! So tell me, girl, how can yer be a good detective in the morning, then in the evening start playing silly buggers?'

'When yer have a visitor, sunshine, who happens to be a neighbour, then yer make her welcome. That makes yer a well-mannered hostess. To make her feel unwelcome, and not wanted, well, that makes yer ill mannered and a lousy hostess.'

Jack and Corker had listened in silence to the dialogue. And now they looked at each other and winked as they each lit a cigarette. What would Nellie's reaction to that be? If she stuck to form, it would be hilarious.

'I didn't say she wasn't wanted, girl. I wouldn't say that to Ellen, she's our mate.' Nellie forced her face to look innocent and hard done by. 'What I said was that she shouldn't be here. She's barged into a private meeting what has nothing to do with her.' She held out her hands, palms up. 'Now I ask yer, that's not the same as saying she's not welcome, is it?'

There was so much laughter, Nellie had to wait for it to quieten down before saying, 'I think the best way to solve this is for Molly and Ellen to go to the pictures to see June Allison, and Corker and Jack to stay here and listen to what has been written down on this piece of paper, by a senior member of the detective agency.'

Ellen feigned horror. Both hands to her cheeks, she cried, 'I'm not leaving me husband with a man-eater who has a voluptuous body. Heaven forbid. I'd probably never see him again.'

'Oh, yer'd see him again, girl, I promise yer that.' Nellie was having the time of her life. 'I can't say he'd be any good to yer when I've finished with him, though.'

'The time has come to get down to business,' Molly said, knowing her mate was in a cheeky mood now, and would have them blushing with embarrassment if they weren't careful. 'Bring that spare chair to the table, Jack, please, and we'll start getting serious. I'm taking it for granted that yer had no intention of going to the pictures, Ellen, am I right?'

Ellen grinned. 'Corker said we'd get more of a laugh off you and Nellie, and I agreed with him. But I'll not interfere while ye're talking business, and I promise that not one word I hear will be repeated.'

When they were all seated round the table, an ashtray placed between the two men, Molly smiled across at Nellie. 'Well, at long last, sunshine, the floor is yours. And we're all eager to hear what yer have to say.'

'And I should bleeding well think so! The next time I get asked to do some detecting work, I'll ask for me wages in advance.'

'What makes yer think yer deserve a wage, sunshine? What yer've done today didn't cost yer anything. In fact yer gained from it, 'cos yer met a long-lost friend.'

'I know all that, girl, but what about compensation for wear and tear?'

Molly raised her brow. 'Oh, and what wear and tear was that?'

'Me shoe leather, girl, that's what. And what about the hole in me stocking, made by me shoe?'

'Nellie, yer had that hole in yer stocking when yer left the house, I saw it with me own eyes. And yer shoes have been down at heel for months. Didn't I say to yer last week that if yer gave up cream slices for three days yer'd be able to have yer shoes heeled?'

Nellie nodded. 'Yes, yer did, girl, I remember. And I also remember telling yer to mind yer own business.' The chuckles and guffaws egged her on. 'If I'd tripped up and landed on me backside, girl, yer'd have had the good fortune to see that the hole I had in me knickers matched the other hole in me stocking. Some women have matching scarves and gloves, but I like to be different.'

'You're full of holes tonight, sunshine,' Molly said. 'Has that piece of paper in front of yer got a hole in? Just out of curiosity like.'

'No, of course it hasn't, soft girl. It's just as it was when yer wrote it out and gave it to me.'

'Then I suggest yer pass it over to Corker. That's what he came for, and he's heard about everything under the sun but that. So be a good girl, and while you're explaining the whys, hows and wherefores, I'll put the kettle on before Ellen dies of thirst. I'd hate her to leave here tonight thinking we're mannerless and pig ignorant.'

'Oh, Ellen won't think nothing of the sort. She knows anyone who uses words with twelve letters in isn't pig ignorant.'

Molly leaned across the table and picked up the paper in front of Nellie. She did it in a flash, too fast for her mate to stop her. 'Here yer are, Corker, you read what we've written and then we'll answer any questions yer might have.'

Jack leaned sideways so he could read at the same time as Corker. And like his neighbour, he was amazed at how clear the details were.

Corker held the paper between his thumb and index finger. 'I can't believe yer've found all this out, it's more than I ever expected.

only asked yer the other day, and I thought with a bit of luck yer might find out the address. Yer've done wonders, and the pair of yer never cease to amaze me. I'd never have found all this out, not in a million years.'

'We wouldn't have done, either, only for a stroke of luck. But that was Nellie's doing, so I'll leave her to tell yer. That is as long as she doesn't stretch it out by adding things that don't really matter. Like how many cakes were on the tray in the shop. Ruthie will be in at ten o'clock, and the less she knows the better.'

'Blimey! You're a fine one to talk, girl! I could have told Corker everything in the time it's taken you to tell me I talk too much.'

Corker held up an open hand. 'Now, ladies, we don't want any fighting or falling out.'

Molly and Nellie burst out laughing. 'Corker, this is normal for us,' Molly told him. 'Never a day passes that we don't argue and insult each other. But we never fall out, not ever.'

'And the last time we had a fight was about twenty-four years ago,' Nellie said. 'That was over the kids fighting, and me and Molly faced each other and rolled our sleeves up, ready to do battle and knock spots off each other. But instead of a boxing match, we ended up with our arms round each other, laughing our bleeding heads off. The neighbours weren't half upset, 'cos they were hoping for high ding-dong. A bit of excitement to brighten up their day. They were disappointed, but that was the day me and Molly made friends, wasn't it girl? Do you remember?'

'Of course I do, I'll never forget that day no matter how long I live. It wasn't that I was frightened of getting a black eye, I was more worried about making an enemy. But, thank God, I made a good pal. We've stuck together through thick and thin, hard times and good times.'

'You don't have to tell me that, me darlin',' Corker said, 'because don't forget I was living in the street when you arrived. Neither of yer had any children then; yer'd just been married. Molly was very slim, with long blonde hair, and Nellie was a slip of a girl with dark hair, all curly.'

'My God, Corker, yer've got a good memory, lad,' Nellie said. 'I can't remember ever being a slip of a girl. And I bet me hair has forgotten how to make a curl.'

'I bet George still sees yer as yer were then, Nellie,' Jack said 'I know Molly hasn't changed in my eyes since the first day saw her.'

Corker glanced at Ellen, who was sitting quietly listening. He' known her for as long as he'd known Molly and Nellie, had eve thought of her as his girlfriend all those years ago. But he'd neve told her that in so many words for he was away at sea more than h was home. And when he landed after a long trip, he was devastate to learn she'd married a man he knew to be a rotter. Much water ha flowed under the bridge since then, and he'd finally claimed her a his wife after her husband died, taking over as father to her fou children. They were one big, happy, much loved family now, bu Ellen had no happy memories of the days Molly and Nellie wer talking about. She and her four children had never known the lov and warmth of a caring and happy home. They did now, though Corker made sure of that.

'My wife hasn't got much to say for herself.' Corker put a hand or Ellen's arm. 'But I remember the first time I saw her. It's a picture i my mind of a very pretty girl with a lovely slim figure, wonderfu dancer and a smile to make yer heart turn over. And she still has th power to do that.'

Nellie snorted. 'Sod that for a lark! All this sloppiness is enougl to make yer want to vomit. If ye're going to carry on, I'm going t fetch my George. And if he doesn't beat you two for compliment and say I was the loveliest girl in the whole of Liverpool, I'll breal his bleeding neck.'

'Stay where yer are, sunshine, 'cos we're getting down to busines now. George can tell yer how beautiful you are when ye're in bec tonight.'

'You don't think we waste time by talking in bed, do yer? Goc didn't invent beds to talk in, He invented chairs and couches for that And come to think of it, if He hadn't invented beds, there wouldn' be anyone to sit on the chairs and couches.'

Even Molly couldn't stop a smile coming to the surface. Wa there anything Nellie didn't have an answer to? And she could carry on all night, without repeating herself, if she was allowed. But tim was marching on, so the subject had to be closed.

'Corker, has the information on that paper given you any ideas?'

Molly asked. 'Will it help yer at all? Me and Nellie will dig a bit deeper, if need be.'

'No, you and Nellie have done very well. Saved me a lot of time. In fact I would never have been told half of these things, for people would be suspicious of a bloke my size asking questions. I could never make meself inconspicuous, I'd stick out like a sore thumb. But to answer yer question, yes, this information will be a big help. I can't tell yer how, 'cos I'll need to give it a lot of thought first. But I will definitely make use of it.'

Nellie was all eyes and ears. 'Yer will keep us in the picture, won't yer? After all, Flora Parker is my adopted mother, so I have more than an interest. You could almost say I'm one of her family.'

Molly and Jack looked at each other and burst out laughing. It was a few seconds before Molly could get control of her voice. 'Nellie, don't yer think Flora Parker has suffered enough, without being adopted by you?'

'It was your idea, girl, so yer can't blame me.'

Corker stood up, folded the piece of paper and slipped it into his pocket. Then he bent down and put his face close to Nellie's. 'Listen, me darlin', yer'll make as good an adopted daughter to Flora as yer do a detective. You and Molly would be top of my popularity list any day.'

Nellie's face was a picture of happiness. 'Ah, that's nice, Corker. Did yer hear that, girl?'

'Yes, I did, sunshine, and it's high praise indeed. We'll have to make sure we're deserving of it. A good start would be a visit to Flora's in the morning before we start our shopping. But not a word about the robbery, what we've found out, or that Corker is involved. All right?'

'Me lips will be more sealed tomorrow than they've ever been, girl. I'll be so quiet yer'll think I've lost me voice.'

Molly was helping Ellen on with her coat. 'What d'yer think of the chances of that happening?'

Ellen grinned. 'I've heard of miracles, Molly, but I wouldn't rely on it. Don't hold yer breath.'

Instead of going down Spencer Street, Corker walked down the back entry until he reached the road that cut across the street, dividing it

167

into two halves. He'd planned to follow the young Blakesley boy, but he'd have to keep out of sight, and that wouldn't be easy. He had a cap pulled down over his eyes, and a scarf round his neck which he'd pulled up to cover part of his moustache and beard. But he couldn't do anything about his height except try to hunch his shoulders. It would only be for the one night, to confirm what Nellie's friend in the corner shop had told her. That the Blakesley lad had a routine every night. During the day nobody knew where he got to, but at night he stuck to the routine. Sometimes he left the house on his own, other times he was accompanied by his mother and father. But he always, without fail, ended up at a certain pub on the main road. The one Corker had been told was run by a crooked landlord, name of Les Simpson.

Corker had been leaning back against a wall, out of sight, but his eyes had never left the front door of number twenty-seven. And when he saw it open, and heard loud voices as three figures stepped on to the pavement, his mind and body became alert. He would give them a few minutes and then follow them. He had to be careful they didn't see him, especially the father, who would recognize him. Ted Blakesley hadn't lasted at the docks for longer than a few weeks, but he would remember his gaffer – Jimmy Corkhill.

Keeping at a short distance, Corker followed the threesome. He didn't have to see them, he could hear them. They had loud voices with a vocabulary containing few words that weren't coarse or blasphemous. And the loudest voice was that of the mother. As the shopkeeper had told Nellie and Molly, they were the family from hell. Corker pitied anyone forced to live near them. Particularly elderly people who would be afraid to complain. The mother was no lady, and the father a lazy good-for-nothing. And the son, apparently, a robber who preyed on all and sundry, especially the most vulnerable who couldn't fight back. Like Flora Parker. An eighty-year-old woman facing a lad of twenty who would take what she had even if it meant hurting her in the process. And the sad part was, he probably thought he was brave to break into someone's house.

Corker watched them crossing the main road, their voices still loud enough to cause passers-by to turn their heads and tut in disgust. Corker was disgusted himself at their behaviour. They seemed to think they had the right to do as they pleased, whether it discommoded other people or not. People like them should be made to toe the line like the majority of decent people. A stint in prison would teach them a lesson, and God knows they must have committed enough crimes between them to warrant a prison sentence.

The noisy trio were nearing a pub on the corner of a street opposite, and Corker muttered under his breath, 'They're going into Les Simpson's, so Bill was right. I've a good mind to go in the pub and tell Les Simpson what I think of him. He'd lose a lot of trade if his customers found out he was not only allowing stolen goods to be sold in his pub, but he was taking a share of the profit.' And the customers would find out, Corker vowed. But his priority tonight was to discover the routine of the Blakesley boy. Did he stay in the pub with his parents? Or was he a cat burglar, who used the darkness of the night to carry out his crooked deeds?

Once again, Corker muttered under his breath. 'I should have asked Jack to come. He could have kept a lookout here, while I followed the lad. Then if I lost sight of him, Jack would know if the parents waited in the pub for him, or if they'd arranged to meet him back home. Still, it's too late to be thinking of that now, so I may as well stand in the doorway of the sweet shop opposite, and see what transpires.'

As he crossed the road, Corker was telling himself it was a good job he'd done what Ellen had insisted on, and that was make sure he had the right clothes on. He needed to be well wrapped up if he was to spend a couple of hours keeping watch. It wasn't raining, thank goodness, but the night air was cold. He'd chance lighting a cigarette later, but for now his main concern was keeping his eyes on the pub opposite. If he let his guard down, even for a few seconds, he could miss the lad who was used to being a sneak in the night. A lad whom he intended to teach that if you hurt and rob an elderly lady, frightening the life out of her, then you owed a debt to society which you must be made to pay.

Corker had been standing in the shop doorway for an hour when Sid Blakesley slipped out of the pub door. He looked left and right, then pulled the collar of his coat up before turning into the street at the side of the pub. Corker didn't intend to follow him tonight; he only wanted to know that Nellie's friend in the shop had the facts right on his routine. He knew now that the lad would leave the pub each night after spending an hour with his parents. He'd be alone tonight, but this time tomorrow night there would be someone waiting for him.

Chapter Seventeen

'We've no time for a cup of tea this morning,' Molly said when she opened the door to Nellie. 'We've too much to do.'

'Ah, ay, girl, don't be so miserable. It would only take about twenty minutes, and we're not that pushed for time.'

'Yes, we are, sunshine, If we're going to Paddy's market, as planned, then we've no time to sit jangling. I want to nip up to Jill's to see they're all right, then over to Doreen's to ask after Bobby and get her shopping list. Then there's our own shopping to do, as well.'

'Just one cup of tea, girl, that's not too much to ask for.' Nellie put on her most innocent smile. 'Me throat is so dry I can hardly speak.' And as an added enticement, she said, 'I'll wash the cups afterwards.'

'There'll be no cups for yer to wash, sunshine, 'cos we're not going to dirty any. And no amount of coaxing or pained expressions will make me change me mind. So stay there until I put me coat on and get me bag and keys.'

Nellie changed from one foot to the other as she waited on the pavement. 'It's coming to something when yer best mate can't be bothered to make yer a cup of tea. If I die of thirst, that'll teach her not to be so mean. And it'll serve her right when she's got no best mate.'

'I heard that, Nellie,' Molly said as she stepped down on to the pavement and pulled the door shut. 'If I ask yer a simple question, will yer give me an answer?'

'I will if I know the answer, girl.'

'If you are so thirsty, why didn't yer have a cup of tea before yer left the house? That's what I would have done if I was so thirsty.'

'Because I thought you'd be making one as usual. What's the point in tiring meself out when I don't have to?'

'So yer thought yer'd tire me out instead, did yer?' Molly was

171

determined not to laugh, even though she could see the funny side. 'So, it's Molly Bennett the workhorse, is it?'

'Now don't be so bleeding bad-minded, girl. I didn't say nothing about any horse.'

'You didn't have to, sunshine.' Molly turned Nellie round so she was facing the houses opposite. 'Your face is a mirror of your brain, and I know yer were calling me all the miserable so-an-sos going. But yer'll be thanking me later, when we've got time to stroll around Paddy's market at our leisure, knowing all the shopping and housework is done, and the dinner prepared. You'll be thankful that yer've got a mate who is very organized.'

'I don't think Doreen would agree with yer on that, girl, 'cos she's been waving to yer for the last ten minutes.'

Molly lifted her eyes to see her daughter standing on the step of the house opposite. 'I didn't see yer there, sunshine. I was too busy talking to Nellie.' She linked her mate's arm and they crossed the cobbles. 'A little matter of a cup of tea, that's all.'

Nellie wasn't letting her off so easily. 'Don't yer mean the absence of a cup of tea? Go on, tell yer daughter how yer wouldn't let me over the threshold, and yer refused point-blank to give me a drink, even though I told yer I was gasping for one.'

Doreen folded her arms and leaned against the doorjamb. 'I'm sure me mam had her reasons, Auntie Nellie. She wouldn't do it just for spite.'

Nellie wagged her head from side to side. 'Yer don't only take after yer mam in looks, girl, yer take after her in – er – in . . . oh, what's the bleeding word I'm looking for?' She looked to Molly for inspiration. 'It's one of those long words what I can never remember. But I'll know it when I hear it.'

Doreen was glad of a laugh. The baby had kept her awake most of the night, but thankfully he was sleeping peacefully on the couch now. 'Mam, have yer got time to go through every word in the dictionary? Yer could be here all day.'

'I think I can help Nellie out, 'cos I'm used to her forgetting words.' She smiled down at her mate. 'Yer said Doreen didn't only take after me in looks, and that's where yer got stuck. Perhaps what yer wanted to say was that she didn't only take after me in looks, but in temperament as well. Is that right, sunshine?'

172

'That's the word, girl, yer got it first time.' Nellie winked at Doreen. 'What would I do without your mam, girl? It doesn't bear thinking about. I'd have to go in shops and point to what I want. You know, like sign language. Just point a finger and grunt.'

'You could write it down on a piece of paper, Auntie Nellie, and just hand the paper over to the shop assistant. And make sure yer've got the right money with yer.'

'Don't be encouraging her, sunshine,' Molly said. 'She'll keep yer talking, even though she knows we want to get our shopping over quickly so we can go to Paddy's market. The drawback with Nellie is that she wouldn't worry if we got back late and there was no dinner ready for the workers when they got home.'

'If yer mean I'm not worrying meself into an early grave, girl, then I'll agree with yer. You can be too fussy, yer know, and it's not good for yer health. And if the dinner wasn't ready when George came in from work he wouldn't think it was the end of the world.' Nellie's chins moved with her head. 'No, he'd just light a cigarette, make himself comfortable in his fireside chair and open the *Echo*.'

'Well, he won't need to do that tonight because we'll be home by half three if it kills me. So if yer've got yer shopping list ready, sunshine, pass it out and we'll be on our way. And I'm sorry yer had a bad night with Bobby, but keep yer chin up and remember he'll be back to normal in a few days.'

'How did you know Doreen had a bad night with the baby?' Nellie was looking quite indignant when she glared at Molly. 'Are yer a ruddy mind reader as well as everything else? I bet that when God was giving gifts out, you pushed yer way to the front of the queue. And while I was asking for a good man, and a voluptuous body, you were asking for a ruddy dictionary.'

'You're a bad-minded so-and-so, Nellie McDonough. For your information I was seeing Jack and Ruthie off to work this morning – same as usual – when Phil came out. I asked about the baby and that's how I know Doreen didn't get much sleep. That's all I know, for Phil was in a hurry to catch his usual tram so he wouldn't be late for work.' Molly gave Doreen a sly wink. 'And what a pity I can't get you to hurry like Phil did! The difference is, you couldn't care less whether ye're late or not. You wouldn't hurry if yer backside was on fire.'

'Ah, now, come on, girl! I'd definitely move like lightning if me backside was on fire. Especially right this minute, 'cos I've got me pink knickers on, and I'd have them off in a flash in case they got scorched.'

Doreen was tickled as her mind took in the scene. 'Yer mean, Auntie Nellie, that yer'd take yer knickers off in the street where all the neighbours could see yer?'

'Sod the neighbours, girl! My pink knickers mean more to me than they do. I can't see them clubbing together to buy me a new pair, can you?'

'No more than I can see you buying them a new pair if the occasion ever arose.' Molly could imagine Nellie's reaction if she was asked to contribute anything towards a collection for one of the neighbours. It was hard going trying to get money off her towards a wreath when there was a death in the street. She'd stump up in the end if it was Molly doing the collecting, but as she was handing the money over she would mumble under her breath that she didn't see the point of buying flowers for someone who couldn't see them. A bottle of milk stout on their deathbed would have been more sensible, then they'd have been in a happy mood when they met Saint Peter.

'Get yer shopping list for us, sunshine,' Molly said. 'Otherwise we'll never make it to the market. It must be nearly half an hour since Nellie knocked on me door, and we've achieved nothing. Nowt, zero, sweet Fanny Adams.'

'Ooh, er, she's getting mad now, girl,' Nellie said. 'I'd do as yer were told if I was you. When yer mam gets one of these moods on, there's no telling what she'll do. So poppy off and get yer list, just to keep her sweet, like.'

The two mates were standing at the tram stop, waiting for the twenty-two tram which would drop them off near Paddy's market. All their chores had been done, and they'd decided on bacon and egg for the evening meal because it didn't need any preparation.

'How did yer say Corker got on last night, girl? It's gone completely out of me head.'

Molly raised an eyebrow. 'How could something I didn't say go completely out of yer head, sunshine?'

This reply needed some working out, and Nellie's face was still screwed up when the tram they needed came trundling along.

'Get on the tram, sunshine, and by the time it comes to our stop, yer'll have figured it out.'

Puffing and blowing, Nellie pulled herself on to the platform and glared at the driver. 'If you were a gentleman, yer'd have got off yer backside and given a lady a hand up.'

The driver knew her well enough to smile while he told her, 'There are times during me shift that I do get off me backside to give a lady a helping hand, Nellie. That's when the lady is young, slim and good-looking. If I gave you a helping hand, I'd do me back in, and I'd be off work for a month. So yer see, Nellie, I'm not only a gentleman, I'm clever with it.'

'You cheeky sod.' Nellie shook a fist. 'You wait till I tell my feller what yer said, and he'll come and sort you out.'

The driver, name of Dave, looked at Molly. 'What's her husband like?'

Molly gave a description of Corker, the biggest man she knew. 'He's six foot five inches, hands like ham shanks and built like a battleship. He'd only have to blow on you, Dave, and yer'd hit the ground hard.'

Dave, who was determined to finish this exchange despite the rumblings from the passengers behind him, smiled at Nellie. 'I was pulling yer leg, queen, to cheer meself up. We don't get many passengers we can have a laugh with, like you. The conductor is upstairs collecting fares, but he'll tell yer himself when he comes down, we enjoy having a laugh with you.'

Is he pulling me leg, Nellie asked herself? Shall I give him a kiss, or thump him one? Better do neither, she silently answered herself. Molly wouldn't approve of either. So nodding to the driver, and ignoring the sighs of relief from the passengers who had visions of being late for wherever they were going, Nellie made her way down the aisle. A hand on the back of the seats either side, she swayed with the motion of the tram until she came to an empty seat. 'You get in first, girl. I'm more comfortable on the outside. And I've got the fare in me pocket, so yer don't have to fiddle in yer purse. You can pay on the way back.'

When they were comfortably seated, or as comfortable as they could be with Nellie's bottom taking up most of the double seat, she said to Molly, 'Now yer can tell me how Corker got on last night, girl.'

Molly rested her head against the window and told herself to keep calm. So she counted slowly up to ten before answering. 'I didn't see Corker this morning, sunshine, so I have no idea how he got on.'

'Didn't yer see him going out to work? Funny that, when yer were at the door waving Jack and Ruthie off. And yer saw Phil and had a word with him.'

'Well, I'm sorry to disappoint yer, Nellie, but I don't stand at the door very long because I'm not dressed properly. Sometimes, when Jack is running late, I've only got a cardi on over me nightie, and if I stood at the door too long in a state of undress, I'd be the talk of the neighbourhood.'

When Nellie's body began to shake with laughter, every head turned towards her. And Molly could feel her cheeks burn when her mate said, in a voice everyone could hear, 'Oh, they'd have a ball, girl. They'd think it was a knocking shop.' Molly wished the tram was nearing a stop so she could jump off. But it wasn't, and she couldn't. So she had no option but to stay put and listen to Nellie's sense of humour running in full flow.

'Ay, can't yer see it, girl? Every morning about the same time, all the doors in the street would open and the wives would step out with their husbands. They'd march them to the tram stop, and make sure they got on the tram and didn't try to sneak off. And you'd be the talk of the town.' Nellie's hearty laughter brought a smile to the faces of all the men on the tram. The women turned to look through the windows, as though they hadn't heard a word.

The conductor rang the bell and called, 'Next stop is Paddy's market.'

'Are we going straight to Mary Ann's stall, girl, or looking at the stalls what sell new things?' Nellie turned her body sideways so she could look at her mate's face. 'We might see something we like.'

'We can't go to Mary Ann's carrying bags with new clothes in, not when she's kept us going in nearly new clothes for years. It would be like a slap in the face to her.' Molly's face showed determination. 'No, I wouldn't do that to her, even if I had money to buy clothes, which I haven't. We've only come to let them see we haven't forgotten them, and ask Sadie about her wedding. I hope we haven't missed it, I wanted to buy her a wedding present. Nothing fancy, like, but just a token to say how grateful I am for how good she's been. And if she's got anything put away on her superior quality stall that I fancy, I might just go mad and treat meself.'

'You've just said yer've got no money, girl.'

'I haven't got money for new clothes, not with Ruthie's birthday coming up. But if Sadie had a nice second-hand dress for a shilling, then I might indulge meself.'

'Ay, girl, that's a good idea.' Nellie's face became animated. 'Our gang are going out the night of Ruthie's party, so it would be nice to get dressed up for a change. Yer never know where we'll end up.'

'It won't be anywhere posh, sunshine, that's a dead cert. But I don't care if it's only the pub on the corner, we always have a good laugh there. And although no one is going to even notice what we've got on, I think I'd feel better if I wasn't wearing a dress everyone has seen me in loads of times.'

When Nellie began to rub her hands in glee, the basket over her arm delivered several blows to Molly's hip before she had time to distance herself. 'Ooh, I hope Sadie's put one away for me, like she usually does when one comes in in my size. We'll be the belle of the ball.'

Molly opened her mouth to say they couldn't both be the belle of the ball, but she asked herself would it be worth trying to explain that to her mate? Single and plural would be a foreign language to Nellie. Then suddenly Molly thought of something that had her chuckling. She could see, in her mind's eye, the little woman looking at her with her eyes narrowed as she tried to make sense of what she was being told. Then in her own inimitable way, she'd shrug her shoulders and say, 'Pull the other one, girl, it's got bells on.'

'What are yer looking so pleased about, girl?' Nellie asked. 'Don't keep it to yerself, share the joke with me, yer best mate.'

'It was nothing, really, sunshine, more hope than anything. Now we've mentioned getting something to wear for our night out, it's bucked me up no end. So let's not dilly-dally, let's get down to Mary Ann's stall, and see what there is on offer.'

'I'm with yer, girl, whatever yer say. Best mates always have to stick together, through good times and bad.' Her brow furrowed for a few seconds, then she said, 'Mind you, that doesn't mean we can't go off the rails now and then.'

'What d'yer mean by that, sunshine? Why would either of us go off the rails?'

'I'll give yer one example, girl, to show yer what I mean. Say, like, Sadie has a nice dress put away that you like enough to buy. But she hasn't got one in my size, and I'm left high and dry, with nothing new to wear on our night out. That's when yer'd see what I mean by going off the rails. I'd be so bleeding mad, I'd rip the dress Sadie was giving yer into little pieces. And then I'd push the stall over, and all the dresses and jumpers would be lying on the ground.'

'Mmm,' Molly put on a thoughtful expression. 'So that's what going off the rails means. I've often wondered.'

'I'm not kidding, yer know, girl. If I can't have a new dress, then neither can you. So there!'

'Ooh, yer can be a real baddie sometimes,' Molly told her. 'I wonder what Sadie and Mary Ann would say if they'd heard that?' She brushed an invisible crumb off her coat. 'Mind you, Nellie McDonough, it's all talk with you. A lot of hot air. If it came to the push, yer wouldn't say a dickie bird to Sadie or Mary Ann. As I said, ye're all talk.'

'Well, if I went round singing all day, people would think I was off me head and they'd have me put away. Which means if I can't talk or sing, I might as well stay in me house all day and twiddle me thumbs. So how would yer like that, Molly Bennett? No one to go to the shops with yer, or keep yer up to date with all the gossip in the neighbourhood? Oh, yer've got a smile on yer face now, but it wouldn't last long if yer were left on yer own day in and day out. No one to tease, or baffle with those bleeding big long words of yours. I'd give yer two days, and I'd bet any money yer'd be knocking on me door, pleading with me to be yer mate again.'

Molly stepped back a pace in mock horror. 'Oh, sunshine, I didn't know we weren't friends. You do surprise and shock me. When did this all happen?'

'Five minutes ago, girl, and don't pretend yer don't know what I'm talking about. What sort of friend would go for a night out in a new dress, when her best friend didn't have one, and everyone in the pub was talking about her behind her back 'cos she looked so

178

dowdy.' Nellie gave a quick nod of her head. 'Go on, see if yer can answer that without feeling ashamed of yerself. Selfish to the core, yer are, Molly Bennett, and I don't know how yer can look me in the eye without blushing.'

'I can't look yer in the eye, sunshine, and that's a fact. And would yer like to know why? Because looking over yer head, I can see Mary Ann's stall, and I can see Sadie's blonde head. So shall we drop what we were talking about, and make our way over there? There seems to be plenty of people at the stalls, so business must be brisk, as usual.'

As though all that had been said was brushed under the carpet now, Nellie's face beamed as she linked arms. 'I've got me mind set on a navy blue, or a brown, with white dots or flowers on. And if I go into town tomorrow, to buy the necklaces for Ruthie and Bella, I can get one for meself what will go with the dress.'

'Don't count yer chickens before they're hatched, sunshine, then yer won't be disappointed. But we've never been disappointed before, have we? Mary Ann and Sadie have always come up trumps. So keep yer fingers crossed while yer wave to Sadie. She's just spotted us.'

Sadie Wilson was a favourite of the two mates, and was very popular with all the regular customers. She was very pretty, with a slim figure, lovely blonde hair and bright blue eyes. Life hadn't always been good for Sadie, but it changed from the day she'd first come to Mary Ann's stall with a sixpence in her hand. The stallholder, who had, of necessity, eyes in the back of her head, had spotted the girl who was too shy to push in between the women, who all seemed to have more than two hands, and very loud voices, and gone to help her. And that was the start of a friendship that would last a lifetime.

'Well, where have you two been hiding?' Sadie's smile would melt the hardest of hearts. 'Mary Ann was only saying yesterday we hadn't seen yer for weeks. We thought yer'd fallen out with us, or come into money and were shopping now at George Henry Lee's. Up there with the big nobs and forgetting yer old friends.'

'Never in a million years, Sadie. If we won a million pound we'd never forget our friends. Would we, Nellie?'

'No, we wouldn't, girl, we'd never be snobs.' Nellie pursed her lips while she was thinking. Then she said, 'Ay, girl, just how much is a million pounds?'

Molly and Sadie looked at each other, and they silently agreed it would be wrong to laugh. They would do that later. 'It's a lot of money, sunshine, more than George and Paul earn in a month.'

'Ooh, I wouldn't like to win that much money.' Nellie seemed very definite about that. 'I'm all right adding up to a pound, but after that I'm lost.'

'I wouldn't worry about it, sunshine, because the chances of yer winning a million pound are a million to one.'

'If you say I shouldn't worry, then I won't, girl, 'cos you know best. But is it all right if I worry about Sadie having a dress in my size, for our night out?'

'Before we do that, Nellie, shall we first ask Sadie about her wedding? I notice she isn't wearing a wedding ring, so we haven't missed it.' Molly turned to Sadie. 'We've been a bit busy lately, what with one thing and another, and were afraid we'd missed the wedding. We would have been upset if we had, 'cos we've told yer we'd be there to see you marry this wonderful boyfriend of yours. I'd never forgive meself if I didn't see you on the happiest day of yer life, and I know Nellie feels the same. So when is the happy day?'

'Two weeks on Saturday, at St Anthony's in Scotland Road, at twelve o'clock.' The very thought of marrying her beloved Harry filled Sadie with happiness that was in her eyes for all to see. 'I can't wait. I'm so excited I can't sleep. Mary Ann keeps telling me to calm down, but I can't help it. I love Harry so much I want to spend my life with him. I'll still work with Mary Ann, 'cos she's been like a mother to me, but I'll be home every night when Harry comes in from work. And with my two sisters and a brother, we'll be like a real family.'

'Where is Mary Ann?' Molly asked. 'It's not like her not to come over and say hello.'

'Who's taking my name in vain?' The stallholder came up behind them. 'It's not me what's been hiding meself, it's you and Nellie! What have yer been doing with yerselves?'

Nellie was fed up being left out. That was the worst of being small, people forgot you were there. 'We're grandmothers now, don't forget, girl. And our grandson, Bobby, has got the measles and isn't very well.'

'I'll forgive yer where thousands wouldn't.' Mary Ann glimpsed a customer lifting a jumper off a stall and holding it against herself. 'I believe in looking on the bright side, Maggie, but if you think that jumper will fit yer, then yer really are looking on the bright side. It'll never go near yer, queen, it would fit where it touched. I mean, be fair, Maggie, I'm losing money by telling yer this, but that jumper wasn't made for a sixteen stone woman. Unless yer only want to wear it on one arm, 'cos that's the only part of yer body yer'd get into it.'

This didn't please Maggie. She knew Mary Ann was right, but she didn't have to broadcast it to everyone in the market. 'Am I hell sixteen stone, Mary Ann. Where did yer get that from? The last time I got weighed I was ten stone, so there!'

'That must have been before yer were married, Maggie, or the scale gave up when you stood on it.'

While Maggie was thinking of a suitable reply, a woman standing near her snatched the jumper out of her hands. 'This won't go near you, yer fat silly cow, but it'll look good on me.'

'Give me that back. I saw it first, yer cheeky bugger.'

The woman laughed in her face. 'Yer've got no chance. I've got it now and I'm sticking hold of it. I don't know why ye're kicking up a stink, ye're too old and too fat for it. So keep yer gob shut or I'll shut it for yer.'

Mary Ann wasn't going to stand by when one of her regulars was being insulted. Maggie had been a customer for years and the stallholder had a soft spot for her, and a lot of admiration. 'I'll be back in a minute,' she told Sadie. 'You see to Molly and Nellie while I sort that little lot out.'

Maggie saw help arriving in the shape of the stallholder. 'I saw it first, and this one grabbed it out of me hand, Mary Ann. I've a good mind to batter her.'

Mary Ann kept a straight face, but, looking at the size of Maggie's huge bosom, she mentally agreed that it would certainly make a good battering ram. 'What's going on here? I don't allow trouble on my stalls, so explain yerselves.'

The woman, a complete stranger to Mary Ann, was holding on to the jumper for dear life. 'I've got it now and I'm buying it. What are yer charging?'

'That jumper is not for sale, so put it down.'

'What d'yer mean it's not for sale? It's on the stall, isn't it?'

'The stall is mine, and the jumper is mine.' Mary Ann's voice was deceptively low. 'And I'm telling yer to put that jumper down, it's not for sale.'

A new voice piped up. 'Maggie should have the jumper, Mary Ann. I saw this flamer snatch it off her.' The voice belonged to Ada, another regular of Mary Ann's. 'Another thing, this one what's doing all the shouting, she's a thief. I saw her stuffing a blouse into her basket without paying for it. She's a bleeding robber.'

The woman was quick in moving her basket, but not quick enough to stop the stallholder from snatching it from her. And sure enough, after a quick search, a pale blue blouse was found and held aloft. 'I won't call the police this time,' Mary Ann said, 'but if I catch yer anywhere near one of my stalls again, I will call a copper. That's after I've finished with yer. So if I were you I'd consider meself lucky and skedaddle.'

The woman vanished in no time, and Mary Ann passed the jumper over to Maggie. 'Here yer are, queen, have this on the house. It'll keep one arm warm at least.'

As the stallholder walked away, Maggie shouted after her. 'Ye're a smasher, Mary Ann, and I love the bones of yer.'

Mary Ann acknowledged that with a wave of her hand as she walked back to where Sadie was attending to Molly and Nellie. 'Yer need eyes in the back of yer bleeding head with some folk. They'd steal the eye out of yer head, and have the cheek to come back the next week for the socket.'

'But you're up to them, Mary Ann,' Molly said. 'Yer handled that very well. But fancy that woman stealing the blouse. I mean, yer wouldn't be bothered for a few coppers.'

'Oh, we get the dregs of the earth, and the best, in here, queen. But they say variety is the spice of life, and we sure see life here. Never a dull moment, and I wouldn't swap me job here for one in a posh shop 'cos I'd be bored to tears. The customers may be as poor as church mice, but on the whole they're a grand lot, the salt of the earth. Am I right, Sadie?'

'Definitely, Mary Ann. I love me job here. It's taught me that there are more good people in the world than bad.'

Mary Ann had bright copper-coloured hair, piled up on top and kept in place by a tortoiseshell comb. She was small and wiry, always on the go, and had eyes as sharp as a hawk. She was kind and generous to the many poor people who were her bread and butter, but woe betide anyone who crossed her. She nodded now to the two dresses laid out on the trestle table. 'Sadie fixed yer up, then, ladies? She's had them two put away for weeks, waiting for yer to come. It's nice to see yer again, Molly and Nellie, and I hope all the families are well. Any more grandchildren since yer were here last?'

'Ye gods and little fishes, give us a break, Mary Ann,' Molly said, laughing. 'Two in one year is enough.'

'Yeah,' Nellie said. 'The men are doing their best, but they're not baby making machines.'

The stallholder grinned. 'I'll leave yer with Sadie, 'cos I can see a few irate women waving to me. But I'll see yer at the church for the wedding.'

'Wouldn't miss it, sunshine. And don't let on we got our dresses from your stall, either, 'cos we'll be acting like toffs. Speaking so far back yer won't be able to hear us.'

Nellie had to have her say. 'Yeah, yer won't know us when we say hello to yer. So I'll give yer a clue. I'll be in the navy dress, the one with white squares on, and Molly will be in the green. The only one looking better than us will be Sadie, the bride.' Then she thought of something. 'Oh, and I'll have a necklace on.'

'Fold those dresses up, sunshine, and put them in the basket while I pay Sadie.' Molly handed over three shillings to the girl, who was radiant with happiness. 'Two dresses for three bob, yer can't beat it. Thank you, sunshine, and I hope everything runs smoothly for yer. I won't say we'll see yer at the church, 'cos we'll see yer before then. Are yer ready, Nellie?'

'Ready, willing and able, girl! Can't wait to get home and try me dress on. Ta-ra, Sadie, girl, me and Molly love yer to bits.'

Chapter Eighteen

'We were lucky getting two dresses that fit us, weren't we, girl?' Nellie and Molly were waiting at the tram stop for a number twenty-two to take them home. 'But then we're always lucky when we go to Mary Ann's stall.'

'It's not luck that gets us the dresses, sunshine, it's Sadie. As Mary Ann said, as soon as they get a new batch of clothes in, Sadie puts to one side any she thinks will suit us. And at one and six each, they're a bargain,' Molly said as she opened her purse and took out the fourpence for the tram fare. 'You take this, Nellie, 'cos you'll be sitting on the end seat. Put it in yer pocket so it'll be handy.'

'I'm looking forward to trying the dress on, girl. I think it'll look nice on me.'

'I'm going to wash mine as soon as I get home,' Molly said. 'I'll iron it tomorrow and put it away until our night out. Then it'll be one less thing to worry about. If yer like, sunshine, I'll rinse yours through as well. While I've got nice soapy water in the sink, I may as well kill two birds with the one stone. Waste not, want not, as me ma would say.'

'Ooh, that's good of yer, girl, 'cos yer know I can't stand long on me feet ironing. The veins in me legs start to stand out and I get tired.'

'Ay, don't be jumping ahead of yerself with the old sob story, Nellie. I never said I'd iron it as well as wash it.'

Nellie put on her most appealing face. 'Well, I just thought, girl, like anyone would, that if yer had a hot iron in yer hand it would be just as easy to iron two dresses as it would be to iron only one.' The chubby hands were spread out. 'It wouldn't cost anything, so can't yer see the sense in it?'

'I can see the sense of it from where you're standing, sunshine, but I don't think I'll see the sense of it when I'm standing with a hot iron in me hand, and me feet are talking to me 'cos they're tired and sore.'

Thinking she'd get on the right side of her mate if she showed some sympathy, Nellie said, 'Ah, I'm sorry about that, girl. What are yer feet saying to yer?'

'Now as you are well aware, Nellie, I do not use really bad language. So ye're going to get a very watered down version of what me feet are saying. The right one is the more bad-tempered because it's got a corn on the little toe. That one said, "Why don't yer tell her to ruddy well sod off and do her own work?" And the left one, "She's got yer for a right sucker. Tell her to get lost." '

Nellie glared. 'I'll get them for that. When they're least expecting it, I'll jump on them.'

'You do that, sunshine, and yer won't stand a snowball's chance in hell of me washing and ironing yer ruddy dress.'

The smile was back on the little woman's chubby face. 'So yer are going to do me dress? I knew yer'd come round in the end, yer always do.'

'Our tram is here now, so I'll see if the rocking from side to side puts me in a good mood. If it's smooth and soothing, I'll do what yer want. But if it's rough and jars on me nerves, then ye're not on.'

Nellie always made a big show of climbing on to the platform of a tram or bus. The step was too high, and whoever put it there needed their bumps feeling. But today there was no complaint or commotion, she hopped on the tram like a young and sprightly girl. And Molly, walking down the aisle behind her friend, was filled with wonder that a one and sixpenny dress could bring about this transformation.

They were nearly at their stop, and Nellie had been as good as gold all the way. No chattering or cheeky exchanges with the conductor, and giving Molly as much space as was possible without her falling off and landing in the aisle on her backside. She even swung off the platform with the aid of the bar, and landed on the pavement before Molly. 'Ye're getting slow in yer old age, girl. I beat yer to it.' She waited until her mate was standing beside her, then, with a cheeky grin, she asked, 'Well, was the tram all right for yer? Do I get me dress washed and ironed, or not?'

'I know I'm a fool for giving in to yer, Nellie, but it's a habit I find hard to break. So I'll go halfway with yer. If you go home to try yer dress on, I won't see yer for half an hour, and I can have mine washed and on the line by that time. So this is my proposal, and yer can take it or leave it, it's up to you. Instead of going home to try the dress on, yer do it in my house, and once yer've tried it on I can put it straight into the water with mine. So it's up to you.'

Nellie didn't hesitate. 'I'll come in yours, girl, of course I will. As long as I can get undressed without you seeing me.' She huffed. 'I may as well tell yer the truth instead of beating about the bush. I've got a pin keeping me knickers up.'

They were halfway up the street when Molly doubled up with laughter. 'What am I going to do with yer, Nellie McDonough?'

Her confession over, Nellie was feeling free of guilt. 'Ye're going to wash me dress, aren't yer? And tomorrow, if me luck's in, yer'll iron it for me.'

They reached Molly's front door and she put the key in the lock. Then she turned to look down at her mate. 'Yer've heard of women doing a striptease, haven't yer, sunshine?'

Nellie did her best to contort her face into an expression of disgust. 'Yeah, I have, girl. The dirty buggers.'

'Well, ye're in a race with them from the minute yer step foot in me living room. They do it slowly, to tantalize, but you're going to do it like greased lightning, to please me. I want the two dresses in water in five minutes flat. Then yer can poppy off home and let me start on the dinner.'

Looking woebegone, Nellie said, 'I can't get out of me dress in five minutes, Molly Bennett, never mind out of this and into the other. It takes me ages to get me dress off.' She put a hand on each of her breasts. 'It's these ruddy things. They get in the way and I can't get me dress over them.'

Molly took pity. 'Look, sunshine, I'll draw the curtains in the living room, so no one will see in. You take yer time taking one dress off and putting the other on. And I'll do the same, but in the kitchen. So yer'll have privacy, and no one will know about the pin in yer knickers, unless you tell them. So come on, Nellie, make a start. I'll go in the kitchen and leave yer to it.'

There was a smile on her face when she closed the kitchen door.

She had more patience with Nellie than she'd had with her children when they were little. But her mate paid her back in other ways, for never a day went by without laughter. She couldn't imagine life without her best mate.

While Molly was thinking this, she pulled her dress up over her head and draped it across the mangle. Then out of her basket she picked the dress from the market. After giving it a good shake she put it on, and was delighted when it fitted her perfectly. She liked the colour of it, too, a lovely soft green with a round white collar. There was no mirror in the kitchen to see herself in, so she'd have to wait until Nellie had sorted herself out. The small pockmarked mirror that Jack used for shaving wasn't a ha'p'orth of good. She could only see about six inches of herself.

The minutes ticked by and there was no sound from the living room. Molly told herself to stay calm; Nellie was probably struggling. But when ten minutes passed by, and there was still no sound from her mate, Molly moved away from the sink with the intention of knocking and asking if help was needed. But as she brought her clenched fist up, she heard a loud knock on the front door. 'Now what do I do?' she muttered. 'This is a fine kettle of fish.'

Molly rubbed the side of her nose, a sign she was flummoxed. Then came the sound of a muffled voice. 'This is a fine bleeding time for someone to call, when I'm neither dressed nor undressed. I'm a right bleeding sight for sore eyes, and the queer one is preening herself in the ruddy kitchen!'

'I am not preening meself,' Molly said as she pushed the door open. 'I've been—' Her words trailed off as she took in the scene before her. Of Nellie's face there was no sign, but her chubby legs were on show, and Molly didn't know whether to laugh, cry, or hug her mate to death. Nellie's lisle stockings were rolled down to the knees and kept up with the help of elastic garters. And a couple of inches above that was an expanse of her blue fleecy knickers. 'In the name of God, Nellie, where are yer?'

'Where the hell d'yer think I am, yer daft nit!' There came another ran-tan on the knocker, and Nellie, face unseen, struggled to find a way out of her predicament. 'If you let anyone in, girl, I'll break yer ruddy neck.'

'Tut-tut, Nellie Mac, those are very strong words for someone in the position you're in. But don't worry, I'll not let anyone in because one look at you and they'd have a heart attack.'

Molly opened the door to find her daughter looking very agitated. Immediately, Molly thought the worst. 'What is it, sunshine? Is it the baby?'

Doreen looked puzzled. 'Bobby is just the same, Mam. It's not him I came about. I saw your curtains closed, which is unusual, and thought yer might be unwell?'

'I'm fine, sunshine, but I'm sorry if yer got a fright. I drew the curtains over because me and Nellie bought a dress each, and we wanted to try them on. We didn't want the neighbours to have a peep show. I can't ask yer in, I'm afraid, 'cos yer Auntie Nellie is in a state of undress.' Molly put a finger to her lips and whispered, 'She'd kill me if she heard me, but yer should see the state she's in. Honest, yer wouldn't credit it. She's stuck in a dress, and can't get it on or off. God love her, I'd better go in and give her a hand. I'll give yer a knock later, sunshine, just to see how Bobby is.'

Doreen turned to cross the cobbles. 'Don't you be giving me any more frights, that's all. And Aunt Vicky, I had her worried, too!'

Molly waved before closing the door and going back to find Nellie still headless. 'Haven't yer managed it yet, sunshine? Here, let me try and help yer. No, Nellie, I can't help yer unless yer stand still.'

The muffled voice came back. 'I can't breathe, girl! Get a pair of scissors and cut me out of the bleeding thing.'

'That will be a last resort, sunshine. I'm not going to cut a good dress up unless it's absolutely necessary. So stand still until I can figure out what's what.' Molly stood with her chin in her hand, 'I can see yer've got one arm down, Nellie, so why can't yer get the other down? I'm sure if yer calmed down yer'd have no trouble, for ye're only making things worse by pushing and pulling. Just take things easy, and I'll try and help yer get the other arm down.'

If Nellie could have seen herself, she would have been the first one to laugh. But she couldn't see herself and was far from laughing. 'Me arm won't go down, soft girl! Don't yer think I'd have tried that by now? D'yer think I enjoy being suffocated? It's not me arm, it's me bleeding breasts. If I could get one past me waistline, I'd be home and dry. Not happy, like, not after all this kerfuffle. But at least I'd be able to breathe proper.'

'Would yer mind if I try and ease one of yer breasts out, Nellie? It won't hurt, I'll do it nice and easy. The way you're going on, ye're only making things worse, and I'm surprised yer haven't ripped the ruddy seams open by now.'

'Ooh, I wish George was here,' Nellie said. 'He's used to me breasts and would know how to handle them.'

'Well, I'm sorry, sunshine, George is not here and ye're going to let me help yer, or yer stay like that until Jack and Ruthie come in from work.'

'If your Jack so much as lays a finger on one of my breasts, my George will kill him.'

Without giving Nellie the opportunity to object, Molly put her hand up her clothes, squeezed it past the waistline and manoeuvred it so she could cup Nellie's breast. 'Now this won't hurt, sunshine, if yer keep still.'

Five minutes later, when order was restored and Nellie able to breathe freely, Molly said, 'Don't ever do that again, Nellie, for God's sake. I don't know why yer decided to take the dress off by pulling it up from the neck. The easiest way is to bend over and pull the bottom of the skirt over yer head. I hope you've learned yer lesson and do it proper in future.'

Her humour restored, Nellie was grinning like a Cheshire cat. 'I was in a state, girl, when you were in the kitchen waiting, and I was struggling. And of course the more I struggled, the worse it got. I won't tell George, though, because he thinks I'm crazy as it is. Besides, if I told him you came to my aid with one of your hands, I doubt he'd see the funny side.'

'You don't tell any one, Nellie, or I'll have yer guts for garters. Certainly not Jack or anyone else in the family.' Molly tut-tutted. 'And after all that, yer haven't tried the new dress on! But I'll tell yer this, Nellie, I'm going to supervise the trying on of the dress. I wouldn't go through that palaver again for a big clock.'

'I notice you've got yours on girl, and it fits yer a treat. The colour suits yer, as well. But you're lucky 'cos you're more the standard size.' Nellie had a rethink, and wanted to change that statement. 'Well, I don't mean that ye're more lucky than anyone else. Like me for instance. I'm one of the real lucky ones. I mean, who else do we know what has a voluptuous body like mine? Go on, clever girl, how many women do yer know who have a figure like an hour glass?'

'Nellie, I've never even seen a hour glass, so how would I know if a woman had a figure like one?'

'It's like an egg timer, girl. You know, what posh people use what are too bleeding lazy to keep an eye on the clock.'

Molly pretended to see the light. 'Oh, I know what yer mean now, sunshine, but I still don't know anyone with a figure the shape of one.'

'Yes, yer do, girl, yer know me, don't yer? Me, Nellie, with a figure like Mae West.'

'I'm out of me depth now, Nellie. Voluptuous body, hour-glass figure and Mae West lookalike!' Molly shook her head slowly. 'But I'm willing to be persuaded. So why don't you put yer new dress on, and open my eyes to all the things I've been missing for years. I might even owe yer an apology for being so blind to your assets, yer never know. So stand up for me, and I'll help yer put the dress on properly. I couldn't go through that performance again.'

When Nellie was standing in the middle of the room wearing an underskirt that had seen better days, Molly said, 'Raise yer arms above yer head, sunshine, and I bet the dress will go on without any bother, and fit yer like a glove.'

And Molly was proved right for a while. Nellie's arms went into the sleeves, and her head popped out of the round neck. And that is when Molly's bet began to go wrong. For the dress stopped at Nellie's breasts and refused to go any further. 'See what I mean, clever clogs,' Nellie said. 'Ye're no better at it than I was.'

'At least yer can breathe, which yer couldn't do before.' Molly's lips were clamped together, which was a sign she meant business. 'I'll get yer into this dress if I have to use a shoehorn. And once we get the hang of it, it'll be no trouble next time. It's only the waist that's too tight, so if there's a decent seam we could let it out a bit. But for now, let's get it on yer and see if it fits everywhere else. However, as I don't want to be manhandling those breasts of yours again, yer can do that yerself. Yer only need to get the waist over one, and yer'll be laughing sacks, 'cos the other will be easy. So go on, sunshine, press in and down, while I pull at the waist.'

The operation was a success that brought sighs of relief from the two mates. 'Was it worth it, girl?' Nellie asked as she did a little twirl. 'It feels comfortable enough, but what a performance getting it on.'

'It was a damn sight easier than getting yer other one off! I've never seen anyone make such a drama out of taking a dress off. If yer'd seen yerself, yer wouldn't have known whether to laugh or cry. The only part of you showing was yer chubby legs, stockings rolled down to yer knees and elastic garters. Oh, yer were a sight for sore eyes, sunshine, and I was wishing I had a camera. But all's well that ends well, and if yer'll get back into yer old dress without doing yerself a mischief, I'll put our two new dresses in water. They'll be on the line in half an hour, and hopefully ready for ironing in the morning. And I'll see if there's enough seam to let the waist out. An inch would do it, then we'd both be ready for our night out.'

'I'm going into town tomorrow, to get the girls their birthday presents from Woolworth's,' Nellie said. 'Are yer coming with me?'

'I want to make a few calls tomorrow, sunshine. Only the usual: Doreen, Jill and me ma and da. And I was thinking of calling to see Flora. We said we'd keep in touch with her, and I'd hate her to think we don't keep promises.'

Nellie nodded. 'It's me what should be keeping an eye on Flora. She's my adopted mother and I should do the job properly. When you visit your ma, I should visit mine. So to save time tomorrow, you go one way and I'll go the other. It'll be quicker, girl, and then yer could come to Woolies with me. I don't like going shopping on me own, there's no fun in it. Besides, yer could help me choose which beads to get for the girls. You know what they'd like more than me.' A smile spread across Nellie's face. 'Now I want yer to put yer hands on the table, to steady yerself for the shock I'm going to give yer. I don't want yer dying of a heart attack on me, 'cos your Jack would be upset if he came in from work and you were lying dead on the floor, and there was no dinner ready for him.'

'Oh, I think Jack would be more than upset, sunshine. But don't let's be morbid, just tell me what your earth-shattering news is, and I'll do me level best not to have a heart attack.'

'Okay, girl, are yer ready for it?'

'Nellie, for goodness' sake will yer get on with it! If I do have a heart attack, it will be caused by the suspense rather than what yer have to say.'

Looking as pleased as Punch, Nellie said, 'Because yer've been so good in offering to wash me dress and what-not, I'm going to treat yer to a cup of tea in Reece's. How about that then, girl? Aren't yer pleased?'

'Over the moon, sunshine, it's very thoughtful of yer. But yer don't have to treat me, just because I'm washing a dress. It's not costing me anything, and I'm only too happy to help. So save yer money, Nellie, or, better still, buy a cake from Hanley's and take it to Flora's. That would be a nice gesture and she'd be really delighted.'

'Ah, ay, girl, don't be putting temptation in me way. I couldn't go in Hanley's for one cream slice. Yer know I haven't got no will power.'

'I didn't mention a cream slice, Nellie, you've got a one-track mind. A doughnut or an Eccles cake, either would be welcomed by Flora. All yer've got to do is go in the shop and keep away from the end of the counter where the cream cakes are. If yer don't see them, then yer mouth won't water and yer won't feel a craving. For heaven's sake, sunshine, surely yer have some control over yer mind?'

'Listen, girl, I can talk to yer now until I'm blue in the face, about how I'll be strong and not give in to a craving. I'll lie me head off to yer, but it won't alter the fact that when I walk in Hanley's shop I'll forget all the lies and promises. Once I see that glass case full of cream cakes, I'm drawn towards it.' Nellie was never just serious when talking on any subject, she had to be dramatic. Eyes fixed on a spot somewhere behind Molly's head, hands always in motion. 'I'm drawn to it, girl. I have no control over me actions. It's as though a blast of wind has come through the shop door, and it blows me to that glass case. And the next thing I know, I've got a cake bag in one hand, and I'm passing money over the counter with the other.'

'Nellie, you really did miss your vocation in life. Yer could have been up there with the best if someone had taken you in hand when yer were younger.'

Nellie would have loved to look pleased at what she thought sounded like a compliment, but curiosity got the better of her. 'What was it yer said I missed in life, girl?'

'I did say vocation, sunshine, but I'll change that to chance, so yer understand what I mean. Yer could have been an actress, a comedienne, anything yer set yer mind to.' Molly could feel the floorboards creaking before Nellie's laughter filled the room. 'What have I said that is so funny, sunshine? Whatever it was, it certainly tickled yer fancy 'cos I can feel the table and floor shaking. Let me in on the joke, so I can laugh with yer.'

Nellie was doubled up. She was laughing so much she couldn't speak, and the tears were rolling down her cheeks. The sound of her laughter was so genuine and hearty, Molly couldn't help but add to it, even though she hadn't a clue what she was laughing at. 'I'm getting a stitch in me side now, Nellie, so will yer cut it out and tell me what we're both laughing at? And if yer say ye're not laughing at anything, so help me I'll clock yer one.'

With her two hands flat on her tummy, Nellie gasped, 'Oh dear, oh dear, oh bleeding dear! I haven't laughed so much since George fell out of bed, and I fell on top of him.'

'I know I'm a fool for asking, and will probably regret it, but how did George fall out of bed and you fell out too?'

This brought forth another burst of laughter. 'He was trying to get away from me, girl, and I wasn't having none of that. He started something and I wasn't going to let him stop halfway through. It worked, too, girl, 'cos he's never attempted to get away from me since.'

A voice in Molly's head was telling her to give in now, for it was nearly time to put the dinner on. But curiosity got the better of her. 'Nellie, that isn't what started the bout of laughing, so leaving George out of it, what did yer find so funny to begin with?'

'Well, girl, it was you telling me I could have been anything if I'd set me mind to it. I know yer weren't being sarcastic, but it was yer timing, girl, it was all wrong. I can't speak proper, can't add up, and can't even get out of a bleeding dress! Can you see Greta Garbo struggling to get out of a frock and showing everyone her blue fleecy knickers? Or Katharine Hepburn or Joan Crawford? Nah, girl, I'm as thick as two short planks and don't care who knows it. I bet we have more laughs than all of them put together, and I'm more than happy with my life as it is.'

'Me too, sunshine, me too.' Molly's smile held affection and tenderness. 'With a mate like you, what more could I ask for?'

'My sentiments exactly, girl. A good husband and family, and a good mate with her family.' Nellie pushed herself to the edge of the couch. 'I'd better go and let yer get on with the dinner.'

'I'll see you out, sunshine, then get our dresses on the line before starting the dinner. And I'll see yer in the morning.'

'Ay, girl, if yer hear anything from Corker, yer will let me know, won't yer?'

'Of course I will. But I'm not going to ask him. Corker will do things his way, and I have every faith in him. He'll do his best, and that's good enough for me. And if he does find anything out, yer can rest assured that we'll be the first to know.'

Nellie was always reluctant to leave, for she didn't like going home to an empty house, with only the wallpaper to talk to. 'And yer are coming into town with me tomorrow, aren't yer? After we've done our shopping and calls, like.'

Molly nodded. 'If we can be finished with our housework by ten, then we'll have plenty of time for what we want to do.'

'See yer in the morning, then, girl. Ta-ra for now.'

'Ta-ra, sunshine.'

Chapter Nineteen

The evening meal in the Corkhill house was always noisy with chatter and laughter. Corker and Ellen sat at each end of the table, Phoebe and younger sister Dorothy sat next to each other at one side, and brothers Gordon and Peter sat facing. It was the one time of the day when all the family were together, and there were always tales to tell of incidents at work, for all six had a job. The two boys were apprentices and on low wages, but the man they were proud to call their father was generous and they were allowed to keep half of what they earned. This also applied to Dorothy, who was nineteen and courting. Phoebe, the eldest, was courting Paul McDonough, and they were saving up to get married. At least, Phoebe was; no one was sure about Paul, who loved to go dancing, or to the odd night at the pictures when Phoebe insisted because she wasn't as mad about dancing as he was. She was crazy about him, but was wise enough not to run after him. They'd had a few fallings out, but it was always Paul who came cap in hand to make up.

'Is everyone going out tonight?' Ellen asked. 'Or is anyone staying in to keep me company?'

'Me and Peter were going to the church dance, Mam,' Gordon said, 'but I'm not that fussy if yer want a game of cards.'

'I'm not fussy, either,' Peter said. 'I wouldn't mind a game of cards as long as ye're not playing for money. Me and Gordon are saving up to buy birthday presents for Bella and Ruthie.'

'I'll help yer out with that,' Corker told them. 'Yer need to buy them something nice, for the number of times ye're allowed in their houses for playing cards, and parties.'

'We don't know what to get them, Dad, so d'yer think we should ask Auntie Molly?'

'I'll ask Molly for yer,' Ellen volunteered. 'Her and Nellie will be in the shop tomorrow, so I'll have a quiet word with Molly. Can yer tell me how much yer want to spend on a present? It would help if yer could. I wouldn't tell Auntie Molly, it's just so I can help with a few suggestions if I know what money yer can run to.'

Peter looked bashful. 'I've got two bob. I know it's not much, but I don't earn much. I'll have sixpence to add to it next week, so that's two and six.'

'I should have four shillings,' Gordon said, feeling quite proud. 'It will buy something decent, I hope.'

Corker raised his bushy eyebrows. 'I'll make the money up to five shillings each. That makes yer even.'

That brought smiles as the brothers nudged each other. 'Thanks, Dad, that's brilliant. Five bob will buy a really good present.'

'I don't know them very well,' Dorothy said, 'I haven't had much to do with them. So would a box of chocolates and a birthday card do?'

Ellen nodded. The dreadful years she and the children had suffered at the hands of her violent first husband were long gone. But she never let herself forget that it was with the help of Molly and Nellie that she was able to survive those years and learn to have pride in herself. And looking round the table now at the happy faces of her children, she thanked God most of all for bringing Corker back into her life. She loved him dearly, and the children adored him. 'The girls will be made up with chocolates and a card. They won't be expecting so many presents.'

Corker pushed his empty plate away and smiled at Ellen. 'That was very tasty, sweetheart. I really enjoyed it.'

'Yes, it was lovely, Mam.' Phoebe stretched her arms to collect the empty plates. 'Me and Dorothy will wash up, you rest yer feet. Put them up on the couch.'

Ellen could hear the two girls chatting as they washed the dishes, and she listened for a while to the boys talking about the blokes they worked with. They were deep in conversation, so she took a chance on asking Corker, 'Are yer still set on going out tonight?'

Corker nodded. 'I won't be out long, love. I'll be back home by nine o'clock.'

'I wish yer wouldn't go on yer own. Why don't yer ask Jack, or Steve, to go with yer?' Ellen was speaking in a low voice. 'Yer don't know what sort of people ye're dealing with, and I'll be worried sick the whole time ye're out.'

His huge hand covered hers. 'I'll not come to any harm, I promise you. The one thing I'm sure of is, there won't be any fighting. I'm trying to find out what the lad did with Mrs Parker's fob watch. If I can get it out of him, there is a chance I'll get it back. If he's pawned it, the pawnbroker won't try to sell it so soon, it would be too risky. Of course he could have sold it to a customer in the pub, and if that is the case, it would be easy to make whoever it was return it. I'd only have to mention the police and it would be handed over.'

Ellen still wasn't convinced. She knew her husband could look after himself, for it would be a very brave man who took him on. But anyone who would break into a house, knowing there was only an elderly lady living there, had no scruples and would stop at nothing. And this thief was very daring to have walked out of Mrs Parker's in broad daylight. 'I still think you should go to the police, Corker, and let them deal with it. Tell them all you've found out, then leave it in their hands.'

'I'm sorry, love, but this is something I have to do. I'm not saying I'm better than the police, but in this case I believe I can sort it out quicker and Mrs Parker won't have the upset of policemen calling on her.'

'Oh, I never thought of that,' Ellen admitted. 'It would bring it all back to her, just when Molly said she's getting better.' She smiled into Corker's face and pulled playfully at his beard. 'You're a good man, James Corkhill, and I'm so lucky to be married to yer. Except there's only that one drawback.'

The big man looked surprised. 'What is that, love? Ye're always telling me I'm the perfect husband and father, so what have I done to change that view?'

'You haven't done anything, love, and I still think you're the perfect husband and father. And the drawback I mentioned isn't your fault; there's nothing you can do about it.'

Corker glanced at the clock. 'It's time I was making tracks, love. I want to be on the lookout for them going into the pub. I could stand on watch for two hours, then at closing time find they haven't been in and I've wasted me time. So be quick and tell me what fault I've got. It'll give me something to think about while I'm standing doing nothing. Whatever it is, I'll remedy it.'

Ellen chuckled softly. 'Oh, there's nothing yer could do to remedy it, love, I'm afraid. And I wouldn't want yer to, either.'

'Is it me beard and moustache? I hope not, for I'm very fond of them. I'd feel naked without them.' Once again he glanced at the clock. 'Come on, love, I've got to move.'

'It's a joke, really, love, and I don't suppose yer'll find it funny when I'm holding yer back. But if I ever wanted to clock yer one, or hit yer over the head with the rolling pin, I'd have to stand on a chair.'

Corker's head went back and his guffaw filled the room. The boys' heads turned towards them and the girls came in from the kitchen. 'What's the joke, Dad?' Gordon asked. 'It must have been a good one.'

'Your mam has a complaint. I'm too tall for her. She can't reach up to clock me one, and she'd have to stand on a chair to hit me on the head with the rolling pin. So if yer have any suggestions, yer can pass them on to her. I've got to scoot now 'cos I'm meeting someone, but I'll be interested in any ideas yer've got when I get back.' Corker stood up and stretched his arms above his head. Then he bent and kissed Ellen's cheek. 'Half nine to ten at the latest, love.' His eyes went from his two sons to his daughters. 'There'll be a shilling for the brainiest suggestion.' He was closing the door behind him when he heard Gordon saying, 'I've thought of a good one.'

Then Phoebe's soft voice. 'I've got one that'll knock yours into a cocked hat.'

Corker's heart swelled with pride. He was lucky to have a wonderful wife and four children. And he couldn't leave out the mother he idolized.

The Blakesley family came out of their house at seven thirty on the dot, and were as boisterous as usual. They didn't worry if the woman next door was trying to get her baby to sleep, or the neighbours the other side were listening to a play on the wireless. The Blakesleys thought of no one but themselves. The state of the house didn't interest them because they didn't know any different. A bone-idle man had married a bone-idle woman, and they were happy to live in filth. They lived on their wits, stealing from shops or from shopping baskets. Ted Blakesley's sleight of hand kept them from starving, and there was always enough money for a few drinks every night. They ran up bills in shops a few streets away, never too near home. And they never paid back the money they owed for goods they'd got on tick. Neither Ted nor Flo worried about anything. They were disliked by neighbours, and didn't have, or want, any friends. They paid their rent for a few weeks, than ran up arrears before doing a moonlight flit. They'd lived in four houses when the baby was born, and it was Ted who gave him the name of Sid. And it was Ted who taught the child, from when he was old enough to understand, that you didn't need to go without anything you wanted, as long as you had a pair of hands. And the young boy was a fast learner. He'd steal from his classmates when he started school, and from the teachers if he had the opportunity. He'd been expelled from two schools by the time he was ten, and had lived in five different houses so the school boards couldn't catch up with him. And he became a full time thief. He would go out each day with his father, and split up in a shop or market, so if one got into trouble, the other was there to cause an uproar and prevent the culprit being caught.

At the age of fourteen, when other children were leaving school and looking for jobs, Sid Blakesley was a full time crook. If anyone had suggested he should be working, he would have laughed in their face, for he was earning far more as a thief than he would earn as an apprentice. Plus he didn't have to get out of bed until he felt like it, and he didn't have anyone telling him what to do. His mother and father encouraged his thieving, for they lived a good life on his ill-gotten gains. They praised his expertise, even kept an eye out for easy targets. He paid the rent on the house they'd lived in longer than any other, and Ted and Flo were wily enough to know which side their bread was buttered on. Like tonight, they were going to the pub and would have as much to drink as they wanted. All courtesy of the son who had been brought up to believe there was nothing wrong with stealing. If somebody had what you wanted, then you took it, by fair means or foul.

'Anything on tonight, son?' Ted Blakesley asked, slapping Sid on the back. 'Anything lined up?'

The boy turned his head to make sure there was no one behind them. 'I wish yer'd keep yer voice down, Dad. There's no need to tell the world.'

'Your dad's not soft, son; he knows there's no one to hear. Got eyes in the back of his head has your father. He's only asking out of interest, in case yer might want him to go with yer. Keep watch, if yer know what I mean.' Flo Blakesley tapped the side of her nose. 'He's not behind the bleeding door, he knows a few tricks.'

'I'm better on me own, Mam, with only meself to worry about.'

His father let out a silent sigh. What was the wife thinking of? His days of house breaking were long gone. He wasn't as fast on his feet as he used to be and the silly mare should keep her bleeding mouth shut. 'I agree with yer, son. The less baggage yer have, the easier to make a hasty getaway. What time are yer leaving the pub?'

'Not too early, 'cos there's always people around. About nine o'clock I'd say. The streets are quiet around then in this cold weather.'

'It's bitter tonight right enough.' Ted moved closer to his son. 'Any chance of a drop of Scotch tonight, to warm up these old bones?'

'To hear you talk, anyone would think yer were an old man.' Sid's grunt was one of impatience. 'Ye're forty-six years of age, Dad, well able to get yerself a job. I'm sure yer could get part time work if yer tried.'

'But yer dad's not a well man, son.' Flo linked the boy's arm. 'He keeps getting these pains from an ulcer he's had in his stomach for years. He should see the doctor and go in hospital for an operation, but he's too frightened. He hates the thought of hospitals, and having his tummy cut open.'

'What did yer bring that up for?' Ted said. 'I was feeling all right until you stuck yer two pennyworth in. Yer've got a mouth on yer as big as the bleeding Mersey tunnel.'

They'd reached the main road by this time, and waited until a car and a tram had gone past before they crossed the road. Sid sauntered along the pavement, his shoulders moving in rhythm. A young man very sure of himself. 'Yer can have a small whisky, Dad, that's all. Then ye're back on bitter.'

'I'll have a small whisky, too, lad,' Flo said. 'It'll warm the cockles of me heart.'

'It's ale for you, Ma, I'm not rolling in dough. And don't make it look obvious when I leave the pub. Not a word out of yer. I'll go to the lavatory, then slip out unnoticed.'

Corker had arrived just in time to see the Blakesley family enter the pub. A few minutes later and he'd have missed them. It wasn't the family he was interested in, they weren't worthy of interest. It was the lad he was after, and he was hoping the pattern would be the same tonight as it was last night. That the lad would leave the pub on his own. If Corker was to accost him when he was with his parents, they were the type to start a noisy slanging match that would attract the attention of passers-by, even the pub customers and landlord. That was the last thing Corker wanted, for if it turned out the landlord knew about the break-in, and the fob watch, then the police would deal with him.

Instead of standing in a shop doorway on the opposite side of the road, Corker decided to stand at the side of the pub, and wait until the lad came out. Then the task he had set himself would be set in motion.

Corker waited for half an hour, a few yards from the pub so he would have enough time to make sure that whoever came out of the saloon door was the person he wanted to have words with. And when the lad came out, whistling softly, Corker bent down and pretended his shoelace had come loose. He timed himself perfectly. As Sid Blakesley was about to pass him, the big man began to straighten up, and as if by accident he bumped into the lad.

'What the bleeding hell do yer . . .' The words petered out as Sid Blakesley watched the man he was swearing at grow into a giant. He was speechless for a matter of seconds, then, cocky as ever, he said, 'Yer want to watch yerself, mate. I could have knocked yer flying.' He would have walked on, but the hand restraining him was the size of a shovel. He felt a flicker of fear and knew it would be unwise to argue with someone who could pick him up with one hand. So he tried to sound pally, and hail-fellow-well-met. 'I'm in a bit of a hurry, mate. Got a heavy date, yer see, and she doesn't like to be kept waiting.'

'Then she's going to be really mad when yer don't turn up at all. Yer see, I want to talk to yer about something far more important than letting a girl down. Not that I believe there is such a girl. What

I would believe is if yer told me yer had a date with a certain house yer've probably been watching for a while, and which you intend to break into. But whether it's a girl or a house, it makes no difference, for you're not going anywhere until yer've answered the questions I intend asking yer.'

Corker was keeping a vice-like grip on the lad's arm as he turned him to face up the street. 'You and me are going to walk and talk. I'll ask the questions and you give me the answers. And a word of warning – they'd better be the answers I'm expecting.'

Sid tried to bluff his way out. 'I don't know what ye're talking about, mister. I've never seen yer in me life before. Yer've made a mistake; it's not me yer want.'

'Oh, I know it's not you I want, lad. I wouldn't touch yer with a barge pole if I could help it. It's something you know, some information, and I intend to get it out of yer tonight. So yer either tell me what I want to know, or I'll march yer down to the police station and they can deal with yer.'

The mention of the police was enough to put fear into the boy. 'How can I tell yer what yer want to know, when yer haven't told me what it is?'

'I'm going to ask you about a house you broke into recently.' Corker heard a sharp intake of breath and knew the lad was scared enough now to co-operate. 'The house of a very old lady who you robbed and left penniless and terrified.'

'I haven't broke into no old lady's house. Yer've got the wrong person. So let go of me or I'll get me dad to sort yer out. He's as big as you, me dad is, and he's handy with his fists.'

'Oh, I happen to know Ted isn't up to fighting. In fact he's never done a tap of work in his whole life. Him and yer mother sit on their backsides all day and wait for you to hand over what yer've pinched. As for being handy with his fists, your father couldn't fight his way out of a paper bag.' They came to a lamp post and Corker brought them to a halt. Holding Sid by his coat collar, he put his face close. 'Yer've got until we reach the end of this street to make up yer mind whether yer tell me what I want to know or you tell the sergeant at the police station. The choice is yours.'

The lad knew he didn't stand an earthly with this man. He seemed to know too much. He certainly knew his dad for what he was, and that was a weak layabout. 'How d'yer know it was me what broke into this house? It could have been anyone.'

'Oh, no, it couldn't, lad, 'cos yer were seen coming out of the front door. I've got a good description of yer, and the witness would know yer again. You stole a purse containing all the money the old lady had in the world. Like the scum you are, you robbed her of every penny.'

Sid Blakesley felt like kicking himself. He never used a victim's front door, it was too risky. But he'd taken a chance that day 'cos the old lady was asleep in bed, and there didn't seem to be any neighbours in the street. What a fool he'd been! The only way out now was to own up and try to talk himself out of being taken to the police station. 'If I give yer the money for the old lady, will yer let me go?'

'Oh, I see yer memory is coming back if yer can remember what was in her purse. Go on, tell me how much?'

The boy was sweating now. How the hell could he remember the amount when he'd robbed several houses since? But he knew he had roughly three pounds in his pocket now, so he took a stab in the dark. 'It was two pound and a few coppers. I'll give yer that now and we'll call it quits.'

'Oh, not so quick, lad, we've only just started. Yer see, we haven't got to the important part yet.' In the light from the lamp, Corker saw the boy wet his lips, and he knew he'd get the truth now, for fear usually brought a loose tongue. 'Besides the money, yer stole a fob watch which had belonged to her late husband. He was killed in the First World War, fighting for his country. He was a hero, you are a thieving coward. But you're the one who will have to live with that knowledge. The fob watch was all the lady had left to remind her of her husband. There was a photograph of him inside the lid. Now, you won't understand this, because you don't know what true love is. But the lady is grieving, heartbroken by the loss of that fob watch. So we'll walk now to the top of the street, and when we get there I want you to tell me what you did with the watch. Who did you sell it to? Yer see, I want to get it back for the lady, and you're going to help me do that.'

'I can't do that!' The boy was really sweating now. 'Okay, I did steal it, I'll admit that. But I haven't got it now, so will yer take what money I've got in me pocket and give it to the old lady to make up for the watch? I can't do any more than that, and the watch wasn't worth more than a few pound.'

Corker's grip tightened. He was so angry he thought the lad should be made to feel some pain, but he couldn't fight a skinny kid who was only half his age and a quarter of his weight and build. 'I would like to give yer a good hiding, for that's what yer deserve, and a taste of prison life. That might make yer change yer ways.' Corker heaved a sigh. 'I'm wasting me time on yer, for like yer father yer will never make anything of yerself. Yer'll go through life stealing a bit here and pinching a bit there. And yer'll never know what it is to have a friend, for good people will always give yer a wide berth.'

'Take me money and let me go, mister.' There was pleading in Sid's voice, but Corker wasn't going to stop until he got what he wanted.

'Tell me who bought the watch off yer? And no lies because I've wasted enough time on yer. I want the name right now, and yer'd be foolish to mess around, lad. Out with it, now!'

'I gave it to the landlord in the pub, and he took it to a pawnshop.' The words tumbled from the lad's lips. 'He only got thirty bob for it, 'cos the pawnbroker said it wasn't real gold.'

Corker's laugh was one of derision. 'A thief among thieves. You, the pawnbroker, and Les Simpson are all of a kind. Liars and thieves. Yer see, that fob watch was solid gold, and worth at least ten pound. And either you, Les Simpson, or the pawnbroker, are going to get that watch to me in the next eighteen hours. If not, the police will be involved and all three of yer will be sent down.'

'I haven't got the watch, mister, so I can't give it to yer.' The lad was near to tears, and Corker was glad he was being made to suffer. 'And I haven't got that much money to buy the woman another one.'

'She doesn't want another one, you stupid boy! She wants to hold the one that her husband held.' Corker pushed the lad away in disgust. 'Just touching you makes me feel dirty. I could talk to you all night and wouldn't be able to make yer understand what love or compassion means. But even though your nearness makes me want to shudder, I'm staying with you until the pub closes. Then, me and you are going to pay a visit to the landlord, and I'm going to teach him the error of his ways. So lean back against the wall and we'll stay out of sight until throwing out time.'

'Les is not going to like this. He can't get the flaming watch back for yer. It's a done deal now.'

'When yer get to know me better, yer'll find I don't talk for the sake of hearing me own voice. Yer father would vouch for that if he was here. He had plenty of reason to know I mean what I say. So listen carefully. I couldn't care less whether Les likes it or not. Or whether it's a done deal, as you put it. And if Les doesn't agree to get the watch back, then he's in for a very hard time. The brewery will come down on him like a ton of bricks, and he'll be out of a job. Then the police will pull him in and he'll end up in jail. You, now, are your own boss, but you'll end up in jail too. And the pawnbroker won't come off much better when it's known he's buying stolen goods. That's three crooked people going to prison because they were greedy, and had no sympathy for an elderly lady whose pleasure in life they took away. And you are all cowards who are going to blame each other. I wouldn't be in the company of any one of yer if I had the choice. I'm here because I have seen what your selfishness and greed has done to a lovely old lady. And I want to see you atone for the heartache yer've caused.'

Corker was dry with anger and talking. They were now leaning against a wall near the pub, and the smell of beer was very tempting. But first things first. He'd give up beer for good if the prize was seeing Flora Parker's face light up with happiness.

205

Chapter Twenty

At ten o'clock the pub doors opened and customers came streaming out in pairs and groups. There were so many talking and shouting goodnight to each other, it was difficult to make out what was being said. But one voice Corker recognized immediately was Flo Blakesley's. It wasn't only the loud, coarse tone, it was the bad language. And one thing Corker couldn't abide was to hear a woman blaspheme. He pulled Sid into the dark entry behind the pub, and whispered. 'We'll wait here, out of sight, until the landlord puts the bar on and locks up.'

'Les won't open the door for yer once it's locked.'

'No, but he'll open it for you,' Corker told him. 'For all he knows yer might have something he can make a few bob on. I bet it wouldn't be the first time he's let you in when the customers have left. But let's be quiet for a while, until the crowds disperse. Then you can knock and tell your partner in crime you want to see him.'

Sid was sick in his tummy. And his head was whirling as he sought a way out of this mess. Right now he didn't know who he was more afraid of, the landlord he was pally with, or this giant of a man. The landlord would make a dangerous enemy, for he had a hold over Sid. He knew too much of his business, and would think nothing of spilling the beans if he was crossed. To get himself off the hook he would spread the word that it was Sid who had robbed several houses in the area.

'You don't know Les.' Sid's voice was shaky. 'He'll kill me when he knows I've told yer about the watch. He's a bad bugger, and he won't worry about no old woman. He doesn't worry about no one.'

'You should have thought of that before you became a thief and a burglar, and got involved with the likes of Les Simpson. He'll hang

206

you out to dry. He'd sell his own mother for a few bob, and he'll lie through his teeth and say everything is your fault and he doesn't know what I'm talking about. I can see him now, looking at me and saying he knows nothing about a fob watch, and what you've told me is all lies.'

'It's not, mister, no matter what he says. I've told yer I stole it, but I passed it over to him.'

'Then if yer want a bit of advice, lad, take heed of what I'm telling yer. No matter what happens, you're in trouble for breaking into a house and stealing from it. And yer can't talk yer way out of it because there's a witness. But don't let Les Simpson pretend he didn't have anything to do with it. Don't take all the blame because ye're frightened of him. Tell the truth and I promise there'll be no comeback from him. And that's not because I like yer; quite frankly yer disgust me. But Les Simpson is a rotter who has been your accomplice in crime. And being older than you, and in charge of a public house, he should have turned you away the first time you offered him stolen goods. You have no doubt broken into the homes of some of his customers while they were drinking in his pub, and he's bought the stuff off yer.'

Corker could feel his anger rising. Fancy a working class man and his wife, sitting in the pub enjoying a drink which was served to them by a man who knew they were being burgled. It didn't bear thinking about, and if the people who drank in the pub knew what the landlord was really like, they'd run him out of town. He'd never dare show his face again.

The customers had gone now, all in different directions, and Corker pulled Sid out of the entry. 'He'll be locking up any minute, so remember, when yer knock, tell him yer've got something for him. Once he opens up, leave the rest to me. But I warn yer, if yer don't tell the truth, all of it, then yer'll live to regret it.'

The bolt on the door was being shot when Sid knocked. A voice from inside shouted, 'Can't yer see we're closed?'

Corker gave the lad a dig, and with a quiver in his voice Sid called. 'It's me, Les. Open up.'

'Can't it wait until tomorrow? I'm busy now.'

After another dig, Sid called, 'No, it's urgent. Open up.'

They heard the landlord calling to the barman. 'Leave the glasses,

Jimmy, I'll see to them. Go out the front door and I'll lock it after yer.'

There were a few noises from inside, then they heard the bolt being drawn back. 'This had better be worth it, Sid, me feet are dropping off.' The landlord was keen to shut the door after he'd pulled the lad inside, and would have pushed Corker out if he'd had the strength. 'What have I told yer about bringing strangers here after we've closed?' The landlord turned after he'd bolted up again, and his eyes nearly popped out of his head when he saw who Sid's companion was. He gawped for a few seconds, wondering if the lad had said anything he shouldn't have. Then he pulled himself together. 'Well, if it isn't Corker! Haven't seen you in a long time.' Les Simpson had a terrible feeling in the pit of his stomach. Corker and Sid Blakesley didn't go well together and the sight was enough to cause palpitations. 'Can I get yer a pint, Corker? Or a tot of whisky?'

Corker looked down on the man who was a foot shorter than him. And there was contempt in his eyes. 'It's more likely you'll need a stiff whisky when yer know why I'm here.'

Les tried to laugh it off. 'Has the boy been up to his tricks again?' He nodded to where the lad stood looking terrified. 'What's he done this time?'

'Oh, grow up, man, before I lose me temper,' Corker growled. 'I know about the housebreaking, the stolen goods that yer flog in the pub, and how you and the lad here share the profits from the stuff stolen. So don't try and come over all innocent, or try and put all the blame on the lad. For two pins I'd take yer in the street and give yer a good hiding. Me hands are itching to pay yer back for cheating and stealing. But before I laid a hand on yer, I'd bring all yer neighbours out so they could hear what yer get up to.'

Les blustered. 'I don't know what he's been telling yer, but it's a pack of lies. He's always asking me to buy knock-off stuff from him, but I chase him.'

Corker moved so quickly the landlord didn't have time to move out of the way, and he found himself being grabbed round the throat and lifted off the floor. 'Now yer can tell me which pawnbroker bought the fob watch off yer? The one the lad here stole from the house of an elderly lady, along with every penny she had.'

'I don't know nothing about it,' the landlord croaked. 'Ask Sid, he'll tell yer. I don't know nothing about no watch.'

The boy gulped before saying, 'He knows all about it, Les. Someone told him. He was waiting outside for me when I left tonight. And he threatened to go to the police if I didn't tell him what happened to the watch. I had to tell him; he'd have taken me to the police station. He knows me dad, and everything. And he said if yer don't tell him who yer sold the watch to, he'd tell the brewery and yer'd lose yer job and go to prison.'

'You stupid bugger.' Les Simpson was in no position to argue, as he could see his easy life slipping away. But he wouldn't admit even to himself that he was responsible for this mess. 'I shouldn't have listened when yer asked me to help yer out. I should have told yer to sod off, instead of feeling sorry for yer. But the police have got nothing on me, 'cos yer asked me to pawn the watch for yer and I did. And I gave yer the money I got for it. I did yer a favour, that's all. There's nothing in the law against that.'

Corker lowered him to the floor. 'I told my wife I'd be home at ten o'clock at the latest, and she'll be worrying by now. And I don't like to worry the wife, or see her upset. So I want the name and address of the pawnbroker now.'

Les blustered. 'I can't remember, it's gone out of me head. I think it was the one in Westminster Road.'

'I'm getting annoyed now,' Corker said. 'The name of the pawnshop or a walk to the police station. The choice is yours.'

It was with reluctance that the landlord said, 'It was the one in Everton Valley, on the corner.' Then, in an act of bravado, he added, 'He'll have sold it by now.'

'I don't think so. He'll hang on to it until the dust settles. And you better hope he has, or I'll make life very unpleasant for yer. I'll take an hour extra for my dinner break tomorrow, and I'll meet yer both here at one o'clock. I'll expect yer to have the watch. In fact I'm warning you to have the watch, or else I'll bring the police in.'

'I can't get it tomorrow. I haven't got six pound to fork out.' Les Simpson slipped up badly when he said that, for it seemed to bring Sid Blakesley to life. 'You rotten liar! Yer told me yer only got thirty bob for it 'cos it wasn't real gold.'

'You keep yer mouth shut, yer stupid bugger. Yer've got us into enough trouble as it is. And yer'd better empty yer pockets, 'cos I can't afford to fork out six pound.'

'I suggest yer pool yer money, the two of yer. But no matter how or where yer find the cash, I want that watch here by one o'clock, or you're both looking at prison sentences.'

Corker bent to draw the lock back, then turned to where the landlord and the boy were standing yards apart and glaring at each other with anger written on their faces. 'What a sorry sight the pair of yer are. The falling out of two thieves, and each one trying to put the blame on the other. Best of pals when all is going well and the money from stealing is rolling in. Now yer can't stand the sight of each other. And it serves yer right, for the pair of yer should rot in hell.'

The door now open, Corker gave his last warning. 'If the watch is not here at one o'clock tomorrow, in my hands, then the police will be here at two.'

As Corker neared his house, he could see Ellen standing on the top step with her arms folded, and Molly leaning back against the wall. 'I'm sorry, love, I know I promised to be home an hour ago, but I got held up.'

It wasn't often Ellen argued with her husband, but her nerves were taut with worry, and she took off on him. 'Yer got held up! I've been worrying meself sick, and all you can say is yer got held up.'

Molly, ever the peacemaker, patted Ellen's arm. 'All right, sunshine, I know yer've been worried sick, but Corker's here now, and I'm sure he's got a good reason for being late. I've been trying to tell you that, but yer'd got yerself in a right state.'

Corker held his arms out and Ellen jumped into them. 'Yer big daft ha'p'orth, I've been imagining all sorts of things happening to yer. When you weren't home by ten o'clock I gave Molly a knock, 'cos I was a nervous wreck sitting on me own.'

'You should have more faith in yer husband, me darlin'. I'll not put meself in any danger when I've got you and the children to think of. Are all the children home?'

'The boys are. Phoebe and Dorothy won't be in before eleven.'

Corker set his wife down gently and kissed her forehead. 'I've got a lot to tell you and Molly, but I don't want the kids to hear, in case they let anything slip out by accident.'

'You can come in mine, if yer like,' Molly said. 'Ruthie will have gone up to bed by now, so there's only Jack there.'

'That's a good idea, Molly, 'cos Jack will be interested when he knows what I've been up to. But you'd better tell the boys we'll be next door, Ellen, in case the girls wonder what's up. They take after you for worrying.'

Ten minutes later they were sat round Molly's table with a hot pot of tea in front of them. They knew what Corker was about to tell them would be of interest, for the big man never did anything by half. But they weren't prepared for the drama as the tale unfolded. The room was silent except for an occasional gasp or sharp intake of breath from Ellen or Molly. It was like listening to a mystery play on the wireless. But not once did anyone interrupt to ask a question. They drank in every word the big man said, and imagined the scene in their minds.

'So there yer have it, the whole story.' Corker sat back and twirled the ends of his huge moustache. 'If all goes to plan, then Flora should have her husband's fob watch back tomorrow.'

Molly was shaking her head in disbelief. 'I can't get my head round it, it's too good to be true. If it comes off, Corker, then ye're a ruddy hero.'

'I'd love to see Flora's face if she does get it back,' Ellen said. 'It would be like a miracle.'

But Jack was looking below the surface, beyond the happy ending. 'There's a lot more to it, Corker, isn't there? How do you explain to Flora how yer got the watch back? All the neighbours would find out, and then the police would have to be told. How are yer going to get round that?'

'Oh, yeah, I never thought of that,' Molly said. 'Are yer going to tell the police, Corker?'

'Not until I've got the watch in me hand, Molly. If Les Simpson and Sid Blakesley get a whiff of me bringing the police in, no one will ever see that watch again. They're not stupid. They know if they are caught with it in their possession they'll be charged and sent to prison. Both of them will lie through their teeth, and the pawnbroker. They'll get rid of the watch, and without that the police have no evidence.'

'What are yer going to do, then, Corker?' Jack asked. 'It's not going to be easy, no matter how yer handle it.'

'I've given it a lot of thought over the last week, Jack, and the first priority in my mind is to get Flora's watch back to her. To make a lovely old lady happy. If she has the watch, she can hold on to the memories that go with it.'

Molly's eyes filled with tears. 'What a lovely thing to say, Corker, and I'm with you on that. Flora comes before anything. Even if it means the thieves get away scot-free.'

'Oh, they'll not get away scot-free, I can promise yer that. They've already had a scare that will put a stop to their capers. They got the fright of their life, tonight, and I'll lay odds they never do business together again. But as for the police, I'll give that some thought when I have the watch in me hand. They'll have to be told Flora has it back, but how it came about needs a very plausible tale.'

'You've done a good job so far, Corker,' Jack said. 'The police would never have got to the bottom of it.'

Corker laughed. 'Ah, but they didn't have the assistance of two of the best detectives in the business. Molly and Nellie found out more from a woman in a corner shop than I ever could have done. They did the brainwork, I did the footwork.'

'I think yer can do some footwork now, love,' Ellen said. 'I'm tired and I want to go to bed.'

Corker jumped to his feet. 'Your wish is my command, sweetheart. Stand up and I'll carry you.'

'I think I'm capable of walking next door, love, but yer can give me a kiss to put some life back in me feet.'

On the way out, Corker said, 'I know I don't have to tell yer, Molly, but mum's the word. Don't even tell Nellie until we see if all goes to plan.'

'Will you give us a knock before yer go back to work tomorrow?' Molly didn't think she could stand the suspense for so long. 'Just a quick call, an aye or a nay, that's all I need.'

Corker swept his wife up in his arms. 'Will do, Molly. Goodnight and God bless.'

At twelve o'clock the next day, three angry men faced each other in the pawnbroker's shop. They were all speaking at once, each putting the blame on the other, in language that wouldn't suit the faint-hearted. Les and young Sid weren't satisfied with shouting at each other, they were at the pushing stage. The owner of the shop stayed behind the counter, where he was safe. He was adamant he wasn't going to hand the fob watch over. 'How can I give it to you when it's been sold? Some bloke put a pound deposit down on it, and he's calling for it on Saturday when he's got his wages. Besides, I gave yer good money for it, so don't come crying to me.'

Les turned nasty. 'It won't be me coming to yer, it'll be the bleeding coppers. I'm not taking all the blame, you two are in it as deep as I am. In fact I was doing yer both a favour.'

'Were you hell's like,' Sid said. He had grown up more in the last fourteen hours than he had done since the day he was born. His mother and father had played merry hell with him last night, especially his father who had looked sick at the mention of Corker's name. 'Give the man his six pound back, and get the watch off him. He can make up a cock and bull story when the man comes for it on Saturday. He can say he was burgled and the watch was one of the items stolen.'

Les raised his brows in surprise. The lad wasn't as thick as he made out to be. 'That's the only way out for the three of us. Either that, or we all end up in Walton jail.' He took a handful of money from his trouser pocket and plonked it down on the counter. 'Pass the goods over and we'll be on our way. And don't argue, for time is running out for the three of us. Yer've got yer money back, so consider yerself lucky it's me here, not the police.'

It was with bad grace the pawnbroker took a box from under the counter. If looks could kill, Sid Blakesley and the pub landlord would have died on the spot. But the lad had no intention of sticking around, and before the other two men knew what was happening, he'd whipped the box off the counter and pushed it into his pocket. 'I'm off. You two can do what the hell yer want. But if I were you,' he glared at Les, 'I'd be back in yer pub by one o'clock, 'cos I don't think that big feller is the kind to mess around. I'll be there, but you suit yerself. It'll be the last time we set eyes on each other if I have my way.'

The two older men watched the door being closed, then both looked down at the money on the counter. It was exactly six pounds, but the man behind the counter whipped it up without counting it. There is a saying that there is honour among thieves, but there was no honour, trust, or even liking between these two men. And Les Simpson walked out of the shop without saying a word.

Molly was on pins when the fingers on the clock told her it was a quarter past one. She was pacing the floor, muttering to herself, 'He should be here any minute. Please God let him have a smile on his face when I open the door.'

There was another reason for Molly's restlessness, and that involved her mate. For the first time, only because Corker had asked her to keep mum, she'd kept a secret from Nellie. And the guilt was weighing heavily on her mind. After all, it was Nellie who got all the information that enabled Corker to nab the crooks. Still, if things turned out as hoped, then Molly would make sure her mate was given the credit, and would heap praise on her.

When the ran-tan came on the door Molly nearly jumped out of her skin. After keeping her ears open for the last half hour, she'd let her mind wander thinking of her mate.

'Come in, Corker.' Molly could see by the expression on the big man's face that his plan had been successful. 'Just for a minute, 'cos I know yer've got to get back to work.'

'Haven't got time, Molly.' Corker handed her a small box. 'I'll explain everything tonight, but here's the watch. I don't want yer to give it to Flora yet, not until I've worked out a feasible story of how it came into my possession. Give Nellie a knock, though, for she deserves to know her information has borne fruit. We'll get together after our dinner tonight and talk things through. I'll have to dash now, though. I don't want to take advantage of my boss's goodwill. See yer later. Ta-ra!'

Molly watched him stride down the street, then leaving her door open she made a dash for Nellie's.

'What's up, girl?' There was surprise on the chubby face. 'The baby's all right, isn't he?'

'Nothing's wrong, sunshine, so yer can relax. Come along to mine, I've got some really exciting news for yer. Just come as yer are, but bring yer door key.'

'Ooh, er.' The little woman's face became alive with anticipation. There was nothing she enjoyed more than a bit of unexpected excitement to brighten her day. Her wide hips touching the wall on

214

each side, she made haste to the glass bowl on the sideboard to pick up her key, then within seconds she was banging the door behind her, and bouncing her way to Molly's.

As she walked through her mate's front door, Nellie shouted, 'I hope yer've got the kettle on, girl. Yer know I like a drink to wash down any news. If it's world-shattering news, then I'll need a tot of whisky in it.'

The kettle was already on the boil, for Molly knew her mate inside out. 'Tea's nearly ready, sunshine, but yer'll have to pretend yer can taste the whisky. It's amazing what yer can imagine if yer put yer mind to it.'

Nellie was about to call back that it would take more than imagination to taste whisky where there was no whisky, but the words remained unspoken when she saw two custard creams on each of the saucers. 'Ay, girl, we're coming up in the world, aren't we? Biscuits twice in one day, that's a record.'

'Don't choke on them when I tell yer the news, sunshine, 'cos yer know I'm no good in an emergency.'

'Blimey days, girl, it would take more than two fiddling biscuits to make me choke. Anyway, what about this exciting news yer've got for me? It's taking yer long enough to tell me.'

Molly half turned in her chair and reached out to the sideboard for the small cardboard box. Then she swivelled back and put the box in front of Nellie. 'Open it up, sunshine.'

Nellie looked at the box with suspicion. 'If this is a joke, girl, I'll break yer flaming neck.'

'What d'yer mean? How can it be a joke?'

'You know what I mean, girl, don't be acting all innocent. It's one of those Jack-in-the-box jokes, I bet. I'll open it up and a ruddy doll will pop up and hit me in the eye.'

Molly made a cross over her heart. 'Honest, Nellie, it isn't a joke. It's a wonderful surprise, and yer'll be delighted. That's when yer recover from the shock, like.'

Now Nellie was filled with curiosity, but still not sure. 'You take the lid off, girl.'

'Nellie Mac, you should have been called Doubting Thomas.' Molly took the lid off the box, and, along with her mate, stared down at the gold watch, which had a thick gold chain at the side of it. Both women were struck dumb, Nellie more so because it was so unexpected. Molly knew there was a watch inside the box, but had no idea what it would look like. For it didn't need an expert to know that it was a special, very expensive watch and chain.

'Oh, my God,' Molly said, 'no wonder Flora was so distraught. It's beautiful.'

It was very seldom that Nellie was lost for words, but now she sat with her mouth partly open, as she tried to understand what was happening. Then she licked her lips before asking, 'Is that the watch that was stolen?'

Molly nodded. 'Corker got it back, sunshine, but don't ask me how. He handed it in at the door, just before I knocked for you, and said he would tell us the whole story tonight, after we've all had our dinner. He did ask me to tell you, because he said it was your information that made it possible. But he was very definite that we shouldn't tell Flora yet, or breathe a word to anyone. He didn't say why, but I think it's because he's worried about the police. If they find out Flora's got her watch back, they're bound to want to know how it came about. And I think that's why Corker wants to see us tonight. You, me, Jack and himself. We'll have to put our heads together and get the story right, otherwise Corker will be in trouble with the police.'

'Oh, we'll come up with a good story, girl, don't worry.' Nellie looked down at the watch and sighed. 'To think, all those years ago, Flora's husband wore that watch. Makes yer feel sad, doesn't it?'

'There's a long story to that watch, remember, sunshine. Before Flora was married, her boyfriend, as he was then, had it bought for him by his mam and dad. And they'd had to save up hard for it 'cos they were only working class folk. And they had a photograph taken of him, to put inside the watch. I mean, there's a history to it, and as Flora is the last living Parker, it should stay with her.'

'Is the photograph still in it, girl? Or d'yer think the robber will have taken it out in case he got caught with it?'

'I couldn't tell yer, sunshine. And I'm not going to look. We'll see what Corker has to say tonight and we'll be guided by him. But I hope the photograph is still in it, for Flora's sake.'

'D'yer know what I think, girl? I think if we had a proper office, like, with our names on the window, we could ask Corker to join the staff, 'cos he'd make a really good private detective. Just imagine how it would look with our names in gold on the window. McDonough, Bennett and Corkhill, Private Detective Agency. Wouldn't that look great?'

Molly kept a smile at bay. 'I think it would look much more businesslike, and sound more posh, if the gold sign on the window said Bennett, McDonough and Corkhill. Seeing as I was founder of the agency, it's only right and proper that I am the senior partner.'

And what did Nellie think of that idea? 'Sod off, Molly Bennett, we'll be equal partners or nothing at all. And that's me last word on the subject. Yer can like it or lump it, or pour me out another cup of tea. Please yerself.'

Chapter Twenty One

'I won't put the kettle on yet,' Molly said as she pulled a chair out from under the table. 'I've only just finished washing the dishes after dinner, and I'm not ready for a drink yet.'

Corker was lighting one of his Capstan full strength cigarettes. 'I'm full, Molly me darlin', and I'll be going for a pint when we've finished our discussion.'

'I'll come with yer, Corker,' Jack said, mentally counting how much money he had in his pocket. 'Just a pint to wet me whistle.'

Nellie looked disappointed. 'It's not worth yer making a pot of tea just for me, girl.' And with the look of a martyr on her face, she added, 'I can hang on for half an hour.'

'Where's Ruthie?' Corker asked. 'Upstairs?'

'No, she's gone over to Bella's, as usual.'

'Then we may as well start. I'll tell you what happened last night and today. Yer'll find it unbelievable, but I can assure you every word is true.' Corker threw the stump of his cigarette in the fire and lit up another one. 'I think better with a fag in me hand.'

After that there was silence as he talked them through the events that started at nine o'clock the previous night, and finished at one o'clock that day. There were questions on everyone's lips, but they held back until Corker had finished.

It was Jack who said, 'Yer warned us we'd find it unbeliev-able, Corker, and if it hadn't been you telling it, I would have found it very hard to believe. Did yer really manage to get the watch back?'

Molly butted in quickly. 'The watch is in the drawer, love. I couldn't tell yer, or show it to yer, while Ruthie was here. Me and Nellie have only seen it in the box, we haven't touched it.'

'What a wonderful surprise Flora is in for,' Jack said. 'She's the one that matters in my eyes. I couldn't care less what happens to the three criminals.'

'They are the ones we need to think hard about. I believe we all agree that they need to be punished.' Corker poked a stiffened finger into his chest. 'I personally would like to take each one down a dark entry and give them a good hiding. But what I would like, and what we need to do, are two different things.'

'They'll go to jail, won't they?' Jack asked. 'That's where they belong, so they can't rob any more poor souls.'

'I couldn't agree more, Jack,' Corker said. 'But I don't think the police would be too pleased that they weren't brought into it when we first found out who it was that broke into Flora's. But then the old dear would have had to go through it all again with police calling to her house. And they'd probably have wanted to keep the watch as evidence, which would have upset her.'

'What do you feel would be best, Corker?' Molly asked. 'You're the one who knows more than we do. None of us have laid eyes on the three blokes involved.'

'The main problem over them, Molly, is that we can't prove a thing. They can blame each other, 'cos we've no proof. Les Simpson, although he helped in getting the watch back, is not going to admit to anything, and neither is the bloke in the pawnshop. And judging from the few words exchanged today when I was picking the watch up, the trio of con men have split up. I honestly think they've learned their lesson, 'cos the pub landlord and the pawnbroker have too much to lose. As for young Blakesley, I wouldn't like to say. He hasn't got decent parents who will help him keep on the straight and narrow.' Another cigarette was discarded before Corker admitted, 'I'd be inclined to say they've learned their lesson, we've got Flora's watch back, so let's leave them now. The only problem with that idea is how to get the watch back to Flora without her asking questions and wanting to tell the police.'

Nellie, who had been unusually quiet as she listened intently, now said, 'I know an easy way.'

Molly didn't believe what her mate said was possible, but wasn't going to discourage her. 'What have yer got in mind, sunshine?'

Nellie loved being the centre of attention, and tried to look important by sitting up straight and lacing her fingers together. 'Me and Molly can call on Flora one afternoon, and while we're there, having a cup of tea with her, there's a knock at the door.' She lifted a finger and said, 'There's two ways of doing this, so see which one yer think is best.' Coughing gently behind her hand, she continued. 'I could answer the knock on the door, and there would be a young lad standing there with the box in his hand. He's only about four years of age, too young to be asked a lot of questions. He shoves the box at me and says, "Here yer are, missus, the man said to give yer this." And he runs away to play with his mates.' Nellie could see her words were sinking in, and felt she should be promoted to having her name first on the window of the detective agency. They didn't have an office yet, like, but they would do, one day.

'That is an idea that could be worked on, Nellie,' Corker said. 'Good thinking.'

'Oh, I told yer I had two ways in me head of how to do this, so listen to the other. It starts with me hearing the knock and opening the door. There's nobody there, and I'm just going to close the door when I happen to look down and see the box on the bottom step. I look in the street, but apart from two young kids playing the street's empty. I didn't know what was in the box, and I was in two minds whether to give it to the kids to play with, or take it in the house. Well, I took it in, didn't I, and the rest is easy.'

Corker was nodding his head and stroking his beard. 'Nellie, me darlin', I think yer've solved the problem with the second tale. If the kids were only toddlers, the police could hardly question them. And I think it would work.'

Jack sighed. 'I've got to say it would grieve me to see the thugs getting off with it, but I'll go along with whatever yer think is best. I haven't contributed, so I'm not in a position to stick my two pennyworth in now. Let the professionals decide.'

Molly had been dithering, but the more she thought of how easy Nellie had made it sound, the more she was drawn to the idea. In fact, she found herself adding her own ideas. 'A family that lives opposite Flora have a couple of toddlers, only eleven months between them. And the mother lets them play in the street just to keep them from under her feet. So there's no lies being told there. And me and Nellie could walk Flora to the police station and tell them the tale. Flora would be too nervous to say very much, so I'd do the talking.

Not that I'm a particularly good liar, but I'd do it for the old lady.'

'If there's any lies to be told, girl, then I'm the one to do it.' Nellie's chins agreed with her emphatically on that. 'Ye're a bloody awful liar, you are. Yer eyes blink fifteen to the dozen and yer go the colour of beetroot. Left on yer own to do it, the three of us would end up in a cell. Mind you, they don't make a bad cup of tea down at the nick.'

'Give it some thought, first, ladies. Don't do anything hasty,' Corker advised. 'Sleep on it. If yer have any qualms in the morning, then drop the idea and we'll think of another way. But could I see the watch now? I didn't have time when they handed it over. I'd asked for an extra hour at dinnertime and didn't want to take advantage of my boss's good nature. So I only lifted the lid off the box to make sure the watch and chain were in it, then I hot-footed it to here.'

Molly left her chair to take the box from the sideboard drawer, placed it in the centre of the table, then took her seat again.

All eyes were on the box but nobody reached out a hand to touch it. Each one was waiting for another to make the first move.

Nellie's impatience surfaced with a shake of her head and clicking of tongue on teeth. 'In the name of all that's holy, we're sitting here like stuffed ducks.' She lifted her bosom so she could stretch across the table for the box. 'The ruddy thing is not going to bite yer.' She picked the watch out of the box and then squealed with horror when the chain remained where it was. 'Oh, my God, I've gone and broke the bleeding thing.' The watch was quickly laid on the table and Nellie's eyes turned to her friends. 'I didn't do nothing. It must have been broken when the buggers what stole it were messing with it.'

'It's not broken, Nellie,' Corker said. 'The watch fits on to the chain. Look, I'll show you.' Within seconds he had the watch attached and dangling from the chain. And all four people present, although they were not to know, were thinking of the young man whom it was bought for, who had died fighting for his country.

Molly was feeling very emotional as she thought of how happy Flora would be when she was reunited with the one thing in life that brought her husband close to her. 'Corker, I don't know if you know how to, but could you open the watch and see if there's a photograph inside?'

Considering Corker had such large hands, he handled the watch with great care. And when he opened up the back of it his eyes dwelled for several seconds on the photograph of the young man who appeared to be staring up at him. Then with a sigh that contained sadness he turned the watch towards Molly. 'He was a handsome young man, and a brave one.'

The tears rolled unchecked down Molly's cheeks, and even Nellie was seen to run the back of her hand across her eyes. And although the two men didn't shed any tears, the lumps in their throat were hard with emotion.

Molly pulled herself together and sniffed a few times to swallow the tears. 'If it makes me want to howl like a baby, what effect will it have on Flora?'

'She's bound to be affected emotionally,' Jack said. 'But it'll only be for a short time. It'll come as a shock at first, then she'll be over the moon.'

'We'll be there with her,' Nellie said, and her chins agreed. 'She'll be fine, you'll see. We'll all have a good cry, then she'll be as right as rain.'

'One thing that's bothering me about the plan yer've come up with, Nellie, is the knock on the door. It's the main ingredient if yer plan is to work, but who is going to knock?'

Nellie looked blank, but not for long. 'What are yer on about, Corker? What ruddy knock?'

'You said there would be a knock on Flora's door, and you would open it and find the box on the step. Who will have knocked on the door?'

'Oh, don't be worrying about that. I'll think of something when the time comes. The knock will be the least of our worries. I mean, like, I can always pretend I heard a knock when there wasn't one.'

Corker chuckled. 'Nellie, after this little escapade, I'll believe anything yer tell me. Getting that wonderful watch and chain back from crooks would never have been possible without you and Molly. And yer friend in the corner shop, she was more than helpful.'

'I'll say she was,' Molly said. 'We were lucky we went in that shop. And once again it was Nellie's brainy idea. So I'll put me money on her. If she says she can get round the knock on the door, then I believe her.'

Nellie was in her applecart with all the compliments. And she smiled when she heard a little voice in her head saying, 'It's that chair what does it, girl. Yer look dead important sitting in it.'

'What are yer laughing at, sunshine?' Molly asked. 'Yer look like the cat that got the cream.'

'I'm not laughing, girl, I'm just pleased we got Flora's watch and chain back. Don't forget she's me adopted mother now, so it's me duty to look after her.'

'We're all pleased about that, Nellie,' Corker told her. 'Apart from the memories it holds for her, it's beautiful. Pure solid gold it is, and just to hold it is a pleasure. I know it's not possible, but I'd love to see the old dear's face when you give it to her.'

'It would give the game away, and take too much explaining if we told her you were the one who got it back for her, Corker. It would mean telling lies, and getting her confused. Better stick to Nellie's plan, that would make it much easier.'

'Yes, yer're right, Molly, we'll leave it in the capable hands of the ladies from the Bennett and McDonough Detective Agency. But when all the fuss has calmed down, I might just walk round to Flora's with me ma. Just a friendly visit, that's all.'

Molly put the watch and chain back in the box and closed the lid. 'I'll put it away in case Ruthie comes in.'

'Me and Jack will be on our way for a pint now, then, ladies, if there's nothing more to discuss. I'll give a knock after work tomorrow to see if there's been any development.' Corker slapped Jack on the back. 'Come on, lad, our pints await.'

'One pint, Corker,' Jack told him. 'We're hoping to have an early night.' He was taking his coat off the hook, and Corker was opening the front door when they heard Nellie's voice.

'Is Jack on a promise tonight, then, girl?'

Jack chuckled as he struggled into his coat, but Corker, with his fingers on the latch, dropped his head back and let out a loud guffaw. And it was just dying down when Molly spoke.

'Nellie McDonough, have yer no shame? Honest, there's times when I wish the floor would swallow me up, I'm so embarrassed.'

Jack pushed Corker out of the door and down the steps. 'Yer heard what the wife said, and I don't want to get the blame for her red face.'

* * *

The following morning, Nellie was knocking on Molly's door half an hour earlier than usual. She was expecting to be told off and sent back home until Molly had finished her housework. But Nellie was prepared to put up some strong resistance if that happened, for her nerves were as taut as a violin string. She'd hardly slept all night, her mind was too active, planning how best to go about giving Flora her watch back without arousing suspicion.

When the door opened, Molly wasn't given the chance of stopping her mate from coming in. She was pushed aside by Nellie's hand, then flattened against the wall by a swaying hip. 'Don't bother waiting to be invited in, sunshine, just make yerself at home. Put yer feet up on the mantelpiece if yer like.' Molly closed the front door and tutted her way into the living room, where Nellie was busy moving a dining chair to make space for the carver.

'I don't care if yer take off and call me all the names under the sun.' Nellie plonked herself down with great determination, as though daring her mate to object. 'I haven't slept all night, and I don't see why I should be doing all the worrying on me own. So just pretend it's half an hour later than it is, and put the kettle on. Like yer would for our usual cuppa.'

'I didn't sleep very well meself, sunshine, so yer weren't suffering on yer own. I'll make a pot of tea, then we'll sit and sort our thoughts out in a calm way. The more agitated we get, the less likelihood there is of us finding the right solution. Anyway, I'll stick the kettle on.'

Nellie waited until she heard the tap running in the kitchen before muttering, 'That was a turn up for the book. I was expecting her to bite me head off. If I'd known she was going to be so pleasant, I'd have come earlier.' She nodded her head at the aspidistra standing on the small table by the window. 'I'd have tried me luck at half past seven, when the men had left for work. It would have saved me making me own breakfast.'

'Some hope you'd have had, Nellie, at that time in the morning.' Molly had poked her head round the door while she was waiting for the kettle to boil, and had heard the conversation her mate was having with herself. 'I wouldn't have been washed and dressed, and I'd have sent yer packing with a flea in yer ear. This is not a café down at Seaforth docks that opens at six o'clock for the dockers to have a breakfast before going in to work.'

Nellie widened her eyes in surprise. 'What are yer talking about, girl? I think yer must be still half asleep, rambling on about dockers and their breakfast.' She swivelled her bottom round to face Molly. 'We need a clear head this morning to plan our next move, so I think yer should swill yer face in cold water. That would wake yer up proper, and yer'd be alert.'

'I'm as alert as I'll ever be, sunshine; I had me cold swill an hour ago. There's the kettle boiling now. I'll make the tea. But a word of advice, Nellie. When I bring the cups in, don't ask why there's no custard creams on the saucer. Yer shouldn't need to ask, seeing as yer scoffed the lot yesterday.'

'Blimey, girl, don't be getting yer knickers in a twist because I pinched a few biscuits. There were only four, at the most.'

'Yes, I know that, sunshine, but they were my four biscuits, not yours. It would have been nice to have had the opportunity of eating them meself.'

'But ye're not that fussy on biscuits. Ye're always saying yer can take them or leave them.'

'Two good words there, Nellie! Take and leave. You had no right to take them because they didn't belong to yer. Yer should leave things where they are when ye're in someone else's house.'

'What a bloody palaver, Molly Bennett. While we should be discussing a very serious situation, all you can think about is rotten biscuits! It's a wonder the ruddy things didn't choke me. In fact, come to think about it, it was probably them what kept me awake all night.'

'It would serve yer jolly well right,' Molly said. 'They do say thieves get paid back for stealing, and perhaps a sleepless night was your punishment.'

'Now the lecture is over, girl, can we talk about some thieves that appear to be getting off scot-free?'

'Wait until I bring the cups in. I think better when I've got a cup of tea in me hand.'

Nellie had her chin resting on a hand when Molly came back, and she told her mate, 'I've gone over and over it in me mind, girl, and I've thought of another way to get the watch back to Flora without too many questions being asked. Will yer listen while I tell yer, and see what yer think?'

'Go ahead, sunshine, I'm all ears.'

Nellie clamped her lips together to stop her thoughts putting themselves into words, the words being, 'All ears and no biscuits.' The little woman thought they were funny, but wasn't going to take a chance on her mate agreeing. 'It's the same as the ones I told yer about last night, right up to the time the knock comes on the door. But instead of me taking the box in to Flora, I was wondering if it would be best to take it along to the police station. I could tell them how we came to have it, and that we hadn't told Flora because we thought they should be the ones to give it to her.'

'That's a bit complicated, isn't it?' Molly looked confused. 'Why go to the police first? Surely the obvious thing to do would be to give the watch to the person it belonged to. That would make more sense.'

'You might be right, girl, but think about it first. We still stick with the story about the knock on the door and that, but say we decided we should ask the police for advice. And if the inspector came with us to hand the watch over, after making sure it was the one what was stolen, then the whole street would know. It would all be out in the open, girl, all above board. Corker would be happy, you and me would be happy, and Flora wouldn't have to know anything, except being so happy to have part of her husband back with her. And the police would be able to close the case.'

'Oh, I don't know, Nellie, the police would ask a lot of questions. They're not stupid.'

'I never said they were, girl, but somewhere along the line they've got to be told Flora has got her watch back. If we ask her to keep it quiet she'd think there was something fishy, and if we didn't, she'd be so happy she'd be telling all the neighbours. And they'd want to know how it came about.' Nellie put on her stubborn face. 'If the police gave it back, no one would question how, when and who.'

'I know why you want to go to the police, sunshine, ye're not fooling me. It's an afternoon in the cells you're after, with a big handsome bobby bringing yer cups of tea.'

'You're only jealous, girl, 'cos you missed out on the excitement of sitting in a cell where a murderer might have parked his backside.' Then Nellie's eyes lit up, and she leaned her elbows on the table. 'Ay, girl, Jack the Ripper might have sat on that very seat.'

Molly didn't think she should be chuckling, not when they had a serious job ahead of them. But the chuckle came and she couldn't stop it. 'It must have been some backside he had, sunshine. It never would have fitted on a seat on the twenty-two tram.'

'How can yer say that, girl, when yer didn't even know him? He might have had a little bottom for all you know.'

'Nellie's, if Jack the Ripper sat in that cell, he must have had the biggest bottom imaginable. Yer see, he didn't live in Liverpool, he lived in London.'

Nellie's tummy saw the joke before she did, and the table bounced up and down. 'Ay, that was a good one, Molly. And it'll give me something to talk to the inspector about. Get pally with him, like, so he won't notice we're lying our bleeding heads off.'

'I won't be lying me head off, sunshine, 'cos you said you'd do all the talking. And I'm quite happy to take a back seat and let yer get on with it.'

Nellie was delighted. 'So yer think me last plan is a good one, girl? Ye're happy to go along with it?'

'I'll go along to the police station with yer, but I'll leave you to do all the talking. I'll back yer up if the officer asks me for confirmation, I wouldn't let yer down or leave yer swinging, sunshine. But what I absolutely refuse to do is share a prison cell with yer.'

'It's a pity about you now, Molly Bennett. We share everything else, so why isn't a prison cell good enough for yer?'

'We don't share everything, sunshine, that's quite a big statement to make. Name the things we share, and yer'll find it's not a very long list.'

Nellie was so sure she was on safe ground she didn't give herself time to think. 'Well, we're mates, so we share that. And we go to the shops together, that's another thing. Then we're grandmother to both baby Bobby and baby Molly.' There was silence for a while as Nellie realized there weren't many more things she could think of. After all, being best mates meant yer shared everything. But she was blowed if she could bring to mind anything in particular. That is until she lifted her teacup, and then her face lit up. 'And we share our morning cup of tea every day.'

Molly was shaking her head even before Nellie had finished

speaking. 'No, yer got that one wrong, sunshine. Yer were right with all the other things we share, but not the last one.'

'Don't be acting daft, girl. What's the matter with yer? We're sitting here sharing a cup of tea, and you're trying to tell me I'm imagining it! Yer want to get a grip of yerself, girl, or yer'll be going round the bend. Ye're at a very difficult time in yer life, when old age is creeping up on yer.'

Molly's jaw dropped. 'Well, you cheeky article! I'm a couple of months younger than you, so if old age is creeping up on me, it's galloping towards you.' She hid her smile by rubbing the side of her nose. 'Just wait until I tell Jack yer said he's an old man, married to an old woman who's at a very difficult age, and likely to go round the bend. That should cheer him up while he's having his dinner. That's if he's got the energy to lift his knife and fork.'

'I was being sarcastic, girl, and I'll tell Jack that if I see him. Just like you were being sarky when yer said we didn't share our morning cup of tea. We're sitting here drinking it, so how can we not be sharing it?'

'Because, sunshine, I am sharing my morning tea with you, and have done every morning for about fifteen years. If it was to be a fair share, then I should have tea in yours every other morning.' Molly knew what her mate's response to that would be, and she was looking forward to a laugh.

Nellie's legs swung faster as her face contorted. 'Oh, my God, she's going back to before the bleeding war. Fancy bringing up every cup of tea I've had off her. I thought I'd heard the last of that the day when tea came off rationing. At the last count it was one thousand, seven hundred and sixty-two cups. And if I'd known they were so begrudged, every one of them would have choked me.'

'You can only choke yerself once, Nellie. And yer got the number wrong, as well. Up to the day tea came off rationing, yer'd had two thousand, seven hundred and twenty-five cups of tea. And that doesn't include the second cups, or the lukewarm ones.'

'I'll make them all up to yer, girl, when we go into town. One cup of tea at Reece's is worth more than two thousand and whatever yer said.' Nellie's mind went back a few years to when food was so hard to come by. 'I know it was a struggle when the war was on, and the bleeding rations weren't enough to feed a mouse. And we had the worry of the boys being away fighting, the ruddy air raids and blackouts. But we got through it, didn't we, girl? We still had our laughs, even though our cupboards were empty and our tummies rumbling. We managed to make a meal of some sort for George and Jack coming home from work, and the kids.'

'And people were nicer, too,' Molly said. 'Don't yer remember, sunshine, everyone was more kind and caring, making sure the old folk were safe when there was a raid on? People pulled together then, and that's how it always should be. But you and me have got a lot to thank God for, Nellie, which we sometimes forget. We got our lads back safe from the war.'

'Which brings us back to why I came here so early this morning, girl. And that's Flora. She wasn't as lucky as us, she lost the man she loved. But we can ease her pain a bit today, by giving her back her most precious possession.'

Molly was nodding as she pushed her chair back. 'I hadn't finished me housework when yer knocked, but it won't hurt to leave it for one day. We're going to have to move if we're to do all the jobs we've lined up. So you go and get yerself ready, sunshine, and I'll do the same. Then it's a quick call to Doreen's, and Jill's, before we head for Flora's. And I'm leaving everything in your hands when we get there. You do what yer think is best.'

Nellie carried the carver chair to its special speck at the side of the sideboard. 'I'll make it up as I go along, girl, 'cos it'll look more real if I do.' She was on her way to the front door when she turned back. 'Don't forget to put the box in yer handbag. Whatever happens, no matter which way it goes, my adopted mother is going to have that watch in her hand today. Even if it means me being locked in a prison cell.'

Chapter Twenty Two

'This is a nice surprise,' Flora said, as she held the door wide. 'Yer don't usually call so early.'

Molly kissed her cheek as she passed. 'We're going into town for the birthday presents for Ruthie and Bella. So me and Nellie thought we'd make an early start.'

Flora got her second surprise when Nellie stood on tiptoe and gave her a kiss. The little woman was more noted for her jokes than kisses. 'Go inside and make yerself comfortable while I put the kettle on.'

Working to the plan she had in mind, Nellie said. 'You sit down, girl, and I'll make the tea. What's the good of having an adopted daughter if she's going to sit on her backside and let you do the work?'

Molly winked at Flora. 'Let her get on with it if she wants to, sunshine. Yer might wait a long time before yer get another offer as good as that.'

Nellie was already on her way to the kitchen. 'I know you both take one sugar, and we all like it not too weak and not too strong. So all I need to find out is what the custard cream situation is?'

Flora chuckled. 'The biscuit tin is half full, but I'd like some left in the tin because I'm partial to a couple of biscuits with me afternoon cuppa, and my night-time drink.'

'She'll leave yer some, don't worry, sunshine. My mate likes her cakes and biscuits, but she's not greedy.'

'Take yer coat off, Molly,' the old lady said. 'Or yer won't feel the benefit when yer go out. I haven't been out meself this morning, but I know it's cold by the draught coming under the doors.'

Molly shook her head. She was feeling uncomfortable knowing that very soon Nellie would begin carrying out the plan she had in mind. And then the lies would come. It would all be done for the sake of the lovely old lady she was facing now, but telling lies, for whatever reason, didn't sit well on Molly's shoulders. 'We won't take our coats off, sunshine, because if we make ourselves too comfortable we'll not want to move. And with Ruthie's birthday being next week, I want to get meself organized. She's not having a big party, only a few of her friends. We grown-ups are going out for the night so they can enjoy themselves.'

Flora's mind went back over the years. 'Sixteen is a lovely age to be. Tell her I said she should make the most of the next few years, and she'll have wonderful memories to look back on in later life.'

They heard the kettle whistling, then Nellie's voice. 'Tea up in a few minutes. I'll let it stand for a while 'cos I can't abide tea what yer can see through. If yer can see the bottom of the cup, then yer've got a lousy cup of tea.'

Molly called back. 'You should know, yer drink enough to be an expert.'

Nellie's head appeared round the door. 'Listen, girl, if me mate tells yer that I've had four thousand cups of tea in her house over the years, don't take no notice of her. She's a fibber.'

'Don't exaggerate, Nellie, I never said four thousand. I can't remember the exact figure, but I've got it written down at home.' Molly could see Flora's expression was one which said she didn't know whether to take this seriously, or whether it was all in fun. So she put a finger to her lips, then mouthed, 'Just listen to this, sunshine.' Then she raised her voice. 'I don't have any trouble remembering the number of cups of tea I've had in your house, though. No need to write it down in me notebook, I can just leave the page blank.'

When Nellie put in her next appearance, she was carrying a tray set with three cups of tea, a sugar bowl, milk jug and plate with some biscuits on. She set it down carefully on the table before turning to Flora, 'Have yer got a notebook, girl? I'll mark the date on the top of a page, and beside it I'll put me and me mate's name. So you can keep tabs on both of us.' She brushed her hands together as though ridding herself of an unpleasant smell. Or, more to the point, the crumbs from a biscuit she'd pinched while waiting for the kettle to boil. 'Nan, I'm only kidding, girl, I know you wouldn't begrudge yer best mates a cup of tea. And I mean, I have thought of inviting Molly into my house for a cuppa, to repay her, like. But on second thoughts I decided not to. It would mean me keeping me house tidy for four thousand days, and just the thought of it tired me out so much I had to go to bed for a lie-down.'

Molly put milk and sugar in one of the cups, stirred it, and handed it to Flora. 'My very best mate has very kindly offered to make up for all those drinks, by taking me to Reece's while we're in town, and treating me to a pot of tea and one of their delicious toasted teacakes.'

'Ay, Molly Bennett, I didn't say nothing about no toasted teacake. I'm not made of money, yer know.'

After giving Flora a very gentle nudge, Molly said, 'Oh, I am surprised and disappointed. I could have sworn yer said tea and toasted teacake. Me mouth has been watering since I got out of bed at the thought of sinking me teeth into the teacake, and the butter oozing out and running down me chin.'

Nellie's face was a study as she sought the correct words to answer her mate. When none came, she thought, oh, sod it, why should I be worrying about what words I use as long as she gets me drift. 'I wish I had your imagination, girl, 'cos if I did, me teeth would be sliding through the thick cream of one of Edna Hanley's cream slices. And it wouldn't be running down me chin, either. I can honestly say, no cream has ever escaped from me. Me tongue is like greased lightning, nothing gets away from it.'

Molly chuckled. 'Not even her husband gets away from her tongue, Flora. Poor George, he has to bear the brunt of it.'

That was the wrong thing to say, as Molly was to find out to her dismay. For Nellie came back fast enough to prove her tongue was indeed like greased lightning. 'Oh, my George doesn't mind bearing the brunt of me tongue, for he says I more than compensate for it in other ways. Like me voluptuous body, which he is quite happy to bear the weight of. Keeps him fit, he says, and healthy. Half an hour in bed with me is better exercise than a ten-mile hike.'

Molly could feel her face burning. 'Nellie, I'm sure Flora is not interested in yer private life.'

Nellie was in a cheeky, daring mood. 'No, well she's lucky, 'cos she lives in the next street. It's the neighbours next door what have no choice but to listen to George keeping fit every night. Not that they complain, like, because they don't.' Her laughter drowned out the creaking of the chair being tortured by her wriggling bottom. 'At least they don't complain to me face.'

The loud laughter was for a purpose, but the two women laughing with her didn't know that. It was when Nellie held up a hand and said, 'Wasn't that a knock on the door?' that Molly's heartbeat quickened.

Flora shook her head. 'I didn't hear anything. Did you, Molly?'

Molly couldn't meet her eyes, so she turned to Nellie. 'It could have been, but we were laughing so loud I honestly can't say I heard a knock.'

Nellie was bustling towards the front door. 'No harm in making sure.' She went through the motions of opening the door, looking up and down the street, then closing the door. 'Not a soul in sight so. I must be hearing things.'

'Don't sit down again, Nellie, help me clear the table.' Molly pushed herself off the chair. 'We'll rinse these few dishes, Flora, then we'll have to love yer and leave yer. I want to get Ruthie's present today, then it'll be off me mind. But if there's anything yer need, we can get it for yer while we're out.'

'Thanks all the same, Molly, but I've got enough in to last me until tomorrow. And don't worry about those cups, I can do them later. It'll give me something to do.'

'Are yer sure? It won't take us a minute.'

'I'll do them. You and Nellie go about yer business. But what yer could do for me while ye're in town is get a birthday card for me to send to Ruthie. Get a nice one.'

Molly gave her a hug. 'I'll bring it with me tomorrow. But there's no hurry writing it out, there's a week to go yet.'

Nellie, determined not to falter in her role as adopted daughter, stood on tiptoe to kiss Flora's cheek. 'I know an easier way of doing this, Flora. You could bend down for yer kiss, meet me halfway, like.'

Flora followed them to the door. 'I'll remember that in future, Nellie. And you take care of that voluptuous body of yours while ye're in town. I'd hate George to lose out on his keep fit exercises.' And the front door was closed on the two friends standing with mouths open.

'Well, how about that, then,' Nellie said when she found her voice. 'I thought they were very strait-laced in the old days. Yer know what I mean, girl, all hush hush, something yer did but didn't talk about.'

'My ma is a bit younger than Flora, and I've never heard me ma ever mention such a thing as sex. And come to think about it, Nellie Mac, I'm forty years younger than them, and I never discuss what goes on behind the closed door of our bedroom. The only person I know who does is you! And I bet George would die of acute embarrassment if he heard some of the things you come out with.'

They were walking towards the main road when Nellie said, 'No, my George isn't going to die, he's enjoying himself too much.'

Don't answer, Molly told herself, yer'll only regret it. So she turned the conversation to a totally different subject. 'Have yer worked out what ye're going to say when we get to the police station? Don't rely on me because I'll just dry up. I can't look someone in the eye and tell them a pack of lies. So I'm afraid ye're on yer own, sunshine. Do yer still want to go ahead with it?'

'Don't ask me daft questions, girl, 'cos yer'll make me nervous. I've got the watch in me pocket, and I'll be glad when it's all over with and Flora has it back in her possession. So let's not bugger about, let's get it over with. And if yer can't say the right thing, Mollie Bennett, then keep yer trap shut and a smile on yer face.' They were only yards from the police station when she asked. 'Oh, what were the names of the policemen?'

'Best ask for the inspector, Nellie, rather than the bobby. So ask at the desk for Chief Inspector Willard.'

Nellie nodded. 'All set, girl, let's go. I haven't rehearsed what I'm going to say, so don't be surprised. I'll just open me mouth and see what comes out. I might even surprise meself.'

'Watch yer language, won't yer, sunshine?'

'Give over, girl, for God's sake, and get up them steps. I'm going to be far too busy to watch me bleeding language.'

The young policeman sitting behind the desk looked up from a mound of paperwork. 'Yes, madam, can I help you?'

'I hope so, lad,' Nellie said to Molly's dismay. Fancy calling an officer lad! But Nellie didn't change her outlook on life for anyone. They were all the same to her. If she ever met the Queen, which was most unlikely, she'd probably say, 'Hello, girl,' while falling over her feet in an attempt to curtsy.

Ignoring her mate's dig, Nellie smiled at the officer. 'We'd like to see Inspector Willard, lad, so will yer tell him Mrs McDonough and Mrs Bennett would like a word with him?'

'Can I ask what it's about, madam?'

Nellie shook her head. 'No, lad, we won't talk to anyone except Inspector Willard. He knows us, yer see.'

The chair scraped the floor as the bobby pushed it back. 'I'll see if he's available. What were the names again?'

Nellie stood to attention. 'Mrs Nellie McDonough, and Mrs Molly Bennett. And would yer tell him it's very important.'

Trying to be funny, the policeman asked, 'Is it a matter of life or death?' He'd never seen or heard of Nellie before, so he wasn't prepared for her answer. With her face as angelic as she could make it, she replied. 'If it was, lad, it would be my life and your death.'

The bobby vanished quickly before he answered back and so started a slanging match. The inspector didn't like raised voices, and was bound to tick the unfortunate culprit off. Nellie turned and smiled at Molly. 'So far, so good, girl.'

'How can yer say that when nothing has happened yet?'

'It's a start, girl, so don't be so bleeding pessimistic. Yer didn't think we would be in and out in five minutes, did yer?'

'I was hopeful, sunshine, just hopeful. And I hope yer don't string it out like yer usually do, 'cos don't forget we're going into town.'

The sound of men's voices grew louder, and the inspector came through a passage, followed by the bobby. 'These are the ladies, guv. Mrs McDonough and Mrs Bennett.'

Steve Willard dismissed the bobby with a flick of his hand. 'I know these ladies. I'll take them to the interview room. You get on with what you were doing.'

Nellie couldn't have felt more important if she'd come up on the pools. 'Yer remember us, do yer, inspector?'

Steve Willard smiled and ushered them through a door close at hand. 'I remember you both very well. Two ladies it would be hard to forget. Now take a chair, and tell me what news you have for me.' When they were seated, he said, 'Before you start, can I ask how Mrs Parker is?'

'That's what we've come to see yer about.' Nellie was getting more excited as the vital moment got nearer. 'It's about Flora, and me and Molly thought we'd better come and see you before we say anything to her. Yer see, we were at her house this morning; we call to see her most days since she got robbed. Anyway, we were having a cup of tea with her when I heard a knock on the door. Molly and Flora said they hadn't heard a knock, but I said I'd go and make sure.' Nellie wriggled her bottom on the chair until she felt comfortable, then she continued. 'I opened the door and there was no one there. I looked up and down the street, and there wasn't a soul to be seen, except Mrs Cosgrove's two-year-old boy, who was sitting on their step. Anyway, I told meself I must be hearing things, and I began to close the door.' The little women stopped, and coughed behind a hand, hoping to add to the drama. 'I just happened to look down as the door was closing, and I noticed something on the bottom step. Being nosy, like, I picked it up, even though I thought it was just something that had been thrown away. A discarded empty ciggy packet or something. But it wasn't, and I bet yer'll never guess what was in the box when I opened it?'

'I'm sure I'll never guess, Mrs McDonough, but you've made me very curious now, for you tell a fine tale. Where is this box? And what was in it?'

Nellie delved into her deep coat pocket and produced the box, which she set on the table. 'I nearly died when I saw it, inspector. I thought I was going soft in the head.' She pushed it towards him. 'Have a look for yerself, then tell me what I should do.'

Steve Willard's eyebrows nearly touched his hairline when he saw the watch, with the heavy gold chain set around it. 'Is this the fob watch that was stolen from Mrs Parker?'

Nellie and Molly both shook their heads. And Molly thought it was about time she spoke, instead of sitting like a stuffed dummy. 'We never saw or knew about the watch until after the burglary.'

'What did she say when you gave it to her? Does she know how it came to be on her front step?'

'Flora doesn't know about it,' Nellie said. 'I didn't tell her I'd found it on her step. Yer must agree that it sounds far-fetched. I was frightened that she might think I'd pinched it in the first place, so I put it in me pocket and said nowt. Then, when we left, I told Molly, and we both agreed it would be wise to ask you what to do. We don't know from Adam who stole the watch in the first place. But if it is Flora's husband's watch, she'll be delighted to get it back. It's the most precious thing in the world to her. She'll probably faint with shock, but it'll be worth the shock to hold it in her hands again. But how can I tell her I found it on the step? She'll never believe that. I can hardly believe it meself. Why would someone do a thing like that?'

'Could be a guilty conscience.' Steve Willard was admiring the watch in his hand. Then he opened up the back and saw the faded photograph of the young man. 'I imagine it was on his mind and he decided to return it without being found out. Or someone found out what a dreadful thing he'd done, and threatened to report him if he didn't give it back.'

'You never found out who broke into Mrs Parker's, did yer, inspector?'

'Unfortunately not. Whoever it was left no clues. But if this is Mrs Parker's watch, then I'm pleased she's got it back. Or will be, when you give it to her.'

'That takes us back to me being worried about finding it on her step. If I was in her shoes, I wouldn't believe it, 'cos it sounds too far-fetched. Couldn't you do it for us? Say it was handed in, or any excuse yer like,' Nellie coaxed. 'I didn't pinch the thing, but I want her to have it back. And she'd be really pleased if you handed it over. She'd believe what you choose to tell her, and be happy. Someone finding it on her doorstep could frighten her, for then she'd believe the thief remembers where she lives and could come back again.'

The inspector nodded. 'There is that to it, Mrs McDonough, you have a point. The main thing is that Mrs Parker gets her watch back, intact, with her late husband's photograph. And it will be my pleasure to be the one to return it. I'll tell her it was found and handed in at the desk here.'

'I hope yer don't think I'm daft for not giving it to her as soon as I found it?' Nellie said. 'I'm not usually stuck for words or actions, but when I lifted the lid on that box, me blood ran cold. I didn't know which way to turn, or what to do for the best. So I stuck it in me pocket until we were out of the house, then I told Molly. And the first words out of her mouth were, "Go to the police, tell them what's happened, and take their advice." '

This pleased the inspector. 'And very sound advice it was. That's what the police are here for, to help people.'

'Oh, my mate is very clever, lad. She doesn't talk much, but she's all there on top. Yer should hear some of the big words she comes out with.'

'I leave the talking to you, sunshine.' Molly was determined to show she wasn't as shy as a mouse. 'You're far more eloquent than I am. You have a wonderful way with words.'

Nellie's face was contorted as she gave some thought to what her mate had said. Then she peered out of narrowed eyes. 'Inspector, what did my mate say I was? No, don't bother explaining, just tell me whether it was a compliment or an insult?'

'Oh, it was a compliment, Mrs McDonough, without doubt.'

'That's all right then,' Nellie told him. 'If it was an insult. I'd have belted her one, and yer'd have had to put me in one of those cells, where they serve yer a cup of tea. It was nice in there, except yer don't have no custard creams to go with the tea.'

'Oh, we'll have to remedy that. Next time you come in, I'll make it my business to see there are custard creams in the canteen.'

'We'll call in tomorrow, then,' Nellie said happily. 'Just to see how yer got on with Flora.'

Molly grabbed her mate's arm. 'We will not be disturbing the inspector ever again. Unless of course something drastic happens. We'll see Flora tomorrow, and find out for ourselves how things have progressed. Good day to you, inspector, and thank you.'

As she was being pulled towards the door that led to the street, Nellie called over her shoulder, 'I told yer she was good with words, didn't I, lad? Some of them even have twelve letters in.'

Chapter Twenty Three

'Well, that went off very well, girl, don't yer think?' The mates had just settled themselves on the seat of a tram taking them into the city centre, and while Molly's nerves were still highly strung, Nellie was as happy and chirpy as a lovely spring day. 'He's a nice man, that inspector, easy to get on with and talk to.'

'I'll probably agree with yer when I've calmed down a bit, sunshine, but right now I'm just glad to be out of that police station without handcuffs on me wrists. Me heart was pounding like mad all the time I was sitting there, knowing we were telling lies. And you calling the inspector "lad", well, that didn't help. He's a high-ranking officer, and you were talking to him as though he was one of yer mates.'

'No matter what he is, he's no better than we are.' Nellie waited a second for her chins to catch up with her nodding head. 'God made us all the same, and a street cleaner, or bin man, is every bit as good as the toffs who talk far back and walk with their heads in the air as though there's a nasty smell under their noses. In other words, girl, you and me are as good as anyone.'

The lurching of the tram was soothing to Molly, and she let her body go with the movement. 'My ma has always told me the same thing, Nellie, but I don't think she would have agreed with us telling so many lies to a police inspector.'

Nellie folded her arms and they immediately disappeared under her bosom. But she'd forgotten she had her handbag on her knee, and without a hand supporting it, it fell to the floor. 'Oh, blast the bloody thing, me bits and pieces will be all over the ruddy place now. And I can't bend down while the tram's going. I'll have to wait until it stops.'

'It's no good waiting until we get to a stop, sunshine, yer won't have time. The driver won't wait for you to get on yer hands and knees to pick up yer belongings. And that's what yer get for having a bad temper. Yer were going to come out with a mouthful, I could tell by yer face. Yer don't like me mentioning the word lies, even though I'm right. When I was a kid, me ma told me yer always get paid back if yer tell a lie.'

'I'm going to have words with your ma when I see her. There's lies and there's lies. When yer tell a fib to help someone, that's only a white lie, and it doesn't count.'

'We'll discuss the merits of telling lies another time, sunshine. Let's deal with the matter in hand first. If you'll get up and stand in the aisle, I'll get down and pick yer bag up. And anything that may have dropped out. Was yer purse in the bag?'

'No, girl, it's in me pocket. Yer know I always keep it there for safety.'

Molly was beginning to have doubts, for Nellie had that look on her face which said there was laughter behind it. 'What was in yer handbag, then, Nellie?'

The little woman put a hand to her forehead. 'Ooh, I can't think off the top of me head, girl. I honestly don't know.'

Molly was now certain she was being taken for a ride. But she was prepared to go along with it. 'Did yer have a handkerchief or a comb in it?'

At the mention of handkerchief and comb, Nellie knew she'd been rumbled. For she never carried a hankie, having no need of one when she could use the back of a hand. And her comb was only used once a day, and that was in the morning. So it would be a waste of time carting one around with her all day. 'No, girl, I don't think so. I've been racking me brains, and I honestly don't think there's anything in me bag.'

'Nellie, you and the word "honestly" make strange bedfellows. But if yer move yer legs round to the aisle, I'll pick yer handbag up. We're nearing Blackler's now, so the next stop is where we get off.'

Nellie's eyes were like slits as she turned her body and legs to the aisle. What did her mate mean by 'strange bedfellows'? She'd never heard that before, but anything to do with bed was always of interest to her. In fact it was just up her street, her pet subject. But after Molly had retrieved her handbag, and discarded the crumbs and bits of fluff that had fallen from it, the conductor was calling out that theirs was the next stop.

'Are we going into Woolies first?' Molly asked. 'Or crossing over to Reece's?'

'We'll go to Woolies first, girl, and we can relax once we've got the birthday presents for the girls.'

'I'm not getting presents for the girls today, sunshine. I'll be seeing Mary about them. We're buying Ruthie and Bella exactly the same presents. Silver dancing shoes and dresses. But the dresses won't be the same; we'll have to get different colours and styles.'

Nellie linked her arm. 'I'll get the necklaces, then we'll go for a nice pot of tea and whatever else we fancy on the menu what we can afford.'

The mates walked through the large door of Woolworth's, and were surprised to find it very busy. 'And they say there's no money about. There's no shortage by the looks of this crowd. They're all well dressed, and they don't look as though they're starving.'

'Most of these people probably work in the city centre, sunshine. They look like office workers to me. And this will be their dinner hour.' Molly pulled her friend to one side so two women could get past. 'Let's look for the jewellery counter and get you sorted out. And I've been thinking that while we're in town, we could get Sadie's wedding present.'

'What are we getting for her, girl? Have yer thought what she would like?'

They were keeping an eye out for the jewellery counter as they talked. 'I'm a bit pushed for money, sunshine, so it'll have to be something cheap. But I was thinking of something for the home, which would come in useful. Like a tablecloth or towels.'

Now Nellie didn't like being pushed, and she didn't care whether the other shoppers were in a hurry because it was their dinner hour or not. No one was going to push her aside and get away with it. So her elbow became a battering ram, and Molly found herself being pulled along much faster, leaving people rubbing their ribs behind them.

'Nellie, watch what ye're doing! Yer can't just barge past people and nearly knock them over. They're in a hurry, we're not!'

Nellie's face did contortions at the injustice of that last remark. 'It's not our fault they're working, girl, is it? I mean, like, they get paid for working. But that doesn't give them the right to expect us to move out of the way for them. They don't own the bleeding shop.'

'Oh, stop getting yerself in a huff,' Molly told her as she practically dragged Nellie over to a counter. 'There yer are, just look at all those necklaces yer've got to choose from. Yer'll be spoiled for choice.'

Nellie's eyes opened as wide as possible. 'Ooh, ay, girl, get a load of them! Yer wouldn't know where to start. Which do you like? The glass beads, or those with different coloured stones?'

'I'll tell yer what, sunshine. You have a good look at them, then tell me which ones yer like best. And I'll do the same.'

Nellie made her way along the counter, pushing every other customer out of the way as she did so. And when she'd walked the full length, she worked her way back again. This time she had the counter to herself, for the unfortunate women whose feet had been trodden on had learned their lesson. She met up with Molly, and asked. 'Have yer seen any the girls would like?'

Molly nodded. 'The silver ones. They'd love those, and they'd match the silver dance shoes they're getting.'

'Where are they, girl? I haven't seen no silver ones.'

'They're not real silver, sunshine, yer can't expect anything that good for sixpence. But I think they're very attractive, and I'm sure the girls would love them.' Molly pointed to the back of the counter. 'There they are. And for sixpence, they're a bargain.'

Nellie's bosom got in the way of her leaning forward, so she hoisted it up. 'Ooh, I like the look of them, girl, I wouldn't mind one meself. George gave me the money to buy meself one.'

'You didn't take a shilling off him, did yer?' The smile on her mate's face told her she was right. 'I don't know how you can lie to George. I couldn't lie to my husband. I can't understand how yer can say Saint Peter is a friend of yours, and in the next breath ye're lying through yer teeth.'

'There's method in me madness, girl, and half of the lie was told on your behalf.'

Molly gave her a look to kill. 'Don't you dare involve me in any of your lies, Nellie McDonough. I had a problem over lying about

Flora's watch, but I feel we'd be forgiven for that because of the circumstances. There's a heck of a difference between telling fibs to help Flora, and telling fibs to help yerself. You could easily buy yerself anything yer want out of the wages yer get off George and Paul. Yer don't need to tell lies.'

'I know I don't, girl, but I can't help meself. They should refuse to give in to me, but the silly buggers hand the money over without a word. If they're so daft with money, why shouldn't I take advantage of their stupidity? I don't steal it off them, they hand it over without even a moan.'

'Your Paul is supposed to be saving up to get married. If you didn't take money off him, he'd be able to get married a lot sooner.'

'You know, girl, yer don't half carry on. And all over a bleeding tanner! It wouldn't even pay for a buttonhole, never mind a ruddy wedding. Anyone listening to you would think I was cadging money off George and Paul every day. It's only every blue moon, for crying out loud, not every day or week.'

Molly knew what was wrong with her, and admitted it. 'I know I've been a pain in the neck today, sunshine, but I worry about things more than you do. Fiddling little things that are nothing at all to worry about. But I'd got meself all worked up about going to the police station. While you can talk yerself out of any situation, I can't. I wasn't even any help to yer with Inspector Willard. That shows how bad I felt, 'cos I wouldn't have left it all to you if I hadn't been a nervous wreck.'

'Well, it's all over now, girl, and what's done is done, we can't change it.' Nellie smiled at a sales assistant behind the counter, then muttered under her breath, 'We're being watched, girl, the woman behind the counter is watching us like a hawk. She looks as though she's expecting us to rob something off the display. So pull yerself together, or we'll be back in a police station before yer know it.'

Molly's head turned quickly, and sure enough there was a stern-faced assistant watching them. She had both hands on the counter, as though ready to pounce. 'I don't think we can blame her, sunshine, 'cos we've been standing here for ages and haven't bought anything. This is turning out to be a fine day of cops and robbers. Let's go and look at the necklaces before the hand of the law falls on our shoulders.'

The assistant stood to attention as they approached the counter. 'May I help you?'

Nellie nodded, and put on her posh accent. 'My friend hand I have been making up our minds which necklaces we like best. We need two, for birthday presents. The girls will be sixteen, hand my friend his of the hopinion that the silver ones would be most happreciated. Would you hallow us to have a closer look, please?'

For the first time that day, Molly felt the urge to laugh out loud. The sea could run dry, the sky could fall, but Nellie McDonough wouldn't bat an eye. Here she was now, standing at a counter in Woolworth's, where nothing in the shop cost over sixpence, and she was trying to talk far back to impress the assistant. Oh, how dull life would be if Nellie wasn't her best mate. It didn't bear thinking about.

'What d'yer think, girl?' Nellie held a silver necklace in her chubby hand. 'Would they like them?'

'They certainly would, sunshine, they'd be over the moon. And they'd love you for ever more.'

That did it for Nellie, who wanted to be loved. 'I'll take two of them, please.' While the assistant was taking a bag from a hook behind the counter, Nellie told her, 'I'd like two bags, if you please. I can't give one in a bag and not the other.'

'Are yer buying one for yerself, sunshine?' Molly asked. 'Yer said yer were.'

'Have yer seen the size of them, girl? I might get one to go round me wrist, but never round me throat.' Nellie's head shook so vigorously that her chins were so alarmed they spread out in several directions. 'No, the shilling will buy us a teacake to go with the pot of tea. That will do me more good than buying a necklace that I can't ruddy well wear. So come on, girl, let's go over the road for a nice sit down, and be waited on.'

'Ay, this is the life, isn't it, girl?' Nellie looked round the large airy restaurant, where nearly every table was occupied. It was one of several eating-places in Reece's, the others serving meals rather than snacks, and a lot more expensive. But to Molly and Nellie this was luxury indeed. They'd ordered a pot of tea for two, and two toasted teacakes, from the waitress wearing the standard uniform of black dress, white lace-trimmed pinny and headdress. 'It's fit for the King and Queen, this is. I bet they eat like this every day, and get waited on. It would suit me down to the ground, just ordering anything I fancied and having it put before me without having to cook it, or wash up after. And being able to eat to me heart's content. What a life, eh, girl?'

'It wouldn't do for me, sunshine,' Molly told her. 'I wouldn't last a day before I was missing me family. And I'd soon get fed up being waited on. Yer can get too much of a good thing. I'd be bored stiff after the first day. I don't envy the royal family one bit. I wouldn't change places with them for all the tea in China. They don't have any manual work to do, and they don't even dress themselves. From what I've heard, they have people called dressers who set their clothes out for them every day, and help them into them.'

Nellie was so engrossed, she couldn't hear the chatter around her. 'Go 'way, girl. Ye're pulling me leg, aren't yer?'

'No, I'm not, sunshine, as far as I know that is the God's honest truth. It wouldn't do for me, though. I'd rather have me two-up-two-down house than live in a palace. And I'd rather dress meself than have a lackey do it.'

'Well, I've never heard the like of it.' Nellie was for once lost for words. 'Who told yer all this, anyway? No one told me.'

'I've seen it on the pictures, when it's been a film about the old days, and they show yer how the aristocracy lived. And sometimes I've read bits in the Sunday paper. It's not just our royal family, it's been the same right down the ages.'

Nellie tutted. 'Just wait until I tell George tonight. I bet he won't believe me, though. He'll think I'm pulling his leg.'

'No, he won't, sunshine, he'll know it's true. In fact you're probably the only grown-up in the country who doesn't know what's going on, and I'm surprised at yer.'

'I was no good at history or geography in school, girl. I was always bottom of the class. I couldn't see any sense in having to learn what part of the world China was in, or about Henry the Eighth and his ruddy wives. And I ask yer, girl, how many people were ever going to ask me what year the Battle of Waterloo took place! Has anyone ever asked you?'

Molly thought the conversation was hilarious, as did the two women sitting at the next table. They each had a hand over their mouth to hide their laughter, and were going to great pains to pretend they weren't listening. 'Nobody has asked me yet, sunshine, but yer never know, it could happen.'

'And could yer give them the right answer?' Nellie didn't wait for a reply, because she was sure she knew what it would be. 'Silly me, of course yer know the answer, clever clogs.'

'You're wrong, sunshine, because I haven't got a clue when the battle took place. And what's more, I couldn't care less. I did know when I left school, because I was quite good at history. But in all of the thirty years which have passed since I walked through the school gates for the last time, I have never once had need to use the knowledge my teacher insisted on pumping into me.'

Nellie fell back in her chair. 'Thank God for that! Here was me thinking me mate was perfect.' She was about to lean forward to add to that remark when the waitress came and put a tray down on the table. And the sight of melting butter on the teacakes was more important than the words she'd had in mind.

'I'll pour, sunshine,' Molly said, setting cups on saucers. 'And I'm going to thank you in advance for the treat. It looks very appetizing.'

'Are we going to T.J.'s for towels, girl, for Sadie's wedding present? They've got stacks of all sizes, and they're the cheapest in town.'

Molly nodded. 'Yes, we can walk to T.J.'s from here, then get the tram home from there. But let's eat these first. Me mouth is watering in anticipation.'

While Molly and Nellie were choosing towels in T.J.'s store for Sadie's wedding present, Inspector Steve Willard was knocking on Flora Parker's front door. He waited for a while, and when there was no response he knocked again. He was giving up hope when he heard the inside hall door opening, then slow footsteps coming towards the front door.

Steve could understand the old lady's caution, and bent down to speak through the letter box. 'Mrs Parker, it's Detective Inspector Willard. Would you open the door, please? I have some news for you.'

The door opened slowly, and Flora's head appeared. When she was satisfied her visitor was who he said he was, the door was opened wider and there was a smile of recognition on the old lady's face. 'Come in, inspector. I'm sorry I kept you waiting, but I'm careful about opening the door these days.'

Steve walked past her, into the tiny hall. 'I can understand that, my dear, and you are wise to be careful.'

Flora closed the front door and waved her hand to tell him to go ahead of her. 'I feel very insecure since the robbery, and reluctant to open the door until I know who the caller is. My neighbours knock on the window so I can see them. And Molly and Nellie shout through the letter box.' She waited until he was seated on the couch, then she sat in her rocking chair. 'You'll remember Molly and Nellie. They were here when you came last time.'

'Mrs Bennett and Mrs McDonough. Yes, I remember them well. Two very friendly ladies. Do they still come to see you?'

Flora nodded. 'Nearly every day. I look forward to them coming because they brighten my life, they are so funny. And they're very kind, too.' She set the chair in motion. 'I'd have been in Queer Street without them. After the robbery I was left without a penny to me name. I was out of me mind with worry 'cos I wouldn't be able to pay the rent man or anybody else, and I'd have starved without money for food.'

Flora stopped rocking so she could think straight. She didn't want to tell the policeman too much, especially about the bet on the horse. So she kept her version of events to a minimum. 'They helped me out with me rent money, and made sure I had enough food in. And they are still keeping an eye on me.'

'They sound like good friends to have,' Steve said. 'And I remember thinking what a jolly pair they were. They put me in mind of Laurel and Hardy. Not in looks, of course, but in manner and humour.'

Flora pressed a hand on each of the chair arms and got to her feet. 'I'll put the kettle on, inspector, then yer can tell me if yer have any news of the person who broke into my house.'

Steve Willard was about to say she shouldn't bother making tea, but then he thought it would be for the best. The watch he had in his pocket would come as a shock, and a cup of tea might come in useful.

He heard the sound of running water, then the plop of a gas ring being lit. And Flora's voice called, 'Do you take sugar in your tea?'

'One spoonful, please. But don't make a fuss, Mrs Parker. Come and sit down while waiting for the kettle.'

'It will be ready in no time, 'cos I've only half filled the kettle. And it's easier for me to stand here than it is to get in and out of that chair. When yer get to my age, inspector, yer'll find the old legs will only do so much. They've got a mind of their own.'

'I think you look remarkably well for your age, Mrs Parker. But I hear the kettle boiling now so I won't distract your attention.'

When Flora carried the two cups of tea in, she was about to put one down on the small table she kept by the side of her chair when Steve said, 'Would you mind if I asked if we could both sit at the table? I have something to tell you, and it would be far easier if we were facing each other.'

When they were settled, Flora asked, 'What news do you have for me? Have you caught the person who broke into my house?'

'No, I'm afraid not. But our enquiries are ongoing, and we haven't given up hope of finding him.' Steve took a mouthful of tea. 'I have better news for you, though, and I believe you will prefer it to hearing we'd caught the culprit.' He put his hand in his pocket and brought out the box, which he put on the table and pushed towards Flora. 'I believe this belongs to you?'

At the sight of the box, the old lady's face drained of colour, and a hand went to her throat. 'Would you open it for me, please? I'm feeling a little faint.'

Steve didn't want to keep her in suspense any longer, and he took the lid off the box that had been in Flora's keeping for thirty-six years, until it was stolen from her. 'A man brought it into the station. He'd found it in an entry and was honest enough to hand it over. It was very lucky that he was honest, for there's plenty who would have hung on to it, or sold it. Then you would never have seen it again.' He saw Flora was numb with shock, but there was no other way he could have handled it. No matter what he'd done, it would have been a shock. 'Aren't you going to take it out of the box and look at it? I imagine that's worth more to you than all the money in the world.'

The old lady couldn't speak. She was trembling all over. So Steve lifted the watch and chain from the box and held it in front of her. He wasn't far from tears himself, and felt very emotional. But he couldn't afford to let it show. 'Come on, dear, take hold of it. It has probably missed you as much as you've missed it. And it is intact, with the photograph.' The tears were slow in coming, but when Steve opened the casing at the back of the watch, and Flora saw the beloved face staring up at her, the floodgates opened and she sobbed her heart out as she held the watch to her cheek.

Detective Inspector Steven Willard wasn't known as a softie down at the station, so if his fellow officers could have seen him then they would have been very surprised. He was strict on discipline, and showed no sympathy for the crooks he came into contact with. He came down hard on bad timekeepers, and those whose uniforms weren't up to his standards. But his colleagues only knew Steve the policeman, they didn't know Steve the loving husband, father, son and grandson. For he had a grandmother about the same age as Flora, and he idolized her.

'Look, Mrs Parker, I'll make you a fresh cup of tea, then I'll have to go back to the station. Will you be all right if I leave you with your memories?'

'I'll be fine, inspector. Another half hour to take it all in, then I'll be the happiest woman in the world. I never thought I'd see this again. I'd given up hope. I can't thank you enough, for this is the best thing that I could have wished for. You'll never know what it means to me.'

'Oh, I think I do, Mrs Parker, and I'm very happy for you. And now I'll make that cup of tea, then be on my way.'

Chapter Twenty Four

The friends came out of T.J.'s store and headed for the nearby tram stop. Molly was carrying a bag containing two fluffy white towels which were Sadie's wedding present, while Nellie had tight hold of the bags with the necklaces in. Both women were pleased with the purchases, and felt that on the whole the day had been fruitful and pleasant. The only niggle on Molly's mind was Inspector Willard's visit to Flora. Had it gone well?

'What are yer thinking about, girl?' Nellie asked, squinting up at her mate. 'Yer face reminded me of that song yer ma sings, about a woman whose brow is furrowed and wrinkled with care. I can't remember the title of the song, but I know it always makes me want to weep. Anyway, that's what you looked like. We've had a smashing day, yet you look as miserable as sin.'

Molly shook off her niggles, and laughed at Nellie's description of her face. 'I was thinking, sunshine, and I'm allowed to do that, surely? And at my age I hope my brow is not furrowed and wrinkled with care. That's an old Irish song I remember me ma singing from when I was a toddler. It's called "Mother McCree", and like yerself, I always want to weep when I hear it. Mind you, I love all the Irish songs.'

Nellie squared her shoulders before saying defensively, 'I love them too, girl, but what about our English songs? They're just as good. How about that one about a woman called Maggie? Anyone who doesn't cry when the man sings, "To me you're as fair as you were, Maggie, when you and I were young" hasn't got any feelings at all. That's the best song ever written, that is.'

'Ooh, I think the Welsh and Scottish people would argue with yer about that, sunshine. They're very proud people, and wonderful songs have been written by them. Yer know what they say, to each his own.'

'Who says that, girl? I've never heard it. I bet yer've just made that up on the spur of the moment.'

'We haven't got time now to argue the merits of songs, 'cos the tram is coming. Besides, a good song is a good song, no matter who wrote it. So let's agree to disagree and get on the tram. Try and get on first, 'cos it looks quite full and I don't fancy standing all the way home. Me feet are tired as it is. The walk from Reece's to here was all uphill, and don't my feet know it. So we'll try for a seat.'

Nellie flexed her right arm. 'Leave it to me, girl, I'll get us a seat.' And Nellie's promise came true, even if half the people in the queue did suffer bruising to various parts of their bodies. Molly felt a bit guilty, but her feet told her not to be daft because they'd been the ones stood on all day.

Sitting precariously on the edge of the tram seat, her bottom half on and half hanging in the aisle, Nellie clung to the seat in front like grim death. Molly had told her to sit on the inside, by the window, but the little woman had insisted she'd have more room sitting by the aisle. She was sorry now, though. With the swaying of the tram she was in danger of slipping off, even though she was holding on to the seat in front so hard her knuckles were white. But it was too late to swap over now, for the tram was packed and the aisle chock-a-block with swaying bodies. Still, it was her own fault, she should have taken Molly's advice. She was too big-hearted, that was her trouble.

The last thought brought a smile to Nellie's face, for she was honest with herself when she silently admitted the last thing she was was big-hearted. She chose the outside seat because she wanted to, not to be kind to her best mate.

'What are yer smiling at, sunshine?' Molly asked. 'The position you're in, well, I don't think it's funny.' She lowered her voice. 'Yer should only pay half fare, Nellie, 'cos ye're only half on. Most of yer body is hanging in space.'

'Are yer being funny, girl? Sarky, like?'

Molly was careful to keep her body still when she laughed. One false move and Nellie would be lying in the aisle. 'Yes, sunshine, I am being funny, 'cos yer brought it on yerself. But sarcastic, no, I am not.'

'I know it's me own fault, girl, but I can't help a little moan coming out if it wants to. Yer see, the one cheek of me backside I

251

can't feel because it's numb, and the other I can't feel because it's suspended in the air! I mean, like, girl, wouldn't you moan if yer were in that dicament?'

'You mean predicament, sunshine. There's no such word as dicament.'

Nellie snorted. 'This is a fine time to be giving me a lesson in English, Molly Bennett. I'd clock yer one if I could take me hand off the back of this seat. I'm stuck in the bleeding middle here, halfway to heaven and halfway to hell. And what do you do while I'm in this dicament? Do yer let me link yer arm so I don't fall off the seat, like a proper mate would? Do yer heckers like. Yer'd rather pick on me lack of knowledge of the English language! A fat lot of good that's going to do me when I'm sitting on air and a prayer.'

Molly moved the bag to her other arm, then offered her free one to Nellie. 'Stick it in, sunshine, and cling on to me and the seat in front as though yer life depended upon it.' Under her breath, Molly added, 'And my life as well. For where you go, I go. Be it on to the floor or through the window. Neither of which appeals to me.'

'Did yer say something, girl?' Nellie's chins were swaying with the tram, and quite enjoying the sensation. 'I thought I heard yer muttering.'

'I was talking to meself, sunshine. Telling meself to get ready, for we get off next stop, thank goodness. I've never known a tram so packed for the entire journey. Usually yer have a few passengers getting off and making a bit of room to breathe.'

Nellie turned her face away, so her mate wouldn't see the wicked smile. For several people had attempted to get past the part of her anatomy that was blocking the aisle, but she refused to be any more discommoded than she already was. And the look she gave that said she wouldn't be responsible for her actions if they tried to move her was sufficient to deter the faint-hearted.

'Move in a bit, sunshine, and let them go first. We'll get off last when the crush has gone.'

'I can't move in any more, girl, or I'll be sitting on yer knee. And if I sat on your knee, ten to one some bright spark would stick a ruddy dummy in me mouth.'

'Don't be awkward, Nellie. Squeeze in and let the people pass. If yer don't, we'll be left on when the tram starts again, and we'll end up at the ruddy terminus. And if we do, you can pay the fare back for being so contrary.'

This brought Nellie into motion, and she was standing on the pavement before Molly. 'What took yer so long, girl?'

'It took me a while to get past the people who were calling you all the names under the sun. That's what kept me, Nellie McDonough. Why do yer rub people up the wrong way? Those women on the tram have never done you any harm.'

'Only dirty looks, girl, what you didn't see. They think they should have everything they want, when they want it. And it's to hell with anyone else.'

'Okay, we'll call it quits.' Molly bent her arm. 'Stick yer leg in, sunshine, and let's put a move on. We'll have time for a cup of tea before we have to start on the dinners. I'm afraid I can't offer yer a toasted teacake, Nellie, but I promise I'll treat yer one of these days.'

'Don't you worry about that, girl. Yer said before that we'll call it quits, well, I'm saying the same thing meself. Yer can count the teacake as payment for those two thousand odd cups of tea yer say I owe yer. So it's all debts settled, eh, girl?'

'You're not soft, are yer, sunshine? But I'll let yer off, seeing as ye're me best mate. Now let go of me arm while I get the door key out.'

When the tea was made, the two mates sat facing each other. 'Shall I leave the necklaces here, girl?' Nellie asked. 'Yer could hide them in yer wardrobe.'

'I most certainly will not! You'll do the job properly, or don't bother at all! They are presents for two girls for their sixteenth birthdays. The necklaces are lovely, and the girls will be so excited about them. The least you can do is wrap them up in nice paper, and hand them over gracefully with a smile and a kiss.'

Nellie chuckled. 'Blimey, yer'll make a lady of me yet. The next thing, yer'll have me saying please and thank you.

It was Molly's turn to chuckle. 'That'll be the day, Nellie Mac, when you say "please" and "thank you". I'd think yer were sickening for something and send for the doctor.'

'You never know, girl, stranger things have happened. I could end up being a real goody-goody, like you.' The table braced itself for an onslaught. And only just in time, for in moments it was being

253

bounced up by Nellie's tummy, and down by her bosom. The floorboards were slow in acting, but they were soon heard to be creaking and groaning. 'Ay, girl, can yer imagine what it would be like if I was as good-living as you? Life wouldn't be worth living, would it? No swearing, and no dirty jokes.' Nellie's face was so creased with laughter, her eyes had disappeared. 'George would think I'd turned into one of those religious maniacs, and he'd have me put in a monastery.'

The table and the floorboards thought that was really funny, and their creaking increased to join Nellie's laughter. But Molly's face remained straight, and not even a titter left her mouth. She was bursting to laugh, and to keep the straight face she'd bitten the inside of her mouth so hard she thought she could taste blood. It wasn't until there was a break in her mate's loud laughter that she spoke. 'Your George would be doing you a favour if he put yer in a monastery, sunshine. You'd love it. It would be right up your street.'

The tears were still rolling down the little woman's chubby face, but Molly's words did have some effect. After wiping her cheeks with the back of her hands, and then wiping her hands down her coat, Nellie croaked, 'What d'yer mean, girl? I wouldn't want to go in no monastery with a load of women what had never married, and don't swear or drink milk stout.' Her chins agreed with her head: that wouldn't be a good life for Nellie. 'No, my George wouldn't do that to me. And how can me best mate say it would be right up my street?'

'Well, yer see, sunshine, yer've got yerself a bit mixed up. A monastery is a place for monks. And as yer should know, monks are men. Convents are for nuns.' Molly waited until her mate had taken in this information, then said, 'If I were in your shoes, sunshine, I'd be having a word with your friend Saint Peter when yer go to bed tonight. Explain and apologize, before he crosses yer off the list of people he has down in his book for a seat on the front row in heaven. Better to be sure than sorry.'

'You're right there, girl, I'll do that.' Nellie lowered her head while wondering what contortion she needed to put on her face to show remorse. When she was satisfied, she faced Molly. The laughter was still bubbling inside her, but to release it now would spoil the fun. And she hadn't finished with her mate yet. 'And when I've said me prayers, I'll tell George to keep his hands off me, 'cos I'm celebrate.'

Molly was flummoxed. 'What have yer got to celebrate, Nellie? It's not yer birthday. And a toasted teacake in Reece's is no cause for a celebration. Unless it's me that's going doolally and forgetting something.' Then Molly understood. It came to her in a flash, but she didn't let it show. 'Aren't yer going to tell me what the happy occasion is that ye're going to celebrate?'

Nellie tutted with impatience. 'What's up with yer, girl, are yer losing yer touch? I'll say it slowly so yer can understand. Tonight I am going to be like those nuns in the convent. Them what have never got married. Now do yer know what I mean?'

Molly kept up the pretence. 'Not really, sunshine. I'm trying to, I really am, but what have the nuns got that you would want to celebrate? And where does George come into it?'

The little woman was really getting het up now. 'I'll say it slowly, girl, 'cos I'm beginning to think ye're losing yer marbles. Nuns never get married, do they? Never have a man, like? Well, I'm going to be like one of them tonight.'

Molly's mouth opened at the same time as she banged a fist down on the table. 'Oh, yer mean celibate, sunshine! Why didn't yer say that in the first place?'

Nellie's eyes narrowed as she ground her teeth together. 'If yer weren't going deaf as well as daft, yer'd have heard me say it.'

'So there'll be no hanky-panky for George tonight? Is that what it boils down to? And that's what we wasted the last half hour on?'

Nellie nodded. 'Yeah, it is, girl. But it was a laugh, and helped pass the time away. I mean it was better than us just looking at each other across the table. It's not as if either of us look like Doris Day.'

'You speak for yerself, sunshine, yer don't have to insult me as well. And it's about time yer were on yer way, so I can start on the dinner.'

With reluctance, Nellie pushed her chair back. 'Are we going round to Flora's after dinner, to see what's happened? If the police have been?'

'Not tonight, sunshine, 'cos don't forget Corker's coming to see how we got on at the police station. He'll be here at half seven, so come at the same time. We'll go to Flora's in the morning and stay with her for a while, 'cos we haven't much on tomorrow, thank goodness. I can get some housework done.' Molly put an arm round Nellie's shoulder. 'I'll come to the door with yer.'

'I'll see yer at half seven, then, girl. Ta-ra for now.'

'Ta-ra, sunshine, and just in case we don't get any time to talk on our own tonight, give George a break and don't become celibate.'

'I'm not that daft, girl. George and cream slices are my luxuries in life. And you're my best mate.' As she waddled towards her house, she called, 'I'm a very lucky woman, Molly Bennett, and don't I know it!'

As Corker closed the front door behind him, he felt a presence, and turned to find Nellie grinning up at him. 'In the name of God, Nellie, me darlin', yer gave me a start. I could have turned round in a hurry and knocked yer flying.'

'I'm only little, Corker, but there's plenty of me.'

'Oh, I know that, me darlin', and I'd not be taking any chances with yer. I'm on me way next door, and as I'm presuming that is also your destination, allow me to escort you.'

'As long as it's not me voluptuous body ye're after, then that's okay with me.'

It was Corker's loud guffaw that had Molly rushing to open the door, and when she saw her mate standing beside him she shook her head. 'Were you at the window again, watching out for him?'

Again Corker's guffaw could be heard in the street. 'No, not the window tonight, Molly. She met me at the front door.'

'Oh dear, oh dear,' Molly said, wagging a finger at her mate. 'Yer'll have the neighbours talking, Nellie Mac, and if Ellen hears ye're chasing her husband, she'll have yer guts for garters.'

With a cheeky grin, the little woman dusted her hands together. 'Oh, I could easy deal with Ellen, she's small fry.'

'Oh, get in, the pair of yer.' Molly held the door wide. 'Ye're both as daft as each other.' Then, when she was closing the door after them, a little demon whispered in her ear that she should share a joke with her friends. After all, that's what friends were for. 'Oh, Corker, if Nellie tells yer she's celebrate, she doesn't mean what you'll think she does.'

Corker greeted Jack, then, intrigued by Molly's remark, he said,

'Tell me more. Yer've aroused my curiosity now. Are yer celebrating, Nellie, or are yer not celebrating?'

Busy lifting her carver chair, Nellie jerked her head at Molly. 'You tell him, clever clogs, then we can all have a good laugh when yer face turns the colour of beetroot.'

Oh, my God, she's got her own back, Molly thought. Trust my mate to turn the tables on me. I should have had more sense.

By this time Nellie was seated comfortably in her favourite chair, and feeling mischievous. 'Go on, girl, don't keep the men waiting.' The little woman would have bet a pound to a penny that Molly hadn't told Jack. She knew her mate well. Even with her own husband she was shy. It was a mystery how she came to have four children. 'Hurry up, girl, or Corker will be too late for a pint the way ye're carrying on. Ye're too ruddy slow to catch a cold.'

Molly made a quick decision. She'd turn the tables for a change. 'I've forgotten all that was said, Nellie, or how it came about. But I do remember it was very funny, so you tell the men while I make a pot of tea. Go on, sunshine, yer enjoy a laugh yerself.' With that parting shot, Molly hastened to the kitchen, telling herself she'd got out of that nicely. And if she put the kettle on a low light, the tale would be well told by the time it boiled. And her blushes would be spared.

Molly leaned back against the sink and folded her arms. She hummed to herself so she couldn't hear Nellie's voice, and when the guffaws began, she hummed as loud as she could. But she had a smile on her face.

Jack poked his head round the door. 'Yer can come in now, love, but I don't know why yer had to hide away. There was nothing embarrassing, just a damn good laugh.'

'I know it was, love, because don't forget I was part of it. But ten to one, I bet Nellie would have added a lot more to it, just to see me blush.' Molly pushed him aside to get to the stove. 'I'll bring the tea through in a minute.'

Nellie's voice sailed through. 'Shall I give yer a hand, girl?'

'No, it's all right, sunshine, I'll see to it. You can be telling the men how we got on at the police station. But leave out the part where yer sat on the detective inspector's knee. Now that was really embarrassing.'

Molly had the teapot in her hand when she heard Nellie say, 'See, she has got a sense of humour. She only pretends to be miserable, but she's not really.'

When the tray was set, Molly carried it through. 'I'm not going to make any comment on that last remark, Nellie McDonough. I'll not attempt to defend the indefensible.' With a sharp nod of her head, she placed the tray in the centre of the table. 'I'll let you pour, Nellie. You can be mother.'

The little woman gave her daggers as she lifted her bosom so she could reach the teapot. 'I'm sure you make words up as yer go along, Molly Bennett. I've never heard nobody else using those long words yer come out with.'

'How many times have I told yer to buy yerself a dictionary, sunshine, so yer can look them up yerself?'

'And how many times have I told you that a dictionary would not be a scrap of use to me. Yer have to be able to spell the bleeding words before yer can look them up.'

Jack and Corker chortled. Nellie had an answer for everything, and it would take a good one to get the better of her. 'Now we're settled with a cup of tea in front of us, are yer going to tell me how yer got on at the police station?' Corker asked. 'It's been on me mind all day. Did it go well?'

'I'll let Nellie tell yer,' Molly said. 'She was the brains, and the actress, today. I only sat and listened. She'll tell yer in her own words. But before she starts, I'd like to say she is a belter. Absolutely brilliant.' She winked at her best mate. 'Go on, sunshine, word for word. Don't leave anything out.'

Nellie was in her element. There was nothing she liked better than being centre stage. And her facial expressions, plus hand motions, went with the words as the tale was unfolded. For once the little woman was serious, and the story could not have been more interesting or factual if it had been told by a highly educated person who would, as Nellie might say, speak with a plum in her mouth.

When Nellie had finished, Corker shook his head in amazement. 'Nellie, you leave me speechless. No one could have done it better, and I'm sure Molly and Jack will agree with me. Ye're a woman with hidden talents, and you don't always do yerself justice.'

Now Nellie loved compliments; she blossomed when being

praised. But she didn't love them more than she loved her best mate, and she wanted her to share the credit. 'That's very nice of yer to say so, but I didn't do it on me own. I wouldn't have even dared walk up the steps of the police station if Molly hadn't been with me. It was knowing me mate was sitting next to me, ready to back me up, that gave me the courage. And we'll both say the same about Inspector Willard: he's a lovely man. Treated us like ladies, he did. No looking down his nose at us, like some in his position would do. Am I right, girl?'

'Yes, sunshine, Inspector Willard is a real gentleman. And he did treat us well. But I don't agree with yer when yer say some would look down their noses at us. It's never happened to me, and while I've been in your company it's never happened to you. I'm fed up telling yer, Nellie, that ye're as good as anyone, and better than some.'

'Hear, hear!' Corker said. 'Ellen aside, I don't know anyone who comes close to you two. And what you did today, well, I don't know a soul that would have had the guts to do it.'

'I wonder how the inspector got on with Flora?' Jack said. 'It would be a terrible shock for her. Wonderful, but initially a shock. It's to be hoped he was gentle with her.'

'Oh, he would be,' Molly said. 'He's a really nice bloke.'

'Do yer think he believed the story yer told?' Corker asked. For it all seemed to have been too easy to be true. 'He didn't ask yer loads of questions?'

'No, he just said he was pleased the watch had been found for Mrs Parker's sake, and that they would still go on with their enquiries, to try and find the culprit. That's about it, really, and I don't think he suspected anything untoward.' Molly sighed, 'Nice as he was, though, I was glad to get out of that station.'

'When will you be seeing Flora again?' Corker asked. 'I know I can't be seen to be involved, but I'd love to see the happiness on the old lady's face.'

'And you should be allowed to.' Molly felt very strongly about this. 'Without you, Flora would never have seen that watch again. You did the hard work, and me and Nellie just did the easy bit. In fact I didn't do anything.'

'We'll be going to Flora's tomorrow, won't we, girl?' Nellie tilted her head. 'We could mention that Corker is always asking after her, and, in an off-hand way, say we might walk round with him one night. How about that?'

'Yes, of course,' Molly said. 'She'd be chuffed to have a handsome man visit her.'

'Ay, ay,' Jack said. 'What about me? Or aren't I handsome enough?'

Molly leaned sideways and gave her husband a sloppy kiss. 'Yer'd win the most handsome man contest if I was one of the judges, sunshine. And Flora would be doubly delighted to have two men visit her. Me and Nellie will see how she is tomorrow, whether she's up to visitors. It may take her a few days to settle down after the excitement.'

Nellie nodded. 'Yeah, we'll meet same time tomorrow night. So set yer watches to the same time.'

'Nellie, you and me haven't got watches.'

'Then we'll watch the bleeding clock, girl! Any port in a storm, as my old ma used to say.'

Chapter Twenty Five

When Molly and Nellie called at Doreen's the following morning to pick up her shopping list, they were in for a pleasant surprise. For Molly's daughter had the list in her hand, and a smile on her face which stretched from ear to ear.

Molly could feel her heart lifting with relief. 'Oh, sunshine, it's a treat to see that smile. Is Bobby better, then?'

'He slept all night, Mam. I never had to get up once for him. And his temperature has gone down, so that's good, isn't it? Phil went to work this morning with a spring in his step. And Aunt Vicky's got a permanent smile on her face. She's been really worried about him.'

'She's not used to babies, love, seeing as she never had a family of her own. What about his rash, has that gone away at all?'

'It has a bit, yeah.' Doreen was as happy as it was possible to be. First baby, and she wouldn't tell anyone because they'd say she was daft, but she'd really thought the baby was going to die. And although Phil had tried to make light of her fears, she knew he was also worried. 'I won't ask yer in today, Mam and Auntie Nellie, but if he's better tomorrow, will yer come for ten minutes? He'll be really pleased to see yer both.'

'I'll be all right to come in, once me and Nellie have done our shopping. I've only got yer dad's dinner to worry about, 'cos Ruthie is going into town straight from work with Bella. They're going to buy their dresses. Me and Mary decided we'd let them keep all their wages this week, as a birthday present. And anyone listening would have thought we'd given them the crown jewels.'

'If Bobby hadn't got sick, I could have made dresses for them,' Doreen said. 'I feel a bit mean about it.'

'Don't be daft! They wouldn't expect yer to make them. Don't forget, Ruthie's got the job you used to have, and she's working on sewing machines. I believe they'll enjoy the experience of buying their own dresses. Heaven knows what they'll end up with, but it'll be their own choice, so whether I like it or not I'll say they're lovely.'

'I don't think yer need worry about that, Mam, 'cos our Ruthie has pretty good taste. She has over hairstyles, and when she's here Aunt Vicky ends up looking like a film star.'

'I keep telling yer mam about Ruthie,' Nellie said. 'I know I make fun and say she's man mad, but that girl's got her head screwed on the right way. She'll get what she wants in life, you just mark my words.'

Molly chuckled. 'I hope she doesn't come to you for advice, sunshine. I don't want her wandering off the straight and narrow.'

Doreen handed her shopping list over. 'I'll be able to do me own shopping on Monday, Mam, if Bobby's rash is better. He could do with some fresh air, and so could I.'

'Whatever yer want, sunshine, is fine with me. Yer know I'm always here if yer want me.'

Nellie piped up. 'And I'll be with her, girl, so yer don't need to go short on anything.'

Doreen stepped down to kiss them. 'Ye're a pair of smashers. Me and our Jill are going to be mates, just like you two. Of course yer won't need two guesses which one will be you, Mam, and which one Auntie Nellie.'

'Ooh, I'd need two guesses, girl,' Nellie said. Then she put a finger on her chin. 'I know, Jill will be me, 'cos we're very much alike in many ways.'

Doreen went into action and stood in front of Nellie. She folded her arms, hoisted her bosom and narrowed her eyes. 'What are yer on about, girl? Our Jill is more like me mam. It's me what's unfortunate enough to take after me Auntie Nellie. I might not have her voluptuous body, but I've got everything else she's got.' The stance, the expression, and the voice had Nellie wide-eyed. 'Oh,' Doreen went on, 'and I like cream slices and raiding the biscuit tin when no one is looking.'

Nellie gave Molly a dig. 'Ay, will yer tell yer daughter that if she thinks she's taking over from me at our parties, then she's got another think coming. She's not a patch on me, and never will be. I mean, where's all the swear words? And can yer see her giving Elsie Flanaghan a belt?'

'I should hope not! I don't want to hear any of my children using bad language, or giving someone a belt.'

Nellie grinned. 'Not even Elsie Flanaghan? Go on, just one little belt, for old times' sake?'

'Not even a tap, Nellie Mac, so don't you be leading the girl astray. And quite frankly, the thought of there being two of you is enough to send shivers down me spine.' Molly winked at the little woman before saying, 'Less of this frivolity now, we've got to be on our way. If it was left to you, we'd never get anything done. I want to call to Jill's next, to see the baby. Then we said we'd call on Flora before going to the shops.'

Doreen stepped up into the hall. 'You be on yer way, then, Mam, and I'll see yer later.'

Molly linked Nellie's arm. 'We might be a bit later than we usually are, because of calling to see Mrs Parker. Is there anything on the list that ye're desperate for?'

'No, I've got enough in for our lunch, everything on the list is for tonight. I'll need the stewing meat and veg before three, to give me time to cook it. But don't panic. Phil doesn't mind waiting, he's very easy-going.'

'Oh, yer'll have everything on yer list by half one, sunshine, and that'll be without me panicking. Ta-ra, and give Victoria and Bobby a kiss from both grandmas.'

Nellie was not going to be outdone, and called over her shoulder, 'Yer can give him two off this grandma, 'cos I'm more generous than the other one.'

Molly pulled her mate along. 'We'd never get anything done if it was left to you. If we're offered a cup of tea in Jill's, then we'll have one. But if she's busy with the baby, don't be dropping hints about being thirsty, or yer mouth feeling like emery paper.'

'Ah, ay, girl, give us a break. There's no harm in me saying me mouth is dry. I bet you often get a dry mouth because yer talk a lot.'

'Well, you cheeky article! I talk to me kids more than you do because they are my kids. But what about last night when Corker was in our house? I hardly spoke, because you were doing all the talking. But I didn't object because it was fair. You had done a good job and I'd only been a bystander.'

They were almost at Jill's front door now, and Nellie sighed a heavy sigh before saying, 'I'll do without a cup of tea here, girl, 'cos I'm buggered if I'm going through another lecture like that, just for the sake of a cup of tea. I'll wait till we get to Flora's, and as she's me adopted mother, she won't mind me putting the kettle on. I'm like a daughter to her, but you're just a friend who has to wait until they're asked.'

'Yer've got a cockeyed way of looking at things, sunshine,' Molly said as she knocked on the door. 'I suppose there's logic in it somewhere, but I'm blowed if I can fathom it out.'

When the door opened, there was a welcoming smile on Jill's pretty face. 'What can't yer fathom out, Mam?'

Molly kissed her daughter's cheek as she squeezed past. 'Yer Auntie Nellie, sunshine. She's a law unto herself.'

'Take no notice of her, girl.' Nellie grinned up at Jill. 'I think she's sickening for something. She's been complaining all morning about having a dry throat. Said it feels like emery paper.'

Jill closed the door, saying, 'I'd better put the kettle on, then, and make her a cuppa.' And when she reached the living room to find her mother bent over and gripping the back of one of the wooden chairs, she thought she must really be ill. 'Mam, are yer not feeling well?' Concerned, Jill put her arm round the hunched shoulders, only to realize the shaking was due to laughter. 'What's going on? Auntie Nellie said yer were sickening for something.'

Wiping away the tears with the back of a hand, Molly said, 'Yer should know by now that yer Auntie Nellie – or yer mother-in-law – is the biggest liar on God's earth. She'd sell her soul for a cup of tea.'

Nellie shook her head, but because her chins didn't agree with her, they went in the opposite direction for spite. 'No, girl, I wouldn't sell me soul for a cup of tea. But if I was offered two custard creams with it, then I'd have to give it some consideration.'

Lizzie was rocking in her chair with baby Molly on her lap. Tickling the baby's tummy, she said, 'It's a lucky baby you are, sweetheart, to have two grandmothers who will fill yer life with love and laughter.'

'While ye're telling her some of the facts of life, Lizzie,' Molly said, 'would you tell her that if she ever needs advice on a serious matter, to come to Grandma Bennett. But if it's a laugh she wants, then Grandma McDonough is the woman she wants.'

It took Nellie a few seconds to work out whether that was a compliment or whether her mate was being sarky. But when she saw the baby kicking her arms and legs, and gurgling with baby laughter, she cast all such thoughts aside and whipped her granddaughter off Lizzie's lap. 'Come to yer grandma, girl. You and me are going to be good pals. And I bet when yer grow up, I won't have to ask yer to make me a cup of tea, yer'll do it off yer own bat.'

'The kettle's on, Auntie Nellie,' Jill called from the kitchen. 'So yer can't complain about the service.'

'I'll answer that when I see how many biscuits are on the plate. Yer have to see something with yer own eyes before yer can say whether the service is satisfactory.'

When the tray was put on the table and bottoms were put on chairs, Molly told Jill and Lizzie of the improvement in baby Bobby. 'Me and Nellie might be able to see him tomorrow, but I think you would be wise to leave it until the middle of next week before taking Molly. Best to be on the safe side.'

'I bet Doreen and Phil are glad the worst is over,' Jill said. 'They must have had a worrying time.'

'Well, it's one worry off my mind,' Molly told her. 'I can concentrate on Ruthie's birthday now. Her and Bella are getting new dresses tomorrow, and silver dancing shoes. I can see our Ruthie acting the young lady, showing off in front of the boys.'

Nellie grunted under her breath, but made sure it was just loud enough to be heard. 'Takes after her mother. Man mad.'

Molly chuckled. 'Yes, Nellie, I was, and still am, man mad. But not any man, 'cos I'm fussy. There's only been one man in my life, and I'm still mad about him. If Ruthie is as fortunate as I've been, then she'll have a very good life.'

'Me and Doreen take after you, Mam,' Jill said. 'Steve's the only boy I ever wanted, and Doreen fell for Phil the first time she saw him at a dance. So it runs in the family.'

Nellie put on her bulldog face as she glared at mother and daughter. 'Aren't you two forgetting something? I have a stake in all this sloppiness, yer know, a large stake, too! It was me what gave birth to Steve. I went through the pain, and you just come along and take the prize, as though it's you what's clever! If it wasn't for me, girl, you might have ended up with a rotten layabout. But do I get any thanks for it? Do I heckers like. The most I get is two custard creams, and that's if I'm lucky.'

'You've got a terrible memory, sunshine,' Molly said, setting down her empty cup. 'Yer always leave something out. I think ye're forgetful on purpose.'

Nellie's eyes disappeared in a frown. Then, glaring through lowered lids, she asked, 'What have I forgot, girl? I can't think of nothing.'

'Well, I'm surprised yer'd forget something so important. But seeing as yer are me mate, I'll remind yer. A year after you were in agony in the labour ward giving birth to Steve, I was in the same ward, going through the same agony, giving birth to the beautiful girl he was lucky enough to marry.'

Nellie slapped an open palm on her forehead. 'Oh, yeah! I remember now. Silly me, fancy me forgetting that! I don't see how I could forget, seeing as yer never stopped talking about how beautiful yer baby was. To hear yer talk, yer were the only woman in Liverpool to have ever had a baby.'

Jill put her arms round Nellie's neck. 'I know you and me mam had to suffer when me and Steve were born, Auntie Nellie, but aren't Steve and I worth it?'

Nellie's expression softened. 'Of course yer are, girl. You and our Steve were made for each other. And although yer mam might not have told yer this, we had yer paired off from the time you were two years of age, and my Steve was three. We used to often talk about how happy we'd be if the Bennetts and McDonoughs were joined together. They say if yer wish and pray hard enough, then yer wish will be granted. And that saying certainly came true in our case.'

'Nellie Mac, I do believe ye're getting sentimental in yer old age,' Molly teased. 'Next yer'll be telling them how we were going to buy the biggest wedding hats in Liverpool, for their wedding.' She chuckled. 'If I remember rightly, yer said yer were going to buy one as big as a cartwheel, to outshine me.'

The laughter this brought had Nellie's chins doing a quickstep. 'Oh, yeah, I remember that, girl. The best of it was, while we were full of big ideas, we didn't have two ha'pennies to rub together.'

Jill moved to hug her mother, while Lizzie watched with a little sadness that she never had a mate as close as these two. 'You and Auntie Nellie managed to have a good life without a lot of money, didn't yer, Mam? While yer were talking about memories, one came into my head that I hadn't thought of for goodness knows how long. And it was like a picture in me mind, of you running down the yard to the entry, and yer had a pan of hot stew in yer hands. Yer said yer didn't want the neighbours to see yer, 'cos you and Auntie Nellie had shared the meat and potatoes for the dinner for both families. Do yer remember that, Mam?'

'I can't remember that one occasion, sunshine, because we shared everything. We'd have starved if we hadn't. Many's the time we've had a pan of stew without any meat in! There was plenty of vegetables and barley, and it was filling. But meat was a luxury we couldn't afford.'

When Nellie laughed, the room became alive with creaks and groans. 'There was one night George came in from work, and he sniffed up and said, "Mm, that smells good, love. What is it?" And I told him it was a pan of stew, and it would do him the world of good. It was when we were halfway through our dinner, he said, "I haven't come across any meat, yet, love, it must be all hiding." When I told him it was blind stew, he thought I was pulling his leg. That's until he'd emptied his bowl, then he believed me.'

Lizzie lifted the baby and held her close while patting her back. 'I never went without because Corker was going to sea and left me a weekly allowance. But while you two had nothing, you had everything. Yer might not have had two pennies to rub together, but you enjoyed life. Yer gave yer children love to keep them warm, and laughter to keep them happy. I believe you've been happier than any millionaire.'

'There's that word again,' Nellie said. 'Just how much money is there in a million pounds?'

'Oh, dear,' Molly said. 'I couldn't tell yer, sunshine, and we don't have time to figure it out now, 'cos we've got to call on Flora before we go shopping. So let's make a start. Jill won't mind us leaving her with dirty cups, will yer, sunshine? But I must have a few minutes holding the baby, so pass her over, Lizzie.'

'Yeah, I'll have another cuddle,' Nellie said. 'We've got equal rights with this baby, don't forget. So it's five minutes each.'

Molly was in her element holding her granddaughter. And baby Molly recognized her, too, for she gurgled and thrashed out with legs and arms. 'Ooh, I love the smell of a baby,' Molly said. 'Scented soap and talcum powder.'

And while Nellie was waiting for her turn, she whispered to Jill, 'Ay, girl, how many pounds are in a million?'

When Flora opened the door to the two friends, she was eager to get them inside. The difference in her was remarkable. Her eyes were bright, her hair was neatly combed, and her movements were more animated. 'Come on in. I've so much to tell you.' She was all of a flutter. 'Sit yerselves down while I put the kettle on, then I can tell yer me news over a cuppa. Yer won't believe it, honest, because I could hardly believe it meself.'

'Whatever it is, it's done yer the world of good, sunshine. Yer look ten years younger,' Molly said. 'If they sell whatever it is in bottles, then me and Nellie will buy a pint.'

'I'll have two pints, girl,' Nellie called, while pulling a face at Molly, which said they were in for a treat. 'Just in case the first pint doesn't work, like. I've got a lot of creases in my face, yer see.'

'I'm sure Flora has noticed that, sunshine. Not that there's anything wrong with having creases, 'cos I think they make yer look more intellectual. More clever and interesting, like.'

'What are yer after, girl? Whatever it is yer can forget it, 'cos ye're not getting it.'

'Blimey, sunshine, I pay yer a genuine compliment and yer throw it back in me face. That's the last time I'll say anything nice about you.'

Nellie was silent as she went over Molly's words in her mind. What were they now? One of them was a long one. She'd never be able to say that, even if she could remember what it was. The one she could remember was the word 'clever'. Now that was a compliment if there ever was one. And she should have thought before she opened her big mouth. Her mate had a cob on with her now, and she only had herself to blame. But how could she put things right? 'Your hair looks nice today, girl. Is that a new style? It suits yer, makes yer look a lot younger.'

'I'll give yer five marks for trying, sunshine, but yer'll not get round me so easily. Not this time, 'cos I'm cut to the quick.'

Flora came bustling in then, with a tray bearing steaming cups of tea and a plate with a variety of biscuits. This was a sight for sore eyes, and Nellie decided they were far more inviting than an apology to her mate.

'You're doing us proud today, Flora,' Molly said 'What are we celebrating?'

Flora set the cups in front of them before answering. She wanted to be seated when she told them her news, so she could see the look on their faces. 'Well, are yer ready for a big shock?'

Molly gave Nellie a gentle kick to remind her that this was supposed to be a complete surprise to them. 'We're ready, Flora. Feet firmly on the floor and hands steady on the table. So let's have it.'

'Inspector Willard was here yesterday, and yer'll never guess what he came for.'

'To tell yer they'd caught the blighter that robbed yer?' It was quick thinking on Molly's part. 'At least that's what I hope he called for.'

'Yeah, me too!' Nellie's face was as serious as she could muster. 'That would be really good news.'

'That would have been good news,' Flora said, 'but what the inspector brought was better than that.'

'Well, yer've got me stumped, sunshine, 'cos I can't think of any better news than catching the robber.'

Flora left her chair and walked to the sideboard. 'I won't tell yer, I'll show yer.'

Nellie played the role of her life. Her show of surprise when Flora stood between them at the table, and opened the box, was nothing short of perfection. 'Oh, my God, Flora, am I seeing things?' A hand to the throat as she'd seen Bette Davis do, she shook her head in feigned wonder. 'I can't believe it. Is this really the watch what was stolen?'

Flora, her hands shaking with emotion, nodded as she picked the watch out of the box. 'It's my Wally's watch all right.' She opened the back casing. 'Look, there he is.'

Molly had no intention of letting her mate get away with that

Bette Davis trick. She knew it was childish, but couldn't help trying to compete. 'He's as handsome as a film star, sunshine, and it's no wonder yer thought the world of him.' She put an arm round the old lady's waist, and squeezed gently. 'This is the best news I've had for a long time, and it hasn't sunk in yet. It's the last thing me and Nellie expected to hear, isn't it, sunshine?'

'It certainly is. I thought yer'd said goodbye to that for ever. How did the police get it back? Did the inspector tell yer?'

Flora rounded the table. 'I'll sit down while I tell yer. And then I'll make a fresh pot of tea, 'cos that one will be cold by then.'

The two mates listened to the tale in silence, except for the odd 'ah' or 'ooh'. They were surprised to learn the inspector had spent an hour with Flora, and was really kind and friendly. She had nothing but praise for him.

'He said he'd let me know if they catch the criminal, but didn't hold out much hope. Anyway, although I think everyone who does wrong should be punished, I'm just happy to have Wally's watch back. I feel nearer to him now. I know it sounds soppy coming from someone of my age, but my love for him is as strong today as it was the day we got married. And having his watch in my hand seems to bring him closer to me. I was so delighted when the inspector showed me why he'd called, I could have kissed him. It's the very best present that anyone could have given me.'

'I'm delighted for yer, sunshine, and I know Nellie is too. Someone up there is looking after you.'

'It'll be my Wally. I bet he's smiling now, knowing I'm happy.'

'I'm glad we decided to call,' Molly told her. 'It's wonderful news and I'm chuffed for yer. It was Nellie's idea really, she's the one who suggested we call before going to the shops. But I'm afraid we can't stay any longer 'cos I get me daughter's shopping in and it's almost closing time. So we'll love yer and leave yer, sunshine, if yer don't mind.'

'Not at all, sweetheart, you see to yer family. But yer will be coming to see me again, won't you?'

'Sure as eggs is eggs, girl,' Nellie told her. 'Remember, ye're my adopted mother now. Yer won't get rid of me that easy.'

The two mates were stepping on to the pavement when Flora said,

'I wouldn't want to get rid of either of yer. Not after yer were so good to me when I needed help. You take care now. Ta-ra.'

On Saturday morning, Irwin's was the last call for shopping, and as the mates stepped out of the shop Nellie said, 'There's Spencer Street across the road. It wouldn't take us five minutes to nip down and have a word with Ena, in the corner shop. Just to ask if she's heard any more about the shenanigans of the Blakesley lad.'

'That's an idea, sunshine, but don't make a meal of it, will yer, 'cos we haven't got a lot of time.'

They looked both ways before crossing the busy road, then linked arms to walk down Spencer Street. 'Let's stay on this side, girl, then we might be able to sneak a look in their window.'

'Oh, I don't fancy that, sunshine. They're not the sort of people I'd like to tangle with. Let's cross over and be on the safe side. We can still run our eyes over the house.'

Nellie whispered through her teeth, 'Ye're afraid of yer own shadow, you are. No one would dare lay a finger on yer when ye're with me.'

'Leave it, Nellie. We're nearing the house now.' Both women slid their eyes sideways, and both came to an abrupt halt. For the house they were looking at had no curtains on the window, and as they crossed the cobbled street they could see there was no furniture in the house. It was completely empty. 'Well, I'll be blowed,' Molly said. 'They've done a flit.'

The door of the next house opened and a woman stepped out. She had a basket over her arm and was clutching a purse. When she saw the two friends peering in the window, she said, 'If ye're looking for the Blakesleys, yer're out of luck. They did a moonlight flit last night, and am I glad! It's good riddance to bad rubbish. A bloke up the street was going on night shift at the docks, and he saw them loading what bit of furniture they had on to a handcart. Thank God for that, is what me and all the other neighbours are saying. They were a blot on this street, the neighbours from hell. I don't know what yer business was with them, but yer've missed them. I hope they didn't owe yer any money, 'cos if they did yer can say goodbye to it.'

Molly shook her head. 'We don't even know them, missus. We

saw the house looked empty and were nosy. A friend of ours is after a house in this area, and she asked us to keep our eyes open. That's all, love.'

Nellie pulled on her mate's arm. 'Come on, girl, we're late as it is.' They waited until the woman was out of earshot, then they looked at each other and grinned. 'Well, that's a turn up for the book,' Nellie said. 'But perhaps it's just as well, eh? They won't be robbing anyone else around here. We'll have to let Corker know.'

'I'll keep me eye out for him coming home from work, and fill him in with all the news. He's usually home half an hour later than Jack on a Saturday, so with a bit of luck me and Jack will have our dinner over before Corker comes. You can watch for him as well, and come down to ours. I don't want you moaning, and calling me a sneak for going behind yer back. Now Flora has got her watch back, and the Blakesleys are gone, we can put an end to the whole thing.'

Nellie didn't say so, but she was going to miss the excitement. Still, never mind. Something else would come along to keep her and Molly busy in the McDonough and Bennett Private Detective Agency.

Chapter Twenty Six

Most factories closed down at twelve thirty every Saturday, and it was a welcome break for manual workers whose jobs were tiring and monotonous. So when Jack arrived home at dinnertime, he was looking forward to a quiet afternoon and a peaceful Sunday, when he could sit in comfort in his fireside chair with his packet of Woodbines close to hand while he read the Sunday paper from cover to cover.

He let himself in, and slipped his jacket off while shouting through to the living room. 'I'm home, love.'

'I heard yer, sunshine,' Molly answered. 'I'm just seeing to the dinner. There's only you and me today. Yer know Ruthie's going straight into town after work, with Bella.'

Jack hung his coat up and walked through to the living room. 'Have I got time for a cigarette?'

'No, yer jolly well haven't! I'm just putting the dinner on the plates, and it won't kill yer to wait until we've eaten before yer light up.'

'Don't bite me head off, love, I was only asking.'

Molly carried two plates in, and set them down so she and Jack would be facing each other. 'It's bacon, sausage and egg, sunshine. I made it easy for meself. No point in making a pan of stew for just the two of us.'

'I'm glad yer did, love, 'cos I enjoy a fried meal. And I'm ready for it. I didn't realize I was so hungry until I smelt the bacon.'

Molly cut into a sausage, then dipped it into the soft yolk of the egg. 'Me and Nellie have had a busy morning, but I'm not going into details now. I'll wait until Corker and me mate are here.'

'Is Corker coming here?'

Molly nodded. 'He doesn't know it himself yet, but yes, he is coming. He's usually home later than you on a Saturday, so I'm hoping we've finished our dinner before he arrives. I'm going to keep me eye out for him passing the window, and I'll give him a knock. And Nellie's watching out for him as well.'

Jack chuckled. 'What have the pair of yer been up to now?'

'All in good time, sunshine. But as I said, there's no point in going through the whole story twice. As soon as Corker arrives, all will be revealed.'

'So what ye're telling me is, I've got to eat me dinner in double quick time?'

Molly pursed her lips, wagged her head from side to side and glanced at the clock. 'Yer don't have to choke yerself and gobble it down, sunshine. I reckon yer've got about ten minutes.'

All the love Jack Bennett had for his wife could be seen in his eyes, and the tenderness of his smile. 'Oh, that's bags of time, love. I bet you and me could have the dishes washed as well, by then.'

'I'll wash, sunshine, and you dry.' Molly returned his look of love. 'We make a good team, you and me. By the time Corker comes, we'll be sitting nice and comfortable, and no one would know about the mad dash we've had. You can be listening to the wireless, and I'll be knitting a tea cosy.'

Jack was speaking with his mouth full. Well, he had to if they were to be finished in time. 'I've never seen yer knitting a tea cosy, love.'

'No, and ye're not likely to! I did enough knitting when the children were little to last me a lifetime. I know me ma still uses a tea cosy, but I think they're a nuisance.' Molly popped the last piece of sausage in her mouth, then pushed her chair back. 'I've got the kettle on a low light, so there'll be hot water to wash these dishes in. I'll start, you finish eating yer dinner. If we're not finished when Corker gets home, why worry? He's not likely to give the place the once over.'

'You get cracking, love, and I'll be with yer in half a mo. Or d'yer want me to watch out for Corker?'

'No need to, sunshine, 'cos Nellie will have her eyes glued to the window. Corker wouldn't have time to get his key out before she was standing at the side of him. She's a woman of many talents, is my mate. She can see through walls and round corners, and is able to smell Elsie Flanaghan from half a mile away.'

Jack put his plate in the hot soapy water, and followed up with his knife and fork. 'I'll finish off here, love; you do what yer have to do in the living room. But yer need to wipe the side of yer mouth. Yer've left a bit of egg yolk there.'

Molly wiped a wet hand across her mouth. 'Nellie's often told me that one day I'd end up with egg on me face.'

'So that's another of yer mate's talents,' Jack said, as his hand searched the water for the dish cloth. 'Is there no end to what she can do?'

There came a loud rattling of a window pane, and Molly hurried to the door, shouting back to her husband over her shoulder, 'She's also clever at frightening the life out of me. Yer'll come home from work one day to find a big gaping hole where the window used to be.'

Molly had her hand on the latch when she heard Nellie say, 'Tell her it was you what knocked on the window, Corker, or she'll carry on something woeful.'

'Oh, Nellie, much as I love yer, me darlin', I don't want to get on the wrong side of Molly. I'm afraid ye're going to have to admit it was your fair hand that had the window frame rattling.'

Molly stood perfectly still, waiting to hear what her mate's reply would be. And a smile crossed her face when she heard the familiar voice.

'Well, is that all the thanks I get for standing like a ruddy lemon for the last half hour, waiting for yer?'

'But why were yer waiting for me, Nellie?' The big man was trying hard not to laugh at the contortions Nellie was putting her face through. 'It's very flattering, but if it happens again all the neighbours will be talking.'

'Sod the neighbours, I don't owe them nothing. And I'm not going to tell yer why I was standing like a lemon waiting for yer, not until we're inside.' Nellie put a finger to her lips and winked up at Corker. 'And neither of us will get inside until my mate turns the handle and opens the door. She's been standing there listening to every word we've said. She makes out she's holier than thou, but believe me, she's far from it.'

Dropping the smile from her face, Molly opened the door. 'Hello, Corker. I see yer've got yer shadow with yer again. The neighbours will be talking about you behind yer back, no matter what Nellie says. She doesn't worry about what neighbours and gossips say, but your Ellen will if she gets to hear that twice this week a female with a voluptuous body has been waiting for yer coming home from work. She'll have yer bags packed in three minutes flat, and she'll open the door wide and throw the lot into the street. You included.'

Nellie pretended to yawn. 'Oh dear, yer don't half carry on, missus, ye're sending me to sleep. Will yer step aside and let me and me boyfriend come in.'

When Corker followed Nellie up the steps, Molly winked, and said, 'I hope yer think what we've got to tell yer has been worth the effort. I believe yer will.'

In the living room, Jack said, 'I'll put the kettle on. I'm sure Corker could do with a drink after working all morning.'

'That's thoughtful of yer, Jack. I'd love a cup of tea. As yer know, Ellen works through her dinner hour on a Saturday.' Corker lowered his huge frame on to the couch. 'The kids will be in, but they'll make themselves a drink and a sandwich. We have our dinner when Ellen gets home.'

Nellie was carrying the carver chair from its speck by the sideboard to the dining table. 'I'll have a cuppa while ye're at it, Jack. If I'm going to be talking a lot, me mouth will get dry.'

Molly tutted. 'Ye're not backward in coming forward, are yer, sunshine? What excuse are yer going to give my feller when yer ask him to put a few biscuits on yer saucer? Yer can't say it's because yer mouth will be dry with talking, 'cos biscuits won't quench yer thirst, they'll make yer mouth more dry.'

'Oh, I don't want the biscuits for a dry mouth, girl,' Nellie said, her eyes rolling. 'I want them so I won't starve to death with hunger. Can't yer hear me tummy rumbling?'

'No, but I can hear the kettle whistling. I'll give Jack a hand with the cups, and I want you to be as quiet as a mouse while I'm in the kitchen. I know it's asking a lot of you, but could yer keep yer lips together for a few minutes? I don't want Corker to hear the news in bits and pieces, sunshine, I want us both to tell him the events in the order they happened.'

Nellie held a hand to her forehead as though giving the matter her consideration. Then she looked at her mate. 'I'll think about it, girl.'

Molly was willing to barter. 'Two custard creams in return for two minutes' silence?'

Nellie's face creased into a smile. 'Yer've got yerself a deal, girl.'

Corker guffawed. 'I don't know why anyone would want to go to the pictures when you two are funnier, and yer don't cost anything.'

Molly's head quickly appeared round the kitchen door. 'What d'yer mean, Corker, we don't cost anything? It costs me a fortune in custard creams. Being best mate with Nellie Mac doesn't come cheap.'

'Oh, she's not getting away with that,' Nellie told herself. The flaming cheek of her! 'Aren't yer forgetting something, Mrs Bennett? Yer've got a very convenient memory, you have. Yer only remember what yer want to remember. Why don't yer tell Corker about the tea and toasted teacake I bought yer? Served by a waitress what was wearing a little lace pinny, and a lace crown on her head. Proper posh it was, with a serviette to wipe the butter which ran down yer chin.'

Nellie turned to Corker. 'Living it up with the toffs we were, lad. Me and Molly were the only two women in that café what didn't have fur coats on. Not that it worried me, like, 'cos I'm used to toffs. In the street where I lived when I was going to school, the woman next door always had butter on her bread, not dripping like all the other neighbours. And she had jam on her bread every Sunday. So I do know how the other half live. I've tried to teach me mate about heticat, but it's like flogging a dead horse. She didn't even know which knife to use in Reece's, she was well out of her depth. Still, she's me mate and I had to stick up for her. The snobs on the next table soon stopped laughing at her when I gave them daggers. Stuck-up cows.'

There was complete silence in the room for a few seconds, then Molly's laughter bounced off the walls. 'Nellie, you are priceless. I don't know anyone who could have made that up without time to read their lines. That was worth every custard cream yer've ever had off me. And I'll never forget Reece's cup of tea and toasted teacake.

And d'yer know why I won't forget? Because yer ruddy well won't let me!'

Jack wondered if there was any truth at all in what Nellie had told them. 'Were all the women wearing fur coats? And did yer get mixed up over which knife to use, love?'

Molly had a stitch in her side with laughing, and she held a hand to it as she answered. 'I didn't see one woman wearing a fur coat, love. We'd have had to go in the restaurant on the next floor for that, where the real toffs go. And as for getting the knives mixed up, I'd have had a job because they only give yer one small knife to cut the teacake with. But Nellie's version of events was much funnier than any I could have come up with at such short notice.'

Corker wiped his eyes with a hankie which was as white as snow and as large as a tea towel. 'Yer should write a book, Nellie. You would make a lot of money.' He grinned. 'I'd buy one.'

Nellie chuckled. 'I would do, lad, if I could spell. I'd fancy being famous and rich. But I've got a very good idea what has just come to me. I could tell me mate what to write, and she could do it for me. The book would have to be in my name, of course, but I'd share some of the money with her. That's if she behaved herself.'

'We'll discuss your desire to become a teller of tales another time, sunshine. Right now I believe Corker would be more interested in the real life tale we have to tell him. The reason for him being here now.'

'Hang on a minute,' Jack said. 'What happened to the tea we promised Corker? I know the kettle boiled, but I don't remember whether the tea ever got made.'

'It didn't, sunshine, and yer can thank Nellie for that. Once she started talking, everything else was forgotten. But it won't take long to boil the kettle again; we can have cups of tea on the table in a matter of minutes. But I think it would be a good idea to put a scarf round Nellie's mouth to shut her up. Otherwise she'll be taking us on another journey with one of her fantasies.'

'You can do that, love.' Jack put his hands up to protect himself. 'I'll see to the tea.'

* * *

'I'll let you start, girl,' Nellie said. 'Then yer can't say I talk too much. But I'll help yer out if yer get stuck, and pull yer up if yer get anything wrong.'

They finally had their cups of tea in front of them, and were ready to start. Jack and Corker sat at one side of the table, with Molly facing them, and Nellie in her favourite chair at the end of the table.

'I don't know where to start,' Molly said. 'There's so much happened I'm afraid of leaving something out.'

Corker nudged Jack. 'I suppose you've been told the latest news, have yer?'

'Have I heck! When I asked Molly what you and Nellie were coming for, and why I had to dash me dinner down, I was told that all would be revealed as soon as you arrived. That there was no point in going over the story twice.'

'She put yer in yer place, did she, lad?' Nellie was feeling mischievous. She wasn't in a hurry, and wanted to stretch the proceedings out as long as she could. That was why she generously offered to let Molly speak first. 'Yer want to put yer foot down with her, or she'll be wearing the trousers next.'

'I know what ye're up to, sunshine, but ye're not on. Yer want to spend the afternoon here to pass the time away. Well, whether yer like it or not, you and me have got things to do this afternoon which won't wait. So try and keep yer lips close together while I fill Corker and Jack in with the news.'

Nellie looked pained, or tried to. 'What have we got to do this afternoon that can't wait?'

'Sadie's wedding present, that's what. And don't ask any more questions 'cos I won't answer them. Corker has been here so long he's taken root, so behave yerself.'

Nellie lowered her head and could be heard muttering, 'I should never have said she could go first, 'cos the power has gone to her head.'

Molly ignored her, for time was moving on, and she wanted to go to the sweet shop for some decent wrapping paper for Sadie's present. Then get the tram to the market to hand it to the girl she'd grown fond of. They might not have time to spare next week, and she didn't think she could hand the present over at the church.

'We called to Flora's yesterday, Corker, and yer've never seen such a change in anyone. She looks a different woman, now she's got her husband's watch back. I don't believe she will ever know the truth about how it came to be back in her possession because we can't tell her, it would spoil the happiness she now has. But if she did find out, I know one thing for certain. You would be a hero to her, and she'd love you for the rest of her life.'

Molly went on to repeat everything Flora had said, and how she had a permanent smile on her face. How she praised Inspector Willard for his kindness to her. 'All she was told was that it had been handed in at the police station. And I think that should be the end of it. We've all played a part in giving her the one thing in life she wanted, some a bigger part than others, and I believe we can congratulate ourselves. And because I know you would like to see Flora, Corker, I'll ask yer ma to walk round there with yer one night for a visit. That would be a happy ending to the story.'

Molly turned to Nellie. 'You can take over now, sunshine, 'cos ye're right about getting a dry mouth when yer talk too much. Start by telling the men what we did when we came out of Irwin's shop this morning.'

Nellie wriggled her bottom until she was sitting on the edge of the chair. Her legs swinging, she rested her bosom on the table and circled it with her arms. 'This is going to come as a big surprise to yer, Corker, so hang on to yer hat.'

Molly tapped her on the shoulder. 'In case yer haven't noticed, sunshine, Corker hasn't got his hat on. It's on the sideboard.'

Nellie glared. 'Then the bleeding sideboard had better hang on to it! And if yer don't mind, girl, no more interruptions, please. I kept me gob shut when you had the floor, so kindly keep your gob shut now.' She held her head in her hand. 'Yer've put me off me stroke now. I don't know where I was up to.'

'Yer hadn't started, me darlin',' Corker told her. 'So begin at the beginning. That's always the best place to start.'

'Good thinking, lad, good thinking.' Nellie, accompanied by her chins, nodded knowingly. 'Well, me and me mate had just come out of the shop when I reminded her that Spencer Street was just across the road. And I asked her if it wouldn't be a good idea if we called in on Ena, that old neighbour of mine. The one what has the corner shop. Me mate wasn't exactly over the moon with the idea, but she gave in, and we crossed over to Spencer Street. And yer'll never guess what we saw when we came to the Blakesleys' house.'

Corker showed interest and leaned forward. 'What were they up to, Nellie? Were they fighting, causing trouble with the neighbours?'

'No, ye're not even warm, lad. Have another guess.'

Molly huffed. 'This is not a guessing game, Nellie, and Corker hasn't got all day. Tell him what we saw.'

'We didn't see nothing, girl!'

'And why didn't we see nothing, sunshine?'

Nellie was getting ratty now. She should never have let Molly tell the first part of the story, 'cos she had all the juicy bits. 'We didn't see nothing 'cos there was nothing to see. The bleeding house was empty.'

Molly raised a hand when she saw Corker open his mouth to speak. 'Leave it, Corker, I'll get Nellie to tell yer this bit if it kills me.' Her smile fixed, she looked at her mate. 'This is the part Corker will like, so tell him why the house was empty.'

The light dawned. 'Oh, yeah, silly me, I remember now why the house was empty. See, Corker, the Blakesleys had done a moonlight flit. Me and Molly were looking through the window when the woman next door came out and told us they'd done a flit last night. Put what bits of furniture they had on a handcart, and buggered off. The woman said all the neighbours were glad to see the back of them.'

Corker was thoughtful as he stroked his moustache. 'That is certainly a surprise. We put a halt to their gallop all right. They'll have moved to another district, and they won't show their faces round here again. We must have put the fear of God into them. Heaven help the next lot of neighbours they get. It would be good if we could warn them, but that would complicate matters. Anyway, they may have been taught a lesson and might change their ways. Not the father, he's too ruddy lazy to change. But the boy could turn over a new leaf and get himself a job. And the same could happen to the manager of the pub, and the pawnbroker. They nearly got their fingers burned, so perhaps the fear of losing their jobs will have given them food for thought. Who knows, they could stay on the straight and narrow path in future.'

'They're fools if they don't,' Jack said. 'My ma used to say that crooks never prosper, and she was right. But the main thing here is that Flora got her watch back. It was worth all the trouble you three went through to get it. It's a story with a happy ending.'

'Ooh, me husband is going all sloppy,' Molly said, leaving her chair to give Jack a hug. 'Ye're right, sunshine, it is a happy ending, and we can go back to our normal daily tasks knowing we've done a bit of good. And our daily tasks are going to start right now. You two men can sit and have a chinwag, with a ciggy in yer hands, and a pot of tea on the table that Jack will make. Or does the pub sound more to yer liking?'

'Molly, me darlin', ye're a mind reader. If Jack will put his coat on, we'll be up to the corner pub and leave you and Nellie to go on your errands. But first I must thank both of you ladies for the part you've played, the tips you've given me, and for keeping me informed. I take my hat off to yer, and next week when all the gang are having a night out while Ruthie is having her party, well, the drinks are on me.'

Nellie sat to attention. 'That's what I like to hear, lad. Just line the bar with bottles of milk stout and me and Molly will get drunk.'

'Ay, less of that,' Molly said. 'I've never been drunk in me life and I'm not starting now.' She wagged a finger. 'And you can get off that throne of yours, 'cos we're off to the shops. I want to be in when Ruthie gets back from town. I'm dying to see the dress and shoes she's bought. So, off yer backside, sunshine, and we'll be on our way.'

'What do we have to buy paper for, when the towels are already in a bag?' Nellie was doing a hop, skip and jump to keep up with Molly. 'It's a waste of money.'

'Nellie, if we're giving a wedding present to a girl we like, and who has been good to us, then the least we can do is make it look presentable in nice wrapping paper.'

Nellie grunted. 'She'll only throw it away, so I don't see why we should bother.'

Molly lost her patience. 'Okay, then, Nellie, you have it your way and I'll have mine. There's two towels and one bag. You keep your towel in the bag, and I'll buy paper to wrap mine in. I hope that satisfies yer.'

Nellie put on her bulldog face. 'How much is this paper ye're talking about, and where d'yer get it from?'

'If yer used yer eyes, Nellie, yer would have seen it in the sweet shop. They have it hanging up, in different colours, and it costs tuppence a sheet.'

'No thank you, I'll stick to the paper bag. I'm not paying tuppence for a piece of paper. If I put a penny to it, I could buy meself a cream slice.'

'Have it yer own way, sunshine. It's no skin off my nose.'

But when Nellie saw the fancy paper, she changed her mind. She watched as Molly took one of the towels out of the paper bag, and coaxed the girl behind the counter to wrap it in the wedding paper for her. And when Molly moved away from the counter, Nellie moved in. 'Here yer are, girl, yer can wrap mine up like yer've done me mate's.' She plonked two pennies down. 'And don't crease the paper.'

'You changed yer mind quick, didn't yer?' Molly said when they were outside the shop. 'Did yer have a guilty conscience?'

'Was it heckers like a guilty conscience! You'd have made me look like a poor relation, girl, and I wasn't having that.'

Molly pinched her mate's chubby cheek. 'Good for you, sunshine, and now if we catch this tram we'll be there and back from the market in no time. I'm not looking for anything to buy; we'll give Sadie her presents then scarper.'

Molly need not have worried about being long at the market, for Sadie and Mary Ann were run off their feet. There was no time for a conversation, so Molly and Nellie waited until Sadie came down to the stall, and they passed their presents over. 'They're not much, Sadie, 'cos we're not rolling in money. But we wanted yer to know we appreciate the way yer've looked after us. We look on you and Mary Ann as friends, don't we, Nellie?'

Nellie nodded. 'We sure do, girl. And we're looking forward to seeing yer getting married next Saturday.'

Sadie held the presents close to her chest. 'Yer shouldn't have bothered, but I'm glad yer did. I'll give yer a big hug next time I see yer. I hope ye're definitely coming to the church, 'cos I want yer to meet my lovely Harry.'

'We wouldn't miss your wedding for a big clock, sunshine,' Molly told her. 'Yer'll be a beautiful bride.' She waved a hand to Mary Ann, who had just spotted them. 'Tell Mary Ann we couldn't stay to talk to her, but we'll see yer both at the church next Saturday at twelve o'clock. Have a good week, and enjoy yer wedding. It'll be the best day of yer life, and yer have my word on that. Ta-ra for now, sunshine.'

Nellie nodded. 'You take care now, girl, and do as me mate said. Ta-ra.'

Chapter Twenty Seven

There was a strong wind blowing when Ruthie and Bella came out of the factory gates, and both girls shivered. But because they were so excited, the cold weather wasn't going to be allowed to spoil the first day they really felt grown up. 'There's a tram coming,' Ruthie said, 'let's run for it. We might have to wait ages for another to come along, and we'd freeze to death.'

So, holding hands, the girls ran towards the stop, and reached it just as the tram shuddered to a halt. 'I'm staying downstairs,' Bella said, being first to board the platform. 'It's too cold to climb those stairs.'

'There's an empty seat at the back,' Ruthie told her, pushing her friend down the aisle. 'You can have the window seat into town, and I'll have it on the way home.'

The conductor came along clicking his ticket machine, and calling, 'Tickets, please. And can yer have the right money ready?'

Ruthie and Bella had the fare clutched in their hands, and they passed it over. They watched the conductor turn the small silver handle on the ticket machine, and both giggled and blushed when he said, 'The sight of two pretty girls has warmed the cockles of me heart.' Then he went down the aisle collecting fares, leaving the two young girls very happy.

'D'yer know which stop to get off?' Bella asked. 'I'm relying on you, 'cos I haven't got a clue. I've only been into town a few times, and that was with me mam. I'd be lost if I was on me own.'

'Well, ye're not on yer own, soft girl, are yer? If we stick together we'll be fine. Me mam said the big shops in Church Street would be expensive, and we should try London Road first,' Ruthie said, her tummy doing somersaults with excitement. She had her wage packet in her handbag, and the two pound ten shillings it contained was all hers. She'd never had so much money in her life. 'The conductor will shout out when we get to London Road, so we'll take me mam's advice and get off there. We're in no hurry, so we can take our time and look in a few shops.'

'My mam said there was a Co-op shop there, and they sell clothes and everything.' Bella was half excited and half nervous. She wasn't as outgoing as her friend, for being an only child she'd been mollycoddled all her life by an over-protective mother. 'Shall we try there?'

Ruthie tossed her head, and her long blonde hair fanned out. 'We can try, there's no harm in that. If we don't see anything we like, we can walk out and try another shop. I'm not buying a dress just for the sake of it, I want one I really, really like. And I know what kind of dance shoes I want, as well.' She grinned into the face of the girl she'd been best friends with since they could toddle. That friendship had lasted all through their school years, and they'd even been able to secure jobs in the same factory. 'I want silver shoes with straps, and heels an inch and a half.' She giggled. 'Amy in work, she goes dancing nearly every night, and she said her dance shoes have got three-inch heels.'

'Is Amy the girl with ginger hair, who works in the dye room?'

'Yes, she's dead funny when yer get to know her. But can yer imagine you and me tottering around on three-inch heels? I couldn't walk in them, never mind dance.'

'Your Doreen always wore high heels,' Bella said. 'I used to think she looked like a film star with her long blonde hair, smashing figure and those shoes.'

'What about our Jill?' Ruthie wasn't having anyone favour one of her sisters over the other. 'She's beautiful, is our Jill, inside as well as outside.'

Bella nodded. 'I know that. I've always loved Jill, 'cos she's so gentle. I don't think I've ever heard her raise her voice. When Doreen was about our age, I used to hear her being stubborn with your mam over being out late, but never Jill.'

Ruthie agreed with a chuckle. 'Doreen was always arguing. She was hot-headed and always thought she was right. But she's changed a lot since she got married. In fact she changed from the night she met Phil at Barlows Lane dance hall. It was love at first sight for both of them.'

The conductor's voice called, 'Next stop, London Road.'

'Ooh, that's us.' Ruthie was down the aisle before anyone else left their seats, and she was standing on the pavement when Bella jumped down from the platform. 'What took yer so long, slow coach?'

'I had to let the other passengers get off,' Bella said. 'I couldn't push them out of the way. As me mam keeps telling me, if I want to grow up to be a lady, I'd better start acting like one.' She looked up at the building behind where her friend was standing. 'That's the Co-op store me mam was talking about. Shall we go in?'

'May as well, girl, as Auntie Nellie would say. We won't get anywhere standing gawping at it.' Ruthie always took into consideration her friend's shyness, and she now held her arm out. 'Stick yer leg in, Bella, and then we won't lose each other.'

'No fear of yer losing me, I'm going to stick to you like glue. Where you go, I go.'

'Don't forget we're not buying our dresses in here. We'll have a look round, see what they've got, then look in other shops. That way we'll have plenty of choice. There's shops both sides of the road, so we'll see what they've got. Then if we see a dress we fancy we'll remember which shop we saw it in, and come back if we don't see anything we like better. Don't yer think that's a good idea? It's better than buying the first ones we see.'

'Have yer made up yer mind what colour yer'd like? I think blue for me, 'cos it suits me.'

'I haven't thought what colour I'd like,' Ruthie said. 'I'll know the dress I want, as soon as I see it. Colour doesn't really matter. Mind you, bright red is out, and black, 'cos me mam would have something to say. I can guess what she'd say, that red was common and black for funerals.'

Bella jerked on her friend's arm. 'Look, there's a shoe shop over the road. Shall we have a look, then we can compare the shoes there with any other shops?'

'That's a good idea,' Ruthie said. 'We'd kick ourselves if we bought a pair of dance shoes in one shop, then saw some we liked better in another shop. And we're not in a hurry; we've got a couple of hours to browse around.'

London Road was a busy road, with trams and buses running in both directions. The girls stayed close to the kerb until there was a break in the traffic, then they made a dash to the shoe shop on the opposite side. But their faces fell when they looked in the window, for half the window was taken up by a display of men's shoes for every occasion. Brogues, heavy working shoes and boots, and walking shoes in fine leather. They were arranged on three of the tiered shelves, the first to catch the eye of window shoppers. Below them, there were two shelves of women's shoes. Those, like the men's shoes, were in brown and black, with Cuban heels. Some were lace-up, and others adorned with a silver buckle.

'There's nothing here for us,' Ruthie said, disappointment in her voice. 'They're all old-fashioned, like me mam and Auntie Nellie wear. They've got no young styles at all.'

Bella had been peering through a side window. 'They've got a lot more shoes inside, and I'm sure I can see a pair of silver dance shoes on top of a shoe box.'

Ruthie joined her friend, and they pressed their noses to the window. 'Oh, yeah, I can see them. But what's the use of one pair? I want the chance of choosing from a selection.'

'It's a big shop inside,' Bella insisted. 'They can't show all their shoes in the window. It wouldn't hurt to go in and ask about the dance shoes. They may have more in the stockroom. And you're the one who said we'd try all the shops, then go back to the one where we liked the shoes best.'

'Oh, go on then, let's go in. But whether I'll have the nerve to ask to see what dance shoes they've got in stock, and then walk out without buying, well, I'm not sure. I know I'm cheeky, but not that cheeky.'

'You could always say we've got shopping to do, and will call back later,' Bella said hopefully. 'I mean, it might be true. For all we know they may have a good selection in the storeroom. We can't tell by standing outside.'

'You're not as soft as yer look, Bella Watson, are yer? Yer've got it all worked out in yer head, but yer want me to do the dirty work! I'll go in with yer, if you do the talking. I dare yer.'

Bella took a deep breath before rising to the occasion. She'd always envied her friend for her ability to hold her own in any situation. How often she'd lain awake at night promising herself she'd come out of her shell the next day. Well, it was now or never. 'Okay, I'll do the talking for a change.'

'Now, this is something I've got to see,' Ruthie said, putting a hand on her friend's back. 'Lead on, McDuff, and I'll follow.'

There were two assistants in the shop, one an older man and the other a woman in her late twenties. Both were attending to customers who were sitting on low stools, trying on shoes with the help of the assistants and shoehorns. The two young girls stood just inside the door and the longer they stood the faster their confidence evaporated. Bella was whispering in Ruthie's ear that they should leave when the female assistant smiled and said, 'I'll be with you in a minute.' Then, true to her word, she left the woman she was attending to, who couldn't make up her mind between two pair of shoes, and approached the girls. 'Can I help you?'

Swallowing hard, Bella told her, 'We were wondering if you have any dance shoes? Silver ones?'

'We don't have a big selection,' the assistant said. 'But if you'd like to take a seat, I'll show you what we have in stock.'

There was little the friends could do but sit down. And as they did so, Ruthie whispered, 'Next time yer have a bright idea, Bella Watson, keep it to yerself.'

But Ruthie was soon to eat her words, for the assistant came out of the stockroom carrying four boxes. 'These are the only styles we have in at the moment, and I'm afraid we only have them in sizes five and six. Have a look and see if you like them, while I attend to the other customer, who seems to have made up her mind which pair she prefers.'

'You take them out of the box, Ruthie,' Bella said. 'It says size five on the box, and we both take that size.'

The first and second box didn't appeal to the girls, but when Ruthie took the lid off the next box, both girls gasped with delight. 'Ooh, these are more like it,' Ruthie said. 'They're exactly like the ones I've had in me mind. Four straps and a heel that's not flat, but not too high. Ooh, I wonder how much they are?'

'I hope there's not going to be any argument, Ruthie, but I like them as well. And we can't very well wear the same shoes when we go dancing.'

'Why not? Most girls wear silver shoes, so unless they get down on their knees, no one will notice ours are exactly the same. And even if they did, so what? It won't bother me. Would it bother you?'

Bella shook her head. 'No, not at all. But you said we weren't going to buy in the first shop, we were going to look around before deciding.'

'I know I did, Bella, but that was me big mouth talking. I'm showing off because I've got me wage packet in me handbag, and all the money in it is for me to spend. It's like a dream and I'll soon come down to earth with a bump. But about these dance shoes, I don't see any point in looking in other shops when these are like the ones I've had in me head. It depends how much they are, 'cos I want to make sure I've got enough for a nice dress. What about you?'

'I'll go along with you. I want a really special dress for the party. And I'm hoping you'll do me hair for me that night, so I'll look me best. I don't want you looking all glamorous, and me like the country bumpkin.'

'Don't worry, I'll make sure ye're all dolled up, and Peter won't be able to take his eyes off yer.' Ruthie grinned into her friend's face. 'Now, back to these shoes. Can yer see any price on the box?'

The girls were holding a shoe each, and the box was on the floor. 'I can't see a price, but there might be one. I don't like picking the box up to look. Anyway, the assistant will be over now, 'cos she's just giving the customer her change.'

The assistant had a pleasant face, and she smiled as she approached the girls. 'Have you seen any you like?'

Ruthie held the silver shoe up. 'We both like these. How much are they?'

'Seven shillings and elevenpence,' the assistant told them. 'They're the dearest, the others are only five and eleven.'

Both girls were delighted. They'd expected them to be ten shillings at least. Ruthie was so pleased she told the woman, 'Me and me friend are sixteen next week, and our mothers have given us the money to buy a new dress and dance shoes. We'll be going to our first dance soon.'

Their pleasure and excitement rubbed off on to the assistant and cheered her up. 'That's nice for you. I hope you both have a happy birthday. And those are nice shoes you're holding, very pretty and smart. You won't find any better.'

'Yes, we're both buying a pair, aren't we, Bella? We're best mates, and we live opposite each other.' Ruthie put on a serious face and announced. 'From next Saturday we'll be young ladies, not girls.'

Bella gave her a dig. 'You looked just like yer Auntie Nellie then. Except yer didn't swear.'

The assistant held out her hands. 'Give me the shoes and I'll wrap them for you.'

'We're both made up with them,' Ruthie told her. 'I hope we're as lucky in getting dresses we like. Can you tell us the best shops to go to?'

'Well, there's T. J. Hughes opposite, and the Co-op. Then there's two shops as you go down towards the centre of town.' The woman hesitated for a second, then said. 'There's also a shop on the other side of the road, and that's the one I buy all my dresses from. It's a one-woman business, but she has some fashionable clothes at reasonable prices. And she's patient, she lets you take your time, and if she doesn't think a dress suits you, she'll tell you so.'

'Where did you say the shop was?' Ruthie asked. 'We could try there first.'

'If you cross the road and walk down a bit, you'll come to a café called Samson and Barlow. You can't miss it, it's got a sign above the window. And right next door yer'll find the shop I told you about. It's worth a try. And now, if you come to the till, I'll put the shoes in a bag and take your money.'

Both girls offered ten shilling notes, and they seemed to grow in stature as they held out their hands for the change. It was the first time they'd spent so much money in a shop without being accompanied by their mothers. When they thanked the assistant, who had been helpful and friendly, she said, 'Tell the lady in the dress shop that Veronica sent you, and she'll treat you well.'

Once outside the shop, the friends looked at each other and grinned. 'Ay, we did well there,' Ruthie said, already feeling like a young lady. 'I thought the shoes would have cost a lot more.' She linked Bella's arm and squeezed. 'We've still got two pound two and a penny. We should get a really nice dress for that.'

'I'm really enjoying meself. It's great going shopping when yer can buy what yer like. When I've been out with me mam, I've always ended up getting what she liked, not what I liked.'

The friends stood on the kerb, and as soon as a double decker bus passed they made a dash across the road. 'We could get a bus home if yer like, instead of a tram,' Bella said. 'There's a stop here that would take us to the top of our street.'

Ruthie was looking at the signs on the shops they were passing. 'I'd rather go on a tram, but we'll take a bus if yer prefer. Makes no odds to me.' She suddenly pulled her friend to a halt. 'This is the café, Samson and Barlow. And there's the dress shop next door. There's not much in the window, though, only a couple of dresses, skirts and blouses.'

'There's probably a lot more inside, otherwise the woman wouldn't have told us about it.' Bella was growing in confidence by the minute. 'If we don't try, we'll never know. And if we've got any money over after we've bought a dress, why don't we be daring and go the whole hog?'

Ruthie's eyes widened in surprise. 'Ay, you're getting cocky, aren't yer? For all you know, we mightn't have enough money for a dress, never mind have some over. And what did yer mean by going the whole hog?'

Bella was feeling as free as a bird when she answered, 'If we've got any money over, we could go next door for a scone and cup of tea. Wouldn't it be great, you and me sipping tea with the hoity-toity? We'd have a lot to tell Peter, Gordon and Jeff.'

Ruthie could feel her friend's new-found confidence and pleasure rubbing off on her, and she was laughing as she nodded her head. 'If we don't have enough money left after buying our dresses, we could go in the café, sit down, and when the waitress comes over we could ask for one cup of tea and two straws.'

The girls were still laughing when they entered the shop, and their pleasure brought a smile to the face of the owner. She moved towards them. 'How nice it is to see two happy faces on such a cold day. A smile is always more welcome than a frown.'

'It's the first time me and me friend have been shopping together, with no warnings from our parents about what we should or shouldn't buy. We're both sixteen next week, and we've been allowed to keep our wages as a birthday present.' Ruthie liked the look of the women, who seemed friendly and kind. But it wouldn't do to tell her how much money they had, for then she could price a dress to suit their purse. Not that she would do that, but better to be sure than sorry. 'Not that it's a lot of money, like, 'cos we don't earn much, but it's the freedom to spend it as we wish, on dresses of our choice.'

The woman nodded. 'I understand, dear. It's a long time ago, but I was once your age. So I'll let you look round to see if there's any dresses you like. I would suggest you start in the room at the back, there are racks out there you can go through. Most of the dresses in this room are expensive and more suited to mature ladies. The dresses on the racks all have a price tag on, so you'll know which you can afford.'

As the girls were walking through an archway to the room behind, Ruthie turned. 'Oh, I nearly forgot, we were told to say Veronica sent us.'

The room they walked into was lined with racks of dresses in every size, colour and style. It was like a wonderland to the two girls, who put the shoe bags on the floor while they searched through the racks. They were going for colours they liked, then slowed down so they could take the hangers off the rails and examine the dresses more thoroughly. Ruthie was the first to give a low cry of delight.

'Oh, look at this one, Bella, isn't it gorgeous?' The dress she held up had a white background, with patterns of blue, red and turquoise bows dotted in the cotton material. It had a nipped-in waist, full skirt, cap sleeves, and a V-shaped neck. 'Don't yer think it's lovely?'

'Yes, it's really attractive. How much does it say on the price tag?'

Ruthie forgot where she was in her excitement, and holding the dress to her she twirled around, half laughing and half singing. 'It's only nineteen and eleven, and aren't I a lucky girl?'

Bella giggled. 'Don't act daft, the woman will think we're both crazy. I hope I can find one for that price, then we'll both have enough for lipstick and powder.'

'I'll help yer look for one,' Ruthie said. 'What colour did yer say yer wanted?'

'I suit blue better than any other colour.'

'Then we'll look for a blue one.' Ruthie was running a hand along the rail of dresses, with the dress she'd fallen for over her arm. When she turned to say something to Bella, she noticed her friend was holding a blue dress as she followed Ruthie along the rail. 'What's the dress yer've got over yer arm? That's a nice shade of blue. Don't yer like the style?'

'I picked it off the rail because I liked the colour, but I haven't had a good look at it yet. You put me off, acting daft and dancing.'

'Then you're more daft than me! Yer've got me looking for a blue dress, and yer've got one over yer arm! Open it up and let's see.'

Bella got herself all hot and bothered as the dress hanger got in the way when she tried to hold the dress up to her neck. 'D'yer think I can take the hanger out, so I can hold it against me, like you did with yours?'

'What are you like, Bella Watson?' Ruthie said, tutting and shaking her head. 'Turn the hanger down as I did. Here, let me do it for yer or we'll be here all day.' She stood back when she'd sorted her friend out, and after gazing for a few seconds, she said, 'Bella, it's beautiful. Honest, it's a lovely dress and the colour suits yer.' The dress had three-quarter sleeves, a pleated bodice, nipped-in waist, and a full skirt. 'I'm dead serious, Bella, it's a lovely dress.'

Bella's face lit up. 'Can we try them on to see whether they fit proper? I really do like this one, so I hope it fits.'

She hadn't finished speaking when Ruthie disappeared, only to come back with the shop owner. 'We can try them on, the lady said.'

The woman, who was very smartly dressed, smiled at the pleasure she saw in the young girls' faces. She pointed to a narrow passageway at the side of the room. 'There are two fitting rooms down there, so you can try your dresses on in there. And there's a mirror in each, so you can see if you like them once you have them on. Come out when you're ready, so I can satisfy myself that they are the right dresses for you.'

Considering Bella was always the quiet one, she was now making up for lost time. She never stopped chattering over the partition dividing the two fitting rooms, and Ruthie, who had always protected her friend from the bullies at school, was delighted Bella was coming out of her shell.

The two fitting room doors opened at the same time, and the girls looked each other up and down before bursting out laughing. 'I think I look devastatingly lovely,' Ruthie said, her nose in the air. 'The boys will be falling at my feet.'

Bella's nose took to the air to match her friend. 'And I look tantalizingly adorable. I don't want all the boys falling at my feet, only Peter.'

Together, the mates walked through to the front of the shop, where two customers were deliberating on the attractions of one dress above another. The owner smiled and walked towards the girls. 'I'm not going to sway you one way or the other. But in my opinion you both look lovely. However, it is how you feel that is important, so don't let me alter your decision.'

Both girls spoke as one. 'We love them, and are going to buy them.' Ruthie's tummy was churning with excitement. 'We're going to knock the boys for six.'

Bella's dress was the same price as Ruthie's, and very soon they were standing outside the shop with a bag in each hand. 'What a wonderful day, eh, Bella?' Ruthie said. 'And as we've got over a pound each left in our purses, let's push the boat out and treat ourselves to a pot of tea in the café? What d'yer say?'

'Yes, let's live it up for the day,' Bella agreed. 'Let's celebrate our first day as grown-ups.'

The girls didn't speak much during their very first visit to a café where the customers were well dressed and spoke in hushed voices. They were enjoying the experience, though, of being served by a waitress, and drinking out of posh cups. They also had a scone each, served with butter and jam in small, separate dishes, and this made them feel very grand, mixing with the hoity-toity.

Ruthie was taking in what was going on around her when Bella said, 'If I say something, or ask yer something, will yer promise not to bite me head off?'

'Anyone would think I was a bully, and yer were frightened of me,' Ruthie said, surprised by her friend's words. 'When have I ever bitten yer head off? Go on, admit I never have. Then tell me what's on yer mind.'

'Well, our dresses and shoes are really nice, and I'm over the moon with them. But I was just thinking they wouldn't show up well in the house. I'd like to show them off to advantage, somewhere where they can really be seen. And I wondered if, instead of having a party next Saturday, would our mothers let us go dancing with the boys? We could really show off in a dance hall.'

Ruthie looked taken aback, then thoughtful, before a huge smile lit up her face. 'Ooh, that's a good idea, Bella! Ay, ye're not just a pretty face, are yer? I think it's a brilliant idea, and don't know why I never thought of it.' She clasped her hands together. 'Oh, yeah, the more I think of it, the more I like it. Shall we finish our tea, pay the bill, and make our way home? I'll get round me mam, and she can talk your mam into it. Oh, boy, I could kiss yer.'

Bella smiled. She knew her idea would bear fruit, 'cos Mrs B could always get round her mam. So roll on next Saturday, when she and Ruthie went to their first dance.

Chapter Twenty Eight

'Have yer got time for a cup of tea this morning, Mam?' Doreen asked on the Monday. 'It's ages since you and Auntie Nellie were both here, telling us all yer news and gossip.'

'Well, it's not our fault, sunshine, 'cos yer wouldn't let us in when Bobby was poorly. But we're not in a hurry this morning, so we can relax for half an hour and get reacquainted with the baby.' Molly took her coat off and laid it over the arm of the couch. 'He looks the picture of health and happiness on Victoria's lap, but I'm going to pinch him off her so I can cuddle him.'

Doreen looked at Nellie, who was standing with her coat still on, and her eyes narrowed. 'You're very quiet, Auntie Nellie. Yer haven't opened yer mouth since yer came in.'

'Well, I haven't had much chance, have I, girl? Yer mother hasn't shut her mouth long enough to breathe. I was beginning to feel like the invisible woman. Now I ask yer, girl, where are her manners?'

Molly, busy tickling the baby's tummy to make him squeal with laughter, looked at her friend and chuckled. 'I left me manners on the sideboard, sunshine. I picked up the door key, and me purse, but forgot me manners. So I humbly apologize to yer, and beg your forgiveness.'

Doreen helped Nellie off with her coat, and whispered in her ear, 'I'll hang yer coat up, Auntie Nellie, and my good manners will make up for me mam. She didn't mean to leave you out, it was because she was so happy to be able to hold Bobby again. He's her first grandchild and she's been missing him.'

'If yer think yer can get round me by making excuses, girl, then ye're not on. I've been missing the baby just as much as she has, yer know.'

'I'll let you have a turn in a minute, sunshine,' Molly said, 'so don't be getting yer knickers in a twist. You can hold him while I fill Doreen and Victoria in with all the latest news.'

'You can just sod off, Molly Bennett, if yer think I'm going to baby-sit your grandson while you sit and have a good gossip. Yer must think I need me brains testing! If there's any news and gossip, I want to hear it.'

'Oh, he's my grandson when it suits yer, is it? And *our* grandson when ye're in the mood. It's a fickle woman you are, Nellie McDonough, but seeing as ye're me best mate I'll forgive yer.'

Nellie took up her stubborn stance, with feet planted firmly on the ground, chubby hands on wide hips, and narrow, glaring eyes. 'What did you just say I was, Molly Bennett? If it's what I thought it was, then yer'd better put the baby down in case he gets hurt when I belt yer one.'

Victoria's rocking chair picked up speed as she waited in anticipation of the antics to come. She'd missed the two mates over the last ten days, for they were a tonic to her. Better than a dose of medicine any day.

Molly lifted the baby up in the air, which brought forward gurgling and baby laughter. 'Shall I ask yer Grandma McDonough what she thinks I said, eh, sunshine? Her answer should be very interesting. I bet she doesn't know.'

'Oh, I heard yer all right, girl, I haven't got cloth ears. Yer said I was a fat little woman – me, yer very best mate. I've a good mind to pulverize yer. It's only the baby what is holding me back.'

Molly handed the baby over to Doreen, then put her arms round Nellie. 'I didn't say yer were a little fat woman, sunshine. I said yer were a fickle woman, and there's a big difference. If only yer'd listened to yer English teacher at school, it would have made life much easier for me.'

Nellie's face took on a look of innocence. 'I did listen to her, girl, when I was in the classroom. But I spent most of the time in the corridor for talking in class. So yer see, it was me English teacher's fault I can't speak proper English. She kept sending me out of the class.'

'Ah, you poor, hard done by, put upon girl. I bet if it hadn't been for your teacher, who couldn't see further than the end of her nose, that you would have been Prime Minister by now. Or, at the

298

very least, Winston Churchill's right hand woman. Come to think of it, yer have a look of Mr Churchill about yer. A look of the bulldog breed.' Molly's chuckle was throaty. 'Before yer have time to mull that over, and clock me one, I promise yer that was a compliment.'

'Oh, I understood that part of it, girl, and I'm flattered. Mr Churchill is a real man in my eyes, the strong silent type what won the war for us.'

'With the help of our soldier boys, Auntie Nellie,' Doreen reminded her. 'Phil, Steve, Archie and our Tommy. They're real men, and they never brag about what they did.'

'I know that, girl, they were all heroes.' Her chubby face creased. 'And now we've gone from my teacher at school right through to the war, are we going to have to wait as long for that cup of tea yer mentioned when yer let us in the front door?'

'I've put the tea in the pot, the cups and saucers out, and a plate of biscuits. So when the kettle comes to the boil, all yer have to do is sit at the table and be watered and fed.'

'I'll have a nurse of the baby while I'm waiting, girl, just so he doesn't forget he's got a Grandma McDonough.'

With baby Bobby now asleep on the couch, and tea and biscuits in front of them, the women talked in low voices. 'Our Ruthie's over the moon with herself, isn't she, Mam?' Doreen said. 'She called in yesterday with Bella, and the pair of them couldn't stop talking about their shopping trip. I suppose I was like them at their age, except the war was on and everything was rationed. I wanted them to show us their shoes and dresses, but they flatly refused.'

'She wants to surprise everyone on Saturday. Her and Bella might be sixteen this week, but going into town on their own on Saturday, and buying clothes of their choice, was a big adventure for them. I haven't seen Bella's dress, but Ruthie's is lovely. And so are the silver dancing shoes.'

'She's the spitting image of her sisters, Molly,' Victoria said, nodding gently. 'And they get their good looks from their mother.'

The custard cream biscuit that was on the way to Nellie's mouth had a reprieve when her hand stopped in mid-air. 'Ay, Victoria, don't yer think my mate is vain enough, without you buttering her up? I'll not hear the last of that, yer know. I'll have the earache all day now. She'll tell everyone we meet at the shops, even Tony the butcher.'

Molly laughed, and immediately her eyes went to the couch. 'Oh, I forgot about Bobby. Have I woken him up?'

Doreen shook her head. 'No, he's fast asleep. Go on, Mam, what's Ruthie's dress like?'

'It's more than me life is worth to tell yer that. I've been sworn to secrecy. But the arrangements for Saturday have changed. She pleaded with me to let her go to the dance on Saturday with the boys instead of having a party at home. And with Bella there, backing her up, I couldn't refuse. Anyway, she had a point. If it's yer birthday, and ye're all dolled up like yer've never been before, then yer want to show off. I had a job convincing Mary, but she gave in eventually, as long as Gordon, Peter and Jeff look after them and bring them right home to the door.'

Nellie had been listening with a serious expression on her face. 'Us grown-ups are still having a night out, aren't we, girl? It doesn't mean because your Ruthie's changed her mind, we've all got to. Not after you and me have got new dresses.'

'Not to worry, sunshine, our gang are still going for a night out. It's only the corner pub, but that suits me fine. And I'm glad the youngsters are not having a party. It would spoil a night out if I had to come home to a mess.'

'How many of yer are going, Mam?' Doreen asked.

'Bella's mam and dad, and Maisie and Alec from the corner shop. So, two Bennetts, two McDonoughs, and two Corkhills. That's ten of us. None of the young ones are coming, and neither are me ma and da. The pub's not big, so with the regular customers, and our gang, we'll be lucky if it's not standing room only.'

'How is Flora?' Victoria asked. 'Has she got over her ordeal yet?'

'I don't think she'll ever get over it properly,' Molly told her, 'but she's happier and more at peace now she's got the watch back.'

The biscuit plate now empty, Nellie was ready to join in. 'She gets more visitors now, does Flora, so she's not as lonely as she was before. Me and Molly call in nearly every day, but we don't need to go today because Bridie and Bob are paying her a visit. And one afternoon Jill is walking round there with the baby and Lizzie.'

Molly was nodding in agreement. 'So, although nothing excuses the person that broke into her house, in a way he's done her a favour. For she's got more going on in her life now than she's ever had.'

'Why don't yer bring her round here one day, Mam?' Doreen asked. 'We'd love to see her.'

'Just hang on a minute,' Nellie told them, in a voice that said she was none too pleased. 'Any invitations to Flora have to come through me. As her adopted daughter, I'll attend to her appointments. So I'll look in our diary and see what day she's free, girl, and I'll let yer know.'

Molly chuckled softly. 'That should be very interesting reading, sunshine, if yer spent half yer school days standing in a corridor. But if yer need a secretary I'll offer me services for free. We could even buy a diary while we're out this morning. How does that suit yer?'

Nellie's face was a picture of pure bliss. 'That would be handy if we open an office for the McDonough and Bennett Private Detective Agency. Just think, girl, I'm sitting behind a big desk, and you're my secretary, showing our clients in.'

'Wishful thinking, sunshine. It'll be equal partners or nothing. If that doesn't satisfy you, then I'll be off, and yer'll be sitting behind that big desk with no secretary and no clients.'

'Ooh, yer drive a hard bargain, girl.'

'I'm going to drive a harder bargain now, sunshine. I want yer off that chair and putting yer coat on in two minutes flat. It's time to start our shopping. So jump to it.'

Nellie gave a smart salute. 'Yes, sir! One, two, three, sir!'

'Before yer go, Mam, what's happening on Saturday?' Doreen asked. 'Is Ruthie doing the rounds, or are we handing her presents in?'

'I thought it would be nice if everyone called in the afternoon. It would be a treat to have all the family together, and I know Ruthie would be pleased.'

Doreen nodded. 'Shall we make it about three o'clock? That would give us time to get the dinner over and dishes washed.'

'That would be fine, sunshine, but keep it to yerself and she'll get a lovely surprise when everyone turns up. I'll spread the word on secrecy.'

* * *

Molly and Nellie arrived early at St Anthony's church, so they could see Sadie getting out of the wedding car with her two sisters, who were her bridesmaids. They wanted to wish her all the best, in case there wasn't time after the service. Molly had to be home by half past two at the latest, for all the family would be calling around that time to see Ruthie.

'Here she comes, girl.' Nellie squeezed her mate's arm. 'I'm glad the sun is shining for her.'

And what a radiant bride Sadie Wilson was. She outshone the sun with her beauty. This was the day she was to become the wife of the man she adored. He used to live next door to her when she was a kid, and was the only one in the street who spoke to her. The other neighbours steered clear because of her parents, who were filthy, foul-mouthed and lazy. But Harry had defied his parents, and always stopped to speak to her, and treated her like a lady. He was her only friend then, and now he was to become her husband.

'You look beautiful, sunshine,' Molly told her as her bridesmaids fixed her veil. 'Your Harry is a very lucky man. And he's as handsome as yer said he was.'

Nellie nodded. 'We peeped in the church and saw him.'

Sadie tilted her head sideways, to the man whose arm she was linking. 'This is Harry's father. He's giving me away.'

'There's a lot of people in the church, sunshine; yer have many friends. Me and Nellie will have to leave early, but we'll be down to see yer at the market soon.' She bent to give Sadie a kiss. 'We both wish yer all the luck in the world. Now don't keep Harry waiting and have a wonderful day, and a wonderful life. We'll be inside to see yer tie the knot.'

The two friends waited until bride and bridesmaids were in the church, and the organ was playing, before they took their seats in one of the back pews. They stayed for the exchanging of the vows, and rings, then quietly slipped outside, happy for the young girl they'd grown fond of.

There was a constant stream of visitors to the Bennett house on Saturday afternoon, and Molly was rushed off her feet making pot after pot of tea. Her head was splitting and her feet killing her. But each time she got to the point where she thought she was near breaking point, she just had to look at the happiness on the pretty face of her now sixteen-year-old daughter to feel better. The room was littered with paper that had been torn in haste from present after present by a young girl who was bursting with excitement. There was chatter, laughter, hugs and kisses, in an atmosphere of family togetherness and love.

Molly leaned back against the sink in the kitchen, and through the open door she viewed the scene. There'd never been a birthday like this before. Her three older children certainly didn't have the fuss and presents Ruthie was enjoying. But that was because money was tighter then. And no one begrudged the happiness of the young girl who had entered the world seven years after Molly thought her child-bearing days were over. She was welcomed and loved then, and still was.

Bridie and Bob came with Tommy and Rosie, bearing stockings and lovely pink fluffy bedroom slippers. Jill and Steve came with baby Molly, and an underskirt in lilac, which sent Ruthie into a state of rapture. And the pretty blue blouse from Doreen and Phil brought tears to her eyes. There was a silk scarf from Lily and Archie, a box of chocolates from Maisie and Alec in the corner shop, and Corker arrived with a nicely wrapped parcel containing a lovely cardigan from Ellen and himself. And he also brought a message from Gordon and Peter that said they'd bring their presents when they called to take her and Bella to the dance. Any other time she would have blushed at the mention of going out with a boy, 'cos that meant it was a date. But she was so overwhelmed by everything she didn't have a blush in her. 'Oh, Uncle Corker, I must be the luckiest girl in Liverpool.' She waved a hand. 'Just look at all the presents. I want to pinch meself to make sure I'm not dreaming. And I got about fifteen cards at least.'

Corker bent down and gave her a bearlike hug. 'Enjoy it, sweetheart, for these are the best days of yer life. Make the most of them.'

He was the last guest, and when he left, Molly sank on to the couch and put her feet up. She looked across to where Nellie was sitting in the carver chair, and said. 'The way my feet feel, I'll never make it to the pub tonight.'

Nellie, who had arrived at half past two so she wouldn't miss anything, pulled her chair nearer the table so she could rest her arms on it. 'Of course yer'll make it, girl, yer can't let everyone down.' She winked at Ruthie, who was stacking her presents into a neat pile. 'Yer'll never forget yer sixteenth birthday, will yer, girl?'

'I won't, Auntie Nellie, because it's been the best day of me life. Everyone has been so good, I feel like crying.'

'Oh, well,' Nellie said in a matter of fact voice. 'If ye're going to cry there's no point in me giving yer my present.'

Ruthie was well used to having her leg pulled by her mother's mate, and grinned. 'Me head is in the clouds Auntie Nellie, but I'm not so far gone I don't know when I'm being wound up.'

'It's a pity yer feel like that, girl, 'cos it means yer best mate, Bella, will really be belle of the ball tonight.'

Ruthie's eyes slid sideways to where her mother was stretched out on the couch. 'Mam, is Auntie Nellie kidding?'

'I don't think she'd pull yer leg over a thing like that, sunshine. Mind you, yer can't be up to her tricks.'

Nellie wagged her head from side to side. 'What a ruddy performance! I didn't have this trouble with Bella. She was delighted with her prezzie, and she gave me a big kiss.'

Jack came through from the kitchen with a cup of tea for his wife. 'Here yer are, love, yer deserve this after all the running round yer've done. Relax and enjoy the tea, we've got an hour before we need to start getting ready.' He dropped a kiss on Molly's forehead, before saying to his daughter, 'Tell yer Auntie Nellie that yer'd be delighted to have another present, and thank her for her kindness. I'll stay here and watch the proceedings, and once you've got the promised present, I'll give Mrs Mac a nice cup of tea.'

Molly was taking a sip of tea when a shriek shattered the silence, and the tea went down the wrong way, causing a fit of coughing. 'Ruthie,' she spluttered, 'I nearly choked meself.'

'Look what Auntie Nellie bought me, Mam! It's beautiful!' The girl was so excited she couldn't fasten the necklace. 'Dad, will yer fasten it for me? And will yer lift me up so I can see meself in the mirror?'

'I can't hold yer any longer, love,' Jack said, puffing loudly. 'Ye're not a baby any more, and I'm not a teenager.' He lowered her to the floor. 'You're no lightweight, love. Another minute and I'd have put me back out.'

Her hand on the necklace, Ruthie put an arm round Nellie's shoulders. 'It's a beautiful present, Auntie Nellie, and I love yer to bits. Not as much as I love me mam and dad, though, 'cos they let me keep all me wages, and just wait until yer see me all dolled up tonight. Yer'll mistake me for a film star.'

Molly handed her empty cup to Jack. 'Be an angel and put that on the draining board for me, love. I'm keeping me legs up for the next hour, otherwise I'll never make it to the pub.'

'You can lean on my arm, girl,' Nellie said. 'Ye're not getting out of going, 'cos I'm looking forward to a night out.'

'I know yer are, sunshine, and I won't let yer down. Even if it means Jack giving me a piggyback,' Molly said. 'But you poppy off home now and we'll see yer at half seven. That's when Corker will be going up the pub to keep seats for us.'

Nellie pushed herself to her feet. 'I'd better get in or George will have a face on him that'll stop a clock. I'll see meself out, Jack, you stay where yer are.'

As she waddled towards the door, Ruthie was close on her heels. 'Has Bella got a necklace as well, Auntie Nellie?'

'Yes, I wouldn't make fish of one and flesh of the other, girl. I wouldn't leave her out. And I hope we see yer in yer finery before yer go gallivanting with the boys.'

Ruthie giggled. 'I don't think yer'll recognize us, so I'll tell yer which glamour girl is me, and which is Bella.'

'You might have a problem there, girl, 'cos in me new dress yer might not recognize me. So we'll let yer mam do the introductions, 'cos she'll know who's who.'

Molly and Jack were ready with their coats on when there was a knock on the door. 'I'll go,' Molly said. 'It'll be the lads for you.'

'Ooh, don't let them in, Mam, keep them talking until we've got our coats on. Me and Bella don't want them to see our dresses until we're in the dance hall.' Ruthie was slipping her arms into her coat sleeves. 'Come on, Bella, me mam and dad are waiting to go out.'

'I'd better open the door,' Molly said. 'Me and yer dad will go straight out, because Nellie will be on pins waiting for us. Come on, Jack, we'll let the lads in before they turn to blocks of ice.'

Jack smiled at the two girls, who were almost sick with excitement. 'Enjoy the dance and the rest of yer birthday. Ta-ra for now.'

Molly opened the front door to see Gordon and Peter all spruced up, with their best suits on, nice white shirts, neatly knotted ties, and sleeked back hair. 'Oh, if I was only thirty years younger. It would be hard to choose which one I'd fall for, 'cos yer both look so handsome.' She glanced up the street. 'I thought Jeff Mowbray was coming with yer?'

'He said he'd see us there,' Gordon said. 'He met a girl he liked on Wednesday, and he promised to meet her there.'

'Let the lads in, love,' Jack said. 'They'll be cold, and we're keeping Nellie and George waiting.'

Molly called over her shoulder. 'Enjoy yerselves, girls, but remember to be home by half ten.' She stepped down on to the pavement. 'Go in, lads, the girls are ready, but yer know how fussy we females are. Every hair has to be in place.'

'We'll look after them, Mrs B,' Gordon said. 'We'll make sure they're home safe and sound by half ten.'

'Yes,' Peter told them, 'they won't come to no harm with us.'

Ruthie came into the hall. 'Are you two coming in, or not? The night will be over before we get out.'

The two brothers had been hiding their hands, but once in the living room they held them out. Gordon passed a small parcel over to Ruthie with a card. 'Happy birthday, Ruthie. I hope yer like the present. I've never bought anything for a girl before, so I'm keeping me fingers crossed.'

Peter nodded as he passed a parcel and card to Bella. 'Me and our Gordon spent an hour looking for something. I hope yer like it.'

'You're supposed to wish me a happy birthday, Peter Corkhill,' Bella told him. 'Your Gordon's got more manners than you.'

'Don't be narky, Bella,' Ruthie said, taking the paper off the parcel. 'You're not allowed a sour face on yer birthday.'

'I was only joking,' Bella said. 'I didn't mean to be rude, Peter.'

'Of course yer didn't,' Peter said. 'Open yer parcel and card.'

It was fifteen minutes later when the foursome left the house, making sure the door was firmly closed behind them. The brothers didn't mind the delay, because their presents were the cause of it. The face powder compacts had been a great success with the girls.

They were filled with perfumed powder, and there was a fluffy powder puff on top. And the mirror in the lid came in handy for the delighted girls to powder their faces. It had been a wonderful day for them, going beyond their wildest expectations, and it wasn't over yet.

Gordon and Peter Corkhill felt ten foot tall when they paid the entrance fee to the dance hall. And when Peter saw his big brother cup Ruthie's elbow and walk her towards the cloakroom, he took Bella's arm and followed. 'We'll wait outside that door for you,' Gordon said. 'That's the dance hall.'

The small cloakroom had many uses. It boasted a few hooks on the wall, two toilets, a cracked washbasin and a small mirror. But the two friends didn't even notice; they were full of nervous excitement as they hung their coats on the hooks. They could only see themselves from shoulders up in the mirror. 'Does me dress look all right, Ruthie?' Bella asked. 'It's not creased or anything?'

'Your dress is lovely, Bella.' Ruthie reached up to fix some of the curls in her friend's dark hair. 'Stand still a minute, the wind has blown yer hair about. And we can't have that, we've got to look our best tonight.' After standing back to make sure there wasn't a hair out of place on her best friend's head, Ruthie said. 'Now you can tell me how I look.' She did a little twirl. 'Is my hair all right?'

'Your hair is always nice, Ruthie, but yer've really gone to town on it tonight. I love the way yer've combed it right back and tied it with ribbon. I wish my hair was like yours. I hate this colour, it's so dull.'

'Don't be daft, it's not a bit dull! You're the lucky one, with curly hair. Anyway, we'd better hurry, or the boys will wonder what's taking us so long. Let's change our shoes and put our working shoes in the bag we brought.'

While they were changing into their silver dancing shoes, Ruthie said, 'Don't forget, we're not going to tell the boys we've been practising dancing in our dinner hour with Amy. It's to be a surprise.'

Bella was getting more nervous by the minute. 'I won't be telling Peter anything, Ruthie, 'cos I'm shaking like a leaf, and I've forgotten what Amy taught us. I'll freeze, I know I will, and I won't be able to put one foot in front of the other.'

Ruthie could sense how nervous her friend was, but she was wise enough not to sympathize. If she did, they'd both spend the night standing in the cloakroom. 'Yer can't have forgotten the steps to a waltz, there's only three! Look, put the bags down and we'll have a little go to warm yer up.'

Bella's eyes went to the door. 'Oh, what if someone comes in and sees us?'

'You don't half look for trouble, Bella Watson,' her friend said. 'Put the bags on the floor and I'll hum while we do a few steps.' Some of her confidence rubbed off on Bella, and soon the two girls were dancing in the small space, laughing at their own antics. Then Ruthie pulled them to a halt. 'Yer see, it's easy when yer know how. But we've kept the boys waiting long enough, so let's get cracking.' She tutted and pulled a face. 'I wish we didn't have to lug that flipping bag with us.'

'I'll carry it,' Bella said, feeling a little more relaxed. 'My mam said when she used to go dancing, girls would put their shoes and handbags under a chair. So we can do that, if there's any chairs in the dance hall.'

'We'll manage, Bella, so don't be worrying. Just put a smile on yer face and act as though yer've been to lots of dances. That's what I'm going to do.'

The two friends had no idea how pretty they looked, until they saw the looks of admiration on the boys' faces as they hurried towards them. 'Yer look lovely, Ruthie,' Gordon said as he cupped her elbow. 'That's a smashing dress, and I don't half like the way yer've done yer hair.'

Peter, at sixteen, was a year younger than his brother, and not so sure of himself. But he made a valiant effort. 'You look lovely, too, Bella. I like yer hair in that style.'

'Gordon, where can we put our bags and walking shoes?' Ruthie asked. 'We can't lug them around all night.'

Gordon held out his hand. 'I'll put the bag under one of the chairs. It'll be quite safe.' And a few minutes later the bag was out of the way, and he was leading Ruthie on to the dance floor. 'Don't worry, it's a waltz. I'll lead yer, and yer'll soon get into it. Just follow my steps.'

Ruthie met her friend's eyes, and winked. 'We're game for it, aren't we, Bella? The worst thing that can happen is we fall on our face.'

'That won't happen, Bella,' Peter told her. 'I'll keep tight hold of yer.'

At the end of the dance, Gordon said, 'Ay, yer both did well for beginners. Yer didn't trip up once.' He took Ruthie's elbow to lead her off the floor, and bent his head to say softly, 'You're the best-looking girl here, Ruthie. I could see all the lads looking at yer.'

'Don't be daft,' Ruthie said, a little embarrassed, but thrilled. 'There's lots of pretty girls here. And yer don't have to stay with me. I won't mind if yer want to dance with one of the better dancers. I'll be quite happy to watch.'

'I came with you, and I'm staying with you.' Gordon sounded very definite. 'If I left your side, another bloke would claim yer in no time. I've waited over a year for this night, Ruthie, and I'm holding on to you tight.' The music started for a foxtrot, and Gordon put his arm round her waist and led her on to the floor. 'I'll hold yer close, and yer'll be able to follow me steps better. And don't worry if yer tread on me toes, it won't hurt.'

Ruthie looked for Bella, and was happy when she saw her dancing with Peter, a smile on her face. She wasn't actually dancing, more like walking, but the main thing was she was enjoying herself, and Peter was being very attentive. It had been a wonderful day all round, but this was the best part.

In the snug room of the corner pub, it was so noisy you couldn't hear yourself think. And who was causing the shrieks of laughter? None other than Helen Theresa McDonough, doing her impression of Two Ton Tessie O'Shea. With the hem of her dress in her hands she went round all the tables, singing at the top of her voice. That she was showing her rolled down stockings kept up with elastic garters, and both legs of her blue fleecy knickers, mattered not a scrap to the woman who loved to be the centre of attention. The laughter she attracted was like music to her ears. And it wasn't only the people in the snug who were being entertained, either. The customers in the saloon had been drawn by the laughter, and decided to stay and enjoy the fun. And, encouraged by the shouts and clapping, Nellie went from Tessie O'Shea to her Mae West impression.

'What would yer do with her?' Molly whispered to Jack. 'I don't know whether to laugh or cry.'

'Just look at the faces around yer, love. There isn't one that isn't laughing. George is laughing his head off, and she's his wife! If he doesn't object, why should you? Look at Corker, Mary, Maisie and the rest of our gang, they're all in stitches. It would be dull without Nellie.'

'Yes, I know. She's a cracker, and I love the bones of her. If only she'd buy herself a decent pair of garters.' Molly grinned. 'I'll buy her a couple of fancy ones for Christmas, then she can do the dance of the seven veils and I won't be embarrassed. And I'll make sure those pieces of knotted elastic go in the bin.'

Nellie passed their table just then, and even though she was out of breath she was still dancing, and showing her legs. 'Are yer enjoying yerself, girl?'

'Having a wonderful time, sunshine. I was just telling Jack I've thought of a good Christmas present for yer.'

Nellie stood still long enough to say, 'I hope it's not a bleeding dictionary.'

The words were out before Molly could stop them. 'No, sunshine, it's a pair of fancy garters.'

There was a loud burst of laughter when Nellie answered, 'Get blue ones, girl, to go with me fleecy-lined knickers.'

Gordon never left Ruthie's side all night. He asked her up for every dance, and when she refused to take to the floor for a rumba or tango, he sat it out with her. And Peter was the same with Bella. It was during a waltz that Gordon plucked up the courage to ask, 'How would yer fancy coming to the pictures with me one night, Ruthie? Just to the local flicks.'

The girl's heart was pounding. She felt she'd really grown up now, being asked for a date. And by the lad she had more than a soft spot for, and thought very handsome. 'I'd like to, but I think yer'd better ask me mam.'

Gordon was riding on a cloud. 'Oh, I'll ask yer mam, Ruthie, and I don't think she'll object.' He grinned. 'If she does, I'll get me dad to have a word with her.'

Ruthie was thoughtful as Gordon navigated a corner. 'What about Bella? We always go everywhere together.'

'Our Peter is going to ask her for a date, he told me. But that's up to them, Ruthie, it's you I want to go out with. It's you I've always wanted to go out with. So if yer mam says it's all right, will yer come?'

Ruthie nodded, her pretty face aglow. 'Yes, okay, I'd like that.'

The music faded, and they were about to walk away when a voice said, 'Stay on the floor for an Old Time Waltz.'

Gordon was in his element when the music started, and he twirled Ruthie round. He caught his brother's eye and winked, before singing along to the tune of 'I'll Be Your Sweetheart'. Round and round they spun, laughing with sheer delight. Then Gordon held Ruthie from him, and looking into her laughing eyes he sang, 'I'll be your sweetheart, if you will be mine?'

She almost sang the answer. 'Yer'll have to ask me mam that, as well.'

Taking his courage in his hand, Gordon kissed her on the cheek. 'Happy birthday, Ruthie.'

The blushing girl was unable to speak for a while, she was so stunned. But stunned in a nice way. Then she wagged a finger. 'I'm going to tell me mam on you.'

'Well, I couldn't ask her if I could kiss yer when she's not here, could I?' Gordon felt as though it was his birthday as well. 'If she's around next time, then I'll ask her.'

'Better not,' warned Ruthie. 'Just ask about taking me to the pictures one night. Ask too much and she'll send yer packing.'

'No, Mrs B won't send me packing. She knows ye're safe with me. On the back row at the Astoria, holding hands, what harm can come to her beautiful daughter?'

'You might just pinch the odd kiss, that's what!'

'Wouldn't yer like the odd kiss?'

Ruthie chuckled. 'I won't tell me mam if you don't.'

This book is to be returned on or before